PUBLISHED *by* PARABLES
Earthly Stories with a Heavenly Meaning

By The River And Beyond

By

Michael Joseph

By The River And Beyond
Michael Joseph

Published By Parables
April, 2021

Printed in the United States of America

Readers should be aware that Internet Web sites offered as citations and/or sources for further information may have been changed or disappeared between the time this was written and the time it is read.

By The River And Beyond

By

Michael Joseph

This book is dedicated to my wife,
whose loving faithfulness and dedication
know no bounds.

By The River
And Beyond

Introduction

2021 is in full bloom. And we are at a new point. With advanced technology, the world has never been as closely tied together as it is now. And in that collective, we find that it's not easy to herd eight billion people together into a system that everyone agrees is good for all. Indeed, the herculean effort just may, in the final analysis, illustrate how naturally provincial we might otherwise like to be.

Perhaps the times we are living in have amply stirred your curiosity about what is truly noble and lasting in life and what is not. As you turn these pages, may that curiosity be in motion. It is my enduring hope that this story may move you toward deeper matters and lasting possibilities as the pages are turned. And may the curiosity that you ride carry you in search of something lasting. For any adventure void of that, no matter how stimulating, will leave a heart lacking.

Desire is one of the wheels of the bicycle that a noble curiosity rides. Ambition is the other. The wheels can carry you along a particular trail that every genuinely good heart seeks to travel. The trail leads to the realm of the enduring principle – to the most important connection in preparation for something, or so it seems – a long principle in the same direction. Emotions will come and go. But the trail to the enduring principle lies open to every noble curiosity.

It is this writer's hope that this story will help you to have a deeper appreciation for what is real and true in life. And may it inspire you to seek the good that is gently tucked inside every affectionate and every challenging reality.

~ Michael Joseph

Time Passage

A Pause

A dead thing can go with the stream,
but only a living thing can go against it."

~ G. K. Chesterton

One

Simeon Mangino, barely twenty-one, began his journey into the unknown when he stood hopeless and helpless with a dead man's head resting on his right foot.

A few months earlier, he and Evans talked about leaving town. Though surrounded by friends and family, both of the young men sensed a call from faraway. When in an inebriated and vulnerable space one evening, Evans floated the idea to Simeon. They batted it around the next day and Evans decided that he was in. And though the idea was attractive, Simeon hadn't gotten that desperate yet. His attachment to family, neighborhood, and friends was laden with sentiments that carried just enough weight to hold his pioneer spirit in check.

Though he couldn't bear to leave home, there was nevertheless a burning in his soul to heed the summons of an unknown call. What began as soft whispers in his childhood morphed into a clear, distinct dog whistle from an unknown origin.

For nearly a year, he ignored the festering turmoil inside. But he could no longer avoid it after the first time his life was spared. The unexpected tragedy that just unfolded right in front of him rocked him to the core. His eyes were the last pitiful ones the dying man saw as he slipped away.

Since the switch to a second high school a few years earlier, Simeon had pursued a path of his own choosing. It had enlivened him at the time. But in doing so, he outdid himself. He traveled the path toting a knapsack full of bad habits that he picked up along the way.

That pathway was the way of the whim. It held little in the way of promise and the potential for enormous unwelcome surprises along with its dopamine rushes. At the entrance of the path was a sign marked: "Uncertainty". At the outset, it held immense appeal to him. After a few years on the path, however, dark shadows appeared along the way.

In all the fun, he couldn't rid himself of the nagging notion that something wasn't right, both in a macro and in a micro sense, inside and all around. He was familiar with the sensation since he was a boy. And it latched on to his inquisitive disposition like a friend in need.

Walks on the wild side as a means to escape the pains of reality had worked for him, at least for a while. But they added heavy burdens to his knapsack. The confusion that was the result of his selfish choices was harder and harder to avoid as the days passed by. Now, merely months since joining the Navy without Simeon, in the fall of 1973, his pal Evans was home on leave.

Two

The Mississipi River weaves its way south through mid-America along hundreds of well-worn bends and curves in the landscape. As it courses south, the bends become tighter. Several large cities are posited as sentries along the muddy waters. The last of these is the city of New Orleans. It is known as the Crescent City for the crescent bends in the river as it courses through the metro area. The neighborhood known as 'uptown along the river' was inhabited by working class men and women after the demise of the small plantations. Family owned grocery stores and barrooms sprouted on many corners there and became neighborhood gatherings.

The rushing, muddy activity of the river carried millions of tons of discard-able materials from the north. Runoff soil, debris, waste, and chemical residue from crops converged in the river on its journey south. When the never-ending waters approached the New Orleans area they were a caramel color according to the mix of mud and contamination. Whether the city's inhabitants worked, ate, or slept, the constant movement of semi-dark, polluted water pushed through its center, dividing the geography of the metropolis. Day and night, for hundreds of years, the flow of brown water went on unabated.

The city dwellers were largely unaware of the rivers workings. They took it in stride in their places like the grocery stores on the street corners, the many barrooms around the city, the French Quarter down river, or the streetcars that carried passengers around town. All the while the muddy, murky water flowed on and on carrying with it things seen and unseen from the far north.

At the lowest part of the bend in the crescent of the river, the Public Belt Railroad station sat at the foot of Lions and Front Streets. It fronted the rail line that preceded the warehouses along the wharf. Fumps Bar was diagonally across the street. It was the front part of a building owned by Simeon's aunt. An upstairs and a downstairs apartment filled out the rest of the building. In the upstairs rooms, a young man was preparing for the evening.

Mockinging birds of the northern variety are plentiful in the arid climate of New Orleans. A significant population of the creatures mock and chirp their way merrily and confidently throughout the neighborhoods. In the spring and summer, the male variety of the species is known to broadcast in the night and early morning hours in order to attract a mate. Its regular, incessant litanies sound forth in a cascade of versatile songs, tweets, chirps, and chits. Its performances blend in with the other sounds across the neighborhood to form the background noise that locals hear, but rarely actually hear.

It was early evening. Simeon prepared to head to Mitts to meet Evans when he heard its sounds. One of the pesky critters went on with aplomb outside the screenless open window to the roof atop Fumps Bar.

He stood, brushing his teeth in front of the open window overlooking the flat, tarred roof. Beyond, across Tchoupitoulas[1] Street, was a still train locomotive. It sat with its engine idling as if in preparation. As the mockingbird continued its versatile, impressive litany of sounds and song he took in a few bars, noting them with mild irritation. He was aware that he stood in the exact place where his momma, aunts, grandma, paw-paw, and great grandmother stood years ago. They lived there long before and looked out of the same window.

He laid his toothbrush down, and walked down the creaky wooden stairs out of the side door onto Lions Street. He was glad to have his old roommate in town for a few days. They arranged to shoot pool and catch up at Mitts that evening.

After catching up, they sat at the bar for some time. As was usually the case, Simeon was in the building for the third time that day. The old, worn floor and walls had begun to seem more dreary and forlorn to him over the past year. That evening, they appeared even more so.

"What's it like, Ev?"

From his tone and demeanor, Evans picked up that his former roommate was as curious as ever about leaving home.

"It's good, man, real good. They teach you stuff dat you really need and is good for you. And they don't let you get away with things. You

____

[1] Pronounced: "Chop-it-ool-lus"

know, you and me need dat, man. You should go down to the Customs House and join. Let's go tommorrow. I'll go with you."

"Naw."

Simeon shook his head and pursed his lips as he spoke. He didn't look Evans in the eye.

"Don't be a chicken head, you stupid Dago. If it can help me, Ah know it can help you."

"Ah'll have to think about it. Let's play some nine ball. Since you're working and Ahm not, you're paying."

"What else is new!?"

Evans grinned as he headed toward the pool tables.

Having deftly weaseled out of the conversation, Simeon practically leaped off of the barstool to fetch a cue stick. In the motion, he turned to his cousin Lan, working the bar.

"Lan! Me and Evans on table six."

"What for? Neither one of ya'll are any good."

Lan looked up as he pushed two beer mugs through a bin of soapy water.

"Ah never thought Ah'd say this, but Ah miss your old dago crumb bum of a cousin."

He chuckled with a sentimental half smile.

"Ah miss all of ya'll. But Ahm glad to be outta hear, man."

Simeon didn't respond.

A short while into their second game of nine-ball, Simeon was aware of the far-away feeling washing over him again. Looking at his buddy, he noted a quieter and more secure demeanor. He was still the same Evans. And there was no hint of some new kind of awakening that he might claim in his new estate. But in his six-foot one frame he seemed more erect, though not rigid, and more relaxed than Simeon had ever known him to be.

"Ev."

The reach-out came as a surprise from its source.

Evans momentarily looked up from his bent-over approach shot on the three ball. Their eyes met.

"Do you remember the night on the corner at Bivi-Q's, when ya'll walked with me to the bus stop?"

He didn't answer, intensely viewing his next shot, which he stroked and missed. He stood up, leaning his curly head of hair slightly with a faraway look.

"On the corner at Bivi-Q's, across from Mel Paines?"

"Yeah. Do you remember?"

"There's something familiar about being at dat spot. We never went into the bar or hung at that corner. So if Ah was there, it would only have been only once or twice. But there's something familiar about standing there. What are you getting at?"

"Early one school night, a bunch of us were at Doraix's[2]. We bought a bunch of quarts of Dixie from Jawje's. Somebody pulled out a can of some kind of cleaning fluid and a small plastic bag. He sprayed the fluid into the bag, closed it up, and began to inhale the stuff through the narrow opening to the bag. Most of the guys tried it out, including me."

"Carabina Cleanin Fluid. Dat's what it was! Ah remembuh. Dat stuff was bad news. Ah can't believe we did dat."

"Did it affect you? Did it get you high?"

"Ah think it did. Ah think it did for all of us. Why are you aksing, Simm?"

"It didn't get me high at all. It made me sick to mah stomach. And mah head too. And that's where Bivi-Q's comes in. You, Betz, and Tweet walked with me to the corner there so Ah could catch the bus home. Ah went home early dat night."

"Oh yeah. Ah think Ah remember dat. We were pretty loaded."

"The three of you had more to drink den Ah did. Plus, ya'll sucked on that plastic bag a lot. Ah only had one drag, and it took me down fast."

Evans' mouth lifted ever so slightly on the edges while he slowly shook his head left to right, holding a far away stare for long seconds. Simeon called him back.

"Do you remember the man standing at the bus stop?"

"There was a man at the bus stop?"

"Yeah. An older guy, maybe in his late forties. You know, our daddy's age."

"You got me on that one. You actually remembuh dat?"

---

[2]Pronounced: "Doe-rays"

"Ah do, man. Ah remember everything about being on that corner dat night. And there's a reason, Ev. You want me to tell you?"

"You got me curious. Ahm all ears, bruh."

"We headed to Tchoupitoulas Street and Napoleon Avenue to catch the bus."

"Why theTchoupitoulas bus?"

"Just a hunch dat Ah ought to go home that way. Ya'll were carrying on the whole way to the bus stop. It was about 10:30, early to go home. But Ah was feeling pretty sick from that cleaning fluid crap."

"Yeah, Ahm remembering this, now."

"When we got there, ya'll ribbed me. But Ah noticed this man on the corner. He was familiar looking in a general way, one like we might find in Fump's, Doraix's, or Mel Paines. Something struck me about the man, Ev. When we got to the corner, he looked at me hard, man. Our eyes met and there was something weird about it, man, Ahm serious. And he had some kind of old, blue folder in his hand. You know how dat corner is lit up by the big Jax Beeuh sign and streetlight. Ah could see duh color of that folder like it was daytime."

"Ah don't remembuh him *or* a folder, Simm."

"Yeah, well go figure. Ya'll wouldn't stop kidding and laughing. Ya'll were getting on my nerves. Ya'll just leaned on my shoulders like ya'll always do and kept carrying on. Anyway, at one point the man made what appeared to be a deliberate attempt to focus my attention on the blue folder."

"Did he ever say anything to you?"

"Not once. And that's the thing of it, Ev. Ah felt like Ah was supposed to be there, and that he was too. And Ah've rarely ever been on that corner. There was something riveting in his expression when our eyes met."

"Was it like a threat or something?"

"It wasn't like dat. His look wasn't threatening at all. It was more like a look of deep concern. It was as if he knew me, like he knew about some uh mah, well, Ah guess Ah can tell you….. like he knew about mah struggles and questions."

"Man, that's freaky, Simm. And you're sure about this after the fact?"

"Ah swear to it, man. Ah recall it like it happened yesterday. The minute we arrived there, Ah noticed him. He looked into my eyes and Ah was riveted, Ev."

Evans stared at the wall but he didn't see it. His mind's eye was on the lighted corner back into their common story that evening.

"And then, Ah heard duh sound of the train horn and bells."

"Wait. There's *bells* after the train horn blows?"

"Yeah. You never noticed dat?"

"Never have."

"Ah thought everybody knew dat. So when Ah heard duh horn and bells…"

"You sure about there being bells after the train horn?"

"Evans, listen to me. There are bells after the train horn, okay? So Ah heard the horn and bells…, you sure you don't remember duh man standing at the corner when we were there?"

Evans paused again, before answering.

"Ah really don't, Simm. What's the big deal about dis guy? Why are you telling me this?"

"Your shot, Ev."

Evans looked over the table to ponder his next shot. His concentration appeared to diminish his attention from the direction Simeon was taking the conversation. So he decided to let it go. Evans and the guys weren't aware of what happened with the man that night at the bus stop. He decided he would hold off on telling him the rest of the story.

After making the shot, Evans continued.

"Why haven't you said something, Simm? Dat's been a few years ago. You know you could have told me, especially me, man. Is this something that's bothering you, Simm? Is it eating at you like thinking about leaving is eating at you?"

He dodged the question.

"Shoot again, Ev."

Simeon was warmed by the talk with his friend. As he took in the moment, a sober thought overtook him. Evans would be leaving in a few days. Uncle Sam had a claim on him for the next four years. And in his own words he presumed he'd never live in New Orleans again. He had the urge to tell him more.

"How'd you like dat straight shot, Dago? Pretty impressive, Ah'd say."

"Not a bad shot for a boy your age, Robertson."

Evans pried a little more in the hopes that he might get his friend to see what was plain to see.

"What else do you wanna get off your sholders, Simm? Ahm only hear a few more days."

He welcomed the inquiry.

"Ready for one more then?

"Lay it on me, bruh."

"You know about the two times our two different friends rescued me from being murdered. You were in one of those scenes, remember?"

"Yeah. For those two reasons alone, you should have left-duh-heck outta hear with me months ago."

"Well, there was a third encounter with death. And another spectacular rescue, or some strange explanation dat Ah can't figure out."

"No way, man. Are you serious? Who'd you tick off this time?"

"Nobody. Here's how it went down."

"One night after you left, Ah was out cold in my room on top of Fumps. Me and Betz missed having you around as a roommate, man. Living on top of Fumps, one block down from Mitt's, we thought we were on top of the world. Anyway, I was conked out in my creaky old elevated porch room where the wind blows through. It was cold and Ah had the gas heater on. All of a sudden, Ah popped awake choking."

"Choking?"

"The smell of gas filled the room and Ah couldn't breathe. Ah was choking and knew Ah was about to pass out for good and be done with."

"No way, Simm. You're the most unlucky friend Ah've ever had."

"Ah had lit the gas heater..."

"'Dat old brown contraption on the floor right next to your bed."

"'Dat one. Apparently, Ah had it on a low flame and the wind coming through the floor boards, window, door, heck,... every darn where in that room.... blew the flame out."

"And the gas was still on. Holy crap, Simm."

"Ah was able to spring up from the bed and get out the door dat led to the small elevated deck and catch my breath. It took me a minute to get mah breathing back. Ah was choking and coughing so much. Ah was a gone pickawn[3], Ev. Then Ah was able to run in and turn the gas off."

His friend stared at him with a caring and pitiful gaze. He felt for his buddy. Why couldn't he read the handwriting on the wall? As if in a trance, his pal had unknowingly locked away what he couldn't bear to lose. It was in that place where folks can store it free of charge, not aware that the charge would come due later. He was to leave in a few days. He knew that neither of them were good at writing letters. Long distance phone calls were very expensive. He didn't know when he'd be back to visit his beloved hometown. And he knew that he was never coming back to live there. He was holding out for one more appeal.

Simeon went on.

"Ah was petrified, man. Even though it was cold up on the deck overlooking Lions Street, Ah was sweating like a pig. Mah heart was pounding. Ah felt numb. Ah remember saying out loud, *'What just happened? Ah almost died again.'* And Ah don't like to admit this, Ev. But just like the other two brushes with murder, the fear that washed over me was palpable."

Evans just sat there. It was his turn to shoot on the six ball. But he waited, giving full attention to his vulnerable friend.

"Why didn't Ah die *this time*? And why is death knocking on my door so often in the past year? Why did Ah wake up, and what woke me?"

He paused for a moment so Evans could take his shot. In telling what happened, he was instantly back there, revisiting a stored image taken down from in the gallery of his mind. He recalled that he had wondered almost out loud to the street light. It stood faithfully, overlooking his upper porch-room window like an undaunted sentry eight feet in front of him. And he wondered what woke him.

"Your shot, Simm. Think about it. Somehow, you're still alive. Somehow, for the third time in the last year, you escaped the menacing grip of death."

Simeon missed on the six ball. Evans began to line up his shot on it. As he did, Simeon found himself back in the experience out on the small, elevated deck, recovering from the latest near-death experience. And as

---

[3] "Pecan", pronounced "pick awn" – traditional New Orleans pronunciation within a traditional New Orleans phrase

he recovered himself outside his porch bedroom in the cold air, his heart began to beat faster again. A slight sweat began to moisten his body once again as he realized the brevity of the events of the past year. The sound of the song striking up on the jukebox helped him to recover himself. The tune that ignited the recovery was a New Orleans original: *"Ain't Got No Home[4]."*

Evans proceeded to make the next three balls in a row. Simeon was impressed at how good he was shooting that day.

"My old pal, Evans Robertson."

He moved in and out of the song's words and his attention to his pal. It wasn't lost on him how close he had come to enlisting in the Navy with Evans a few months before. If he had left with his friend he would no longer be living above Fump's Bar. The experience with the brown gas heater would never have happened.

"Nine ball, side pocket, Mangino."

He missed.

"Close. Your shot, Simm. You're gonna have to bank dat nine ball, you know. Is it gonna be one rail to the near corner, or three rails to the far corner pocket. You used to be pretty good at dat one rail shot. So what's it gonna be?"

"Three rails to the far corner pocket, just to give you a chance, Chump."

He took his time to line it up for the long, difficult three-rail bank shot. He shot it perfectly online, but he didn't strike the ball nearly hard enough. It rolled to a stop well short of the far corner pocket. The cue and the nine balls stopped at the exact same spots on the table as they were lined up for Simeon's shot. But they were on the opposite half of the table. This left Evans the same choice that Simeon had.

"How do you like dat? Same shot, opposite side of the table, Ev. What's it gonna be?"

Simeon presumed his friend would take the much easier one-rail shot to try to win the game. But he didn't.

"Three rails in the far corner. Just like you, Simmie Boy."

"Have you ever made dat shot before, Ev?"

---

[4] Clarence "Frog Man" Henry

"Maybe Ah have, maybe Ah haven't. But Ah tell you what. If Ah make dis shot, which is highly improbable, Ah want you to swear on this pool table that you'll go with me down to the Customs House tomorrow and join the Navy. We'll see if you can ultimately get orders to the same place Ahm stationed at. And we'll get your dago cousin over there behind bar to come and be a witness."

A moist, cool fear came over him. Simeon had seen Evans shoot pool many times. He was certain he would miss the difficult shot. But an uncanny strength of conviction upheld his confidence in the moment.

"And if you miss it?"

"All bets are off."

He paused, frozen by Evans' unexpected boldness, faith in himself, and courage to express such a deep concern for him.

"Ahm not comfortable basing a major life decision on a pool shot, Ev. Though Ahm certain you have mah best interests at heart."

"Awe-right, Simmie. Three rails to the far corner pocket."

Bending down to line up his shot, Evans Robertson's jaw was set with a confidence he hadn't had on any other pool shot that evening. He had a look in his eyes that Simeon had witnessed on only a few occasions in the past. In a split second, the cue ball struck the nine ball with a telling authority that Simeon hadn't noticed in any shot Evans took that evening. The nine ball obediently caromed off of the long first rail. It took a confident ninety degree right toward the short rail that held the two corner pockets on either end. Once it kissed the short rail, it parted right again, and began its steadfast journey to the long rail that was opposite the first long rail. It headed straight toward the now standing Evans who looked down on the proceedings with the aire of an artist in midstroke. The thick, yellow stripe in the middle of the nine-ball rolled over and over again atop the ivory sphere as it continued its forward motion. Upon striking the third rail, it rebounded left at a hard angle. It proceeded with determination in the direction of the far upper left corner from the shooter. Evans continued to eye his shot with a look that made certainty feel ashamed of itself. And Simeon watched with utter amazement as the nine ball dropped neatly and comfortably into the far corner pocket, like a baby chick waddling home under its mother's wing.

His pal, his buddy, his friend, turned to look at him. He had never looked on his Italian friend, his former roommate and companion in mischief, with such sympathy and concern. Their eyes locked in a long, silent pause.

"Now Ah aks you, mah good Dago friend. How many more chances with life do you think you're gonna get?"

Time Passage

Exploration

"Your conscience is the measure
of the honesty of your selfishness."
~ Richard Bach

Three

It was the Saturday before Halloween, 1968. The New Orleans fall
weather was as humid as it had been that summer. The side door to the
two-story home was open. A worn screen door fronted it, forbidding
never distant mosquitoes a blood meal. Looking in that direction,
Simeon saw his cousin, Trae, bounding up the steps. Without knocking,
he opened the screen door and walked in.
"Anybody home?"
He saw his cousin reading the newspaper at the kitchen table.
"What are you reading in the paper, Simmie?"
"Ah was catching up with what's goin on in the Vietnam War."

"You've been watching and worrying about wars since we were kids. Where's Paw-Paw Jacomo?"

"He went to see Aunt Shirl and Uncle Duckie?"

"Where's my Aunt Maria and Uncle Julian?"

"They're making groceries[5]."

"Where's Pokey and Shairee?"

"'They're at Aunt Mae and Uncle Gasparo's"

"You here all by yourself?"

"You writting a book, Trae? You didn't aks me about the dog. He's in the yard."

"Just because you grew an inch, shorty, don't think you're getting tough now. And any way, me and Lan were here first, don't forget."

He was encouraged that Trae noticed the growth.

"So what's going on with you?"

"We ain't seen each other for a while, Simmie boy. You wanna go for a walk and catch up? Let's go get some Barq's Root Beers from Nawby's. We can talk there, then walk to Audubon Park and catch up. Sound good? You got any money?"

"Ah got two dollars."

"Good, cause Ahm broke. You buyin."

The pathetic gaze Simeon proffered his cousin was followed by a slight purse of his lips and shaking of his head.

In a matter of seconds, the two sixteen year olds were into an early sweat as they turned to walk down State Street. The tower bells from Saint Francis announced that it was twelve noon.

"Ah don't remember those bells sounding at noon when we went to school there. You, Simm?"

"Ah think dey refurbished dem after we left."

"You see any of our old teachers,the nuns, living about seventy feet away across the street from them?"

"Hardly ever. Though sometimes Ah feel like Sistuh Eugene, Sistuh DeChantel[6], are Sistuh Ross are looking at my upstairs windows from their windows."

---

[5] "Making groceries" is an old New Orleans expression meaning "going to the grocery store"

[6] Pronounced 'Day-Shahn-tel'

"Good thing you didn't live across the street when we went there. Dat would have been creepy, Simm."

"Right on, Trae. Yes indeed."

The sounds of a mocking bird caught Simeon's attention as they stepped off the curb crossing Patton Street. It came from the direction of the nun's convent across the street. He noted the short, rapid-fire imitations that proceeded in four-second chirps and chatter bursts. But his thoughts went back to his cousin.

"Are you having girlfriend problems again?"

"Why are you aksing me dat? Did Cath call you again?"

"What do you think, Trufant[7]?"

"Why does she keep doing that? Ah don't care, really. Ah just hate dat she's talking about me. Ah guess Ahm glad she tells you instead of other people."

"Do you think shes gonna say anything about you dat Ah don't already know?"

"Ha-ha. No. We know each other too well, don't we, cuz?"

"Way to well, cuz. Since duh crib."

"So how awe you liking things at Redemptor? At least it gets you around girls more."

Simeon didn't answer.

"What's wrong, man? Ah aksed you how you're liking it at Redemptor. Why didn't you just stay at Saint Ignatius?"

"Okay, second question first. Ignatius was tough, man. Ah did good the first year. It got harder in the second year. We had to take Latin and French. Hours of homework every night. Ah had to take three buses and the street car each way. You know dat. It was getting old."

"You still talk with Barry Q., Derbs, and Crisp?"

"Naw. Not since Ah left Saint Ignatius."

Silence ensued for a moment.

"You know what Ah miss, Trae? Ah miss neighborhood, king cake pawties, and crawfish boils. Corner bars and grocery stores where everybody knows everybody else. Where you walk down the street and see a lot of folks you mostly know. Families getting togethuh…."

---

[7] Pronounced 'True-font'

Trae was silent. And he wondered if he was teasing something inside of him as he talked. They walked past The Sugar Bowl Confectionary where the kids from Saint Francis stopped to get candy on the way home from school. The majestic oaks that populated State Street looked down on the two familiar fifteen year olds as they passed beneath. The mimicking, mocking sound of the mockingbird was as loud as it was when they were a block behind. It had apparently landed again along their path in one of the oaks.

"The old Sugar Bowl."

He thought he heard a hint of affection in Trae's announcement. He welcomed it.

"If Ah tell you something, you gotta promise none of our parents, aunts, or uncles ever find out."

Trae's eyes lit up.

"You got it. Is it a nice, juicy piece of gossip?"

"Naw. We'll get into some uh dat later. Okay. Ah never told you what happened at Ignatius, with me leaving and all uh dat."

"Nope."

"It was a thing of beauty, man. Ah've been dying to tell somebody about the secret scheme Ah manufactured to get outta there."

"Ahm all ears, cuz."

"Okay. Momma insisted dat Ah stay there, but you already know dat. She wants me to have a good shot at a future and thought dat staying there would give it to me. But Ah wanted out. So Ah self-designed a slow-fail plan dat kept me at the point of nearly failing out of school by mid year. The secret to the scheme is to not have your grades so high by mid-term that you have to tank it real bad at the end. Dat way it looks like you're trying to fail, which Ah was."

"Dis brilliant, Mangino. Ahm takin notes, man."

"Momma was hurt. She works hard outside the house so we can afford tuition and all uh dat. But Trae, Ah just had to get outta there."

Trae could only stare at his cousin with sheer admiration.

"Ah wanted to give the impression, and Ah said so to momma, dat Ah was gonna work hard to get my grades up by finals time."

"But you were planning on doing the exact opposite. Clever, yes indeed."

"It was tricky by the third grading period. Ah had to show some improvement, but not enough so dat it would be hard to fail for the year."

"A true master. Ah'd tip my hat if Ah had one on. Ah knew you had a conniving bent inside. Ah've known you as long as Ah've known me. Ah also have known you to be lazy, crazy, wild,… want me to go on?"

"Naw, dat's okay. Ah'll remember you said those things about me when we get to Nawby's, and Ah get mah Barqs Root Beer and play pinball alone with mah two dollars."

"Okay, okay. You know Ahm just kidding."

"Can Ah go on now?"

"When the last grading period began, mah grades were perfectly situated to pass or fail by for the year. And Ah know it's mean to mah momma, but she's over it now. Ahm at a good school. And you know, Trae, after seeing the plan through, Ah look back with a sense of pride on the accomplishment."

"In your weirdly wired way, and mine too, as we both fall from the same tree, you need to think of this as a masterpiece of devious scheming and cunning. Mah congratulations to you, Simmie boy."

"Congratulations accepted, Trae."

The clouds above moved rapidly across the crescent city skyline. Patches of the rolled, bright, white mass glided rapidly across the blue background with breaks in between. They appeared to be in a hurry, or so Simeon thought. He noticed that the train of clouds continued uninterrupted across the horizon. They continued to come forth from beyond the mix of oak, cypress, and magnolia trees and from beyond the rooftops as they walked. In his inquisitive way, he wondered if the rapidly moving immaterial masses might somehow be a means of transport in a larger story.

Trae changed the subject.

"What do you wanna be, Simmie? Ah mean, when you're done with school and all uh dat? What do you wanna do?"

He wasn't shocked by the question. He and Trae had leaned into deeper spaces before.

"Beats the heck outta me, man. What about you?"

"Ah got no idea either, cuz. Hear's Nawby's. Whaddya say, two Barq's Root Beers and with the rest, we hit the pinball?

Simeon rubbed his chin, feigning to ponder the proposition his cousin so generously proffered with money that wasn't his.

"Okay, good. Glad you agree, Simm. Let's go in."

"Wait till Cath calls me again to complain about you. Ahm gonna tell her how you teased me outta mah two dollars."

In bed that evening he remembered the questions that Trae put to him: *"What do yuh wanna be, Simmie? What do yuh wanna do?"*

He wondered why he couldn't answer the questions. Crisp could. So could Derbs and Barry Q.. A lot of the guys and girls could. Some probably weren't sure. He thought of Ranny, Sturgis, and Oss-kuh. He knew they wanted to go to college. But he didn't even know that.

Ambition for anything that required persistence and effort toward noble achievement was a stranger to him. And desire for a career was nowhere to be found. He presumed that he would know it when it showed up at his door with a large Capital A written on its ballcap, announcing his designated career slot. Or, he presumed he would stumble on it by sheer luck.

His thoughts began to fade. In seconds, he slowly bobbed in and out of the early phase of falling asleep. He was aware that his thoughts seemed to be perking, before settling down and fading. And within minutes, the intensity of his attention began to diminish. Almost effortlessly, it began to travel the familiar bedtime journey from real-world thoughts into quasi-real-world thoughts. There, the effortless regression continued.

His awareness leisurely slid down into a small boat on a peaceful, still water. Once there, the boat began to drift gently into the unknown netherworld known as 'sleep'. It was finally detached from the mooring of his conscious thoughts, where it floated in and through the realm of his sub-conscious. As it drifted deeper into the realm, a single, clear, and distinct image suddenly appeared in his mind's eye. It formed seemingly out of thin air and went into motion like it was playing on a gigantic movie screen.

In the dream, he saw what he knew to be a national television news anchor from the future. He was normal in every way except that he had giant earlobes. His left earlobe was an extremely bright blue, such that it was almost too bright to look at directly. He noted a room full of men and women watching the newsman. Their earlobes were extremely large as well. Many of them showed varied shades of darker or lighter blue-lit left earlobes. One or two of the blue-lit lobes were as bright as that of the newsman's. A few of the others had their large *right* lobes lit in dimmer to brighter shades of *red*. Several of those were an extremely bright red light.

There were no sounds until the image began to fade. As it did, he heard a voice muttering a short, faint sound. He barely heard it, but thought that sounded like *"Mo"*. And its sound was imprinted as an image on the front of a ball cap.

Four

"Up and at 'em, you three."

Julian moved rapidly as he passed through the upstairs bedrooms the following morning. Within minutes, Simeon was bedecked in his bland school uniform. His younger brother, Pokey, was a freshman at the same high school. He poked around the bedroom, rubbing his eyes and mumbling. He couldn't find his pants.

Shairee, his baby sister, prepared for the start of her eighth grade school day at Saint Francis. It stood seventy-five yards across the street, behind the convent that faced their home.

His dad, Julian Mangino, and momma, Maria, were busy about their morning routines. His maternal PawPaw, Jacomo, sat downstairs at the kitchen table. He was relaxed, leaning back slightly in the circular-armed wooden kitchen chair. His upper left arm rested flat on the table. His forearm extended upward with a lit cigarette extending from his fingers like a fading beacon.

Simeon opened the top drawer to his chest of drawers in search of a comb. When he moved a shirt, he uncovered a black and white photo taken in 1954. In it, he sat as a two-year old on the lap of his paternal Paw-Paw, Tino. It got his attention. In a millisecond, he was drawn into the distant past beyond the day it was taken. Instinctively, he was on the wonder trail in search of his ancestors.

His Paw-Paw peered from the photo as their nearest ambassador. He was part of him, and those who came before him. His Paw-Paw Jacomo was downstairs. Parts of his family's DNA made up who he was as well. Unseen factors were at work. He couldn't fathom the science of it. But in the moment, it kindled his sense of being, of home, and of place.

Skipping breakfast, he headed out the door to catch the bus for school. With the sentiment still fresh, he walked past his family members and took note of each one. Their presence fit, as did each household item, in its placed or misplaced location. Every familiar presence was a stamp of familiarity that affirmed his nimble hold on meaning. Each was a marker. Every human touch, every word and look, fortified something inside. Every routine item and passing place deepened an imprint already there.

He walked past Ranny's house next door, and past Osskuh's behind Marquette's Hardware Store on the corner at Magazine Street. The bus stop was there. And within minutes, he was seated on the Magazine Street bus, a mere block and a half from his front steps. He was on his way on a one-bus ride down the river to Redemptor High. It was his new place of adventure and discovery for the next three years, and the only co-ed parochial high school in the city. He welcomed the change.

A mile and a half down Magazine Street, the bus stopped at the corner stop at Bourdeau Street. As the bus slowed to a stop, Lan, his paternal cousin, stood to enter the bus. On the left, he noted the old neighborhood bar that was once run by Trae's uncle. Lan and Trae, though not related themselves, were like cousins to one another. Though the three of them competed and prodded, they didn't know life without one other.

Lan made his way to the back of the bus. When he came to the seat where his cousin sat, he stopped.

"Push over."

Simeon shook his head as he slid over next to the window.

"In case you didn't notice, the seat across from us is open, as are most of the seats around us."

The remark dripped with an attempt at sarcasm, which he knew from experience, wouldn't stick.

"Ah just wanted to give you the chance to experience once again how good it is to be close to me. You've been lucky to have dat chance for sixteen years now, since you were born. And never forget, me and Trufant were here two months before you."

"How could Ah forget, you two keep reminding me."

The bus picked up speed again. The cousins sat in silence, trading yawns both large and small that imtermittently erupted in unison.

"You coming around tonight, cugino[8]?"

"Maybe. Are you and Betz going around Doraix's tonight?"

"Ah guessso, Simmie boy."

---

[8] "Cugino" – Italian: male cousin

A dozen or so yawns later, the bus neared Simeon's departure stop at Jackson Avenue. He rose to head to the rear door. So he could access the aisle, he nudged with his knee one of the two cousins whom he could never forget, was "here first".

"See if you can scrounge up seventy-five cents, Simmie. Me and Betz will too. We can walk down to Jaw-jes and get a few quarts of Dixie[9]. Why don't you pass by my house and we can walk over to Betz's on the way down there."

"Awe-right. Ah'll give Evans a call. See you later."

Simeon got off the bus and headed for school.   In less than ten minutes he crawled into the back of Coach Theaux's[10] homeroom several minutes late. The venerable old baseball coach and math teacher caught him sliding into his desk seat.

"Mangino! You're late!"

"Sorry coach."

"This is gettin old, boy. Something the matter, son?"

"Nope. Just late, coach."

"You come on the Magazine bus?"

"Uh-huh."

Every Ram in the room anticipated the anointing. One month in, he was getting baptized.

"Catch the earlier one tomorrow, you damn fool!"

And with that, he was officially part of the Redemptor student body, a Ram forever. He had heard that a young man didn't have the total Ram experience until Coach Theaux called him a "damn fool".

The room erupted with yuks and chuckles. He released an easy grin when he caught the nods of approval from a few of the sophomore boys. He had crossed a hurdle, been given a rite of passage. Coach Theaux had finally called him a "damn fool".   In the secret chamber where the ego lurks, he congratulated himself.

There was a noticeable similarity among the folk who grew up on the river side of Magazine Street. The aroma of local crabs, crawfish, and shrimp boiling behind the local bars, or in backyards, was a familiar

---

[9] An original New Orleans brew

[10] Pronounced: "Thay-o's"

scent. The seasoned smell was familiar to one and all in the neighborhoods where most of the houses were a mere thin alley apart.

During the Great Depression, Monday was wash day for New Orleanian housewives. Because kidney beans were cheap and easy to cook, it became a tradition to boil a potful for the day while they did housework. The tradition of eating red beans and rice for Monday suppers lived on. And the spicy meal's weekly appearance added more flavor to the feeling of home and place for every homeboy and girl.

The corner barrooms generally stayed open into the early morning hours, and often, all night on weekends. And if a bar was across from, or down the street from one of the playgrounds, it brought another dimension of life and activity to the neighborhood. Softball and baseball leagues were active along the river and their fallout spilled into the local establishments.

Multifaceted and fluid interaction wove effortlessly among a people who had much in common. Yet, in the economic boom that Simeon and his baby boomer generation grew up in, many set their sights on moving out to the surburbs. But a small few would not so easily disengage from the world they clutched onto for meaning.

Far above Memphis, the Mississippi meandered south on its long trek to larger waters. As it did, newer water moved through the crescent city each passing second. And while the locals went about their business day and night, the muddy, murky water of the Mighty Mississippi flowed on and on, carrying many things along the way.

A few hundred yards inside the crescent turn of the river, Simeon randomly applied himself at his undefined craft. As the weeks went by, he distanced himself further from most things related to his Old Oak Tree and the meaningful experiences when he was a boy on a bike. But he could never stray too far from what happened to him in the first grade.

Each experience hung as a marker in the near hallway of his mind. He placed each one there just after they occurred, knowing they were significant in his story. But one was closest to the doorway leading to his conscience. That one was an image of a bird silhouetted against a blue sky. Deep in his soul, he never wanted to not be able to recall the image if he needed it to hang on to. Something deep, personal, and profound happened that hot, early September day. The spark was ignited by words and kindled by that bird in the sky.

The image hung in the back of his mind like a treasure that no one could steal away. But the six year-old became a sixteen year-old. And like a wound up toy with a very tight spring, he was loose to charge into adventure on a whim. So he did.

He spun, whirrled, and rolled. He hopped and leaped, and repeated. There was no indication that the spring was going to finally unwind. And he presumed that there was nothing in sight that would slow his momentum anytime soon. A bird in first-flight realizes adrenalin it had not known before. Instead of laboring over the homework that Ignatius would have required, he was on the street corner in front of Doraix's, drinking Dixie Beer and being cool.

He was able to be served in most of the bars along the river. But he was forbidden in two – Mitts and Fumps. They were the two that were closely associated with his family. His Paw-Paw Tino worked at Mitts and lived across the street from Fumps. The two sat as bookends, each occupying an end of the same short block. And he told the proprietors to not let any of his grandsons in until he let them know they had turned eighteen. Until then, other establishments, street corners, and adventures did nicely to maintain the adrenalin first seized in his maiden flight.

Mitts was the place where a large concentration of eighteen and older young men hung out days and nights. It was attractive to Simeon to be part of that crowd. It had a history as the place that their daddies and uncles hung out in their younger days. His older cousins went there. And on occasion, their dads would drop in for a drink or two.

He rode the momentum into the lifestyle that his forefathers had forged growing up in the neighborhood. He looked forward to the day two years into the future when he would be able to be part of the crowds at the two establishments. And come what may, it was into the life of that short city block, where the two corner placeholders held many secrets about his roots, where he intended to continue his journey.

Five

"Okay, class. I'll read a few paragraphs to help us continue our discussion on abstract thinking. Now I want all of you to turn to page fourteen. I see Mr. Felgoux[11] doesn't have his book, hee-hee-hee."

"Yeah, Sis-tuh. Ah, ugh, well,….. Ah left it on the Magazine bus."

"Now you know, Mr. Felgoux..,.."

"A.J."

"A.J'? Did you say *A.J.?*"

"Dat's what everybody calls me, Sis-tuh."

"Oh. Hee-hee-hee, oh."

"Dat's not true, Sis-tuh. Most of us call him 'Buddy', 'Buddy Felgoux'. And did you know dat him and his sistuh, Jo-Annie, have fourteen brothers and sistuhs? Sixteen kids. You know his sis-tuh Jo-Annie, right?"

"Well, ugh, yes, … Hee-hee. And well, my goodness. Thank you, Mr. Mangino. I didn't know that, Mr. Felgoux. Congratulations. Hee-hee. Now, what was I saying…?"

Sister Peter Mary Fouriere[12] looked up and rubbed her chin.

"If my recollect recollects correctly, Sis-tuh, Ah believe you were getting ready to read to us from page fourteen."

"Yes, of course, page fourteen. Thank you, Mr. Mangino."

While she turned the pages, Simeon and A.J. slipped a gentle low five hand slap from their seats.

She began to read:

> "She hadn't learned enough from life to realize
> that Ambition was humming steadily along. It lurked
> beneath what she and others could see or know about
> herself. Ambition was powering her soul like the
> hormones that governed her body's chemistry. Along

---

[11] Pronounced: "Fel-goo"
[12] Pronounced: "For-ee-a"

with Motive it served to give her a cohesive, hidden power source and abstract internal support structure for her actions. Motive and Ambition were alive and serving to move her thoughts, words, and actions toward a particular end, having a goal in mind."

"She was an adolescent. She wasn't at a point in her mental and emotional development where she could discern what her Motives and Ambitions were. No doubt vast numbers of adults aren't able to either. Some of her teenage friends were maturing. They were motivated by obvious noble pursuits that required time, attention, and positive energy. And the end of their Motives and Ambitions would be noticeable virtues and strong character. Her motives, however, led her into a hot pursuit of misguided adventure. She was committed to find herself through good times, friends, and having fun in her community. And its culture not only sanctioned that lifestyle but offered up its next generation at its altar. She had not yet learned maturity's first motive. That is, Motive and Ambition need to be intentionally channeled in a good direction with noble intentions and guided by high moral values."

The soft spoken nun finished reading. She looked up over her reading glasses and spoke.

"Well, class, how might these ideas help us to be more aware of what abstract thinking is?"

A thinly participated in discussion began. Simeon listened silently. He looked over at the stack of books along the shelf below the window. Various works were on display. Hawthorne, Emerson, Dickens, and Frost were among the names whose works they were to read in the months ahead.

"Fairly interesting, Ah guess."

He was surprised to hear the words whispered softly from his mouth. They leaked out as if he had something on his mind that he couldn't fully

disengage from. Some were engaged in the discussion with the teacher.
And he wondered why he wasn't. The topic was interesting. He wasn't
ready to go abstract with his thoughts in real time with them. But
something resonated with the words Sister read. And the discussion was
helping him to probe new places.

But his quest down vanity lane held greater appeal. He leaned back,
almost in defiance, with his chin on his fist. His eyelids closed. The
shifty side went into gear, ready to carry him down his familiar path. He
picked up his heavy knapsack to head toward Neverland again. It was a
whole lot easier.

But he couldn't nap. He was preoccupied, trying to distance himself
from the discussion. It extended possibilities for a life he abandoned.
As a boy on a bike, he was always uncertain if his organic growth was
going to bear fruit that satisfied. So he left the garden in search of
something else that might. Now, he was coming into a time in his
journey when his knapsack was getting heavier from the experiences he
packed into it. On his chosen path, he was taking the slow turn that
would lead him to discover what people of the night often do. He was
heading into the space where he encountered the first approach to the
dark void.

"What chall doin Frahday night, Dago?"

The whispered question surprised him.

The old nun looked up in their direction, then went back to her
discussion. Simeon replied with a whisper.

"Nothing special. Some of the guys are gonna hang out around
Doraix's."

"Ah think Ah'll join ya'll. Ah'll walk by your house at six. And we
can take the Magazine bus."

"Okay."

The coveted weekend came. And Saturday afternoon was absorbed by
early evening. The boys pitched in their coins and dollar bills. They
stood around and drank beer. Occasionally, others with cars drove to the
corner and mingled. By midnight, they were down to their last two six
packs, eight bodies, and one car.

"It's hot as h-e-double toothpicks out hear. And it's hot midnight. Let's go down to Audubon Pawk and sit in the fountain pool near the zoo. We can drink our hot beer there and cool off."

Finding Simeon's idea agreeable, the boys headed there. He led them to the cement kiddie pool.

Twin rows of mature white oaks ran from Magazine Street to the fountain, which sat peacefully at the end of the rows, spaced between the last two oaks. A lone mockingbird applied itself assiduously nearby in the musty summer night air. Its litany was composed of varied chirps, tweets, and chitters. And they were tantalizing to Simeon's ears. He recalled one of its kind along the route that he and Trae walked a few blocks away, on the way to Nawby's. While the gang bantered about nothing and everything, he willingly engaged with the sounds coming from the tree.

"Are you mocking, little critter, or just showing off your talents? Sounds like mocking to me, even in the middle of the night."

No one heard his thoughts.

Momentarily, he was alone with the winged pest as he stretched out in the warm water below the thick, mossy, canopy overhead. The last two oaks guarded either side of the concrete pond. Their thick branches spread over the shallow water from either side of the cement pond. They met affectionately in the middle and invaded the space of the other like caring, competing cousins who were born and raised next to one another. From one side of the fountain pool wherein the boys lay, a steady flow of water poured forth into the night air. The water lazily charged upward into the night air before arriving at its arc and rapidly diving into the twelve inch concrete pond that held the lads. Twin park lamposts revealed the after-hours presence of the late teens wallowing there. Already into his reflective side, Simeon began to leak his freshly stirred abstract proclivity on his buddies.

"So why are we sitting hear at one in the morning in our underwear, in the fountain at Audubon Pawk?"

"You forgort to add dat we are drinking hot Dixie Beer, Simmie, you dumb dago."

"Dat's right, Sturgis, tell him. He's aksin us why we're here. When it was his idea to come here and strip down to our drawers."

"Shuddup, Trae. You didn't complain when Simmie suggested we come here to the fountain to cool off. It's ninety degrees at one in the morning. You know the fountain feels good in here."

"Yeah ,but Ah just saw a frog jump next to me, Graves. Ah hate those slimey suckuhs. And mah daddy's a cop on patrol in the neighborhood right now. If he catches me, Ahm dead meat."

"Shuddup, Trae. I'll handle your old man. Leave him to me."

"Yeah, Felgoux, if your momma finds out we were in this slimy water at one in the morning, let's see what you get."

"Ah know if Officer Art Trufant finds out his son was sitting in this fountain drinking beeuh in his underwear, we're all gonna be in trouble."

"Dat's what Ahm trying to tell them, Lan. But your cousin, Simmie, keeps talking us into doing stuff in our drawers."

"*My* cousin? He's your cousin too, Trae."

The rest of the testosterone-laced, uptown teens erupted with laughter in the fountain pool.

"Yeah, and how come we always let Simmie talk us into doing stuff in our drawers out in public late at night?"

"You mean like - *right now, Tabes*?"

"Yeah, Stick. Like right now."

"Ya'll are just jealous dat Ah always come up with the good ideas."

"Whatever you say, Simm. Whatever you say."

The piercing cry of a flamingo penetrated the silent, humid, early morning air. It came from a place deep within the zoo that abutted the fountain pool where they lounged in the lazy morning darkness. And Simeon wondered as its cry echoed through the large park.

The herd of long legged pink birds couldn't fly away. Their wings were clipped. For much of their lives, they stood on only one leg in a fenced-in area of the zoo. They could protest with their signature high-pitched 'finn-ARK' sounds to no avail. They were confined to their cages until their last breaths.

When the echo faded, the nearby winged vertebrate resumed its nighttime concerto. Simeon picked up with it where he left off.

"Mocking, mocking, always mockin, little fella. Who are you mockitn tonight as me and the boys relax in this pond?"

His thoughts were interrupted by a second cry of a flamingo resounding through the dark, soupy air. And he wondered if the mockingbird heard the flamingo's cry and if he was mocking them all in their confinement to a specific place. And he reasoned to himself, with more than a slight touch of introspection:

"Its wings aren't clipped. It can fly away any time it wants to."

Six

It was July 20th, in the year 1969. A group of teenage males moseyed along the choppy brick sidewalk. It was mid-evening, and each of them wore a thick veneer of sweat in the humid evening air.

"How much money ya'll got, fellas?"

"Ah got fitty cents, Ray Bay."

Betz grinned large at the suspicious accountant.

"Awe-right, Betz. Who's next?"

"How bout you, Lan?"

"Ahm not saying yet."

"Evans?"

"Come on, Lan. Ah got ninety five cents."

"Tabes?"

"A dollar forty-five."

"Dago number three, … Flip?"

"What do you mean, number three? Ahm dago number one, man. Ah got two dollars and eighty cents, man. Ah ain't no number three, man, Ah…"

Ray Bay cut him off.

"Simmie? How bout you?"

"Ah got eighty cents. And Ah know Betz has more than fifty cents. See how he grinned when he answered you. He always says 'fitty cents' when you aks him."

"Okay, okay. Ah got two dollars and fitty cents tonight."

"Dat's more like it, Betz, you sorry rascal. And back to you, Lan. You in?"

"Count me in for a buck and a half."

"Timmy Norris?"

"Ninety-five cents."

"Joey?"

"Five dollars."

"Nice. Tweet?"

"Eight dollars. Ah won in the poker game last night at Mel Paines."

"Duh jackpot! Yeah you rite!"

"Shatt?....... Shatt! What are you looking at over there, man? Ahm talkin you. We're doing the count. How much you got Shatalein?"

"Ah got tree bucks."

"Tree bucks is good."

"Izzi?

"Two and a quarter. Ah busted the piggy bank."

"Oh yeah, Izz. Nice. And Ward, last one."

"Two dollars, and Ahm ready to git dis show on the road, baby. Let's git while the gittins good."

"Eh labas[13]. Well, we're sitting pretty tonight. Okay den. Dat should do us easy for some quarts at Jaw-jes and quite a bit for something else after."

They strolled down to Georges Bar, where they served through the side window. Old Man George, an ex-New Orleans cop, left to fetch their cold beverages. They could see the television broadcasting a fuzzy black and white image through the window. It was televising the first man to walk on the moon. The boys crowded around the window, nudging one another out of the way like pups on their mother's nipples, trying to see and hear about the historic event.

With cold quart beers in hand, the lads proceeded to walk back to the corner at Doraix's, consuming them along the way. When they arrived back to their street corner perch, they bantered about the moon-walk and miscellaneous other important teenage interests and random neighborhood gossip.

It was a midweek school night. Those who hadn't dropped out of high school to work would be certain to not miss school the next day. Their parents would see to that. Each of the boys sported a slick head of hair combed back or to the side off of their foreheads. Most of them had a comb at the ready in a rear pocket. And if one were to ask to borrow the esteemed item, the young man could produce it in the blink of an eye. The thin-toothed accessory was as important in the wardrobe as the chosen pants that were lucky enough to cradle it that particular evening.

---

[13] Pronounced: "A-lah-bah"; a Cajun exclamation of agreement or positive affirmation.

The occasional use of it to two-handedly re-slick the hair back into place was an acceptable image-enhancing move.

Not unusually, Simeon found himself quietly cherishing the evening with his whimsical and tease-happy friends. Testosterone was leaking into the steamy corner air and macho male bonding was crackling among them like embers on a stoked fire.

The group of young men were known as The Laurel Street Gang, though by definition of what a 'gang' was they hardly qualified. The moniker was bestowed on the boys by one of the girls in the neighborhood. The mischievous and fun-loving crew was made up of a fluid crowd. Lan was a constant presence in Simeon's life since birth. And like Trae, he was always aware, and didn't mind saying so, that he and Trae were two months older than him. He bonded with Betz at Redemptor. Tabes Benjamin introduced Evans Robertson to the scene. Joey Groves, Tweet Pertoit[14], Timmy Norris, and Flip Grosscano lived within a short stroll to Doraix's. Ray-Bay Nichols , Ward Peters, Shattelein, and Ike Izzi lived close to Audubon, near Simeon and Trae.

These were the suspects that loitered on the corner that first-man-on-the-moon evening.   As the evening wore on, a New Orleans Police squad car from the Second District pulled up to the corner. Officer Mervin Bates, a Redemptor grad ten years Simeon's senior, gave the look to the boys on the corner.

"What are y'all up to, boys?"

The venerable, pain-in-the-twat neighborhood cop wasn't known to cut much slack. The boys mostly looked away and down, hands in pockets. Some shuffled their feet. One or two spit on the ground, a universal sign of toughness.

"Nuttin", "Takin it easy", "*Ah* dunnno'" and other slippery, non-committal replies were heard coming from the LSG boys.

"Ya'll not planning nuttin stupid, Ah hope."

"Nope", "Who, *US*?", "No way, man".

None of the corner denizens made eye contact with the familiar policeman.

"Who's bottles of Dixie are those over there against the wall?"

---

[14] Pronounced: "Per-twah"

"Mussbe some of the old men in the bar, Mervin, Ah mean, Officer
Bates. They must have left them out here. Ah think they're empty.
Want me to show you?"

Tabes was full of himself, and something else.

"Don't be a smart-aleck. And don't let me catch ya'll drinking on this
corner. I'll take *all* ya'll in, you hear me?"

And with that he was off till the next shakedown.

"Let's head over to Mel Paines."

Everyone was in with the idea. And as Tweet bounced down the
sidewalk in front of them, without a whisper to the contrary, the whole
lot of them got up and began to follow him.

Tweet Pertoit, hardly the leader of the crowd, was an easily well-liked
and congenial cut-up in the neighborhood. He had an air of toughness
with thick, wavy, greased-back auburn hair and a rabid pep in his step for
a stocky guy. But he had a soft heart beneath his tough veneer. He was
quick with a laugh or a joke and the universal tease that all uptown men
along the river wore as a badge of honor. He also had a wild side. He
loved adrenaline and most of the means that brought it in life, especially
fast cars and motorcycles.

With Tweet leading the way, the small group of young bucks headed to
Mel Paines. It was three blocks away on the corner of Napoleon and
Tchoupitoulas Streets. It stood across the wide street from BiviQ's Bar.
On the way, the boys took an inventory of the kitty. Joey Groves was
nineteen and out of high school. He worked steadily in television repair
and was generous. He always made sure the boys were covered.

After a few beers, Simeon, Betz, Evans, and Joey got into a discussion
about the war in Vietnam, world events, and the world's future. Simeon
perked up as they dove into the topic.

Joey was of the impression that the world was just fine. The war in
Vietnam didn't indicate that the world as a whole was in danger. After
all, wars have always been around. Betz and Evans went back and forth
on the idea that the world was headed for a bad place. Evans, especially,
thought that might be the case. Simeon, for his part, was *sure* that the
world was becoming more and more of a hostile place. As a matter of
fact, and he didn't mind saying it, he believed that the world might, no

would, end in his lifetime. The declaration made, the other three in the discussion stopped and gazed at him.

"Yuh really think so, Simm?"

"Ahm sure of it, Joey."

"How can you be sure?"

"Just am."

"Come on, Simm, you can't know dat. Nobody can."

"Ah can't tell you how Ah know, Betz. Ah just know it."

"No way the world's gonna end by the year 2000, Simm Mangino."

"Tell you what Joey. Ah'll bet you fifty bucks dat the world will end by the year 2000."

With the statement, Joey broke into a giant grin. He quickly offered his hand for Simeon to shake.

Which he did.

"Eh labas! I'll see you in the year 2000, Simmie boy."

"Simm, there's now way you can win that bet. If you win we'll all be dead and outta hear."

"Yeah, Ev, and will Simm have any money to pay up in the year 2000?"

"Ah won't have to worry, Betz, because Ahm right."

And with that, the debate ended when one of their favorite songs, *"Lipstick Traces"* began playing over the juke box. It was sung by one of the many famous local and beloved New Orleans musicians, Benny Spellman. Feet began moving and voices joined in.

As the evening wore on, the rambunctious lads ventured out of Mel Paine's. They walked a half mile through the tightly-packed uptown streets for one final stop before calling it a night.

They tussled along. And each familiar old house they passed, and every crease and bump on the street where they tread, were markers for his place. But they were no match for the steady flow of adrenelin that accompanied his bond with his friends.

In no time they were about to enter Huntster's Bar, not fifty yards from Lan's front door. It sat across from the fenced-in cage protecting home plate at Wisemar Playground, one short block down from Mitt's.

Approaching Huntster's, the boys came upon Put Smith, an African American man in the neighborhood. Old Put was the same age as their daddies. They knew him since they were young boys. He was short, on the thin side, and always wore a flat gatsby hat with a short rim. He was never seen without his shirt tucked inside his baggy pants and wore his belt high onto his waist. What could be seen of his closely-cropped Afro hairdo was graying along the temples. He was dark-skinned.

Put was mostly quiet and soft-spoken, that is, depending on how much he had to spend on shots of wine. He purchased them at the side window of one of the three barrooms on Lions Street - Huntster's, Mitt's, and Fump's. He was a regular on one of the three corners most of his afternoons and evenings. Each day, he spent what little he had to buy wine at one of windows. He depended on handouts after. Simeon had known of Put since he was a kid. He lived the first five years of life a short half a block away, behind Lan, in the old slave quarters annex of the old Plantation home.

The man Put was a fixture in the two block area of the community. And when he was juiced up on the fruit of the vine, he became quite gregarious and verbal.

"Dey call me *Put*! P-U-T! Sounds like FOOT! Yuh oughtta have a qwawtuh fuh Old Put. And you can put it right-cheeuh."

And with that Old Put would extend the palm of his hand right side up, hoping to receive some coin for another drink.

Simeon often wondered about Old Put. Locals sometimes made fun of him behind his back. Some teased him. And many dropped quarters in his hand. Those who served him at the barroom window engaged with him some until he got so drunk he began to aggravate them. Stories went around about him. But no one seemed to care one way or the other about him. He was often spotted knocked out on the sidewalk on one of the corners or between his house and the bars. More often than not, the poor, old gentleman was taken for granted, like one would walk by a telephone pole, or a parked car.

He paused to look back to him before going in to Hunster's.

"Good Old Put."

With the pause, he felt a shove in his back.

"What are you doing, Simmie. Why are you standing in the doorway? Go head in."

An hour later, the boys stumbled out of Huntster's. The sound of a train horn traveled across the neighborhood. Simeon's attention was stolen away from the ribbing going on between the guys. It went to the sound of the train horn from the railroad tracks two blocks away. He thought he heard the familiar sound of a bell that rang a few times after the horn sounded.

He looked down the block to where Lan lived. And he remembered the black and white photo in the top drawer in his bedroom. The little boy in the photo sat on his Paw-Paw Tino's lap in the yard a half block away. It was taken fifteen years earlier.

"This is my home."

The sentence was closer to a pledge than a statement.

He and Evans walked the fifty yards to Lan's house. When they left him, he couldn't help pause to stare into the yard behind the house, where he lived as a child, and where the photo was taken of him on his Paw Paw's lap. As they stepped toward the bus stop, the train horn blew again, followed by the bells. It seemed for an instant as if something so routine and familiar was meant to point to something else. But as in all things, his attention to the notion easily faded. Other things were more important.

And the nearby river flowed on and on from the far north.

Seven

By his seventeenth birthday, there was a new pep in his step.

He had a car, thanks to his daddy, who handed him the keys to his 1961 serviceable Chevy Impala. Off-and-on part time jobs helped pay for some of the expenses. When in an off-again season, he ramped up the fun. Adventure was out there waiting. And he was all in.

Yet, there were a few times when he allowed himself to recall what life was like as an innocent boy on his bike in the neighborhood. Somewhere inside, there were vestiges of hunger and desire for something else. And his curiosity was stirred one afternoon, while driving through the neighborhood.

One rarely drove down the block that Simeon turned onto that cool, late fall afternoon. It was on Constance Street, one block from Audubon Park. On the left, stood a home for special needs adults. The Order of the Poverty Servants, a kind and compassionate religious order of nuns, lived in the structure on the right. It occupied the entire square block and was completely surrounded by a nine-foot high brick wall. A taller brick structure inside the compound stood out above the high outer wall. It gave that entire square block the look of a fortress.

When he turned, he saw The Old Oak Tree. Impulsively, he locked onto it like a kid who had misplaced a valued item.

As a boy, he often rode under it alone or with others. Coming into adolescence, he and his friends rode their bikes under the tree with him to sit on Gerry LeClerc's frontporch. She was his first girlfriend in the days of innocence. In the moment, the time containing the memories seemed like another life ago, a life he walked away from.

The particular stretch of Constance Street did something for him, not only due to the memories of recent youthful times past, but also because of The Old Oak Tree that was there.

The venerable Old Tree guarded the front of the special needs home. In the days of his youth, it was showing signs of slow decay. It wore considerably more Spanish moss than it did leaves. Its main trunk extended upward with a slight lean toward the street, before its appendages sprouted toward the heavens in all directions. Its appearance and slight lean gave the impression that the beautiful organism had seen its better days.

His initial attraction to it was due to its abundance of Spanish moss. The soft gray, curly fungus overpowered its leaves, adding charm to the serene street that displayed it. The thicker fungus also gave it a somber appearance that intrigued him. The Old Tree appeared to be tired. Yet, there was something splendid and mysterious about it.

He parked his '61 Chevy and gazed at his Old Friend. And not unusually, he was aware of something. What it was he didn't know. But it was real. Not because of a New Age spiritual idea of an impersonal voice from nature and the cosmos speaking to the god in everyone. He knew there was no god in him. But he was aware that he was more than just a body.

Something was happening once again as he sat beneath it. And it was as real as something else from his past, from his early years. But he withdrew from all such experiences, as if looking for life in easy possibilities, rather than in the nurturing of fruits from some of the rich experiences in the days of innocence.

Mere blocks from where he sat, Old Man River scurried along. From the Carrollton Street flood gauge south, past the Nashville and Napoleon Avenue Wharves, it moved along. Toward the the Jackson and Canal Street ferries, to the crescent turn at Harmony Street beyond the French Quarter, the muddy water churned through the city. It pushed on toward its ultimate destination, always carrying with it material from the past. And always moving on to the future, an unknown future.

Eight

"Why are you going home so early, Simm? It's only ten o'clock."

"Ahm not feeling good, Betz. Dat stuff ya'll been sniffing got to me."

"But you only took one hit."

"One too many, Tweet. Walk with me to duh Tchoupitoulas bus stop, guys."

"Ah'll go with ya'll. Ha-ha. Ole Simmie can't take the heavy stuff. Come on, Betz, Tweet. Let's get him on the bus."

"Okay Evans, you crazy son-of-a-gun. But why's Simmie taking the Tchoupitoulas bus? Ya'll always take the Magazine bus."

"Ah don't know, butt-head. But dat's what Simm wants and he's not feeling good. Let's get him there, heh-heh. Man, mixed with Dixie Beer, dat stuff gets you pretty giddy, eh Betz?"

"Whoooh, baby."

Betz's eyes and grin were sending signals that challenged the street lights. Evans and Tweet wore the same expressions. But Simeon was dizzy and nauseous. He wanted to be in bed.

Unusually, he headed for the bus stop that was on Tchoupitoulas Street at Napoleon Avenue by the river. The bus stop was just outside the door of Bivi Q's Bar and across the neutral ground[15] from Mel Paines Bar. One month before, he wrecked his 1961 Chevy Impala. He was back to catching busses again.

The four boys walked unsteadily toward the bus stop. Evans had his left arm around Simeon's shoulder the duration of the three block trek. He, Betz, and Tweet teased and shoved one another along the way. Loud laughter went in all directions.

They approached the corner at Napoleon and Tchoupitoulas to wait for the next bus. The three escorts continued their friendly provocations, oblivious to the surroundings. When they arrived, Simeon noticed a man standing there. He appeared to be waiting for the bus.

---

[15] The New Orleans term for 'median', the divider in the middle of a street

Above them hung a well-lit street light and a large lighted 'Jax Beer' sign. The building was to the left of the boys. To the right, he saw the man standing in the night. He was leaning, with his right arm extended and his fingers wrapped around a steel pole that extended upward from the concrete sidewalk. On the top of the pole was a metal sign with the words "Bus Stop" printed on it.

The man looked in the direction of the train tracks. Tucked under his left armpit was the protruding edge of a blue folder. Out of view, he held a lit cigarette in his left hand near his pants pocket. He stood ten feet away. Simeon's attention went to the blue folder, partially viewed under the man's far armpit.

The man wore dark hair combed off of the forehead. He appeared to be in his late forties. He was wearing a light colored button shirt tucked into his dark, baggy trousers. The sleeves of his shirt were rolled up to just below his elbows. He sported a small pouch at his midsection and had the overall look of one of the many men in the neighborhood who worked the docks of the Mississippi River in the fall of 1972. Many drank beer in one of the many corner bars along the river.

Bivi Q's was a mere five blocks down Tchoupitoulas Street from Fump's Bar, the place of his family roots. The stranger on the corner turned to look at him. Their eyes met for what seemed like a long, deliberate stare.

There was something riveting about the man. As they stared at one another, he had a strange feeling. He felt a slight threat from his presence before quickly realizing that the perceived threat came from within. In the seconds this transpired, his three friends continued their free performance unabated.

He looked over to the man again. He was now turned slightly to the right, toward Simeon and the boys. As if waiting for him, the man took the old, worn, blue folder from under his left armpit with his right hand before lifting the cigarette in his left hand to take a draw from it. As the man exhaled the smoke from his mouth, he turned his head slowly and deliberately upward and to the right. He paused, as his eyes burrowed into Simeon's. The blue folder was now in his right hand at his waist. It was in full view.

It appeared to be old, with worn edges. And it held his attention for a moment. Its worn, yet well preserved look gave him the impression that he was holding a folder made out of papyrus. He had read that in ancient times papyrus was the material that was used for the written word. It was made from a plant with long, thin, rod-like reeds. The combined elements of lignin, cellulose, and uronic acid were what purportedly gave it its enduring quality

His appearance was rugged, and the image he was cloaked in announced that he was a rough man with streetsmarts. Yet, there was a knowing look of concern on his face as he locked onto Simeon's eyes. He didn't smile. Neither did he not smile. It felt to Simeon that the man might know him.

Their eyes engaged for a few long seconds. In the short span of the engagement, and for the first time in his life, he was vaguely aware of a blurred lens through which he viewed life. The man broke off with him as he slowly, and deliberately, turned his head down so as to look at, and draw attention to, the old blue folder at his right side. He paused, looking down at the blue folder for several seconds. He reversed the motion, slowly bringing his head back up and toward Simeon. As he did, his eyes once more locked onto Simeon's.

Was he one of the men in the neighborhood who knew his parents or grandparents, aunts, or uncles? Did he find out about Simeon from some of the neighborhood men in the bars? Was he aware of his many questions about life? Was he aware that he had strong notions of matters that involved the whole world but rarely spoke of them? He wondered with notions that didn't form into words confined to language. The wonder languished, overcome by the lure of his the stare.

He turned his head quickly at the sound of Tweets' loud exclamation.

"Neithuh one of ya'll can handle me on a pool table!"

He went back to the man with the blue folder. The instant their eyes met again, he heard the sound of a train horn across the street. The horn blew a short, abrupt, three-second toot followed by six crisp, clear dings of a bell. He had lived all of his twenty years along the railroad by the river and heard the sounds countless times since he was an infant. This time there was something different about the sounds he was hearing.

They were the same sounds, same tones, same toot, and same dings of the bell that he had always heard. But this time, the sound of the train horn and bells were more than just vaguely heard background noise in the neighborhood. They were more crisp and distinct this time. He had never heard this clearly before what he had always heard in the background. It took him back to the experience he had in the first grade. That seemed so long ago.

And he also realized for the first time that the clear sound of the solo train horn was followed by a total of six distinct rings of the bell. He had never before been aware of the number of times the bell rang after the toot of the train horn.

"The train horn blows its three-second toot, followed by six distinct rings from the bell, ... huh."

For some strange reason and for the first time, this time, when he heard the sounds, he had the unique sensation of them having the purpose of a call-to-preparation, a summon to muster attention.

His attention went back to the mysterious man holding the worn, old blue folder on the street corner. He was aware that no bus had come. He was also aware that the entire scene in front of him had lasted for about two minutes. He quickly surveyed the scene for the man who stood at the bus stop. There was no man.

Nine

He was facing the door to the barroom the whole time. The man couldn't have gone in. If he had walked down the sidewalk or across the street in any direction, he would have been able to see him. No bus had come. He simply vanished.

He wondered if he might be dreaming. So he did a quick review to confirm that he was in real time. The boys were still with him. Everything else was normal as well, including his nausea.

In minutes, a bus arrived. When he boarded, he was still puzzled. But he was adept at dismissing matters that didn't fit the moment as he thought it should be. His full-bore obsession with all things mischief and fun trumped everything.

The next morning he sat at the kitchen table, drinking a glass of orange juice while reading the newspaper.

"What are you reading in the paper every morning, Boo-boo[16]?"

"About the Vietnam War and what's going on in the world."

"You think its bad out there?"

"Yeah, Ah really do, Paw-Paw."

"Me too, Simmie,… me too."

Jacomo Bonamo was too young to fight in the first world war. He was too old to enlist in the second. He lived through the Great Depression and worked as a dock clerk along the river. He was an astute and aware man who thought deeply.

"As you grow, you see a lot of things. The world's changing, Simmie. People are more selfish and wanting things. There's more and more taxes and laws. We are getting into more and more wars around the world. What's it gonna be like when you are in your early seventies, like me?"

"Ah don't know, Paw-Paw. Ah wonder. Ah do wonder."

---

[16] A broad New Orleanian cultural term of endearment

"Look at the time. You better get off to school, so you can eat your books and read your lunch. Pokey and Shairee got tired of waiting for you. They already left to catch the Magazine bus."

The familiar play on words humored him. And with that, he was off.

In religion class that morning, Mister Encalaige asked the class what they thought about the wars that were being waged at that moment. He offered that the Bible had mentioned the second coming of Christ to the earth. Simeon usually slept through the class next to Betz and Felgoux. But when he faintly heard what was said, he snapped out of his light doze and lifted his head.

He was fascinated. Fancies, thoughts, questions, and sensations abounded. But his attention faded. He slipped back into his nap.

That evening, he headed for home with Betz, Lan, and Evans before midnight. They crossed the corner where Put was sitting on the sidewalk. His back was against the outside wall of Huntster's. His head was down, resting on his folded arms that were held up by his knees.

As they approached, Evans belted out a cheerful greeting.

"Where Ya'Att, Put!"

Startled, the poor old man struggled to respond.

"Awwwe right,... Yeah you.... rite."

Looking up, he recognized the four young fellas and snapped awake. Instinctively, he let go his time-worn, ever-ready pronouncements.

"Eh labas! Dey call me *Put*! P-U-T! Sounds like FOOT! You ought to have a quarter for old Put."

Seeing Simeon, he halted for a moment.

"*SIMMIE* BOY! *SIMMIE* BOY! DAT'S mah, mah *SIMMIE* BOY!"

"What tahm is it Put?"

Lan eagerly waited for the patented answer.

"Eleb'm - Seb'mTeen - Twenty-Two!"

The venerable old uptown man had his cheer back.

"Yeah you rite, Put."

"Who's dat?"

Betz pointed to Simeon.

"Dat's mah *SIMMIE* BOY!

"Dat's right, you old Put. What you got to say to us tonight, Bruh?"

The boys stood over their elder, the man they knew to be whom everyone always knew him to be. They waited eagerly, with wide grins. Evans and Betz each leaned on Simeon's opposite shoulders. Lan looked at them agreeably before looking back down at Put. They waited for one of Old Put's humorous and time-worn quips.

But Ole Put was slow to respond. He appeared to retreat to a more somber place. Their expectant grins slowly faded into slight frowns that were anointed by disappointment.

He steadied himself while rising. Standing, he applied two shuffled half steps, one right, and one left. One by one, he looked Lan, Betz, and Evans resolutely into their eyes before softly and deftly speaking to them in his raspy, throaty, thick, New Orleans accent,

"Mah *SIMMIE* Boy got dem Pwohtohc."

The four lads stood puzzled.

"What'd he say?"

Evans looked at Lan, Betz, and Simeon with a furrowed brow.

"Heck if Ah know. What did you say, Put?"

Lan's question came out in a slightly higher pitch.

"Mah *SIMMIE* Boy got dem Pwoh-tohc. Yeeeaaah, dazz right."

"You know what the heck he's saying, Simmie?"

"Donk if Ah know eitther, Lan. Awe-right Put. We'll see you tomorrow."

"You think old Put's messing with us tonight, Simm?"

"Yeah, dat was weird, Ev."

And with that they went into the night.

Finally in bed, Simeon went nostalgic before he nodded off. It wasn't an unusual pastime.

Pokey was asleep in the twin bed five feet away. Shairee was asleep in the room next to them. Directly across the street was the Convent. Some of the same nuns who taught him in elementary school were fast asleep on the second floor. Their windows were a mere forty yards away from where he slept. And the experience from Sister Mary Imelda's first grade class happened just beyond that, another forty yards behind the Convent. It happened right across the street from where he lay, now pondering the words from the mouth of Old Put one hour earlier.

"Mah Simmie Boy got dem Pwoh..., or something like dat. What the heck is dat supposed to mean?"

He wondered, as his mind lingered in the deep corridors of his memory where the former, meaningful images were stored. As the images began to linger, blur, then fade, his thoughts slowly drifted. The hour was half past midnight.

Well into the early morning hours, Simeon popped out of what, until that moment, was a deep sleep. As he turned, he heard the sound of the Public Belt Railroad train horn five blocks away along the river. Within seconds he was fast asleep again.

In the morning, Shairee wobbled into her brothers' bedroom rubbing her eyes. She approached her oldest brother gingerly to ask if he would drive them to school in his newly purchased used Plymouth.

"You gonna wait for me and Pokey this morning?"

"Yeah. But we gotta get going. Let's get Pokey outta bed so we can go. Where'd he put his pants this time? Look for his pants while Ah get him up. We gotta pick up Felgoux and Betz."

"Okay."

With pants secured and Pokey taking his time foisting them, he opened the screenless window to the upstairs bedroom. The noise from the traffic on State Street rushed into the room. He saw an early morning mockingbird land on the single story roof just below. It sounded off immediately, and its expressions filled his ears despite the noise from passing cars. The barrage quickly became a source of irritation, so he slammed the window shut.

"Pesky bird. You can cackle to a closed window."

Ten

They sat at the varnished table next to a window in Fumps. Betz, Evans, and Pick took up some small talk.

"Ahm thinking about breaking up with Janet."

"How come, Pick. She's easy to look at."

"Yeah Betz, but she's not mah style."

"You ain't nevuh had style, Tweet."

"Shuddup, Evans."

Simeon found himself wandering in and out of the conversation. He hadn't had a steady girlfriend since sophomore year. He and Evans dated several girls over the time period, but no one steady. The chatter was fading. He was wandering someplace else.

Old man Fump meandered over to the table and took up a chair. The three young small- talkers continued to wax on about their love lives. Simeon was looking around. The song *'Blue Monday'* swooned over the sound waves throughout the old bar room, into every local patron's ears, head, and heart. They were born in the neighborhood that supported the establishment. And the early 1960's tune by a fellow New Orleanian[17] was taking them on a stroll down memory lane. Simeon was in the front of the line.

No one noticed when Fump pulled up a chair next to them.

"Anybody home?"

He looked around at the three late teens. His loud, scratchy, throaty voice had not garnered their attention. They were leaned into one another at the table, absorbed in small talk, girls, some laments, and the encroaching influence of beer. He tried Simeon, engulfed in the photos on the wall.

"What's up, little dago?"

"Oh, hey, Fump. How long you been sittin there?"

"Oh, about an hour. What are you daydreaming about?"

He stared at the son of his longtime friends, Julian and Maria.

---

[17] Fats Dominoe

"Just thinking about family, and all uh dat."

"Yeah, dat's right, Ah remember dose days, boy. Yuh momma and Trae's momma grew up here, upstairs. Your Aunt Shoilee too."

His ultra thick glasses magnified his eyes from the outside looking in. They seemed to magnify his growly voice as well.

"How's yuh momma an nem[18]?"

"Everybody's good. How's your sistuh, Miss Mary? Ah saw her down at Huntster's a few weeks ago with Manny. She awe-rite?"

"She's fahn."

The growl was soft, and unusually tender.

"What comes to your mind sitting hear with me, Fump? You grew up living across the street. My momma lived in this building. My daddy a few houses away, and Ahm sitting hear all nostalgic."

"Well, for starters, you rascal dago, your momma's grandma owned dis building for a long tahm. She owned it when Ah was a kid across duh street, here on Tchoupitoulas. Yuh uncle Peck took it over and ran the baw. Ah came in hear to shoot pool. Yuh momma and aunts lived in the back wit cha Paw Paw Jake Bonamo. Me and him got along good."

He gave his scarred vocal chords a break before abusing them once more with a long drag from his ever-present cigar.

"Fump, do you remember me and Trae running around hear when we wer little? And Footsy, and Cat?"

"Yeeaaah."

The question sent him somewhere. He stared straight ahead through the wall and into the past. Many hours of his life passed in the building and along the street blocks outside. And the wall that he peered through offered glimpses of his story, as well as Simeon's parents, in the black and white photos it held. Their stories ran parallel. And the opportunity to hear more about the people he loved and the places where they were formed was a treasure.

He had been in and out of the building since infancy. Early childhood images of the living spaces were embedded in his memory. He recalled running the floors upstairs and downstairs with Trae. There were two upstairs porch rooms. The larger one held a very old wash tub with a

---

[18] Local New Orleans expression: 'Your momma and them' – referring to 'the family'

mechanical lever. It stood in place since the early 1900's, when his great-grandparents used it. The creaky, smaller porch room had a door that opened onto a four-foot square elevated deck. It had a wooden rail and overlooked the sidewalk adjoining Lions Street. There was a brown gas heater on the floor in the room. At seventeen years of age, the room held out a strange appeal to him. He didn't know why.

"How's Mistuh Tibby?"

"He's awe-right. He's comin in early to man his mop."

"Is anybody living upstairs right now?"

"Yuh Aunt Katie ain't been able to rent it. You should move in."

"Ahm still in high school, Fump. You know dat. Can you imagine me living up there?"

With the release of the question, the thought boomeranged back into his mind and found a crease to lodge in. The narrow space was carved out by whispers of steady winds that came downriver from the north. He heard them sometime in his early adolescent years. He listened for them and welcomed them.

Fump growled more scratchy words for the welcoming ears of his teenage listener. His coarse voice coaxed out memories from the wall that contained them and which held his stare. It released story after story about Simeon's family which the young apprentice tried hard to record.

Not long into his musings, the side door to the bar swung open with authority. The right hand of Graves Condale was planted on it. The gregarious uptown teen bounded into Fumps with a galactic grin. He was followed in order by a parade of uptown characters, eight total in all - King Mischief on sixteen legs.

"Where Y'Att, boys!"

Graves and company slapped the palms of the boys at the table. Various greetings and testosterone-laced ribbing broke out among the newcomers and the four boys at the table. With the addition of the eight hearty teenagers in the room the noise volume rose quickly. Loud interruptions and bursts of laughter happened as if someone flipped a switch.

In time, the boys moved around. Some sat at the bar. Some sat at tables. . Graves found a spot at the bar. Simmie eventually moved around, talking with each of the boys for a few minutes here and there.

He ended up on a barstool next to Graves. Fump was his typical happy-to-have-the-business but don't-get-in-my-face self.

An hour later, Simeon stepped outside for a moment to get a break from the smoke and noise. He noticed Old Put leaning against the ledge at the window. An empty vino glass sat on it, waiting to be filled.

"Mah, mah, mah *SIMMIE* Boy! Dat's mah *SIMMIE* Boy!"

"Whey Y'Att, Put. You want a quarter for some vino?"

"Yeah you rite, mah Simmie Boy, *y-e-a-h* you rite!"

He perked up, taking the coin.

"Yuh momma and yuh daddy know'd who Ah is. Ah knowd who dey is too. Lived right cheeuh. Ah knowd dem and dey knowd me. And Ah know'd you too, Simmie Boy. Ah know'd who you is, doe you don't neeuh know'd it fuh yuh own seff."

He looked around the lighted corner to see if anyone saw him confiding in Old Put. The telephone pole grew out of the sidewalk below the street light, too far from the banquette[19]. It obstructed the walkway.

He leaned closer to whisper to the venerable icon of the corner.

"Is that so, Put? Then who am Ah? Cuz Ah don't know it mahself."

The good-hearted man replied softly in kind, clearly and succinctly.

"Ah cain't tey yuh, mah Simmie Boy. But Ah'zza gonna keep sayin it. And one day you's gonna fahnd out who you is. And it gaw be good, mah boy. You gaw see. Yuh heeuh me nah?"

The man struck a chord in the confused teenager's heart.

"Ahd give you another quarter, Put. But Ahm flat broke. Mah friends are gonna have to take care of me from here on."

He went back in and replanted himself next to Graves. A cold draft beer appeared in front of him on the counter.

"It doesn't get any better than this."

The silent pledge did a u-turn back into his soul like another freshly driven nail to fortify a desire already firmly fastened in place.

In time, some of the guys left. A few still mingled, while Simeon remained at the bar, seated next to Graves, who was in an intense private discussion with a very large dude on his left, a stranger. Simeon was to his right. He and Stick were yapping about nothing with Fump when

---

[19] Pronounced: "Bank- ette": Old New Orleans term for "curb".

Graves poked him in the left side and turned his face slightly to the right, toward him.

"Get ready, dis guy's huge."

Simeon rose up from his bar stool and turned to lean left. Graves turned to his left as well, still seated. In the same moment, the large man stood, turned right, and cocked his right hand behind his hip. Noting the fist fast approaching his face, Graves dove down. The stranger's powerful haymaker rapidly approached the now vanished jaw of Graves. The space that Grave's inebriated jaw previously inhabited was now occupied by Simeon's inebriated face.

In a flash, he absorbed the full force of the royal haymaker that was aimed for the face of Graves. As the heavy blow smashed into him, he saw a flash of light. Instantly, he was aware of intense pain in his face. And he was aware of the sensation of descending down a dimly lit, long and winding, narrow slide.

The slide was set inside a blue colored tube that was covered with a slick, silver, steel bottom. As he slid uncontrollably down the winding tube, he began to slide faster. He wound around steep curves and bends. His backside swerved along the walls around each bend. The sensation was of going down a water slide, except for the length, and the speed. The longer he slid down, the faster his slide became.

Around each bend in the slide there was another bend, then another, then another. At stretches, the slide straightened out and this caused his movement to accelerate more rapidly before hitting more tight bends and steady curves. The pattern repeated itself in what seemed to be an endless and uncontrolled experience.

He felt nauseas and dizzy. Panic gripped him as he slid down the chute at increasing speed. He was aware that he was completely helpless. There was nothing he could do but settle into what was happening and brace for whatever awaited him at the end, if there was one.

He was overcome with fear as his breakneck speed increased. He felt a rapid increase in his pulse. His heart was pounding harder and harder as he began to have the sensation of flying in between the tight bends. He hit each one with such speed that it felt as if there was a ready hand in them that shot him into the next part of the course.

He began to tumble and roll in the slide. He was aware of pain in his face and head. Fearing that his descent might end with a devastating crash, he wanted to shout. But who could hear? He desperately wanted to stop. But how? He wanted out. But to where? What was this thing connected to? Was there any connection to this and the real world? And if he could get out, in what world or dimension would he find himself?

He was reeling. He was sliding. He was spinning out of control. He was bursting and coming apart from the inside out while in the free-slide, spinning and rolling, faster and faster. As he accelerated, he heard the faint sound of a humming noise. It grew louder and louder. Pressure built in his ears and squeezed his brain more intensely as the sound grew louder. He was at his end. He looked for a towel to throw in.

"No more, please. Can't take it."

He was fading, diminished in the explosion of noise and speed. His jaw and head pounded with pain. Total darkness ensued, blackness in full bloom. His movement ceased, though he had no sensation of having come to a jolting stop, or of steadily slowing down. He felt human hands, forearms, and arms under him, on him, around him. Voices, yelling, scuffling, confusion. He was on the move again, though slowly this time, very slowly. Cared for appendages were on him, grasping, pulling, moving. He felt them. And then ....

Eleven

It was as if he awoke from the unwelcome trauma event only to find himself someplace else. Where he was he couldn't say. It was somewhere familiar. And it contained a hint of future possibilities with a connection with the past, or so it seemed to Simeon in his chaotic and painful state.

Many soldiers were making their way up the outside of his right leg. He could see them in his mind's eye. In one instant, they were the size of the toy soldiers he, Pokey, Trae, Lan, and Parry used to play with when they were boys on their bikes. In the next, they were large and imposing and real, very real.

He knew them to be coming for him. And he realized they were from a different flag, a strange flag that was not of this world, from an unwelcome realm. They were confident, cocked, and loaded.

In the image, his torso was a hill that they were marching up to get to him. He was at the top of the hill, in the right shoulder area. He was trembling with fear, awash in a cold sweat. He had the idea to run but knew that he had nowhere to run. The shoulder-neck-head area was the end of the line.

He knew them to have a menacing determination, motivated out of utter evil, propelled by seething anger and uncontrolled hatred. Their conviction in the pursuit was intimidating. He felt fear.

They came slowly. He thought he felt sweat dripping from his temples and all over his torso, and that he might be shaking.

He thought he heard the short, punctuated sound of a train horn nearby. But where was he? Was he lying on the floor somewhere? Was that blood he felt coming from his nose?

"Where am I?"

As the soldiers approached, those in the lead reached to take him. And he panicked. He was aware that his face and head throbbed, then nothing.

When he awoke the next morning, a Saturday, he lay in his bed. The left side of his face was swollen and the back of his head hurt badly. He touched what felt like dried blood on his nose. He remembered getting up the previous evening to assist Graves. And then he saw a star, accompanied by instant facial pain. And he had a dream. *Was that a dream?* There was something familiar about it, whatever it was.

He checked the clock next to him. It was 11:17 a.m., with the second hand striking twenty-two the moment of his glance. His thoughts ran to Old Put, much wiser, so Simeon always thought, than he was imagined to be.

As had happened several times in the past few years, he had no idea how he got home and into his bed. Later that afternoon, he found out that some of the guys drove him home. They used his side door key to carry him into his house while his parents slept. He was carried upstairs and laid on his twin bed next to Pokey's. They woke him to tell him what happened to his brother. And they urged him to not tell his momma and daddy.

That evening he caught up with some of the boys back at Doraix's.

"Why did you duck, Graves?"

"Sorry, man. Ah didn't know a punch was coming so quick. And by the way, why didn't *you*?"

"Ah didn't know it was coming either."

With that both of the boys, along with the others standing around, got a hearty laugh from the incident.

"Fella gets up to back up his friend in a fight. Friend ducks his head. Fella takes one to the face and is out cold."

With the teaser, Grump Guilleau[20] erupted into his yukity laugh.

"Glad your face was there for my face."

"Yeah, Condale. Next tahm a fight's coming, me tell me to run. Ah'll be better off."

Others joined in. Several reached over to poke him in the side.

"Get ready, Simm."

Somebody slapped him on the back, calling him:

"The Candle Kid – one blow and he's out!"

"Awe-rite, awe-rite, Ah get it. So Ahm a victim of soy-cum-stances, like Curly. Right?"

---

[20] Pronounced: "Gee-yo"

"Yea you rite," "Yes indeed," "Oh yeah!" were the replies.

"Next beer's on me, dago."

 Graves grinned as he leaned on Simmie's left shoulder with his right forearm.

"Even though you went down fast, you stood up for me, ... literally. Dat's my boy, Simm!"

For his part, Simmie Mangino basked in the macho male bonding while gently massaging the side of his face. When he reached to turn off the lamp and go to bed Sunday evening Pokey was snoring loudly.

"POKEY! Come on, man."

He reached over and poked him in the side.

Little brother grumbled and turned over.

He was tired. And his face and head were still tender with the pain. He rolled over on his side and began to fade just as the sound of a train horn travelled through the neighborhood. It was the familiar sound, familiar enough that one didn't actually hear it much of the time. He briefly entertained the notion that he had been more attendant to the sound of it lately. With the thought, he heard the ringing of bells behind the sound of the horn.

B E L L S S S S S..........

Twelve

He had waited for the day. But when it finally arrived, he was nervous. He paused before he opened the side door to Mitt's bar and pool hall. A new day would dawn when he stepped across its threshold. Outside the door, he could hear the sound of the ivory balls as they caromed off of one another.

He opened the worn side door with the anticipation of a groom walking out to receive his bride. And with tongue in cheek and an impish look on his face, he strode in as if he owned the place. Tino Mangino was bent over the cooler behind the bar. As his just-turned-eighteen, fifth of twelve grandkids walked into Mitt's for the first time, he gave him a grin. Mayeau, one of the owners, was there also. He knew who Simmie Mangino was. He knew that he was one of Tino's seven grandsons in the neighborhood. He gave Simeon the look.

"It's allright. He's eighteen today."

Tino continued to grin as he addressed Mayeau. But his eyes were on his grandson.

Simeon headed straight for an empty pool table and grabbed a stick.

"Rack!"

He belted out the summons he had silently rehearsed multiplied times. As Willie, the rack boy, set the balls for the game, his Paw-Paw Tino smiled once more from behind the bar.

"Ready to lose?"

Trae strode in from the barroom side of the poolhall.

"Ah heard you were coming and Ah thought Ah'd drop in and teach you a lesson on the pool table. Ahm still two months older than you, just like Lan, sonny boy. And we've been practicing."

"Straight pool, loser buys, Trufant."

"Ahm so gonna kick your tail, Mangino."

He was glad that Trae showed up. It made the moment more special than it already was, if that was possible. The adventure at Mitt's was underway.

He felt drawn to Mitt's like no place else. In the days ahead he became a fixture there. His Paw-Paw Tino worked there. His older cousins, Gasp, Lonnie, Jaw-gee, and Footsie, frequented the place. Trae and Lan were in there as much as he was. His daddy and uncles occasionally stopped by. A large number of twenty and thirty-something young men in the neighborhood dropped in regularly. Workers from along the river, from the Public Belt Railroad, and from the Public Grain Elevator were constantly in and out of there. And in time, most of the boys who hung on the corner at Doraix's and who frequented Fumps became part of the scene at Mitt's as well.

He had arrived. His circle of uptown acquaintances and friends would expand from his interactions at Mitt's. So would his experiences.

Within a few months after turning eighteen, he, Betz and Evans moved into the upstairs apartment in the building that held Fump's bar on its front end. He would be staying in the same rooms where his grandparents, his momma, and her sisters grew up. He felt like a chicken that had come home to roost. He was firmly planted where his story began. And it felt right.

Fump's was downstairs from where he lived. Mitt's was not seventy-five yards away, down the block. Huntster's was an additional short block down the street. And these were where many of the young men collected. Most of the activity and the main staging area for weekend evening forays into the metro area formed in Mitt's. And Old Put was just outside one of the windows of the three bars along the two short city blocks. He was now firmly planted in the middle of it all.

Simeon was constantly in and out of work. He was often in the place and available if some of the guys wanted to do something. In time, he spent more time with Tweet. Like Simeon, he was often in between jobs.

It was a cool, late winter evening in 1971. He was a senior at Redemptor, and like always, in Mitts on a Saturday..

"Lan, you're gonna give me and Tweet a bite of your roast-beef po-boy when it comes from Hunstuh's?"

Lan was working the bar at Mitt's. Simmie was in a typical mood as he prodded his cousin in the early evening hour.

"No way. Ya'll get your own sandwiches."

"We ain't got no money, Mangino. Just a bite. Come on, man!"

"Ah didn't eat any supper, Tweet. I'll let ya'll watch me eat it though. Ya'll know how good Miss Hunstuh's po-boys awe."

He gave Simeon and Tweet a sarcastic wink.

As he moved to the barroom side of the establishment, Tweet leaned over with an eager grin. He grabbed Simmie's shirt at the chest with his two hands. He pulled him closer and whispered.

"Simmie, Ah got an idea. You know how picky he is about his caw. It's down the block by Hunstuh's. As soon as the sandwich comes in, Ahm gonna step out on the caw-nuh. Den Ahm gonna bust in and tell him somebody's messing with his caw down the block. When he runs down there to check it out, let's each eat half of his po-boy. But we gotta throw it down FAST, you hear me?"

He was tickled with delight, and eager to pull the caper on his cugino.

At the sound of the news, Lan high-tailed it down the block in his apron, oblivious to was about to happen to his sumptuous supper. While Lan was on his puzzled mission to nowhere, the gravy-laden creation steadily shrunk into the faces of the two giggling thieves. In less than two minutes, their sloppy work came to a close, despite the irrepressible giggling that competed with their overtaxed digestive systems. With no time to clean up, the evidence Lan needed to convict them was all over their hands and mouths. Come what may, they vigorously mashed the last chunk into their leaking faces.

Lan returned with a puzzled look.

"Nobody was there when Ah got to mah caw. You sure you saw…?."

His eyes went to the open, and sloppy, paper-wrap on the bar that previously supported his piping hot po-boy. With the look of a famished wolf about to devour its prey, his eyes darted to Tweet and Simeon. His surprise now burst into a boiling anger, he witnessed firsthand the guilty now giggling down the last remains of his foregone supper.

"YA'LL ATE MAH *PO-boy*?!?

In seconds, he was all over the two culprits, pushing them, and punching them in the arms. His agitation still unspent, he repeated the action. Not a few expletives and unkempt remarks accompanied the pummeling. Tweet and Simeon could hardly contain their satisfaction. Their combined childish delight was fortified by their uncontrolled laughter, which sustained them against the physical and verbal abuse that they they presumed would be forthcoming.

A second po-boy arrived from Huntster's twenty minutes later. Orleans, co-owner of Mitt's, was highly entertained at the entire spectacle, as were the other patrons in the joint. And by the time Lan knocked off from work, he was laughing at the caper with everyone else. He was one of the many uptown sportsmen. He was a victim of such pranks and initiator of similar ones on others. Every neighborhood male was. Lan Mangino told the story to one and all who came in to the place over the next week.

"Can you believe doze two? Boy, boy, boy, Ah was so *mad at them.* Ah had to order me another po-boy. Doze *knuckle*heads."

The evening wore on. And like most things impulsive and extremely amusing, the experience wore off, though it would live on for years in the annals of uptown neighborhood storytelling. Late that evening, the crowd at Mitt's thinned. It was warm outside, quiet and peaceful. The boys let the evening's time slip away without regard. They had plenty to spare. And as lazy new moments continued to float by, one of them became a ripe one for the mischievous of mind. Still juiced by his and Tweet's recent shenanigan, Simeon had a fresh idea.

"Let's drive out to the lakefront and jump off the bridge by the canal."

"What do you mean, Simm? We don't have bathing suits."

Simeon and the rest of the boys stared blankly at him.

"Think for a minute, Stick. It's midnight and Simmie just suggested we do something involving water."

"Ha-ha-ha. Dat's right. Am forgetting, Graves. Awe-right, Ah get it now. We gonna jump off the bridge and the seawall in our underwear. It's Simmie's idea. Right, got it, well, okay, let's roll."

It was shortly after midnight when the boys drove out to Lake Pontchatrain on the northen edge of the city.

"Let's frolick and play duh New A'wlins way."

Tweet was on one of his hormonal highs. The activity was right up his alley, though only slightly satisfying on his adrenalin scale. Yet, he and his pals enjoyed themselves. When they were done, Graves wanted food.

"Let's get some groceries, guys."

"Some of us ain't got any money, Graves."

"Dat's awe-right, Pick. Ya'll can wait in the caw for us while we eat.
We'll get it fast so ya'll won't have to wait long. Come on, less-go."

In the quiet of the evening, the boys headed to one more late night spot
where opportunitiess for the child in some of them might present
themselves yet again. Within minutes, they drove to a locally owned
hamburger joint on Saint Charles Avenue. When the boys went in,
Simeon and Pick sat silently in the front seat listening to the radio. All
the while they were waiting, and quite bored. As if in search for
something to rescucitate his adrenalin, an idea formed in Simeons's
imaginative head.

"Pick, Ah got an idea. There's no way they're gonna hurry inside
there. They're gonna take their time and eat. We were gonna just sit in
the caw and wait for them. We are already in our drawers and no shirt.
Let's skip on in there, holding hands like kids, and give em a show."

Pick fell into a giggling frenzy. He could hardly wait to capitalize on
the macho bravdo behind the not so macho action.

"Ahm in, you crazy dago. Lessgo."

In seconds, they were on their way. No sooner had the two boys
skipped into the joint when several patrons, noting there attire, or lack
thereof, spontaneously got up and left. Simeon took a seat at the counter,
asking for a menu . Pick sat next to him, giggling like a school boy.

"Ya'll gotta leave, or Ahm calling the cops."

"Aw, come aw, man. Ahm hungry."

"Simmie, let's get outta hear before the cops show up."

"Just a minute, Sturgis."

"Uh-oh, look outside, Simmie. It's the fuzz."

"Okay, Tweet. Ah guess we'll go now, suh. No hawm meant."

And with that the uptown boys headed to the door to face the music,
with two in their number still scantily clad in their scivvies.

When they walked out, Graves spoke.

"Ahm gonna take a shot at dis, ya'll. Cross your fingers."

He didn't want his buddies to get hauled in for the night. He was going
to make an appeal. When he realized that he knew one of the officers, he
doubled down. It worked. After a few minutes of animated appeal, with
his arms going every which way, and his voice laden with exaggerated

tenderness and steroidal level earnest, Graves and the two officers strode over to Simeon and Pick.

"Get your clothes on, buttheads. And get the heck outta here."

"No argument here, office-uh."

Pick giggled every syllable of the happy rejoinder while Graves pulled him away toward the car.

When they dropped him off, the amusement still lingered over Simeon. He sat on the mattress which lay on the floor of his small enclosed porch bedroom. It was on the end of the upstairs apartment above Fumps. On the floor next to his bed was a brown gas heater. The small room had a window overlooking Lions Street and the old Coney house across the street. A door opened onto a very small and elevated wooden deck with railing on all four sides.

As he mused and chuckled over the activities of the past few hours, his heart was warmed by the sense of significance and belonging that he felt. And he almost thought out loud that there was nowhere else on the planet that he'd rather be than where he was and who he was with.

He could hear the music coming from the juke box in Fump's below. Though it was the early morning hour, he wanted to make Tweet aware of something. He headed downstairs to the bar to use the payphone to call him, thinking him to be home and awake. He dropped a nickel into the wall payphone and dialed.

"No, baby. He's not home yet."

Tweet's sister didn't ask where he might be.

"Just tell him Ah called."

He saluted a good night to the grumpy old patron smoking his stogie behind the bar. Back in his porch bedroom, he fell onto his floor mattress. In seconds, he was out cold.

Though he was oblivious, Old Man River moved slightly more swiftly and stealthily through the city that early morning hour. Beyond the lonely, quiet, empty train tracks and the dark warehouses, it carried many things. Some were very much more unwelcome than others.

Thirteen

It was close to 10:30 in the morning when Simeon was abruptly awakened. He heard someone calling his name loudly from the sidewalk below his elevated porch bedroom. He went through the door into Betz's room to open the larger window there. When he opened the window he leaned out to stare down to Graves.

"WHAT! You woke me up!"

"Ah got bad news, Simmie. Tweet's dead."

He was stunned. He leaned further out of the screenless upstairs window to hear more. The noise woke Evans. He walked weakly toward the window and leaned toward it, nudging Simeon and leaning out of the same window pane.

"What's going in, Ah mean, going on?"

"Tweet's dead."

Graves repeated the news in the same somber tone.

Evans' jaw fell. Drowsiness fled at the words. His eyes looked as if they were going to leap from below his temples. He turned to Simeon and just looked at him. Simeon looked back into his eyes. Both of them saw disbelief and shock in the eyes of the other. Graves just stood below, silent.

"Where's Betz?"

"He's working."

"What *happened*?"

Disbelief and shock carried the question.

"He was on his motorcycle headed back out toward the lake and got hit by a truck. He died on the spot."

The three friends lingered. They didn't know what to say.

"Ah was in Mitt's. Mayeau was talking about it. Mervin the cop told him."

"Why did he get on his motorcycle and head back out there by himself at 2:30 in the morning?"

Evans didn't conceal his anger with the question.

"He was so crazy on that stupid bike. Ah wish he would have listened
to me. Ah told him to lay off on that thing!"

Tears began forming in his eyes.

They began to form in Simmie and Graves as well.

"Ya'll coming? Ah'll be down at Mitt's. Hurry over."

Graves walked away.

Evans and Simeon left the window and sat in the bedroom quietly.
They took turns muttering their disbelief. They were not only at a loss
for words, they were actually lost. The unwelcome visit of Death itself
had awakened in each of the two young New Orleanians a sense of
longing that each of them had grown accustomed to run away from. The
two friends had drawn closer over the past few years. They had
something in common. It was a stirring, a simmering discontent that
they were feeling. The sudden loss of one of their own reawakened what
was below the surface.

Simeon's thoughts went to his early morning call to Tweet. He
wondered if Tweet's death might have occurred at about the time he had
called his house. A haunting feeling overcame him.

"Let's go down to Mitt's."

"Lessgo."

They were eager to break the momentum that the twin emotions of
dread and confusion had begun to gain.

The young men sat at a table in Mitt's. Some sipped cokes. No one
said anything. Mayeau, a tough and no-nonsense Coon-Ass from
[21]Lafource Bayou, felt sadness for the guys. He couldn't say it. But his
expressions and the retreat from his hard approach were his way of
letting them know he cared. Several of the others showed up…… Pick,
Grumpy, and Tabes. Flip followed, and soon after Stick, Joey, and
Carolla trickled in.

No one said anything. A few cried. Simeon and Evans were among
them. A sad song played on the jukebox. It stirred latent emotions in the
rough, but sentimental, young men.

"It wasn't supposed tuh be dis way."

----

[21] Pronounced: "Luh-foosh By-yoo"

Simeon heard himself think the words. He wanted to ride the wave that was free-spirit and invincibility forever. Nobody was supposed to die, especially none of his buddies. It wasn't right in anyone's world. It cut deep and hurt bad. Hearts bled. His heart bled. And it wouldn't stop bleeding. Tears trickled down his cheeks and onto the table. Pain he'd not known before introduced itself inside and built a nest for itself. The active and realized emotion put a temporary hold on his automatic response to painful, difficult experiences.

Lan walked in. He sat by his cousin and said nothing. He welled up with tears as well. When the guys slowly began to leave the pool hall, Simeon, Lan, and Evans headed back to the apartment over Fump's. As they turned right outside the door from Mitt's, they saw old Put leaning against the building. His left arm rested on the ledge that extended from the side service window.

"Whey-Yatt, *babe*!"

The tone told them that he was sober.

"Awe-right, Put."

Simeon couldn't hide the sadness in his response.

Undaunted, Old Put continued like he was going somewhere.

"Dat, dat, dat's mah *SIMMIE* boy!"

"Not today, Put. We lost one of our own last night."

Lan wasn't in the mood. Nobody was.

Old Put just looked at them. He didn't say anything. The three lads lingered with him, the poor black man who everyone took for granted. In the moment they felt a strange and unfamiliar bond with him. To Simeon, it felt like a meeting of hearts in the space where mutual understanding begins to bring people who are different, and who look different, closer together. It was a place of unwelcome pain, hardship, and challenge. Old Put knew it well – since birth. It was a place where he and most people of color lived in their everyday experience. And now the three young white men were in the neighborhood, if only for a moment. They didn't know how to say it. But they felt it.

Old Put Smith didn't announce who he was that day. He didn't thrust forth his hand to ask for a quarter from the three hurting young men he was very familiar with. He sensed their pain. He felt it too, not only in his own story, but now in theirs as well.

As the three boys turned to head down the block, Old Put spoke again. His parting words were from a full presence of mind. He spoke without exclamation or overdone inflection:

"Ya'll be sad tuhday, Ah knows it. Ooom-hmmm. But mah Simmie boy got dem pwo-tohcs, yeeeessss indeed. Not nah, but dey's a comin. Ah know itch-izz,… *yeeaaahhh* you rite. Watch out ya'll, foh he knowd dem day's. Oh yeah, yes indeed, suh. Ya'll hee-uh me nah. Ah know bout dat, Ah sho do. He not knows nah, but fuh sho will when Ah be dead and gawn. Yeeesss indeed, Ah know itch-izz."

The three young men heard him. And they sensed his sincerity and good intentions. They knew he felt their pain and they appreciated it. Because he regularly singled out Simeon in his address, and because they were still reeling inside, they didn't give his words close attention. Lan and Evans assumed he was going on as he normally did, though perhaps not as soaked with vino that early in the afternoon. Simeon was more deeply affected by what old Put said. He was hurting too bad to catch everything he just heard. But he recalled old Put saying something about him, about 'products', or something like that, in the past. *But what was that other stuff that he just said?*

Fourteen

"Yeah, Uncle Joo. He's here. Ahm sorry to hear about Mistuh Jake.
Tell Aunt Maria for me, okay? Ah'll get him to call you."
"SIMM-*MIE!*"
He was by the pinball machine with Izzi, Flip, Ward, and Shatt.
"Call your daddy."
"You think it's about your Paw-Paw?"
"Ahm afraid so, Izz."
He stepped outside to call home from the payphone. His daddy
answered.
"You're Paw-Paw Jake just passed away. We're at duh hospital.
Momma's here with Aunt Katie and Aunt Shoilee. Is Trae there?"
"Yeah, he is."
There was a great sadness in Simeon's reply.
"His momma aksed me to tell him too. You two get home to see your
momma's dis afternoon, you hear me?"
"Okay, daddy."
"Amavi tuo papa nonno. Andrai tutto bene[22]?"
"Sì, mio padre. Io sono[23]."
Trae was shooting pool with Sturgis. He paused for a moment, before
telling him about their Paw-Paw. He stepped outside. He wanted to be
alone for a few minutes. He walked across the street through the open
chain-link gate that led to left field in Weismar Playground.

His Paw-Paw grew up in the neighborhood. He was born in 1902, four
short city blocks away. He worked along the docks that stretched along
the river from uptown to downtown. And he never left the
neighborhood.

Instinctively he looked to the sky. Heavy gray and white clouds
occupied the airspace. The grays were various shades of dark. The
darker shades claimed most of the sky. It appeared that a rainstorm
might be in the forecast. But he wouldn't have known. He never paid

---

[22] Italian: "You loved your papa grandfather. Are you going to be allright?"
[23] Italian: "Yes, my father. I am."

attention to the weather report. He went by what he could see and experience. All things subjective were the data for his intuition, his northern star, whether right or wrong. He liked flying by the seat of his pants. And intuition afforded him that leisure. It was less tedious and less time consuming than careful thought, fact-checking, research, and consideration.

Reaching third base, he wondered about his life. At the moment, he had little motivation to pursue a career. What would his life count for when his time was up like his Paw-paw's? He had secured a number of jobs since he was fifteen. And within a short time, he quit every one of them. He had little confidence in his ability to apply himself toward college. And he could think of nothing that he wanted to do.

He approached the first base line and the close-together shotgun houses[24] just beyond the fence on Laurel Street. As he did, he heard the progressive singing of a mocking bird. He noted the beauty in the short-lived bursts of bird-songs and critter-sounds that the amazing critter had stored and replayed.

"How do they do that?"

In the beauty of its soundings he wondered if the creature was, in fact, actually mocking the creatures whose sounds it recorded and played back.

"Are you mocking others, you little scoundrel?"

He stopped with his foot on first base as he spoke out loud to the speechless bird. His feet played the same first base position he now stood on when he was on a team at age eleven. He didn't see this day coming.

"Are you mocking me, you little neighborhood pest? Or maybe you're not mocking at all. Maybe bird people don't really know what you're doing when you sing out all the sounds you've recorded. They say you're singing to attract a mate. But maybe you're not. Maybe you're celebrating all of the critters that we humans think you're mocking."

"Were you around nine years ago when Ah stood on this spot playing first base? Were you singing then? If so, were you mocking me den? Are you mocking me now because Ahm not amounting to anything, or

---

[24] A term to describe a New Orleans home where there were no hallways, and one room led into another front front to back..

*have no prospects or ambition? Are you calling me a loser? Or, were
you celebrating me standing on this spot when Ah was eleven? And if so,
are you celebrating me now?"*

In his state of mind, he finished his thoughts half-believing they might
contain a ring of truth. Then he turned to head back to Mitts. As for the
versatile winged recording artist, it kept on doing what it always does.

When he got back to Mitts he spoke to Trae. Lan had already told him.

"Ahm sorry Ah wasn't there, as hard as it was to be there when Ah last
saw him. You know what Ah mean, Simm?"

"Same for me, Trae. Mah daddy said you should call your momma.
We should probably stay around the house with them a few days to see if
we can help. Dey might want us around just to be there, you know?"

"Ah was already gonna do dat, Simmie."

At the age of twenty, Simeon was not unacquainted with death. As a
church altar boy in grade school, he had been called out of class
numerous times to attend with the presider at funeral services. He had
stood facing open caskets containing dead bodies numerous times. But
the loss of Tweet hit him in a deeper place. He was so young. The loss
of his grandfather was a blow as well. He had lived with his daughter
Maria's family since Simeon was seven years old. He often cooked for
the family and told stories about life in the neighborhood when he was
growing up. And he seemed to know when Simeon needed a word of
encouragement.

His momma told him that he took after her father. Jake Bonamo lost
his wife when she was thirty-two years young. He knew what it was like
to survive carrying the burden of the heaviest of losses. He was a deep
thinker and was full of ideas, most of which he kept to himself. He was a
man of simple ambition and didn't mind living a simple life. Simeon
didn't know whether or not he took after his maternal grandfather. But
he knew that he cared for him deeply.

When he went home that afternoon his momma was lying across her
deceased father's bed. He touched her shoulder.

"You awe-right, momma?"

"Ahm allright, dawlin. Ah just need to be alone for awhile."

He stayed around the house a little more than normal for a few days.
In no time, he was back on track, seeking to catch the next wave that

would carry him at its crest into a future with an unknown goal. Some experiences touched him deeply. They were invitations to pause, to think, to consider. Instead, he instantaneously recorded each one, before storing it the gallery of his mind. He had programmed himself that way. He was an expert at it. The exercise was effortless.

Yet the sadness that began to surface at Tweet's death did not totally leave. It operated undercover after his grandfather's death. But it settled into a low-level painful emotion in his psyche. He began to get in touch with it in the quiet and lonely spaces where the unsettled soul wanders in the early morning hours after yet another evening of self-absorbed pursuits. He had become familiar with the world of the night, and its enveloping darkness. Well into his fourth year in that world, the wee morning hours felt like a less-attractive space to him. Having already abandoned the potential for meaning in the light of the day, his experiences in the dark of night were beginning to feel unwelcome as well.

Several months after his Paw-Paw's death, he staggered to the door that led to his upstairs apartment. He couldn't wait to fall onto his mattress on the floor of the leaky porch room. He heard the blow of the train horn a mere block away across the street. Its sound was sharp and clear. After its three-second wail he heard the crisp, clear, and distinct ring of the train's bell. It struck six times.

In a few hours he had to get up for work at the Grain Elevator a few blocks away along the river. Within seconds, he was asleep.

In what felt like no time at all, he was abruptly awakened by the familiar loud thumping coming from beneath his second-level porch bedroom. Ten feet below him, Tibby stood in the back yard behind Fumps Bar. He knocked hard on the floor of Simeon's bedroom above with the long end of a broom stick.

"Oh *Simm*-MIE!"

His patented, piercing, high pitch yell did the job.

"*Simm*-MIE! TIME FUH *WOIK*! *Simm*-MIE! GIT UP, BOY!"

"AWE-RIGHT, AWE-*RIGHT*! *THANKS*, TIBBY!"

Tibby Trufant walked away, satisfied that he'd done what he was asked. Above his head, Simeon rolled over and was instantly asleep again. As an uncle to his cousin, Simeon felt a neighborhood bond with

Tibby. He appreciated his efforts to help him get up for work. But sleep felt better.

Early that afternoon, he walked into Mitts to begin his daily routine. He was prepared for every possibility for the day, with no prospects for anything gainful. When he sat, his Paw-Paw Tino approached him from behind the bar. He glared at his grandson every step he took that brought them face to face. Simeon looked away.

"You missed woik again?"

"Yeah, Ah guess Ah did, Paw-Paw."

"Did Tibby wake you dis morning?'

"Yeah, he did."

"Den why are you not at woik?"

"Ah don't know why, Paw-Paw."

He glanced up at his Paw-Paw briefly, before looking away.

"Boy, you better figure out what you wanna do. Nobody's gonna make it if dey live life duh way you're living it."

"Ah know, Paw-Paw. Ah know."

"You know your Paw-Paw Jake wouldn't have liked dis either, right Simmie? Non si vuole essere una disgrazia per la famiglia.[25]"

"Ah don't, Paw-Paw. You're right, Ah don't. Tu parli cose buone me, Papà Nonno.[26] I'm gonna figure it out. Ah promise."

"Just remember, you can't keep saying 'tommorrow' forever when it comes to things dat require action 'today'."

And with that he turned to serve another customer.

That weekend, when he dropped his dirty clothes off to his parents, he took a walk through the neighborhood. He crossed the street and headed for the walkway between St. Francis Church and the Parish Convent.

His thoughts went back to the old annex building that formerly occupied a place on the current playground. It was in that building that where he had the most deeply meaningful experience of his life in 1958. It was in the first grade, in Sister Mary Imelda's class. She read from the Bible. It was the first Bible verse he had ever heard.

But he wasn't prepared to linger long in front of the stored image in the gallery of his mind. He turned to leave. When he crossed the street, he

---

[25] Italian: "You don't want to be a disgrace to the family.

[26] Italian: "You speak good things to me, Papa Grandfather."

turned to walk toward Audubon Park. He walked down Constance Street toward the brick-walled compound of the Order of the Poverty Servants. He was headed in the direction of a special place.

The benevolent old tree caught his attention like cool water for a thirsty soul. He was surprised by the sight of it. And he was surprised at his surprise when he saw it. Doubly surprised, he marveled how his beloved Old Oak Tree was so far removed from his consciousness. He noted the slight lean to the trunk of the kind Old Tree.

The notions that he always sensed there were came alive. And he was glad for it. He allowed himself to recall the days a few years earlier when he was a boy on a bike. He retrieved a breath of innocence stored in some of the images in the gallery of his mind. It was refreshing.

He recalled having questions when he was a boy. And whatever was going on then was deep and personal. It held out notions of a life beyond, beyond the far reaches of Old Man River coming down from the north. And it reached back, up the river, and into the future. His Old Tree was draped in thick, full, dull-gray, curly Spanish moss. And it wore the fungus like a thick, full, gray beard of an aging, wise sage.

Standing in its shadow, below its thick mossy branches, he began to realize something. His experience in the first grade and his experiences as a boy on a bike under the Old Oak were of the same genre. They had a common thread that he couldn't trace. The same, real, wordless Voice that spoke inaudibly that day, while he sat in his desk in the first grade, was connected with the same still, small, silent Voice related to his beloved tree.

In addition, he sensed that something was being extended toward him pertaining to the world that he lived in – that every human lived in. He didn't understand what it was. But he was aware that he had an interest, a very strong interest, in history, the future, and the connections between the two. He had the interest as far back as he could recall. And as he stood there, he was tucked tightly inside a narrow space between a subject and an object. He was at the same time both initiating something and receiving something. And he knew it, and he didn't.

Fifteen

He wouldn't have admitted it, but things were changing in his heart.
He had steeped into a world where he thought he could find answers.
But he found out that he had more questions. He was into his twentieth
year and five years into an aimless existence with no end in sight.

He was confused. He didn't know what to make of himself. He did
well at what he applied himself to until he lost interest. It was ironic that
the one thing he applied himself to he thrived in. But it wasn't the kind
of experience one would list on a job application.

On a paltry summer evening in 1973 he sat at a table in the pool hall
with some of the guys. Though he wasn't the only one who wasn't
working, he was 'between jobs' more often than any of the rest of them.
He was looking through the employment section of the newspaper when
some of the boys began ribbing him.

"Hey Simm, you can write on your job application how good you are at
getting us together to have fun. And you can write down about all of the
good ideas you get. You know, like when you got the idea for us to jump
off the bridge into the the lake in our drawers. Or when you got dee idea
for you and Pick to skip into the hamburger joint in your drawers
holding hands."

"Flip's right, Simm. You can put down on there how you get your best
ideas at about one in the morning when we are getting bored and looking
for something to do."

"Ah agree wit Grump. Like the time you talked us into going to
Audubon Park at 1 a.m. wit some six-packs of Dixie. We sat in the
fountain in our drawers and drank em. It was a good idea. It felt good
sitting there, cooling off."

"Ever notice, Stick, dat so many of the things Simmie talks us into end
up with us in our drawers in public places?"

"Yeah you rite, Tabes. Simmie, dat's a special talent you got there.
You should put those things on your applications."

"Shaddup, Graves. Ya'll leave Simmie alone."

Evans leaned his head back with an attitude and looked down his nose at his pals.

"Ya'll are just jealous. Simmie gets us together.. And he gets us out and about doing stuff dat happens to be unique. Dat's our boy. Now, Ahm hungry. Let's go get some groceries."

"Ahm in."

"Me too, Shak."

"Ah ain't got any money, guys.".

"We already know dat, Simmie boy."

Trae slapped him on the back and grinned.

"Less-go. We'll figure something out."

"Ahm paying for our cousin, Trae. He's on me tonight."

"Thanks, Lan. Ah'll get you next time."

"Don't worry about it, Simmie."

While he thrived at the one thing he was good at, it unfortunately brought him no substance in return. For the umpteenth time in the last five years he would find soul-meaning in the early morning hours. And in turn, he would feel another deep pang in his soul as he realized that his aimless life was getting him nowhere as a man.

Feeling more and more dissatisfied, he and Evans began to talk more. Evans was getting ansty. So was he.

"Let's join the Navy and go in on the buddy system. Dey have dis program where you can go to boot camp and your first duty station together. Let's do it, man. Let's get outta dis place, you and me."

Simeon was enticed but hesitant. Evans, knowing his reluctance, joined up without him. And before he knew it, his friend was gone. Evans was gone. And his absence was a heavy loss.

Several days later he sat at the bar in Mitts.

"Ready for another one, cugino?"[27]

"Nah, thanks, Lan. Ahm okay."

"Hey, dago."

Both Lan and Simeon turned toward the voice. It was Mixy Palsamo.

"Mistuh Mixy. You callin *us* a dago? With dat dago name you got?"

He ignored Lan and continued.

---

[27] Italian for male cousin.

"Can you believe dat Sammy O'Coule? He's still livin off his momma and daddy and he's twenty- fahve years old. Dat son-of-a-gun needs to get out and get himself a job. Nobody who lives around here makes a lot of money. His momma and daddy can't take care of him. He needs to grow up."

Lan walked over to where Mixy sat and continued the dialogue. Simeon got up to walk outside. He was uncomfortable with the conversation going on a few feet away. He turned to walk across the street to the playground.

"Ain't no way dat's gonna be me, Mistuh Mixy. Mah momma and daddy don't give me any money. You know dat, they are friends of yours. All they do is wash mah clothes and feed me some times. Ah don't get to eat much these days, but dat's okay. You'll see. Dat's not gonna be me. Ahm gonna figure it out soon."

The familiar sound of the mockingbird broadcast from the wire overhead. He reached down deep to find a resolve that had been dormant in him since he was a kid. It had been rearing its welcome head over the past few months when he tried to lean into his heart.

"Go head and mock me, little critter, but Ahm not buying it. Ah never really did. You made me wonder. And Ahm still wondering. But Ahm starting to get mah bearings a little."

He walked back down the block toward Fumps. When he got to the door to go upstairs he walked past it and opened the door next to it, the side entrance to the bar. He was surprised, and very glad, to see Betz seated there.

"Simmie! Ah been waitin for you, man. Ah went down to Mitts. Lan told me you left. Ah figured you'd show up here. Sit down. We gonna have a few drinks and catch up. We been passing in the night upstairs. How you doing, roommate?"

He was touched. He and Betz, though friends, hadn't talked solo about anything personal for a while. And he was ready.

"Ah'll aks you, Betz. How are you?"

"Look, man. Ahm the same as always, working and partying,… with you guys a fair amount. Ahm good, but Ahm worried about you."

"How you mean, Betz?"

"Come on, Simm. It's me. You don't think Ah know you and Evans talked about leaving? And he left without you. Heck, you told me all about it. Remember? Evans did too."

"Yeah. Ah guess Ah do."

"So tell me about what's got you down. Ah know you almost as good as Trae, Lan, and Evans. So lay it on me, man. You need to, and Ah got all night. Did it all start dat night dat dude was gonna kill you down the block at your girlfriend's house?"

"You been reading my soul, Betz? Tweet's death was the starter. Den Ah lost mah Paw-Paw. And then, there was dat first time Ah was gonna be killed."

"You are one lucky, sucker, man. If Stick hadn't walked outside of Mitts dat very second and talked him out of shooting you, you wouldn't be here. Dat dude was gonna shoot you dead."

"When Stick confronted me the next day and told me, Ah was in shock, even though Ah tried to hide it. Could you tell, Betz?"

"Yeah, me and Ev thought you were covering it."

"And then, there was the second time, by the bus bawn[28]. Evans was with me dat time, Betz. You remember dat, Ahm sure."

"Ah know. And if Keith Klane hadn't walked out of the Friendly House at just the right second, those ten dudes would have cut you open. Didn't they jump ya'll and hold you down?"

"Ten on two. They held me down and broke a bottle to jab into mah face. The dude with the broken bottle said, 'Ahm gonna kill you.'"

"In that first experience it was a strange feeling, Betz. Stick chewed me out good for picking a fight with a stranger Ah didn't know was dat desperate. To hear the next day dat somebody talked somebody else outta killing you is a rude awakening. But Ahm too thick-headed to pay attention, apparently."

"Dat second one was more in the moment. Ah thought Ah was done. We were fighting, and gettin the worst of it with ten of them on two of us. All of a sudden, Ahm on the ground with four guys holding mah hands spread eagle and the dude waving a broken bottle in mah face. As soon as he put the period on the sentence dat ended with 'kill you', Keith

---

[28] "bus barn" – where the local city transit buses were parked and serviced

Klane comes tearing into the crowd and takes the bottle out of his hands. 'Let him go,' he said, 'Dat's mah friend, Simm.'"

"And how lucky can you be, Simmie? Dat guy was Keith's first cousin. Somebody's watching over you, you lucky dago."

"And then, there was that last time. It was when the flame blew out in mah brown gas heater on mah breezy, cold, porch bedroom."

"Oh yeah. How could Ah forget dat. Wow, Simm."

"What's going on with me, Betz? Ths is mah home. But Ahm having a hard time here. What's wrong with me, man?"

"Ah don't know if 'wrong' is the right word. But you're definitely struggling. Ahm not good at advising people, Simm. Ah tried a little before with you, you know, about working and all uh dat. But Ah know you're struggling. Ah hope just talking and getting it out is helping in some way. And Ah know you're gonna figure it out."

"Thanks, Betz. This is helping, it really is."

Several months passed. It was late fall, 1973. Simeon arose late, his usual practice. He stepped outside from his doorway onto Lions Street on the warm, fall day. Sweat leaked from his pores the moment he walked down the sidewalk. He began his routine walk with a slow gait. He wasn't in a hurry to go anywhere and proceeded on automatic pilot, like a robot. He was increasingly aware that he was tired. Loneliness was his constant companion even though he was surrounded by family and friends. He was 'in between jobs' once again. Feelings of shame and failure were never far below the surface.

When he stopped by home, his parents saw it. Trae and Lan did as well. Fump and Orleans saw it too. He was feeling sorry for himself. But he felt trapped. He simply couldn't let go. But he was at a loss to find any motivation or ambition for anything if he stayed. So he did what he always did, the only thing he knew to do. He headed for Mitt's.

Ominous, dark gray and bright silvery clouds hung overhead along Lions Street, as he walked. They appeared to be getting darker.

It took less than a minute to walk from the side door of the building that was Fump's bar to the side door that led into the pool hall side of Mitt's. As he approached the side door, Hilton Memke and Sturgis walked out of the barroom front door of Mitt's. It opened up onto the

point of the corner of the block, across from Wesimar Playground. After
they greeted one another, Hilton looked across the street and quickly
turned to Simeon. He had a look of disbelief on his face.

"Did you see dat, Simm?!"

"See what?"

"Dat guy across the street just stabbed the other guy!"

He wore wide eyes and a look of disbelief.

Hilton bolted inside to get a call for help while he and Sturgis stood
stunned.. Unsure what to do, Simeon stepped toward the young man,
who appeared to be about his age. He was staggering toward him with
his left hand over his chest. Blood was coming from beneath his hand.
As the desperate young man approached him, his mouth was moving.
He was struggling to breathe.

Simeon was mortified. He felt compassion for him, but he didn't know
what to do. Coming close, he stumbled and fell to the ground at
Simeon's feet. As he fell, one of his untied, Ked's shoes slipped from
off of his foot. When he hit the ground, his head landed on Simeon's
right foot. When he looked up, he was face to face with Simeon, who
stood frozen in place. He was in shock and heartbroken pity. For an
instant, the victim tried to say something. But he couldn't. And within
seconds, his breathing subsided. He died looking straight into the eyes of
the young Italian whose foot was frozen to the concrete.

Almost instantanelously, a squad car arrived, while Simeon was still in
shock with the young man's head on his foot. They placed his body in
the back seat of the car and drove away. When he, Hilton, and Sturgis
went into Mitt's, they mostly talked about what just happened. Simeon
said a few words about the man's head falling on his foot. Lan was
working the bar with Orleans.

Simeon went to the table by the pinball machine and sat there alone. It
was the same chair where he sat sobbing eighteen months before when
Tweet died. He took turns staring down at the light gray table and the
pinball machine. His head was down. But his stare went to unknown
places far away. Orleans noticed and asked him if he was okay. He
knew that Simmie had been having a tough go of it. Lan walked over to
him wearing his white apron. He looked down on his beloved cousin.

"You awe-right, Simmie?"

"Ah don't know, Lan. Ah don't know."

"How bout a drink. It's on me, cugino."

"Not now, thanks."

In one motion, he pushed back the chair with uncommon resolve, and stood, turning toward the side door. The old and worn hinged barrier welcomed his familiar hand print one more time. The imprints of his palm stood out above every other imprint on either of its sides. They were markers by the most regular of patrons who hoped that he would find something elusive each time his hand coaxed it open, entering or leaving. In seconds he was on the move.

He walked out slowly and turned away from Mitts. He knew where he was headed. And the knowing stirred up questions that he forcefully chose to dismiss. All he knew in the moment, and going forward, was one thing.

An image hung just inside the doorway of the nearest hallway in the back of his mind. It was safeguarded there by his deep conscience, having received his most earnest pledge as a six year old. It was to be on standby for instant review whenever he wanted to retrieve it. The original experience moved him to hang it in the first position.   But he rarely did. Too many other things blocked the doorway.

Dark clouds ruled the skies when he opened the door to leave Mitts. Ever so slightly, they began to blow to the south as the door to Mitts stirred the air when it closed behind him. Rolls of thunder reverberated in rapid succession from somewhere upriver toward the near north. They too, began to slowly diminish in their intensity and rapidity with each determined step that he took. And the sights and sounds of the panorama could not steal him away for a reflective second this time.

The murky, muddy Mississippi River moved through the crescent city a few hundred yards away. Something like a silent call hastily abandoned its current. It blew stealthily into the neighborhood past the train tracks and Front Street. It crossed Tchoupitoulas Street and breezed up Lions Street. Fumps Bar guarded the corner, where it stood like a museum, holding a family's memories. It proceeded toward Mitts Bar and Poolhall where a young man was walking toward it with an unfamiliar determination. And as the silent call of the wind met him, it caressed his face and gently wrapped around him. In its embrace, he realized that something good was out there waiting for him. And he marked the moment.

A mockingbird began to give the business from somewhere close by. But before its sounds reached Simeon's ears, they were calmly escorted away by the gentle breeze of the silent call. With the rescue, its mission was complete. And like a honeybee which plants its deadly stinger in the invading insect coming into the hive, it peacefully flew away to die.

 For the last five years he had parked his soul in the batter's box hoping to get some big hits. Home plate was his uptown New Orleans roots. Every time he thought he hit a good one it ending up tailing off outside the foul line. Time after time, he had a good cut at some nasty pitches only to make enough contact to foul the pitch off.

He had no swings and misses until the last six months. Then Stick Bergeroux was inexplicably able to be at the right place at the right time to save his life. Swing and a miss - Strike One.

After more foul balls, Keith Klane pulled arms and hands off of him, and the bottle out of the executioner's hand. Swing and a miss - Strike Two.

A few foul balls later, he miraculously woke from a drunken stupor, choking from the natural gas filling his room from a brown gas heater. Swing and a miss - Strike Three.

Out at the plate, he was rightfully done and should have walked away from the batter's box. Instead, he held up the game. It took the desperate last gasps of air and terrified gaze of a poor, dying stranger, whose head lay on his foot, to get his attention. It finally woke up his sleeping soul.

He couldn't take it any longer. He had enough. It was over.

Time Passage

Re-Entry

"A definition is to a description as an outline is to a portrait."

~ Ron Bennett

Sixteen

"Honey, come check this out. This is unbelievable!"
The fifty-three year old raised his voice from the living room toward
the kitchen. Seconds later, his wife came in to get the weather update.
"Wow."
The simple word said it all.
The weather update for August 28th, 2005 showed the color image
radar for the tropics. The entire Gulf of Mexico was one giant monster
mega-storm. And it was headed straight for New Orleans. It had
exploded into a massive mega-storm on Saturday. A moving van was
scheduled to be at their home Monday to load their possessions for their
move to New Orleans.

"We can't go now. This one could be a game-changer. The city might not recover if this stays on course."

His eyes had a faraway look when he spoke.

"Well, we can't unpack everything, Simeon. Our house is still on the market, so we can still stay here. Let's just unpack some of the basics and we'll see how long this goes on. What's your mom gonna do?"

"I was just getting ready to call her. I wanted to wait till the latest update before I did. I'll call her first. Then I'll call the moving company and tell them we have to cancel. We can't go down there yet. We don't know what's going to happen over the next few weeks."

"What about Aunt Katie and Aunt Mae?"

"I'll call Momma, Pokey, Shairie, Trae, and Lan. They're probably already getting out. I just wanna be sure. It looks like our stay in Ohio will stretch a little longer."

It was almost a year later, May, 2006. Simeon was asked to give a personal update for his final appearance at a gathering of peers in the Midwest. He was introduced by his friend, Rich.

"Some of the gang know you better than others, Simm. Give them a quick update on your history since leaving home."

"Okay, Rich. Thanks. I'll finish off the matter of our staying here in the north a little longer, before heading down to New Orleans. After we realized we couldn't move to my hometown the same time a major hurricane was coming, we continued in our work with students at Columbus University in Columbus, Ohio until the end of this school year, 2006. One month after Hurricane Katarina, my beloved momma, Maria, passed away. She struggled with a heart condition that was magnified in the heavy stress of evacuating and waiting to return home after the storm. My cherished daddy, Julian, died in my arms in 2002."

"It was a bittersweet departure when I left home in early 1974. Though it tore me apart to leave, it was unquestionably the right thing to do. Within three months of my breakaway departure, my life changed. It was apparent to me then that it took a drastic change of scenery for that to happen."

"When I left for Navy boot camp in San Diego, it was the first time I was more than a few hours from home. Yet I was fully committed to

leave home for good. My entire future was up for grabs and open ended.
It would begin under the authority of the U.S. Navy. After a life-
changing three year stint as a sailor at sea, an experience I'll forever
cherish, I attended college at Madison University in Virginia. I met and
fell in love with a pretty Virginia country girl there. Many of ya'll know
Lily-Grace Briggs, now Mangino. We were friends for several years
before we began spending more time together. My stock rose when she
entered my life. And with her, it only increased in value over time.
Ken?"

"Yeah, Simm. I just want to affirm what you just said, that your stock
rose sharply after you married Lilly-Grace. We all agree."

"A very appropriate affirmation, Ken. Especially considering it comes
from an Indiana man. If there are no more obvious statements to
make....?"

"After marriage and graduation from Madison, I worked on the campus
there for a year before moving to Norfolk, Virginia to work on the
campus of Dominion University. Our three children were born there in
the 1980's. Bran, Jermaine, and Liza added spice and adventure to our
busy lives, as have your children. When I recall my life in New Orleans,
especially my late teen years, I am blessed to have the three of them. I
never dreamed I'd have the opportunity to be married to a woman the
likes of Lily-Grace. And I never imagined how good it would be to be a
father."

"Ten years after moving to Norfolk, we moved to the campus of
Stemson University in South Carolina. It was my first and only
experience in a rural setting. We bought a home there with an in-ground
swimming pool, another unforeseen blessing. Six years later, in 1998,
we headed north to work at the Columbus University campus – Yankee
land. This is our and Lily-Grace's first adventure living in the north.
Now in my early fifties, while at Columbus U., I began to get weary
from campus life and its energy. Over a several year process of
questioning and discussion, we decided to move to my beloved
hometown in 2005."

"Like most of you, into the cup that is our marriage relationship, both
Lily-Grace and I add who we are as people. Some of my New Orleans-
rooted ways spice it. The same is true of what were some of Lily-

Grace's rooted ways. Like all marriages, the cup that we pour from is uniquely us."

"Let me add that I've thoroughly enjoyed the eight years I've lived in the Midwest and shared a common cause with each of you. I am challenged by the good hearts in every one of you. And I value the friendships I've been privileged to gain. Thanks for hearing my story. And may our paths cross again in our shared journey, until the time."

Over the next few weeks he, Lily-Grace, and Liza accomplished their move to his home town. Living in the place of his roots was a different experience his second time around. He was a different person than the confused young man he was when he left. His native temperament was still intact. But he was a more settled person. And things had changed in the lives of most of his cherished friends as well. Almost everyone left the uptown part of town where they grew up. A few of them left the metro area. Most lived in the bordering parishes that made up metro New Orleans.

He found the time to take the fifteen minute drive from his upriver home to the old uptown neighborhood. And when he did, his heart and mind were flooded with cherished memories of youth and adolescence. There were painful memories as well. He caught up with Lan on the phone a short time after settling in.

"It's strange to see most of the neighborhood corner grocery stores made into homes now, Lan."

"There are a lot of strange things you're gonna see, Cugino. You've been gone so long. We caught up some over the years. But you've missed a lot, son. Yet, some things never change. Ahm referring to the fact dat me and Trae are still two months older than you."

"You don't know how much I miss hearing that, cugino. And Fump's is now the F & M Bar, after Fump and Mister Manny. Mah momma told me dat Fump died not too many years after Ah left home."

He momentarily flipped back into old New-Awlins-speak.

"Yeah, Simmie. And you heard dat Crisp Herdanez runs Mitt's now. It's not a pool hall any more. But it has some of the old look. We'll have to get over there soon for old times sake. Gasp was wondering if somebody would be interested in putting on a Mitt's reunion. You interested?"

"I am. I'll call Gasp and see what we can put together. Who's still around from the old crowd, Lan?"

"A lot of guys are in the area. We don't congregate much. Lessee, you knew dat Betz died shawtly after you left. Den Pick died. Graves died years later. And just recently we lost Grump."

"I knew about all of them from you and momma. Their deaths broke my heart, Cugino."

"And of course, our beloved Pokey. Ah sure miss him, Simmie."

"Me too. My little bro, Pokey. That one was the hardest, Lan. It seems like he's not gone, you know? Like he's going to walk in the door any minute."

They were silent for a moment.

"What about Evans, Lan? I tried my best over the years to track him down. But I can't find him anywhere."

"Nobody. The same with Tabes. And then, oh, of course, Flip, RayBay, Timmy, Halligan, Frankie, Ward, Joey, Gerry, Izzi, and Sturgis are still around town. And of course, me and Trae, your two hero's."

"I see you're still taking the high ground with me, eh Cugino?"

"Always. Me and Trae were here first. Never forget dat."

"I won't. I can't."

Affectionate, low level laughter spilled naturally and easily over the phone connection between the two lifelong friends since birth, who happened to be first cousins.

"Simmie, have you kept in touch with Ranny, Derbs, Crame, Crisp, BarryQ, are Sturgis?"

"I have with Ranny and Sturgis. Just a few times with the others. It means a lot to me to keep in touch with friends from our formative years. They are part of our stories and I cherish those guys, Lan. Let's try to get them together again."

He meant it. And in time, he saw to it that it happened. Each of them, as well as the larger uptown crowd along the river neighborhood, were special to him in their unique ways. The experiences he had with them, both the gratifying and the challenging, were part of their bonds. And they helped move and shape his life toward what was becoming a meaningful journey in a vibrant story.

A few weeks later he sat across from a special friend from the Saint Francis years. He had kept in touch with Ranny from time to time since leaving home. They set up a lunch to catch up.

"Can you believe that we live in the same neighborhood again, after all these years, Ranny?"

"Ah know, it's like déjà vu all over again. It sure is good to have you back home, Simmie. It really is."

"I'm glad you're nearby, Ranny. It feels like when we were boys on our bikes, in our St. Francis days again."

"Yeah you rite. Now, recap your experience for me one more time. We've kept in touch some. But give me duh Cliff Notes on it again."

"Okay, Ranny Boy. Gladly. The life change that I experienced three months after leaving home was a spiritual one, which you already know about. When I finally broke away from home, I was able to clear my mind from the distractions that I cultivated in those early years. What we were taught at Saint Francis helped me foment a spiritual-consciousness that never left me. Though I openly questioned things when feeling my oats as a cocky adolescent, I suspected deep inside that my roots were healthy. Often, when alone with my thoughts, I went to the space one reserves for a sense of self. And even though my self-sense was off-center, my spiritual sense was like an infant in the womb. It was embryonic, growing toward a birth. Though stirred early in life, it went underground. I denied my awareness of this. Yet the seed that was sown in both of us in grade school was sown."

"Ah'd say the same thing about myself, Simm. Doze early years were foundational, though there was more to the story dat Ah didn't understand."

"Remember riding our bikes all around the neighborhood, Ran? There's an Old Oak Tree on Constance by Audubon Park, just a few blocks from our old houses. It's across the street from the Poverty Servants. That Tree became a special place for me. There was something about it that's hard to explain, but especially meaningful for me in my story."

"Really? How many times did we ride past dat spot? Ah never knew dat."

"And over the years I've driven by that Old Oak Tree when I came home to visit with my family. In the thirty-two years that I lived away my venerable Old Tree aged significantly. Its trunk began to list slightly toward the street. And its leaf output also shrunk noticeably. But it's thick and curly Spanish moss was as noteworthy as ever. And it never lost its lure or its sense of Voice to me."

"Voice? Explain that."

"Not an audible voice. But a Voice that seemed to come from beyond to my soul. Not some kind of new-age, eastern mysticism thing. But there was something life-giving in my story at that aging Old Tree, in that obscure spot. I never told anyone, Ranny. And the only other person who knows of this is Lily-Grace. In the first few years after I left home, I went to my Old Oak Tree, knowing that I was different inside. The times I stopped by there were newly fresh and vibrant. I began to realize that, what was Voice to my soul there as a boy on a bike, was a real response to my desire for a life that I longed for."

After he left Ranny, he continued to ponder his draw to the Old Oak on Constance Street. He realized that his attraction to it didn't wane after he found the life that he realized he'd been missing. Voice still beckoned him whenever he found time to be there, just like when he was a boy on a bike.

His continued draw to the Old Tree dripped with enticements about his future, and the future of the world. Though the enticements were vague, they were undeniably real. He regularly asked himself if these were merely subjective attractions due to his interest in history and world events. But he couldn't deny that the thoughts were inside of him since he was a kid.

Not long after their phone call, he met Lan at Mitt's. The two nostalgic cousins readily recalled the old days and their neighborhood friends. After going down the list mentioning many of the old guys, Put's name came up.

"Good ole Put."

Lan offered a tender smile and a slow shake of his head while he looked down.

"'Dey call me PUT! P – U – T! Sounds like *'FOOT'*!"

Simeon joined in with a slight smile of affection of his own.

"Anybody ever hear what happened to the old guy?"

The question was attended by an air of expectancy mixed with affection.

"I never heard anything, Simmie. As faw as Ah know, nobody knows what happened to him.

"I've thought about Old Put over the years I was away, Lan."

"Mah *SIMMIE* Boy! Remem-buh dat, Simmie? Remember how he use to call you dat?"

"How could I forget? It was one of the many highlights of my life in the old neighborhood."

"We never knew dat much about him. Our daddy's knew him as kids. He was just always around. He lived across Magazine Street, Ah think. Remember how he use to say strange things about you?"

"Yeah. That's part of why I thought about him over the years."
"Really?"

"Yeah. In a way I always wondered if he knew something. You know, maybe he knew something that nobody else knew."

His eyes went to the old service window.

"Almost like he saw some things that others didn't see, things coming from someone you'd least expect."

As he spoke, he watched Lan to see how he would react to the statement.

"You never know, Ah guess."

With the words, Lan shuffled slightly in his seat. He raised his eyebrows and tilted his head slightly as he spoke. He took a deep breath and continued.

"Ahm sure dat's possible. But's it's beyond mah pay grade, cugino. You'll have to figure dat one out."

Simeon looked at the window where Old Put used to stand outside, waiting to be served his shots of vino. But his look went beyond the window he knew so well at the old Mitt's place.

For a moment, he thought he saw the elder statesman leaning on the shelf on the outside of the window. He thought that he almost heard the venerable old fellow let loose with an 'Eh labas!' But he knew it was only the image of him in his mind.

In the image, Old Put looked through the window into his eyes as if he wanted to get his attention. He turned his head down, then slowly back up, before he fixed his bloodshot eyes on Simeon's again. In the image, Simeon thought he saw Old Put nod his head up and down, slowly and deliberately. It was like an affirmation of two interlocking stories from the early 1970's.

As he beheld the image of Put, the window appeared to transform into a picture frame. Old Put's image faded, and the picture image that he saw in the frame was one of looking down on the world from outer space. As he looked down on the round object, he saw the world's seas in shades of blue. The continents were visible in shades of brown and green in varying places. The world appeared to be slowly rotating from right to left. He thought that he saw flames above the continents. It paused, and began rotating in the opposite direction, this time from left to right. It did this several times. The flames appeared and reappeared above the continents. While he gazed at the image in the picture frame, the frame itself appeared to transform into a mirror.

He and Lan had been sitting facing the window at Mitt's. In the mirror image facing him, he looked directly at himself. He caught his own eyes there. Now in his fifties, with a one-hundred-and-eighty degree change of heart and perspective, some things were beginning to become clearer to him.

"Ah heeuh dat."

The words barely leaked from the mouth of a man who was, in that moment, still moored to a fawaway place through the window. And in the attachment, he easily leaned back into the old NewAwlins-speak that always lingered just below the surface in his psyche, everywhere he had lived.

Seventeen

Over time, Old Man River had carried countless billions of gallons of new water past the spot where the crowd mingled. The water of time past had moved along every second of every day, carrying with it many things. And it was long gone from the days when each one in the festive gathering grew up just off its banks.

The crowd at Mitt's swelled to nearly two-hundred and fifty old uptown people. After living away for thirty-two years, Simeon was eager for the event. As he sat in the building where he had spent so many days and evenings in his former days, he swelled with emotion. He had started his own family, began a career, and returned home. He held back tears. It had been over three decades since he was among his uptown New Orleans friends. Memories of his now deceased momma and daddy flooded his soul, as well as those of his grandparents, aunts, and uncles.

He was caught up in the moment when Gasp, Lan's older brother, walked over to him. Seeing his cousins' approach, he came back to the present. Trailing him, was a very large fifties-looking man with a confident stride and conspicuous smirk on his face. He looked determined. Gasp appeared slightly shaken, like he was politely holding back what he could easily let loose. When he approached Simeon, he stepped aside to allow the large and imposing man to walk right up to the chair where he sat. The stranger glared down at him with the palms of his hands planted on each hip.

"Dis is mah cousin Simmie, duh one Ah was tellin yuh about."

His words were normal, but their delivery was not. Gasp appeared flustered.

"Simmie, dis is Vincent DeMaso. He's not from the neighborhood, but knows some-uh-duh guys. He went to Ignatius like you did for a couple of years. We got to tawkin. And the more we talked, Ah should say, began to debate, Ah told him about choo. Ahm gonna let you and him tawk for a little while."

And with that, he disappeared into the crowd. Simeon thought he detected a look of relief on his cousin's face.

As he looked up at Vincent Demaso he felt the urge to stand. While seated, he felt small and far from him. When he stood, it shortened the distance, slightly. Still feeling quite small, Simeon offered his right hand, angling it sharply upward.

"Simeon Mangino, I'm thinking that I know you. Your name is familiar."

Vincent withheld his hand for a moment before cocking his head sharply to the side and reluctantly extending it.

"Ignatius High School, freshman yeeuh, 1966. Ring a bell?"

Simeon paused for a few seconds and furrowed his eyebrows. He momentarily stared beyond Vincent.

"It sure does! I remember you! You sat to my left near the front. Didn't you play football?"

"Yeah, Ah did, and basketball too."

The answer came out like an announcement.

"I only did two years there. Were we in second year class together?"

"No, Ah was with the other group den. Ah was with your grade school pals, Derbs, Crisp, and BarryQ. Dat was the smarter group, remember?"

There was emphasis in his last sentence.

"Yeah, that sounds right. So how yuh doin Vincent? I guess its 'long-time-no-see'. Not many guys from along the river went to Saint Ignatius. And few ever came to Mitt's."

He was glad for the chance to re-connect with someone from the Ignatius days. But Vincent didn't appear as keen on the renewal.

"What brings you to our old neighborhood gathering?"

"You."

Vincent stood there as if waiting for another question. Simeon offered one up, dodging the terse reply.

"You have friends here?"

"A few acquaintances. It's you I'm here for."

"Well, allrighty then."

Simeon suddenly found himself seeking to ease what he felt was some tension coming from the man.

"So it's me who brings you here. I almost can't wait to hear what that's about."

"Ahm not sure you're gonna say dat after we finish talking. Sit down. Let's talk."

It wasn't a suggestion. His words, glare, and countenance told Simeon that he was about to go on a wild, though not totally unfamiliar ride, this time with an old classmate.

"And what makes you say that?"

He eased into alert status as he and Vincent sat down at the table. It wasn't that he was afraid in a physical sense. He had more than enough friends within a few feet.

"I hear you are a spiritual fella. Is that so?"

The air around Vincent became frosty as he got right to the point.

"Who told you that?"

"Doesn't matter. What matters is dat Ahm here to help you. You hear me?"

"I'm listening to you, Vincent. I'm not sure where this is going but I'm listening. How'd you and Gasp strike up a spiritual note?"

"Ah just dove right into it with him. Ah heard he was your cousin, a so-called spiritual guy too, so Ah stawted with him."

"Why didn't ya'll just finish it then? Why did Gasp want to bring me in?"

"Ah steered him to bring you up because Ah know about you. Ah heard you speak at The Mission a few times. Dat's when Ah decided to find you and get into it with you. Ah didn't see you because of the large crowd. Ah knew he'd lead me to you."

As he spoke Simeon noted his tenacity. An admirable quality, he presumed.

"Ah sniff around the metropolitan area on the lookout for whatever things and whoever persons say things that Ah think are disruptive or harmful to the greater culture as a whole. Ahm a socially conscious person, Ahm proud to say. Ah check out who speaks at The Mission every now and then. Dat's how Ah stumbled upon you."

"Okay. So you have some interest in what goes on in culture, and I'm assuming for the greater good of all. And that's what motivates you to keep your eyes and ears open. Am I reading this right?"

"Mostly, but don't think you're gonna get to me with some kind of pseudo kindness, or what ya'll might call 'sacred listening' technique. Ahm onto you all's 'I'll be kind and gentle, letting them know Ahm listening so they'll think Ah care for them kinda thing', and all uh dat crap. It ain't gonna werk on me, you hear me, Mangino?! Don't even try it."

Simeon looked at him, unaffected. Impulsively, he gave full attention to the words that came from Vincent's mouth. As he listened, he studied Vincent's face.

His hair was thick and white. He combed it straight back without anything to wet it. His face was round and worn with piercing blue eyes. He studied the man's face in the attempt to recall anything about him as a fourteen year old freshman in high school. As Vincent spoke, he finally located the image of his freshman face from 1966. He made the connection. And he remembered what happened to him in the schoolyard.

"So before you even begin to presume that you're gonna size me up, better be careful. Don't try to get a bead on me. Don't think you're gonna take me down into your antiquated spirituality and prophetic mumbo-jumbo, and make something outta me dat Ah don't wanna be."

He stared a dagger into Simeon's eyes, looking down his nose at his target.

"Don't even think about it. Stop dat right now, you hear me, man?"

Simeon said nothing. He held Vincent's stare and merely lifted his eyebrows. With their eyes locked, he saw rage in those that held his own.   He broke the stalemate.

"What is it that you've heard me say that raises alarms in you?"

"How much time yuh got?"

"I'll tell you what. There are too many folks here that I want to visit with and time's moving on. Let's hook up soon somewhere when we have some time and can talk. I can meet you during your lunch hour or for breakfast, or whatever."

"You don't remember anything about me, do you?"

"It's been a long time, Vincent. I switched high schools, joined the military, went to college, and moved three more times after that before coming back home. My life is divided into chapters. I don't remember much about you, I'm sorry to say. I'm sure that's more of a reflection on me than it is on you."

"Now *they're* you go."

He slapped the table as if throwing down the trump card in a game of booray.[29] After expressing himself, he leaned back in his chair. He folded his giant arms while cocking his head back and staring down his nose again at his far away adopted enemy.

"A sign of humility. Ah thought you knew it all, all about duh future, and all-uh-dat. But you see, you really don't know everything now, do you?"

With the expression, he leaned forward with a sadistic grin. His face became red, and his eyes appeared as if they were going to explode out of their sockets.

For the first time, Simeon felt a chill wash over him.

"I'm not sure where this is coming from, Vincent. But I sincerely mean it when I tell you I'd be happy to hear you out on these things. Whaddya say?"

"Ahm retired and financially quite well off, if Ah don't mind saying so. Ah got time to spare. Let's talk dis week. And yuh better pray yourself up or whatever it is you people say you do. Cause you gonna need it. Mah business is done here."

"Thanks for the reminder, friend. Do you know where Pomilesi's is, a few blocks down the street? One o'clock on Friday. How's that?"

"I'll be there. And be ready."

"And by the way, I'm the organizer of this shindig. Stay as long as you like, mingle, and eat and drink to your pleasure. I'm paying for your admission."

"Ah already paid."

He couldn't hide the scorn in his tone.

"Just a minute, Vincent."

With that, Simeon headed to the registration table and returned with some cash. Here's your admission fee back. I want you to be my guest. I paid for you. Visit for a while. Eat and drink up. And I'll see yuh during the week."

---

[29] Cajun version of the card game, *"Spades"*

Vincent stood. Simeon followed, as if pulled up in his wake. As he did, he extended his right hand outward and up at the level of his face. The tall man looked down on his adversary and stared blankly. He grunted with a forceful huff before walking away.

Several in the vicinity saw the man spurn his handshake. Ward Peters saw it go down and felt the tense vibes from where he stood. He walked over.

"What wazzat about? You know dat dude, Simm?"

"Kind of. I remember him from Ignatius High School back in the day."

"Well, if he knows you, it doesn't look like he cares much fuh you."

"I'm getting that feeling too, Ward."

When the event came to a close at midevening, Simeon walked to his car, parked down the block beside the old Fump's Bar. It was quiet and still. He looked up at the small, elevated deck just outside the door to his old porch bedroom. The corner was lit by the same lightpole that he addressed from the deck that long ago early morning many years ago.

His thoughts went next to the barroom that he stood beside. He recalled the night when poor old Graves Condale nudged him, telling him to 'get ready' only to end up knocked out cold on the floor. And he had that dream when he was out. The soldiers were coming up his leg. They were after him. It had a familiar ring to it then.

He heard an evening mockingbird across the street, on the roof of the Old Coney shotgun house. It had been years since he heard one. The context of its soundings stood in contrast to the times when he heard them in younger years. The sounds were the same. But many things were not.

He thought of his Momma and Daddy. He recalled Fump's raspy, throaty, call to come down to receive calls from the payphone in the barroom. He looked up to where Mister Tibby Trufant woke him up by banging beneath his room with a broom handle. He could almost see Evan's charcoal black 1948 Oldsmobile parked in the clamshell covered parking spot where he stood. He recalled someone taking a picture of him, Evans, and Put in front of the Oldsmobile there.

He walked to the corner. The irregularly placed telephone pole stood where he remembered it. It had been positioned too far from the banquette into the walkway of the sidewalk when his parents were kids.

And it remained. Like the images stored in his mind, the awkwardly positioned telephone pole was positioned in its place and time for a purpose. It was not in the most convenient place in the story of every one who had to walk around it. But its awkward placement, like the unexpected timing of most of life's lessons, strengthened its import in the memory.

Having stored them in his memory, he was able to go back to the experiences he had hung in his mind and feel some of what he felt when they originally happened. But he was no longer governed by the feelings and youthful perspectives that he had when they first happened. In addition to feeling some of what he felt in the original experience, something else was waiting for him. It was a new kind of inner strength to embrace the meaningful experiences, whether perplexing, pleasant, or painful. He was able to rise above the original feelings with the strength and maturity of a more mature self. From the new perch as a more objective and more mature observer, he could re-visit the experience when a young boy on a bike, a teenager, or a young man. He was now armed with the right kind of objectivity and the right amount of empathy for how fragmented and confused he was back then.

He could then extract the rich nectar of life lessons that were stored in the petals of those experiences. For years, decades for some of them, they hung as frozen images in the background of his mind and soul. They lay in storage, soaked with potential in his life. They hung in the gallery like masterpieces which, upon completion of the last stroke, were immediately swept away and hung in a hallway which no one else had access to.

He was now a man, a husband, a father, and a Paw-Paw. He had found the meaning of life and a purpose within it, even though there was still an unfolding mystery in it. He knew that it had something to do with the future of the world, a topic that enticed him for a long time.

Across Tchoupitoulas Street, the Public Belt Railroad locomotive was revving its engine and began to inch along the tracks.

"How timely."

A peaceful calm dropped in from somewhere along the lazy, brown river nearby. He closed his eyes to take in the moment, when he was interrupted by the sound of a single, short, and loud blast of the train's horn. It was followed by a total of six distinct rings from a bell. At the sound of the bells, he snapped his head impulsively in the direction of the train.

It had been a long time since he last heard the sounds. And he was impressed again that the bell always rang six times. The sounds led him to take down an image from the gallery of his mind. It was from the experience outside of Bivi Q's over thirty years ago.

He recalled the man at the bus stop on the corner. And the blue folder that he held in his hand. He was brought back to the determined look the stranger gave him after looking down at the blue folder. He was in a time zone, realizing again the stunning sensation he had when the man simply vanished. All the while, Betz, Tweet, and Evans were carrying on, oblivious to it all.

He recalled realizing something that was strange to him back then. When he heard the familiar sounds of the six bells that evening, he had the unique sensation that their rings had a larger purpose. It seemed to be associated with a call-to-preparation or a summons to muster attention.

He looked at his watch. It was time to head home. He stepped into his car just outside the side door of the living area of the building. He glanced at the familiar old entry door to the up and down living spaces. It opened into decades of records from the annals of time when DNA common with his own passed over its threshold thousands of times. And as he drove away from the sentimental doorway, the peaceful, passing waters of the river nearby whispered through the faded sounds of the bells. They spoke in hushed tones of future things from the recesses of the north.

Eighteen

"How are things in New Orleens?"

"Interesting, as always. You recall your experience here, right?"

"Colorful and lively folks for sure. Any new developments related to your curious lifelong question?"

"Not certainly, and yet 'yes', in a way, Ron."

 He paused, knowing how that sounded - not clear at all.

"I'll explain."

"I still have thoughts about the macro world. That hasen't faded. It surges with ebbing and flowing degrees of intensity. But I'm still not clear as to what this is all about. It goes underground. But it's never too far below the surface."

"Well it's important that we live by priorities. I'm glad that you still do, Simm. And as you do, you'll have interests that you'll want to pursue. I believe you when you say that these matters have consistently been coming to you for fifty years, since you were a child."

"And good for you for not jumping to conclusions, for trying to prematurely make judgments about the things that have happened. Too many folks do that, though not all of them. You've been patient about these things for a long time. You do well to be patient still. Don't be in a hurry. Let understanding come as you follow and trust. Keep doing what you regularly do and be faithful."

"That makes sense, Ron."

"And what was the 'yes, in a way' response about?"

"Yeah, that. I was at our Mitt's Reunion, the one you came to town for last year. You remember my cousin, Gasp. He brings this guy to meet me. The man goes at least 6'8" and 380. And he carries it well. He was reluctant to shake my hand when I introduced myself. It turns out that he knows about me. And he's also got it out for me."

Simeon leaned back. He lifted his feet onto the chair next to him.

"It turns out that we were in the same class freshman year at Saint Ignatius. I didn't remember him at first. But when he jogged my memory, it came back to me. We spoke here and there about this and that. But I don't recall that the guy didn't like me. We didn't talk long at the reunion but agreed to get together for lunch this coming Friday."

"So what's out of the ordinary about that? You meet people for lunch often."

"Except for the fact that he was pretty hostile toward me. He scouts out the Mission where I go to serve. When he heard me speak on the prophets, he took exception to things. He apparently has marked me as someone not to be trusted."

"It is a little weird that he scouts around looking for folks to disagree with."

"True. But he didn't come across as being totally disconnected from reality. He said he was retired and well-off financially, with time to spare. I'll find out more about him soon. It wasn't difficult to notice and feel the anger coming from him – and toward me. But I, well,… we'll see how it goes."

"So what did you say that upset him?"

"I did a series on the prophecies and the Lord's return. He's suspicious of folks who give him the impression that they might be a disturbance to the public good by propagating negative thinking. When he thinks he's found someone who does he takes it upon himself to give them the business. Apparently, I'm his latest project. He was one step short of literally being in my face. Verbally, he was already there."

"Do you feel physically threatened by him?"

Ron didn't know if he would ask the question when it first came to his mind. But now he wanted to.

Simeon thought for a moment before answering.

"I'll get back to you on that one, Ron."

"Well it looks like you've found a new friend. You've been in the game for a long time, Simm. I know that you know this was no accident."

"I do. And thanks for the reminder.

Ron Partel knew him well. Their friendship had developed around a common cause. He was good listener and knew how to help his friends get to the crux of a matter with penetrating and well-timed questions.

"Like you said, Ron, meeting Vincent was no accident. It was meant to happen. The very thing he's perturbed about concerning me is the topic of my curious lifelong question. Others have broached the subject with me before. But they are usually folk who know me and know that I have an interest in world events and the prophets. This guy walked in out of a time passage with a giant chip on his shoulder. And he's overtly hostile. This isn't normal. It has the feel to me of a simmering trial that might become a challenge. But like all trials, small and great, it appears to be timely, appropriately fitted, and ripe for this time and place."

After talking with Ron, his thoughts went back to the encounter with Vincent at the Mitt's Reunion. He leaned back in the swivel chair in his study.

In front of him were shelves filled with books. Several different translations of the Sacred Writings stood side by side. They provided him with a warm and secure sense of priority. A dictionary and thesaurus announced their significance to him as consulting companions. Several journals, with thoughts since his days in the Navy, college, and the years after, leaned against one another. They sat like close-knit siblings in the bonds of shared experience and affection, like they belonged together in a shared story.

He was aware that there was a progression associated with each of the works on his shelves. The resource works and the personal journals were tools that helped him progressively understand meanings, associations, and life application. The Scriptures provided objectivity, guidance, and understanding, as well as subjective guided spiritual exercise. He took down a journal and paged through it. It was dated June, 1976, when he was aboard the USS John F. Kennedy. He read a line that he had written in there.

It read: "Wait like a farmer."

He closed the journal. He didn't need to go any further.

He got up for bed, acknowledging that it was one more good night to entrust all things to the Father Of All Nature.

The next morning he chatted with Lily-Grace in the kitchen.

"Today's Thursday, Simeon Joseph, your turn to pick up Liza, right?"

"Yeah, I'm gonna leave early and sit at Wendy's on St. Charles. It's close to Saint Marshall's and I can work there for a while. And tomorrow, I'm having lunch with that guy Vincent I told you about."

"Yeah, the hostile giant. Be careful."

Saint Marshall's Resource School was downriver from where Simeon grew up. Their daughter Liza had Down syndrome. Saint Marshall's was a school for special needs kids. They specialized in their education and development.   Simeon sometimes brought his study-work to a nearby restaurant on the days he picked Liza up from school.

It was mid-afternoon. The lunch crowd diminished and he had a notebook open in front of him. He noticed that the seating area was empty except for he and another patron seated a few away. The music that normally played in the dining area was unusually silent. There was an unusual and noticeable, peaceful stillness in the air.

One other patron, an elderly-looking man, peered down where he sat. There was no food or wrapping on the table before him. There was no drink cup. Several yellow napkins lay flat in front of him. A pen was at the ready in his right hand. His left hand was on a napkin. Simeon rose to go to the restroom beyond where the man sat. As he walked past him, he noticed that the man was writing on one of the yellow napkins. He appeared to be intensely focused on what he was doing. In no time, he was back at his table and deep in thought.

Minutes later, he was aware of a presence. When he looked up, he was surprised to find the napkin-writing man seated at his table, directly across from him.

He appeared to be in his early seventies. He wore a dark, checkered flat Gatsby cap. Strands of thin hair showed from beneath the cap and extended over his ears and behind them. His face wore large rimmed eye-glasses. A rough-looking tweed sports jacket covered a worn v-neck sweater with an unkempt shirt collar showing. He had the impression that he was facing a nerdy college professor.

Their eyes met. The stranger placed both of his forearms on the table so that the palm of one hand crossed over the back of the other. He leaned slightly forward before he began to speak. As he did, he held an air of confidence devoid of arrogance or pretense. His demeanor was relaxed. And for some strange reason he seemed eager and enthused to be sitting there. Before Simeon could process how the perfect stranger pulled off the silent caper, he began to speak. He made no introduction. There was no explanation. He began shortly after their eyes met, like he was waiting for his listener to partially collect himself in order to engage.

"Do you believe that Jesus Christ is coming soon?"

Simeon was utterly seized by the question. He went mentally lame for a moment, and his mouth opened in the pause. Before he could answer the question, the professor began his lecture. He began with a detailed and confusing explanation about scientific discoveries on the ocean floor, where the Gulf of Mexico meets the Atlantic.

"Who is this guy? What the heck is he saying? And why is he talking to me?"

The stranger continued to expel a confusing litany of scientific facts about the oceans and past civilizations. Then, he pivoted to explain in broad terms how oceanic history dovetails with ancient history. As he opined on, Simeon lagged behind.

Things were going down quickly. He couldn't process his thoughts the way he normally would. He hoped the man would slow down. He wanted to hear every word. And he couldn't wait to ask questions. In the moment, the whole scene felt like it wasn't real. Emotions and thoughts were colliding. And the collision caused all time to stand still.

From the beginning, he was aware that something noteworthy was unfolding. He didn't lack the desire to apply extraordinary import to the man's words. But he couldn't keep up.

The stranger waxed on. His hearer was wedged between a familiar question and its elusive answer. It was the same place he had been since he was a boy on a bike under his Old Oak on Constance Street. The space was a lifelong void. And he realized that it was being filled in a little more that very moment. He was crawling again across the hyphen that connected considerations to possibilities. And he wondered if the universe might be pausing so he could take a snapshot of a blurry image to store in the corridor of his mind. But he had to fend off the encroaching confusion that seemed intent on trying to entangle him.

"Don't pay too much attention to your thoughts. You might miss something. He's talking so fast."

Their eyes were locked in. But he simply couldn't follow the man. He was moving too quickly around the race track. He sensed there might be meaning in the man's words, so he tried to stay focused. But the material was over his head. His subconscious had kicked in instantly like an automatic generator when the power goes out. Thankfully, he would have a fairly good recording of the experience.

Imperfect, yet, seasoned intuition told him that he was inside of a defining moment. Fifty six years of growth through the trials and tests of life had helped him get to this point. He hadn't perfected all of the intricate steps of the kind of dance he was doing. But he had been practicing what steps he knew for a long time and was committed to learn the rest. From the first second, he was able to marshal his senses and battle through his internal distractions. All systems were online and functioning. But it took a herculean effort to maintain them throughout.

The stranger rounded the far turn into his stretch run. And his sentences accelerated to come at an even faster pace. He began his closing point with an oblique nod to the science of the skies and the atmosphere. He sprinted into his stretch run for another thirty seconds as he gained on the finish line.

Suddenly, like current charging through wire to power a lamplight, the switch was flipped off. He crossed the finish line. And having finished his sprint, the professor man abruptly stopped talking.

Without blinking an eye, he leaned forward toward the middle of the table, directly toward Simeon. He continued to keep eye-contact as he did. The eagerness and enthusiasm that carried him around the track up to the moment gave way to a sober and serious look. His eyebrows furrowed as he gazed deeply through Simeon's eyes and into his soul. In the same motion, he gently slapped both of his palms on the table top as he spoke.

"That's how we know that Jesus Christ is coming soon."

He left the period to dangle and dry in the air. While it did, he stood deliberately and turned to his right to leave. Simeon was compelled to reach across the table to grab him. He wanted to entreat him, no, to command him, to sit for awhile. He wondered what the man thought he was doing, and why he said what he said. He wanted an explanation for all that was said. And he wanted to know if they could meet again, and not to mention - an introduction.

No time passed. He was utterly perplexed. And his stultified state of mind held at bay the mounting excitement that was waiting to take command of him.

The stranger took a sharp left turn and took a step to walk past him. He was headed for the door fifteen feet away, to Simeon's back. Simeon turned quickly to his left to address him as he brushed past. He didn't know what to say, but he intended to say something. When he turned, he thought to reach over to offer to shake his hand. But he wasn't there.

Nineteen

He slowly sank down in the chair. He was not new to life-defining moments. But few were on the level of the one that just happened. He sat for long minutes, absorbing what had just taken place. His journal was in his bag. He reached for it and began to write:

"A strange old fella just showed up at my table in Wendy's. He went on and on about things hard to understand. The surprise way in which he showed up, spoke, and then simply vanished, has left me totally astounded."

A familiar numbness and confusion is lingering. It's a reaction to the unhealthy influence of doubt. Something incredible just happened. A man was here. He spoke. I looked into his eyes and heard his words. The numbness I feel invaded me when I fathomed the relevance of the unexpected encounter. As well as the profound nature of the whole thing. Now, doubt is telling me that this was just a coincidence.

I don't want the surprise visit by this professor guy to cause dissonance in my soul. Like everyone, I prefer to have harmony there.

The encounter with The Professor was a surprise in its formation, but not in its content, given my propensity and interest in the state of the world my entire life. But I never anticipated what just happened. Rather, I am pleasantly surprised by it. I won't let doubt vanquish any future impact from what just occurred. Nor will I allow vanity and vain-glory to creep into this part of my story. There is something I am to glean from this. I'm sure I'll discover what it is as I walk."

He didn't have a chance to ask The Professor a question, or to even nod in agreement. And he had many, many questions he wanted to ask him. He swept into his life on the wings of the mundane, ordinary grind of daily life. He was there, spoke his mind, and then vanished.

"This must be the way it was supposed to go down, I presume."

His words were to Someone unseen.

Middle-age was in full bloom in the story of his life. Early-on old age was on the horizon. He was not about to miss out on whatever was to be gleaned from the brief, yet profound encounter. The image was freshly stored under his sub-conscious. It was next to the image of the first grade experience at Saint Francis, in 1958, and to the Denver experience in 1974. Still affected by the encounter, he realized it was time to pick up Liza. He gathered his things and headed out.

That evening the phone rang at the house.

"Simeon, are you gonna get that? It's probably Lan. He called earlier."

"Okay."

"WheyY'att, Cugino."

"WheyY'att, Cugino."

"Hey, boy. Ah got a message for you. Mah momma wants you to come by. She said she's been meaning to talk with you about something. Ah aksed her what it was about but she wouldn't tell me. So you'll just have to come, not knowing what it's about. She says it's something between you and her. Ah don't know why she's being so secretive, but dat's her prerogative, Ah guess."

"Allright, Lan. What my Aunt Mae wants, my Aunt Mae gets. I'll drop by Saturday evening. Does she have any of her potato salad laying around?"

"Ah get first dibbs if she makes it. Me and Trae were here first, remember dat. If you walk away from your potato salad, Ah might chomp it down like you and Tweet did to mah poh-boy sandwich at Mitt's years ago. Ahm still mad about dat."

"Good ole Tweet. Just be sure you save me some of yuh momma's potatosalad. Ah'll see you den."

The slide into NewAwlins-speak was unintended.

Friday came. He was anxious when he pulled up in front of Pomilesi's. He had experienced varied levels of antagonism for The One he stood for. But it felt different with Vincent. His anger was as intense as that which he had been the target of in the early days, as a sailor and a college student.

Vincent was seated at a table when he walked in. He appeared the way he did when he walked away from Simeon the weekend before at Mitt's. It wasn't a good sign.

He approached the thick, glass door to the familiar old neighborhood bar and restaurant. As his hand went to open it, he spoke to The Unseen.

"Please go before me. Let me know that you're with me. And please work behind me after I part with this man today. And help me to love the guy."

He walked in. James, the bartender, looked up. He, his siblings and cousins attended Redemptor High when Simeon was there.

"Whey Y'att, Simm. You hear to see Miss Dot?"

"Hey, Whey Y'att, James. If I have time. I'm meeting a friend for lunch."

He quickly reprocessed the just-spoken, upgraded classification of his relationship with the man he was meeting. *"It's better, anyway it goes, if I presume the posture of a friend, even if he obviously doesn't.*

As he looked to the corner table, the massive body of Vincent DeMaso dominated the table area. He pushed past all feeling and walked over to him.

"Awright, Vincent, awright. Hah yuh doin?"

When he spoke, he coaxed out a friendly grin. He offered his hand to the large man.

"Nevuh mind all uh dat."

Vincent folded his thick arms and tilted his head back in one motion with the words.

"And don't presume to offer to buy lunch. We'll each buy our own. Ah already know what Ah want,... you?"

"In the early sixties I lived two blocks away. In fact, I lived there when we were in freshman class together in 1966. This place hasn't changed in fifty years. Miss Dot still lives through that door leading into the house connected to this barroom. Me and some of the guys were in there talking with her last month. As a kid, I played in the backyard here with my cousin Trae while my Aunt Katie visited Miss Dot. I know this menu and the food it represents like I know my wife's good cooking. Yeah, I know what I want. Let's order."

When they returned with their food they began to eat quietly. Gravy from their sandwiches dripped onto their plates with each bite. Sharing lunch together was having the effect of moving the cold connection towards warmth, slightly. The bond of good food shared didn't hurt. Simeon wasn't sure it would last.

After a few bites and more spilled gravy, Vincent began.

"It's well known that most things are difficult before dey are easy. You shouldn't think you can say controversial things and not tick some people off."

Simeon took another bite. Gravy spilled onto his hand.

"They say dat it takes around ten years to realy master a subject. Do you have a degree in what you believe about the world and where it's headed?"

"I don't. My degree is in the arts."

"Den become a painter."

Simeon looked outside. The sun was no longer bright. Clouds were gathering.

"How's your po-boy, Vincent?"

"Listen to me, Mangino. In order to be an expert in the matters of which you speak, you need a background, son. You didn't even go to seminary. Ah checked you out. Have you been pondering sensations, notions, and ideas about the future of the world for a long time? Maybe you have, since you were a kid living around the cawnuh over there. Or maybe you haven't. But how many chunks of knowledge regarding history as a basis for the future has your mind gathered and stored over the past fifty years? You should be an encyclopedia by now."

"Have you read, listened, observed, studied, and questioned? Have you discussed and dissected matters concerning werld thinking and events from many angles in all uh dat time? In your fifty plus years of life have you carefully weighed various options about the future in view of duh prophecys in your sacred book?"

"Have you consulted the findings and opinions of more than a few others who are more informed than you about their subjects dat relate to the future, both secular and spiritual? Are you trying to be holistic in the way you've followed your curiosities? And most important of all, are you careful to try to not jump to conclusions, to keep an open mind?"

Simeon swallowed his food.

"You are asking deep questions, Vincent. And I'm glad you feel free with me to ask them."

"Den think, Mangino. *Think.* Why do you try to stir fear in people? There's already enough of that going around with more coming around every day. And don't answer my question with another question. Just answer duh joking question!"

Simeon swallowed again, this time without food. His brain was churning, processing each of the challenges freely thrown his way. There was nothing new in any of the concerned and intelligent questions that Vincent asked him. Each of them was silently replied to with the silent affirmation of a clear conscience.

"You're right, there's enough fear-mongering going around. And I'm aware that you've heard me speak once or twice regarding the prophecies, the world, and the return of Jesus. I'm also aware that there is very much more that I say about life in my classes, in close-encounter groups, and when with one other person. What you heard is part of a larger story that my life and story revolves around. It has a larger context. And much of that context involves dialogue. I'm not standing before a large gathering to speak to a crowd all the time. Much of what I do is person-to-person and in smaller, more intimate groups. When you've heard me you are taking in monologue. In other contexts there is dialogue, give and take, interaction between everyone."

"Who gives a rip?! What's dat got to do with mah question?"

A heavy clump of gravy dropped to his plate as he picked up his po-boy.

"Here's where it comes in Vincent. If you were with me in all of those contexts on a consistent basis, you'd find that I'm more than the person you hear when I'm speaking publicly on a topic. And a colossal and controversial topic at that. And contrary to what you might believe, I don't talk about that subject all the time."

"Whatever. It doesn't change the fact one iota dat you're attempting to arouse fear in people on what is one of your favorite subjects. You said so yourself in one of your talks. You said it was one of your favorite subjects. Ah heard you. And Ah heard you say dat you like to write. Ah bet you write about all uh dis end of the werld junk too. Right? Am Ah right?"

"Let me answer each of the presumptions. First, I'm not attempting to arouse fear in people when I speak before an audience about the second coming of the Lord Jesus. Second, you did hear me say that it is one of my favorite subjects. Because seven years after we were in freshman class at Saint Ignatius, it was that very subject that led me into a new life. And the old one was becoming a mess, real fast. And third, you heard me say that I like to write. It's a hobby. And lastly, I haven't written anything on the subject."

"You're a fear monger, you and everyone else who tries to get people to follow your religion, whatever your religion is. Ah could feel the vibes coming from you when Ah heard you talking from the microphone. You were trying to make me afraid. Ah could feel it as sure as Ahm sitting here. If you keep wanting to deny it, dats on you, son. But Ah ain't gonna let you. You, and others like you, are gonna hurt our culture and are bad news in our country. Ah love our culture and Ah love our country. Ah ain't gonna stand for all your negativity. You are bad news,… *bad* news."

He forced himself to stop so he could take another bite of his juicy po-boy. More gravy fell to his plate. It was accumulating.

Simeon just sat there. He had the urge to get defensive. But he moved beyond it. He wanted to counter. But he held back. His heart was on alert. But it was not in battle position. He wanted to look on Vincent the way Someone Else did. And he recalled the incidents at Saint Ignatius. He couldn't help but wonder about them.

There was a long pause while the two men ate. Several patrons looked their way when Vincent's voice grew louder. Simeon noticed. He noticed James and several of the old neighborhood sandwich makers looking their way after one of Vincent's minor eruptions. He felt a surge of embarrassment when the heat from Vincent's voice disturbed the seating area. In the moment, he didn't know what to say or do. He felt attacked and misunderstood before a familiar peace swept over him.

Vincent wondered if he had provoked an acceptable level of fear in his victim. So as not to leave it at that, the massive man went for the convincer.

"Mah purpose for meeting you today is accomplished. Ah'll tell you what Ahm gonna do, little one."

He mopped up the roast beef gravy from his plate with the last piece of his French bread.   Simeon noticed that Vincent's plate appeared shiny and clean when he did. He had wiped away every vestige of what he intended to completely consume from the first bite.

"Ahm gonna cut you a break, boy. You watch what you say from that podium. Back away from talking about where you think duh world's headed and all-uh-dat. You refrain from writing about any of this and how it relates to so-called prophecies and end of the werld mumbo jumbo, and Ah'll back off. Ah'll be watching, and listening. And Ah know plenty of people around town. You know some of the same folks Ah know. You're on my radar, you and several others. But mostly you. If you don't, Ah'll be your worst nightmare. You hear me, Mangino? You hear me?"

"I surely do."

He looked down at Vincent's sparkling clean plate.

"I most certainly do."

Twenty

Saturday evening came, and Simeon rang the doorbell to his beloved Aunt Mae's house. Lan opened the door.

"WheyYa'tt, son. Come on in. Momma's waiting. Ah'll get you a drink."

"Okay, Cugino. I'll make myself at home."

Since childhood, he allowed himself to enjoy the pleasant affirmation of the family bond that swept over him everytime he strode in the door of one of his aunts. The pleasing certainty was well established by the time he grew to be a boy on a bike. And it was re-fortified all over again after he moved back home.

"You been doing that since we were born in 1952, when you lived right next door. What else is new? Go head in there and go see momma."

He gestured toward his momma, who was standing in the next room looking down at something on the table.

"Hey deyuh, Aunt Mae!"

New Orleans-speak eeked out as he pulled her close for a long embrace.

"How's mah girl?"

"Hey, mah dawlin. You know how it is. Ahm getting up deyuh. Still kicking, though. Trying to get by, you know. Needing a little more help deez days. But Ahm making it, Simmie, thanks to Lan and Jinnie. And how are you, dawlin? How's Lily-Grace, Liza, and the boys. And those grandkids?"

"Everybody's well, Aunt Mae, thankfully."

"All seven of them, right, Simmie? Ya'll got seven grandkids. Right? And let me tell you their names, honey. Lesssee, there's Noah, Ezekiel, and, lessee,... Evelyn and Ruby,... and Eli,... and last but not least, the two oldest, Blake and Avery. How's dat?"

"You got it, Aunt Mae. Still sharp as a tack."

"Ahm trying, mah dear. Crossword puzzles help. But listen, baby, can you stay a little while? We can catch up more on other things after.

But Ah want to talk with you in private, okay? Lan, leave me and Simmie alone for a little while. We need to talk."

"Okay, momma. Ah don't know what duh big secret is but, if dat's what you want, Ah'll let ya'll be."

Lan closed the door as he left the room.

"Sit down, Simmie."

She seated herself at the table.

Simeon was puzzled. The whole thing wasn't completely unusual. His aunt held confidences with him before. He was close to her. Yet something felt different.

"You know me and your momma were close, honey."

As she spoke, she placed her left hand on the top of his right hand with its palm down on the table.

"We were two months apart and were married to those two Mangino brothers, your daddy and your Uncle Gasparo. And you know how rambunctious doze two were."

She grinned momentarily.

"You know dat me and your momma talked on the phone a lot, sometimes for hours. Ahm not telling you something you don't already know, dawlin. Ah just get choked up when Ah think of her."

She wiped her eyes with a tissue and went on.

"Ah've had something for you dat your momma gave me before she died. It breaks me up just to think about all-uh-dis. Because, not only am Ah talking about the sis-tuh Ah never had, but also because of the story dat goes along with this."

She paused to wipe her eyes again. Simeon felt a lump in his throat. His eyes misted. His aunt's hand remained on his.

"Something strange happened to your momma that pertained to you, honey. You don't know about it, because your momma didn't know what to do about it. But she did confide in me about it. Den, before she passed away, she wanted to, ... well, ... let me back up and go back to the beginning."

She removed her hand from her nephews. She straightened up in her chair, while clearing her throat and looking down on the table. She appeared to peek at the newspaper on the table.

"Dis has been a long time coming, Simmie. Ahm just gonna go ahead and start talking. Ah've been wrestling with how to talk with you about dis. And Ah know dat now is the time. Ah've been aksing the Lawd about dis ever since you came back home after yuh momma died. Now is the time, honey."

She touched his hand again. In a moment, she removed it.

"Ah trust you, Aunt Mae. Ah've always trusted you. You, Aunt Katie, and Aunt Shirl have always been mah second momma's."

He was overcome, and in full New Orleans-speak.

"Ah know dat, dawlin. Really, Ah do. So, here we go."

She took one more deep breath, looked down at the table again, and began.

"A few months before she died, Ah got a call from your momma. She was calm but confused. Something happened dat she needed to talk about."

"Her doorbell rang. When she opened the door, she saw a man standing there, a stranger. He appeared to be in his early seventies or so. He had a flat cap with thin hair coming over his ears. He had eye-glasses with large rims. He wore a tweed jacket with an old sweater underneath. She said he looked like a professor. She aksed if she could help him, and he said he had something fuh you."

He couldn't believe what he was hearing.

"Fuh *me*? He said he had somethin *fuh me*?"

He was aware that he might be coming across as eager, like an orphaned child about to be told something about his unknown family. He tried to stay calm. So he relaxed back into the chair.

"Yes, fuh you, honey. Your momma tried to explain to the man dat you had lived away for over thirty years. She told him you were trying to sell your house in Ohio to move back home to NewAwlins. She said the man was so polite and very calm, peaceful, and convincing in his way. When she told him about you selling your house to move back home, he only said, 'Ah know, mam. Ah know all about it'."

"Now, dis really suhprised her. Now she was wondering how he knew dis. So she aksed him, 'Do you know mah son, Simeon?' But he didn't answer duh question, Simmie. He only replied, 'Please give him this for us.' And he handed her something."

He froze in the attentive state, caught up in the moment. He hung on every word that proceeded from the mouth of his precious aunt. His eyes went from hers to the wall beyond. A painting of the Last Supper[30] hung there. Jesus sat at the middle of the table. Six of his men were on either side. He thought of how pivotal that night was.

He wanted to grab his aunt by the shoulders and ask her if it really happened. He wanted to ask limitless questions so as to extract every bit of possible information about what went down with The Professor and his momma. He wanted to understand because he had so little understanding of what happened at Wendy's a scant short time ago. But he didn't. He looked back at his Aunt Mae. She knew he must be processing something. In her wise way, she waited for him to return.

"Ah know you must be wondering about dis, Simmie. You poor momma was too. She didn't know who the man was or where he came from. But she said dat she knew in her hawt dat he was a good man and felt dat something special was happening. When he came to her door, she thought dat it was something special happening, something straight from Gawd to you, Simmie, from Gawd to you. Dat's what your momma was thinking. And that's what Ahm thinking too."

She reached over to put her right hand on Simeon's left shoulder and gently looked into his eyes. Mutual tears formed in their eyes. She removed her hand and continued to speak.

"Your momma took what he offered her. She aksed him what it was for and would you know about it. She said dat the kind man said the strangest woids. He said:

'Everything in it's time, in it's time - everything.'"

"Well, you know dat, by now, your momma was confused. And it looked like the man was beginning to step away, like he wanted to leave. But she still wondered who he could be and how he might know these things. So she aksed him how he knew you and how he knew you were trying to move back home. And he said again:

---

[30] Reference in The Writings to Jesus' last meal with his twelve apostles the night before He was crucified on the cross.

'Everything in it's time, in it's time - everything, Miss Maria.'"

"Except dis time, he said her name, Simmie. Like Ah said, your momma said he was so polite, honey. And she wondered how he knew her name. She looked again at what he gave her and looked up only to find him walking away beyond her porch wall. She never saw or heard anything from him again. He came and he left. And he left something fuh you, dawlin, … fuh you, Simmie. Your momma left it for me to give to you when Ah knew it was the right time. And now is the right time."

With that, Mae Mangino reached over and picked up the newspaper directly in front of her on the table. She placed it on the table away from the edge where it had been right in front of her. It was now further to the middle of the table and away from her. Where the newspaper had previously been, there, in plain view, was an old, worn, blue folder.

In an instant, Simeon's recall retrieved an image from the hallway of his mind. And it replayed as if he had gone into a time warp back to 1968. The friction from the warp speed-like replay of the past experience froze his body in place. His mind seemed to be the only piece that was working. And it was transfixed on the blue object. Every other sense caved in to the space where utter disbelief and absolute certainty collide, leaving all but his mind momentarily paralyzed.

As the seconds passed, he regrouped. He was able to marshal his faculties, which allowed his soul to leap to attention. He was poised and alert again. His anticipation ranged from expecting the next biggest surprise of his life to never being surprised again. He was at the table. The mysterious blue folder was before him. And he had no idea what to do next.

He looked up again, beyond his aunt, to the picture of the Last Supper. Above it was a crucifix. He saw the image of Jesus dying in agony on a cross. He recalled gazing at the large crucifix in Saint Francis church as a first grader. God seemed so real to him then, evermore so now.

"Dis is what your momma gave me. It's nothing but an empty old folder. But it's not made out of normal paper. It's some kind of different material, more durable. It looks old, real old, and worn. And like your momma, Ah know it must mean somethin to you, honey. She aksed me to give it to you whenever Ah felt it was the right time. Ah believe with all mah hawt dat dis is duh right time, Simmie.”

He sat, staring in disbelief at the strange, yet familiar folder. He wanted to move. But f he did, he might wake up from a dream. With forward motion paused, he didn’t know what to do. In his sixteenth year, folder was in the hands of a man who vanished on a street corner. Now, at the age of fifty-six, it sat on his aunt’s table before his very eyes. It couldn’t be real.

“Simmie, its okay, dawlin. Ah know something is going on here. So why don’t you take the folder and go on. We’ll catch up later. Ah won’t tell Lan and Ginny, or Gasp and Josie, or Shairee, or anybody else, unless you tell me to. Now, you go ahead and go out the front door. Ah’ll tell Lan you had to go.”

She picked up the mysterious folder and offered it to him. His hands were on his lap. But he couldn’t move them to take it. The action seemed irreverent, sacrilegious. It prompted so many questions that he didn’t know the answers to. He was at once both eager to embrace it and mystified by it.

“It’s okay, Simmie. Go ahead, take it.”

When he heard her kind, soft words, he recalled them coming from her when he was a child. When he had scraped a knee or been pushed around by her two older sons, his cousins. He was back in the mid nineteen-fifties. He welcomed the soothing words of a caring elder who knew him from the womb. With his momma gone, his last living second momma was filling in like she often did when he and Pokey were playing with Lan and Parry as kids in their shared yard.

“It’s okay, dawlin. Don’t be afraid. Gawd is gonna guide you.”

And that’s what he needed to hear.

In moments of blurred confusion, a soul at times needs to hear from the voice of a caring elder, what are already his deeply practiced convictions.

He picked up the mysterious folder. He stood and gave his aunt a long embrace. Confused, yet encouraged and empowered, he quietly slipped out the front door.

Twenty One

"Don't forget to call Ted."

"That's right, today's Tuesday. I don't know what I'd do without you, babe."

And he meant it. Though they were as different as night and day, Simeon had grown to appreciate more than ever how the night and day were meant to be parts of a unified life cycle. They were meant to complement one another. One did for a twenty-four hour earth rotation and life cycle what the other didn't, and couldn't. So were he and his Lily-Grace. When they were functioning out of who they really were, they were a good team. In those times, their best laid moments were like the blend of two synchronized voices harmonizing nicely in a pleasant song.

Ted Kuvelich was a counselor friend. He was keenly insightful, with an alert mind and native intuition. They were seasoned and honed through many years of engagement with The Sacred Scriptures and equally as many serving people.

Simeon dialed the number.

"Simeon! How's it going?"

"I'm hanging in there fairly well, my friend. How go things with you?"

"Great. I just had a few hours with my grandkids. They brighten my life in all kinds of ways."

"I'm glad for you, Ted."

"Thanks. How are your kids and grandkids?"

They shared generally about their families over the next ten minutes before they transitioned into talking about more personal matters.

"I've been thinking about what we've been talking about, Ted. I'm understanding my motives more clearly than I've been able to up till now."

"That's interesting. In my story, I've seen that it often takes trials and challenges, life's hardships, to compel me to be willing to delve into the world of my motives."

Simeon twirled the chord to the land-line receiver at his ear.

"I think that's true for for everyone, Ted. Tell me your angle on the connection between ambition and motives."

He paused for a moment before answering.

"Motive relates to the underlying reason that we act or pursue something. I understand ambition to be the desire-fueled drive to practically act and pursue it. "

"So a motive remains alone, unless and until ambition teams up with it to coax it to act in the real world. And they are hard-wired to desire. Is that how you see it working out, Ted?"

"I think so. How's that playing out in your world?"

"I hope that the trials of life find me open to be aware of my motives and ambitions when I realize I'm not responding well in the trials. I've been allowed a new challenge through the entrance of someone new in my life. I guess you can say that he is proving to be someone I have to reach down deep in order to love. I've been down this road before with individuals. But it's been a while. The ongoing experience with him is stirring reactions that invite me to take a look at my motives and ambitions."

They continued their discussion for another twenty minutes before wrapping it up. When he hung up the phone, Simeon sat at his desk for a long while. He sensed that there was more to be gleaned from their discussion. He opened his journal and began to write.

"Now, in my late fifties, I'm understanding myself better. And perhaps how my self-serving nature works as well. All of my actions are the effects of intentions within me. The intentions relate to my Motives and Ambitions. I can see these things clearer than I could when I was a younger man.

I'm growing in understanding my Motives and Ambitions over time. But I realize that neither I, nor perhaps any human being, have totally mastered this very personal endeavor. And I mustn't presume to know the motives and ambitions of anyone other than myself.

My recent acquaintance with Vincent has pressed me into the exercise more intensely. His demeanor, attacks, and force of character arouse negatives in me that compel me to look inside if I want to grow. And when I do, I see that when I don't respond in love to the 'unlovable', that it says something about me. What is my motive when I don't?

My talks with friends like Ted, Dett, and Ron are priceless. They help me probe the hidden spaces and to know myself better in my innermost being[31]. It's there where Motive and Ambition reside, embedded and disguised as part of an internal deep state in the recesses of my life. And all this takes me back to the ticklish little image that Dett and I came up with in college to capture an image of this. Yes indeed."

When he returned from his journal, he went to the iconic blue folder on his desk. The mysterious item was born into his story in his wandering years. He had seen the man at the bus stop outside of Bivi Q's forty years before. The man held a blue folder exactly like the one his Aunt Mae just revealed to him.

"Is this the same folder?"

Like a man who had worked hard to dig a needed ditch, he took a mental break. He went out for a bike ride. Before long, he pedaled his way uptown along the levee top. On the left was the traffic along River Road. Below, on the right, was the mighty Mississippi River, lazily flowing around the bend toward the Gulf of Mexico. With no forethought, his eyes went to the brilliant tropical cloud formations that stretched across the panorama of the sky. It displayed a striking array of

---

[31] Psalm 51:6

fluffy bright whites with various shades of gray. The crisp blue color of the sky proclaimed its majestic presence beyond, where the clouds parted. At intermittent moments along the way, his engagement with the firmament alternately informed and refreshed him, as it always had, everyplace he'd ever been.

As he pedaled, like a boy on a bike, the lazily moving clouds moved in the same direction as the centuries old north to south flow of the river. The crisp, clear beauty of the heavens stood in stark contrast to the muddy and murky appearance of the water as he moved along the levee top. And he wondered, if at the moment, he, along with the dirty waters and the majestic clouds, were moving in harmony through space and time. In thirty minutes he found himself turning onto Constance Street, in his old uptown neighborhood. Straight in front of him, he beheld his friend, his Old Oak Tree.

"Yes indeed, this is where I need to be."

In minutes, he was seated on the sidewalk against the high brick wall of the Order of the Poor Servants, beneath the outstretched limbs of his beloved tree.

An hour later he looked at his watch. He rose from his place. And he was pleased that he couldn't recall ever leaving there disappointed. Life's conditions didn't always immediately change after his forays there. But his heart did. He couldn't recall ever having left there unsettled, ever since he was a boy on a bike.

He hopped onto his faithful, two-wheeled friend as he did in days gone by, on a different one. He was headed up the levee to go home. And once there, he knew what to do.

When he entered the house he found her in the den.

"You got a few minutes or an hour?"

"It depends on who needs the time. For one person I might only have a few minutes. For someone else, I might have an hour."

"What if it's for me?"

"Then I'll split it in half. I'll give ya half an hour."

She weilded her teasy face with the comment.

"I'll take it. So just relax. There's something that I haven't told you that I've been waiting to tell you. It happened just a few days ago. And you may have a hard time believing me until I show you something that's on my desk. I've been in a fog about this whole thing and now that my head is cleared, I'm ready to catch you up. And I'd also like to get your advice."

His wife looked away momentarily before looking back at him.

"Ohhh – kayyy. I guess I'm ready. Let's hear it."

And with that he began to recount his visit with his Aunt Mae. He ended by letting her know about his dilemma with the folder and the mixture of turmoil, excitement, and confusion going on inside of him. When he finished, Lily-Grace sat staring at him. He knew the stare well. It held all the trappings of a look that described someone sitting on a fence. On one side was total skepticism. On the other utter shock.

"Well, I guess I'm wondering what's sitting on your desk."

He had saved the clincher for the last moment. He retrieved the worn blue folder from his study.

"Oh my g-o-o-d-n-e-s-s......"

In the ensuing dialogue, he filled in more of the details about the encounter with the man at the bus stop years ago. And he caught her up on the exchange between his momma and his aunt. He concluded by describing his interaction with his aunt in vivid detail. They exchanged thoughts about the materialization of the blue folder and the re-emergence of The Professor. When he finished, they sat in silence. There was a long pause. Nothing was forced. Neither of them was in a hurry.

Simeon spoke.

"I'm going to the secret place again, this time with you."

He began.

"Father, I know not what to do with the mysterious treasure that has shown up from my long ago silent encounter with a stranger at a bus stop. Is this like a piece to a puzzle that is coming together? I presume this to be the folder the stranger held and pointed out to me before vanishing. It was handed to my momma by my mysterious friend, The Professor, who approached me at Wendy's not long ago. Then He vanished. I presume that You know about that. It was given to Aunt Mae who has passed it on to me. The Professor said it was for me. Since I asked for none of this, I presume all of this to be from You. Does it have

something to do with my long-time thoughts and questions? If so, please let me know. I'm listening. Help me be attentive."

Lily-Grace offered her agreement.

"Amen."

Simeon was quiet, staring hard at the papyrus folder. He was not far removed from a still lingering state of shock and disbelief.

"Okay, here's what I think you should do right now. Get up and go to the Wendy's on St. Charles. I think that if you go there something will happen. Or you'll just know what to do next. Just go there."

"Huh, and I'm thinking that you're saying this because that's where The Professor man first showed up, right?"

"Right."

"And I'm also aware that Saint Marshall's is nearby and that today is your turn to pick up Liza. Is that also right?"

"That might be true as well. But look at it this way, Simeon. You should go there because it might help you. And you can help me too."

She held on to her straight face as she spoke. But the tone in her words belied it.

"I'm sure you're only trying to help me, and that's the only reason you're suggesting I go to Wendy's. Let me see if your left earlobe is a bright blue."

"Of course my earlobe isn't lit bright blue."

She covered her ears as she spoke, and held fast her straight face. But a powerful urge to laugh was growing incrementally. As he playfully tried to pull her hands off of her ears, the barely contained urge burst through the seams of her containment control. She let go of the pent up laughter along with a self-proclaimed victory statement:

"Best get going, Simeon Michael."

He was swept along the coattails of her giddyness and celebration with a burst of laughter of his own. Then, he expelled the words known to every husband who has more than met his match in the moment.

"If you insist, my dear."

When he entered the Wendy's on St. Charles Avenue, the place was empty. During the drive, he imagined if he might find The Professor sitting at a table there once again. Or perhaps he might show up if he waited. He ordered a snack and sat down. He pulled out his copy of The Writings and began to muse. But he had a hard time focusing . Every few minutes he looked up in anticipation to see if his mysterious friend had shown up. But he had not.

The time drew near for him to pick up Liza. He stood and looked around the empty lobby. No one was in sight except for the young man who was sweeping the lobby. He turned to walk to the door when he noticed some yellow napkins on one of the tables. He had been seated at the same table, in the same chair, where he sat when The Professor sat across from him. The napkins were on the table where The Professor first sat months before.

He had the urge to turn back and go to the table that held the napkins. When he got there, he picked them up. He thought to drop them back onto the table. But the young man who had been cleaning the lobby spoke.

"I was going to pick those napkins up and save them."

"Why is that?"

"Some old dude was sitting there writing something on them a couple uh hours ago. He was sitting there. And when I looked again, he was gone. He must have left in a hurry and forgot them."

"But these napkins are blank. There's nothing written on them."

"Think again. There's writing on the other side of each of them."

Simeon turned them over. He saw the writing and glanced at his watch.

"Did you say the man who had these napkins was an old dude?"

"Yeah, kind of a nerdy old professor-looking dude, with a flat Gatsby-hat thing going on. Yuh feel me, man?"

"Yeah I feel yuh, bruh. Did he have a tweed sport coat on?"

"An old tweet sport coat too, man, like he's had it since the 1950's. And he wore these glasses with large rims. You know him?"

"You might say I do. Or more accurately, he knows me better than I know him."

He turned to leave with the napkins in hand.

"Wait. You can't take those. I was going to hold them for the dude in case he comes back for them."

"It's okay. He left them for me."

"But how'd he know you'd be here to get them?"
"It's a long story, a very long one."

Twenty Two

When he returned home, he retreated to a quiet place. With shaky hands, he carefully took out the yellow napkins that he picked up from the table at Wendy's – from The Professor's table. His heart began to pound. He handled them with utmost delicacy as he turned them like loose pages. For no known reason he cleared his throat as if about to read a recital[32]. He gingerly turned back to the first napkin and began to read………

THE PROTOCOLS

Of

THE ESSAYS

Of

Saint Anon

Words of Warning ride Whispering Winds
Deposits on listening ears
Timely seedlings for THE ESSAYS
Devono essere scritti di nuovo[33]

An old folder of blue
A life is a hard field to plow; Five is of twelve

Soldiers on the appendage
The siren howls over the playground
Wars, wars, and wars

---

[32] Recital: Here, referring to the reading of a formal statement in an auathoritative document

[33] Italian: 'They must be written anew'.

Fifty is lost; Still the heart knows

Inizia a scrivere[34],   Il tempo e' vicino[35]
In latter years, Scrivi[36]; Newly for times, as in the
past

Dal libro![37]; Sixty-six writers of forty works
Secondo le Scritture![38]

Broken seals at the foot of heaven's throne
Cinque in numero[39]
For such a time as this - Numero Sei[40]; / Scrivi

Dark clouds in the east, Forebodes of John's beast
Clarion whispers to the least

In the field, In the field, In a hardy field to plow
Seeking the City that will descend from the cloud

Blue sky, lone bird in the Whispering Wind
A man is smoking on a pole; An angry man has a gun
One clenches a broken bottle
But the head on the right foot changes everything

An appointment with a champion
Yellow napkins on a nearby table
An old man is face-to-face
And a butterfly from behind on the right

A horn by the river with six dings of a bell
A slow-dying Old Oak with uncommon allure
And the sky's clouds, Always,... the clouds

---

[34] Italian: 'Begin to write'.
[35] Italian: 'The time is near'.
[36] Italian: 'Write'.
[37] Italian: 'By the book'.
[38] Italian: 'According to the Scritpures'.
[39] Italian: 'Five in number'.
[40] Italian: 'Number Six'.

> **Humanity's Convergence and then**
> **That Day....... Il tempo e'vicino**
> **One mind, Of The Lie, Unitary Planetary Adversary**
>
> **Broken seals at the foot of heaven's throne**
> **Humans despairing, wishing to die**
> **'Hide us, fall on us! Fall from the sky!'[41]**
> **Scrive,........ Certamente, Il tempo e' vicino![42]**
> **In every language, Watch, Be on the alert**
>
> **To eyes that are looking and ears that are hearing**
> **Angelino stands where the bus stops**
> **Scrive, ... Atem lo levad.[43]**
> **On yellow napkins,**
>
> *~ Songieux*[44]

When he finished, he read them again, this time more slowly and deliberately. He dove into them again, a third time, picking them apart piece by piece. Finally done, he sat in silence.

"The Protocols....,"

He spoke softly, almost reverently, so that he could hear himself say the words. He repeated them.

"The Protocols. Of course."

He slipped into a twilight zone. On the one hand, he was utterly amazed at their existence. On the other, he almost knew of them all along. And he couldn't explain why, or how.

He remembered that good old Put Smith had said something about him many years ago. It had to do with something that had a similar sound to it. He paused in silent reflection to cherish and respect the man whose life touched his own in a perplexing, yet moving way.

---

[41] Revelation 6:12-17.

[42] Italian: 'Indeed, the time is near'.

[43] Hebrew: 'You are not alone'.

[44] Pronounced: "Sawn-zhou".

"And what of the name 'Songieux'? Is it The Professor's name? And is this telling me that 'Angelino' is the name of the man with the blue folder who was at the bus stop that long ago night in 1968? I should have waited until tomorrow morning to read this. I'll be up all night."

He looked down at The Protocols. The hour was well past midnight. And he realized that he had been sitting alone in silence for two hours. The yellow napkins were still in his hands.

On the wall facing him was a large canvas painting. It was a dazzling-colored piece by the hand of his son, Jermaine. The image was inviting, with a brilliant mix of bold, bright colors. The cluster of colors was slightly wider at the top and arced slightly inward and down. Most of the color lines were small and appeared as pudgy, fluffy strands with tight curves. They were skillfully stroked by the artist along the canvas top to give them a fluffy, feathery look. A dominant black was interspersed at the wider top and appeared like a cover for the brilliant collection of colorful arcs. The blacks thinned as they merged with the bright, fluffy colors flowing downward toward the center of the canvas. Light shades of pink, blue, gray, yellow, and beige appeared to expel from the middle of the canvas where the bright arcs tapered off. They were almost flat on the canvas and displayed as stand-alone, small colored rectangles.

In one moment, he saw the shape of a flower vase on the canvas. It was filled with a colorful array of violets, roses, lilies, daffodils, carnations, and more. The pedals were set at different levels in the vase so that all of them were displayed. As he continued to gaze at the painting, that particular interpretation faded, giving way to a brilliant Native-American head-feather piece. Sparkling colored feathers adorned it as they were arranged bottom to top.

Jermaine explained that his art was meant to draw the observer in so that she could see what she might see. The two images he saw in the painting were not seen by Lily-Grace or Bran; or by their daughters in law, Megan and Shaneen. They and others might see different images in the piece, or none at all. A lot went into how one saw something. And one's seeing was no doubt influenced by what he had previously seen, and in many cases, come to know.

"All my life, I've come to know, without concretely knowing, that I'd be where I am now, with these things happening."

He spoke the words. But it was late. He finally set the napkins down. After letting the experience bake in his thoughts, he reasoned that he would tell Lilly-Grace about it - but no one else. At least not yet.

"This is way too other-worldly. Who's going to believe it?"

The words were spoken out loud as if someone might walk in and answer the question.

He went to the secret place.

"You are the Keeper of all of promises that You make. You are my Light in this dark world. You know that I've never asked for any of these things. I never asked for the dreams and sensations that I've had since I was a child. I've never presumed special significance for any of these things. But I know that You are with me. And I am with You. Guide me, please. Teach me. Show me. I remain continually surrendered, no matter the cost. I trust You. My times are in Your hands."[45]

For the time being, he understood that much of what was written resonated with his story. And the rest seemed barely beyond his ability to comprehend in the moment. Perhaps that would change in the future. He had to try to sleep.

Not far away, Old Man River continued its constant flow on the way to the first bend of the approach to the Crescent City, near his house. And while its waters were as brown as usual in the nightime, the night itself wasn't as dark. Every gallon of the mass of passing wetness bobbed and flowed by. And the darkness that rode upon it and did its bidding along the way, though still mature in the early hours, was ebbing little by little in time, very slowly and surely giving way to the encroaching light of the morning.

---

[45] Psalm 31:15a

Twenty Three

"Hey Hun, are you going to your Wendy's before you pick up Liza today?"

"I had a mind to. It's been a few weeks since I've been there."

"What cha working on these days?"

"I've been collecting ideas for the men."

"To help with your classes, and with those in the groups?"

"Yep."

"For new friends you might make?"

"All the above."

When he sat to eat in the Wendy's lobby the crowd was thick. But he was able to get the table that he had grown attached to. In the weeks since he picked up the napkins there, he spent time reflecting on them. He was deep in thought when he felt the presence of another person. He looked up, startled. To his surprise, there stood Vincent.

The massive man looked down at him. He helped himself to the chair opposite him and sat with his large arms folded high on his chest. His elbows were pointed toward Simeon, and they momentarily held his eyes. Their large, round points were poised like twin missiles aimed down toward his head. And he had the sensation of being out in the open and exposed. Their owner's head was tilted slightly backward up and beyond them. It was home to eyes that glared down his nose at the target across from him. For several long seconds the two men looked into each other's eyes. Simeon broke the frosty air with a slight, but polite, smile.

"Vincent, what a surprise."

"Yeah, me too. What brings you here?"

"I have to pick up my daughter from school."

"Why dis Wendy's? You don't live near here."

"I don't. My daughter goes to Saint Marshall's nearby. I'm camping out here before I get her. So you know where I live?"

He didn't answer the question.

"What brings you to this Wendy's on the Avenue, Vincent?"

"Just stopped in for lunch. Was in the neighborhood. Or maybe Ah was stalking you."

He laughed in short, punctuated bursts and grunts. His entire elephantine torso moved up and down as he did.

"You been behaving yourself, son?"

"Why are you asking, Vincent?"

"Well Ahm aksing. And Ah don't back down as Ah hope you are aware of. You know what Ah mean?"

He didn't know how to respond.

"You been paying attention to what's going on in the world?"

He thought that he might be being goaded. But he went along.

"Once or twice a week."

"Yeah, things are getting interesting, Ah'll say. Dey sure are. Times are controversial out there. We have a lot of bigots and folks who want to impose their ways on everybody else, causing a lot of trouble with their unwelcome controversy. A lot of folks who want to jold the werld back and keep us in the stone age. Know what Ah mean?"

He listened. He watched and listened.

"Ah heard a man on the so-called 'christian' radio network talking about the end of the world, another bigot type of guy. He's trying to get us all scared and get us to join his religion, kinda like you."

Vincent was getting worked up. His voice was getting louder and his eyes were getting larger as he leaned slightly forward.

"What's dat blue folder in front of you, Mangino?"

An alarm went off inside Simeon. He was careful with the blue folder. This was the first time he took it out of his house. The mere thought of someone else being aware that it even existed made him uncomfortable.

"It looks old. Dat's not a paper folder is it? It doesn't look like paper. Lemmie see it."

He reached over and picked it up.

Panic came over him when he realized that the only copy of The Protocols that he possessed was inside the folder on the original yellow napkins. Looking around, he noticed that several patrons lingered at their tables.

"Best to not show alarm. Relax. Look casual. Don't make a scene."

He thought to reach inside for calm's relief. But he groped to find it.

Undaunted , Vincent opened the folder and pulled out the yellow napkins.

"What's dis? Something written on these yellow Wendy's napkins. 'Duh Protocols of Saint Anon'."

He looked up and far away before his eyes went to Simeon. His eyebrows furrowed. He looked angry. What little calm Simeon could feebly arouse was fading in his entangled state. And his discomfort was growing incrementally by the second.

"What's dis about?"

The question was slow and deliberate, with a demanding tone.

"Just some stuff somebody gave me."

"So what's it about?"

His tone didn't soften.

"Some stuff I'm reading."

He didn't like his answer.

Vincent bore down into the material, reading intently. His eyebrows moved up and down as he read. He winced several times and dropped menacing looks onto the napkins. He went back and forth between the napkins, comparing words. When he flicked them, he did so impatiently. Simeon feared he would tear them. He shook his head several times. He groaned more than once. Simeon prayed silently.

When he finished, he looked up at Simeon.

"Did you write dis?"

"No, I didn't."

"Den who did. Where'd you get dis?"

"Someone gave it to me."

"Who? Ah wanna know."

"Just a friend."

"Ah have a hawd time believing you didn't write it. It sounds just like you. You're not supposed to lie, Mangino. If you do, you're gonna go to hell. You know dat, don't you?   So, one last time, did you write dis?"

"I didn't write it Vincent. A friend gave it to me."

He was battling to harness a tornado of emotions as he spoke. He wanted to reach over the table to calmly take possession of the materials once again. Or he might ask for them. But he didn't want to appear desperate, or worse, tear them.

"Well, if you didn't write dis and you won't tell me who did, Ahm gonna keep this stuff until you tell me who did. Ah might just burn this mumbo-jumbo. Dat will serve to keep you and your wacko, bigoted friends from publishing this kind of crap."

He sat frozen and helpless in his chair. He was overwhelmed and felt puny before the intimdating giant in front of him. Back in the day, he might have at least made an attempt at the folder. As he pondered the option, Vincent began to cough violently. When he did, he laid the materials on the table in front of him. Simeon seized the moment and picked up the folder with his right hand. He held it to his side.

Seeing it, Vincent composed himself and spoke up.

"Give me duh folder, Mangino."

He stood up. The six-foot eight frame and what appeared to be just south of four hundred pounds of massive flesh didn't require a nod of recognition from his countepart.

"I can't give this to you, Vincent."

He quickly reached down with his right hand to grab Simeon's left hand. He pressed hard against it, carrying it above his its owner's eyes. Simeon tried to resist and pull it away but he couldn't. Without warning, he violently crashed Simeon's left hand down on the table with the knuckle of his thumb absorbing the force. Instantly, he felt an intense, pulsating pain. Impulsively, he let go of the blue folder in his right hand and grabbed his left thumb with it. He squeezed it tightly, attempting to hold back the throbbing pain. Vincent moved around the table to pick up the folder, while Simeon rocked back and forth in his chair, groaning in pain. He looked down at his thumb. It was the size of a golf ball. He couldn't speak, but Vincent could.

"Ah hate you, you bastard. There's more where dat came from."

And with that, Vincent hastened to his car. He flung the papyrus folder onto the passenger seat before he sped out of the parking lot like someone being chased. He wondered if the few customers still seated in the lobby had seen what he had just done. And he calculated if Simeon would call the police. He didn't think he would.

"Maybe dat'll make him think, duh little imp."

As he drove the expressway home, he wrestled with surges of intense anger. But rather than work through the negative emotion, he went on the offensive in a different direction. His guilty conscience wanted to vent, so he let it go.

"It's his own fault. Why do people like him presume to have all the answers? Maybe there is a Gawd. Maybe there isn't. But if there is, he surely doesn't care. Ah knew that by the time Ah was six. Duh religious types can say all they want. Dey have no idea what others have tuh go through."

His phone rang. It was his second ex-wife.

"What is it?"

His expression shot through the phone like an arrow aimed at the heart.

"I see you're in one of yuh good moods. I was cleaning up and I found some of yuh dad's things. Do you want them?"

His anger, most recently channeled toward Simeon, once again traveled the well-worn easier path. He chose long ago to never acknowledge its original flare-up point, the initial space of his deep pain. Rather, he allowed it to once again, strike out at the most recent imagined violater of his precarious peace, an innocent stand-in. It returned in a rush, and with a vengeance.

"Throw duh stuff away, you stupid little…. Ah don't even want to see it!"

His teeth were clenched. His palm squeezed the steering wheel hard. He fought the urge to hurl his phone out the window.

"But it looks like it might be valuable stuff, Vincent."

"Ah don't give a rip!"

"You need to deal with your bitterness over what happened to you, Vincent. You know that by now. When are you going to bite the bullet and get the help you need? We're not together any more, but I still care for you."

"Just shut your…. You crazy, whakko, …. Just shut up! Okay?! Why can't ya'll just leave me alone. Ah don't care what yuh do with all uh dat stuff. Just leave me alone."

He ended the call.

Ten minutes later, he pulled into his driveway. When he walked into his spacious home against the lakefront levee, he found his youngest grandson out cold on the sofa. It was mid afternoon. The very tall, lanky lad's feet languished well beyond the edge of the sofa. The last shreds of a giant pizza sat in a greasy cardboard pizza box. Crumbs were all over the box, the coffee table, and the floor in the otherwise well-kept den. Several empty beer bottles sat next to them. He was comatose with his mouth open. The giant-screen television played loudly.

"Great. Another productive day at the DeMaso home. At least Ah know dat he's down and will no doubt sleep through duh night. At least Ah won't get any early morning phone calls to bail him out again. Maybe tonight Ah'll get a good night's sleep for once."

He walked into his rear den. A large window revealed his manicured yard abutting the levee. A resident hummingbird zipped into view. It bounced back and forth between the honeysuckle and jessamine. He looked directly at it as it paused, suspended in space, going about its work in the pristine surrounding of his beautiful garden. But he didn't see it.

Twenty Four

He fought feelings of anger and hatred toward Vincent. He worked through them only to be found that he was still without the now familiar blue folder and its yellow contents. What had seemed so timely and meaningful now seemed like a total loss. Only an empty feeling remained.

When he walked out of the doctor's office, his eyes went to the sky. They beckoned him once again, like a continually open book, that invited him back into a story that wasn't over. A lone, large, gray-shaded, rolled cloud greeted him. It had a funnel shape, like a tornado, and appeared to be just above. The right edge was a bright orange, like it was burning. And its relative proximity made it appear large and near, very near, in the eyes of its viewer.

The always ready view of the sky constantly reminded him of the words of Someone Whom he admired more than anyone else. He advantaged the moment to engage in his ongoing trust with Him.

He would wait, as hard as it would be. He would continually choose to trust every time he found himself dissatisfied with the circumstances. The blue folder and its contents were never far from the forefront of his mind. Several times, he kicked himself for not making copies of The Protocols, and for being careless with the blue folder. He completely ruled out reporting Vincent for theft and assault. When he thought to do that, he reminded himself where he would be if he were nailed for all the stupid stuff he had done in his life. Rather, he chose to continually be thankful for the trial, as challenging as it was. And it was easy to be thankful for pain medication, very thankful.

He stepped into his car. Before he could start the engine, his phone rang.

"Sim*MIE*...., what's goin on, cuz? "

"Trae. Hey, what's up?"

"You've been after me to have lunch with you for awhile. Let's do it today. You wanna do it? You got time?"

"I sure do, and yes. When and where?"

When the call ended, he looked down at the thick bandage covering the brace on his thumb.

"How am I going to explain this?"

He asked himself the question out loud, hoping to come up with an answer.

When they were seated for lunch, Trae got right to it.

"What happened to your thumb? Did you break it?"

He didn't want to worry him. He knew that Trae would want to defend him and that it would disturb him if he knew what happened.

"You know how it is. Sometimes you're not being careful and you end up getting hurt. That ever happen to you?"

"Yeah, you remember when Ah fell off duh latter a few months ago and hurt mah back?"

"Sure do. How's that back, anyway? Is it still hurting you?"

With the intended deflection, their talk pivoted to health and family. By the time the food arrived, Trae began to talk about current events. Simeon listened for some time while Trae talked, thankful that his dominant hand had a whole thumb. He joined in with short comments along the way. Midway through the meal Trae began to ask questions.

"Ah heard you talk and interact before. And me and Lonna have been in a few of your group sessions. You try to help people learn how to walk with the Lawd by having daily time with Him in the Scriptures and talking and listening to Him, and the importance of sharing life together and all uh dat. And Ah've heard you tell your story. Heck, Ah was in that story with you,... still am. Ah know that the matter of the Lawd's return played big in how things changed in your story. Right?"

"That's right, Trae."

"With all that's going on how come people don't like to tawk about the Lawd's return? A lot of mah friends are patriotic and all this here stuff. But when Ah bring up the Lawd, Ah get crickets from them. But Ah can talk with you about it. So Ahm gonna. And if you don't wanna talk about it, too bad. You just gonna have to listen. But Ah know you, you lil dago. Once Ah get you started, you're not gonna shut up about it. And Ahm not gonna have a chance to say anything, because you 're gonna take over. And Ahm gonna be sorry Ah ever brought it up. But you know Ahm just kidding, cuz. If Ah can't kid you like we used to, and always have, then it ain't fun."

"Ah here you bawkin, cuz. And Ah couldn't agree more."

The easy-flow N'Awlins-speak proceeded from his heart in dialogue with another whose words could easily turn a key to unlock it.

"Awe right, Simmie. So you do all uh dis people work, and teaching and speaking. And you don't always talk about duh Lawd's return and the prophecies, right? Just every now and then. So how did all uh dis start, your interest in current events and stuff?"

"I appreciate the interest, and the question, cuz. And you don't know how much it means to me that we've been tied together from the crib. And our connection now has a spiritual component to it."

"And don't forget, me and Lan are still two months older than you. Okay, it took me a while to listen to you, but Ahm finally there with yuh, cuz. Ahm one of His now, too, as you now know."

Simeon couldn't hold back a grin that would not be restrained.

"So okay, Mangino. How did it all start?"

"It's hard to pinpoint exactly, Trae. Do you remember the Cuban missle crises in 1962? We were walking home from school and I was worried about a nuclear war. You were teasing me about it."

"How do you remembuh dat? Ah don't remembuh dat."

"I can't tell you when it first started. But I've been drawn to what's going on in the world since I was a kid. I had scary dreams back then."

"I remember Uncle Duckie, mah daddy, Uncle Gasparo, and your daddy telling stories about the things they went through in World War II. They talked about the guys in the neighborhood who were killed in the war. They talked about the horrors of war. I used to read the front page of the Picayune daily to get the report of the war in Vietnam. I'm not sure how or why, but I've always been aware of the evil in the world."

"And after I left home, I found real answers to the reasons behind the things that I've always been concerned about. And then there were the subjective things of the human condition that I became aware of in my personal life. Those were my best teachers. Inside of me I saw the potential for both good and evil. And I knew well from the habits sowed in my younger years that the potential for selfishness knows no bounds."

"And everyone I interacted with had the same tendencies, especially you, who just happened to be the ugliest little boy I've ever seen."

Trae looked up and laughed.

"Ah *knew* you couldn't resist zinging me at least once."

"I couldn't resist. I set that up so beautifully, too. Anyway, I realized that everyone else had the same tendencies, whether they wanted to admit them or not. Their imperfections affected me and mine affected them. Left to ourselves, over time, we naturally hurt, offend, and incite one another."

"Like you just did me?"

"Exactly, I can tell I scarred you for life. And over the years the world has come to be more closely tied together than it has ever been. The consensus is that this is good. But though there is some good to it, the deeper effect is not good at all, especially in the long run."

"In the decades following my exodus from home, the world grew smaller. As technology grew, possibilities became almost limitless and brought almost everyone into the open. And it brought almost everyone together. And those in power rose to become bullhorns and thought police. In our lifetimes, a world consensus has emerged. And those who cling to old beliefs and systems are increasingly becoming outsiders. As I've watch this unfold I've had to endeavor to not be swept along by it."

"You know, Simm, hearing you talk makes me excited to be alive at a time like dis. And at the same time, it's sobering. Does that make sense?"

"It sure does, Trae. I'm right there with you."

Several weeks after the incident with Vincent, Simeon received a phone call. He recognized the voice.

"Ahm sorry about your finger."

"Thumb. It was my thumb you broke."

"Yeah, your thumb. Ah figured it must be broken."

Vincent passed the palm of his left hand around the still steering column as he sat in his parked car.

"Well I forgive you, Vincent."

"Ah wasn't aksing for fuhgiveness. Ah was just calling to see if you were allright."

"I am. I'm fine. Everything's allright."

There was a long pause. Vincent's left hand continued to glide around the steering wheel without turning it.

"So where do we go from here, Vincent?"

"Ah don't know. You tell me."

"Maybe we're supposed to be friends from all of this."

"Friends? Don't kid yourself, Mangino. We ain't dat. But Ah don't want to be duh kind of person dat gets so angry dat Ah hurt someone. Ah feel bad about dat. Ah got strong feelings about things. Ah don't know why Ah get so emotional. But Ah do. Ahm sure you incurred expenses from doctor bills or medication from what Ah caused. And Ah want to pay for dem. You have mah number. Call me and let me know what it cost and I'll reimburse you. It's what Ah wanna do."

"Insurance covered it, so it's done."

Silence.

"Ahm still not real keen on knowing you're out there, saying all uh dat stuff about the end of the world, and all uh dat. Ah guess you still know dat."

"Sure I do. But remember, I don't talk about that very often. But you are right in that it is still a very vibrant interest for me."

"But why, Mangino? For the love of Gawd, why, man? Don't you know how divisive dat kind of stuff is? Can't you see dat? Don't you care?"

"I never really thought about it being divisive, Vincent. And, frankly, I don't want that. I've just thought about it being a reality."

"How can you say dat, about it being a reality? It's what you think, man. Don't confuse what you think with what's real."

"I know that it can sound subjective. But there is a 'knowing' that is internal, intuitive, if you know what I mean."

"Dat's putting too much emphasis on intuition. Come on, you know dat any logical person can't put all his money on his intuition."

"Allright, then maybe 'awareness' is a more acceptable word in this context. It can have a connection with 'intuition'. And it easily connects with fact checking, as well. Ituition is a subjective thing. People who claim to have it can't always verify what they say. And logically minded folk don't easily embrace another person's intuition. So, let's keep it on the level of 'awareness' and not focus on 'intuition'. We can probably agree that the best awareness is supported by facts."

"Sure. I just get upset when people say things with no facts tuh back it up."

Vincent paused from sliding his hand around the steering wheel.

"Okay. Then it's critically important that the facts are known. We started down this path when you asked me if I cared about speaking on matters that some might disagree about, causing division. And I said that I'm not focused on that, nor interested in causing division. I said that I think about what Jesus and the prophets spoke of as being realities. And that's where 'awareness' comes in, and, I might add, 'intuition' as well, if you're so inclined."

"So you saying that you became aware from looking for the details, the facts. And that, from where you sit, your convictions regarding what's been going on in the world for some time are based upon what you know to be true in the details of world events."

"Through history, leading to where we are now. And personally, I'm not dismissing the role of the sensory element, meaning 'intuition', related to these things."

"Ah suppose a fella like me would only consider the intuition of another person if Ah saw something in him or her dat made me willing to trust dat person. And you might presume I should always check out the facts myself, to see what's what."

"Yes, and may I add one more thing?"

"Go head."

"It's important that we all get to look at the same pile of facts, otherwise this whole discussion breaks down. If we're not looking at the same set of facts, what does that mean? If we both had the same set of hard, verifiable facts – and let's call that 'the truth' – then we might potentially arrive at similar final conclusions from our intuitions. And I use the 'potentially' carefully. Because there's no guarantee that we will. But it increases the possibility that we might."

"So whose facts are duh real facts? And how does one go down that path?"

"That's the million dollar question, Vincent. And personally, since I was a kid, I've been willing to consistently invest a portion of my mental capital to find the answer to it."

When the call ended, it wasn't hard for Simeon to think about The Protocols. Nor was The Professor, Songieux, as he professed to be named, far from his thoughts. Vincent said nothing to him of the material that he confiscated from him. Simeon longed to ask. *Did Vincent destroy them? Were they lost forever? If not, did Vincent intend to return them to him?* But he thought the better of it. He would trust, and wait.

He stepped into the back yard. He walked around, admiring his wife's creativity. Numerous tropical plants populated the spaces behind the house, along the fences and around the garage. A trellis stood near the side fence and opened onto a narrow stone path. The path was bordered with bushes and plants along both sides. A blood-orange tree guarded the trellis on the right. A lemon bush protected the end of the stone path. Several monarch butterflies flitted and bounced atop the bushes and plants. They hovered around some of the blooms, taking turns landing on the milkweed plants that were positioned at the corners of the house.

He walked to the bench that sat below the orange tree. A familiar mockingbird applied itself high above. It was in the branches of the large oak that stretched overhead from the neighbors' yard.

The rambunctious, feathered recorder was well into a smorgasbord of sound bites of songs and sounds. He listened, as the diminutive critter went on, applying his creativity to attract a mate, rather than to mock a young man full of shame. Every brief expression of the recorded sounds it sang out was different from the other.

"I remember, little bird, when I heard your sounds long ago as a teenager. I thought that you were mocking me then. Today, I only hear beauty, longing, and creativity coming from your tiny body. Thank you, my friend."

With a renewed resolve, a one-word message showed up in the inbox of his mind. It read "Scrive". Not to be left out, his mind's eye went to work. It visualized, first, an ink pen, then, a keyboard. And he recalled seeing the word written several times in The Protocols.

Twenty Five

"Don't you have some time off coming to you?"

It had been a while since Simeon caught up with his old friend. In their long overdue talk, he decided to tell Dett the latest.

In their college days, he and Dett had become best of friends. They worked together in the summers, visited one anothers' families, and explored the prophecies together. They convened student discussion groups as well. Dett was aware that Simeon's simmering interest in the prophecies and world events was ongoing.

"I suppose that I do, old friend."

Simeon leaned back in his office chair. He raised his hand to his chin and cradled it in his right hand. His finger scratched back and forth over his day-old whiskers.

"I suppose that I do."

"Why not take the time that you have coming to you and record some of your thoughts? Just start. Heaven knows that you've got a lot of pent up things to say. I knew it thirty years ago. After all this time and with so much that has happened, just let it go, Simm. Lay it all out and see what it looks like, how it feels. Run it by a few people. Let me see it. See what happens, what comes out. Maybe you'll realize it was all about nothing. Or maybe you'll realize that what comes out is confirmed by all that has recently happened with you. Just go for it."

"That's easy for you to say, Dett. You're as concrete as a sidewalk. There's no in between with you. And you know how to operate wisely that way. But for some of us there are abstracts to weigh."

"Yeah, I know. You're right, heh-heh."

Dett's easygoing chuckle took him back to the many hours they were together as students at Madison University.

"There've been times, and I know you've witnessed some of them, when I should have looked for the in-between. It would have served me to do that. But you can't let yourself stay in the in-between forever if things keep happening like they've been happening to you, for a long time. You've got to fish or cut bait."

"Okay. You know me as well as anyone. Your idea about the time off is intriguing. To use it to do that is a new thought. I sincerely have never thought that I'd do anything like that. What comes out might be a little controversial. It might be the kinds of things nobody wants to think about."

"I know, I know. I know you, remember? You're usually not afraid to line up alongside an unpopular opinion if you know its right. You have to do what you need to do to be true to Him and to yourself, in that order. All I'm saying is that if you get it out maybe you'll see it and know what you need to know."

"Okay, talk to Bethany. She knows me almost as well as you do. See if she agrees and let me know what she says. I'll run it by Lily-Grace too. I want to go the extra mile on this."

Vincent tried to watch TV. But unusually, his conscience was bothering him. He was worn out from the activity of the previous evening, when the police came to arrest his grandson for the third time in the past year. He had violated his parole again and was going to jail for an unspecified time. He was out of contact with his daughter, the mom. They had not spoken in years. And the grandson's dad was in prison. He tried hard to help his grandson, attempting to get the help he needed, but to no avail. He continually went back to his addictive lifestyle.

He sat in a chair next to the window. Through the window, a pair of hummingbirds darted back and forth among the salvia, iris and impatiens bushes in his pristinely kept back yard. They busied themselves among the colorful flora, darting and hovering between the flower bulbs on a misson. Then, as if receiving a summons, they sprinted through the air to somewhere beyond the window. In minutes, they were back for more.

A melancholy bench sat at the edge of the garden. It was accompanied by a rusting and worn antique lamp post. Part of the lush, green color of the manicured lawn bordered the edge of the garden. It too, could be seen from the window. The end of a hanging branch from a cypress tree moved gently in the breeze just above the lamp post and bench. It occupied the upper left corner of the window view.

But Vincent didn't notice. He never noticed. Nor did he ever extend an ounce of energy, much less his own sweat, to upkeep his fine yard.

He paid someone handsomely for the service. Had he taken the time to do the kind of work that would produce beauty around him, he might have taken notice of the beauty through his window. And he might have noticed beauty in other things. But he didn't. And he couldn't. He didn't know how to. He looked out of the window. He saw what was there. But he didn't take in its beauty. Like most other times, he was either too pre-occupied or too angry. This time it was the latter.

For the first time in many years, he felt a tinge of loneliness. Dormant despair saw an opportunity and hitched up to follow in its wake. The emotions were uncomfortable to him, not only from the pain they caused, but from the unfamiliar visitors that they were. He wasn't accustomed to allow their kind in. But when he attempted to show them the door, they opted for seats in the living room. The large, imposing figure of a man began to feel overcome. Anger, his go-to coping mechanism, left the building. After a long struggle, lonliness and despair, building strength inside since his childhood, rose up to force it out momentarily. Deathly afraid of them, he began to panic. And the aweful nature of the panic only contributed to his mounting anxiety.

His palms and forehead were sweating. He gripped the arms of his chair. And he had the sensation of his nerves shaking inside. His pulse felt faster than normal, and he began to feel dizzy.

"What duh heck? Am Ah having a hawt attack or something? Dis all started when Ah began to dwell on what's going on with mah grandson. And all the junk he's taken me through. And all the junk dat's gone on in mah life for a long time."

With the admission, he felt a weak, but noticeable sensation in his throat. It was accompanied by an unwelcome surge of feeling that began in his chest. It effected the formation of the lump in his throat and alarmed him. Without warning, unfamiliar tears formed.

"Phew, Ah need to get a handle on this. Dis ain't like me. Dis ain't good for me."

But he couldn't.

His pulse increased. The sweat poured, unaffected by his efforts to calm down. A portrait of The Sacred Heart of Jesus tenderly peered down at him from the picture frame on the wall.

"Ah've heard of nervous break...downs. Ah must be... having one, having one. But Ah, ...Ah've never had one before. Come on, DeMaso. Get a handle... on it."

His breathing was getting heavy and his mind was now in a slow spin. He realized that he was feeling faint. He thought to call 9-1-1 and reached for his phone. But it wasn't on the table next to his chair. The room began to blur and the panic grew stronger. He now spoke out loud.

"What'd Ah do...with dat... stupid... phone?!"

He tried to get up but he fell back in his chair. His eyes rolled back into his head and his eyelids slowly closed. Out loud again:

"Ahm..... going..... fast. Ah .... need ...."

Simeon had the urge to walk past his desk into the den. He didn't know why he went in there, but he did. He had planned on making a few phone calls, but something didn't feel right. He sat down and began to think. Out of nowhere he had the unfamiliar urge to call Vincent DeMaso. Momentarily, he dismissed the thought. He had never called the number that had called him numerous tension-filled times. But he had saved it.

"Why would I do that? I'm not in the mood for more abuse at the moment. And besides I need to make those other calls."

But the provocation persisted. He looked down at his phone and went to his contacts. He found Vincent's number. He lifted his finger to press the call button. But he hesitated with his finger in midair.

His thoughts went to his desk. There were a pile of papers awaiting his attention as well. A call to Vincent would be an act of courage. And he wasn't' feeling courageous at the moment.

"Should I head for the desk or call Vincent?"

With all the mental, sensory, and spiritual meta-data he knew to access being instantly processed at warp-speed, he stood in the presence of an occupied Throne that was so far away, yet so very near. He went to the private space that contained the on – off switch to every choice, his God-Alone given human will. It was time to decide. He took a long, deep breath and pressed his finger down on the call button.

With the fading thought, Vincent was startled when he heard his cell phone ring. The jingle came from beneath his right leg on the chair. The sudden sound momentarily lifted him out of his demise into a vague sense of his surroundings. He gingerly reached for his phone.

"Whoo...is....dis?."

"Hello, Vincent. This is Simeon."

"Who? ...Who is ....?"

"Simeon. Simeon Mangino."

"Simmm ..eee...onnnn, uuuggghhhh........"

"It's me, Vincent. It's Simeon. You don't sound so good. You're groaning. Are you in pain? Do you need help?"

"Not gooooood. ... Uuuuggghhh, ... Ah......."

Vincent's phone dropped to the floor. His head fell softly to his chest.

Realizing something wasn't right, Simeon ended the call and dialed 9-1-1. He gave the operator Vincent's cell number so the police could track the number to his name, and then ascertain the location of his phone. The operator could not give Vincent's home address to him for legal reasons. And he didn't know where Vincent lived.

Within minutes, the police and rescue squad were at the door, which, unusually for the DeMaso home, was unlocked.

Three hours passed. Vincent lay in a hospital room

"How did Ah get here?"

"You called 9-1-1 and were brought here. Your vitals were a little shaky for a minute, but you're gonna be fine, Mister DeMaso. We're gonna run a few precautionary tests. Any history?"

"You said dat Ah called 9-1-1? You sure about dat?"

"No. But somebody did, because you came into the ER in a rescue vehicle."

"Ah rememberuh feeling weak and dizzy. After dat Ah don't remember anything. Uh, yeah, some high blood pressure and Ahm taking something for blood sugar. But nothing like dis has ever happened before. If Ah didn't call 9-1-1, den who did?"

"Are you under a lot of stress, Mister DeMaso?"

He didn't answer.

Twenty Six

It was several months since Simeon last saw the blue folder with its contents. He had a working recall of The Protocols. But there were gaps in what he remembered. As he sat under the thick fir tree he welcomed the cool, dry Colorado breeze. It was a welcome break from the early fall New Orleans heat. Before him, a herd of big-horn sheep meandered across the manicured grass field toward a cluster of tall pines. Beyond the pines, the tall red rocks stood like proud guardians of the glen they protected from the nearby highway.

For a long time something had eluded him. Voice often came to him in whispers through daily images in the routines of life. Was it Afflatus[46]? Steadily, continually, generously, irregularly, and unpredictably, it came sprinkled along the long, winding trail in his story. It came as unmistakable, though inaudible, promptings to his soul through people, experiences, sounds, and images. And it always came by way of a river, a river he was never far from.

He had grown to be profoundly aware of the reality of evil. He could feel it in and around his uptown neighborhood. It had a home in him, and he saw it in the news. It pervaded the air like oxygen. He didn't know how, but he felt like he had breathed it in through the mysterious New Orleans air, itself not unaffected by unseen things coming from the river that coursed through its center. And he began to understand that its control and influence had slowly invaded every culture over time, like steady moving lava to the crater top.

As he sniffed out its scent along the trails of history and in his own time, his conscience was marked for life. Its deceitful, putrid stench left an indelible mark along the trail of his psyche. And no matter what trail one walked, its odious smell could be traced by anyone who cared to be aware of it. For it had left its stench on every trail.

He was seated on a bench beneath an aspen tree. He wrote some of the thoughts that had been fomenting in his mind since his twenties. They

---

[46] Afflatus: A divinely inspired word or thought.

flowed easily, like water that was damned up and held back for a long time. The experience was relatively new. But it was endorsed by the recall of his Oak Tree on Constance Street, twelve hundred miles away.

He remembered the sound of the train horn along the river back home. And the six dings of the bell.

"The six dings of the bell.... Why six? It was always six that I noticed. What has been going on with these images? First, it was the clouds. And then it was my Old Oak Tree. Clear, visible images... of what? And why? And the sound of the train horn with its bells. Why have they endured?"

"And what of the man on the street corner at Bivi Q's? He was there with the blue folder, and then he wasn't. And my friend,...my friend? Can I even call him that? Mister Professor, Songieux, as he is referred to in The Protocols. He actually spoke to me face to face! He was there and then he wasn't. And didn't he speak to me of what burns in my heart? And has that not burned in my heart since I was a child? And why was that? Where did that come from? And didn't it continue up to that day when I was alone in my room in the barracks at Leary Air Force Base in 1974?"

"Is there a convergence happening of things that have been forming in my life? Am I shaped and positioned to respond to it all? Is that the sum of why I consider adding my voice to other voices?"

"And who am I? Am I not an intellectual and positional novice? Who wants to hear anything I have to say about these things? When I've occasionally tried in the past, it has only stirred discomfort among some of my colleagues and peeers. Sure, individuals and small audiences have engaged to degrees. But those were only sporadic eruptions that fit a context. And what would I have to say anyway? And how would I say it? And in what form?"

"It's such a tall task. It's too new. I like what life has served up for me to glean from all that I've experienced, heard, and learned. Maybe I'll just leave it at that. It's all helped me in my life with God, my relationships, and my work. All of what has happened to me for me to experience, sense, and know in my heart has been worth it for those contexts. It's best I leave it at that."

And with that, he laid aside thoughts on the matter and used his last few days in Colorado to read, hike, and refresh himself with friends. But he couldn't dismiss the fact that he wondered what happened to Vincent after he called the rescue squad to get him. And he continued to feel the void in his soul after having the blue folder with The Protocols taken from him. He was constantly amazed by their providential appearance in his life. And that was only diminished by his bewilderment at the swift injustice that was foisted upon him. It was apparent that he might never possess the materials again, even if it were for sentimental reasons alone. He couldn't change the fact that they were taken by a warlike human being whom he was now pressed to love.

He was physically afraid of Vincent, and for good reason. But he resolved to call him. Hopefully, he was alright after his recent spell. And he wondered if he might ask about retrieving his precious items.

Vincent shuffled through the stack of papers that populated his cluttered desktop. In one of the piles he found the blue folder that he had taken from Simeon. He was surprised.

After seizing the item, he laid it aside. When he thought about it, he felt a shame that he hadn't known for a long time. He didn't recall intentionally piling things on top of it. But the stuff of life had a way of burying all things painful for the one skilled at avoidance. And along with his surprise in finding it again, the shame that was previously avoided made an appearance again.

He felt less of an urge to harass Simeon in the days that followed. He was perplexed as to how the rescue squad showed up at his home. And he was almost certain that he locked the door that evening.

"Darndest thing."

He picked up the folder and took out the yellow napkins.

"The Protocols."

He spoke the words as he began to read them for only the second time. It was the first time that he had looked at them since the day he violently took them from Simeon. When he finished reading, he sat in the chair to further consider the content. But his phone rang.

"I'm calling for Vincent DeMaso."

"You're talking to him."

"I'm the Most Reverend Sister Elder of the Priori. Your sister stopped by our shop a few weeks ago. She mentioned that you had some old family religious statues and icons laying around. She aksed if we might be interested in them. I didn't know at the time if we would be. But I think we'd love to have them."

"Dat's right, Ah remember. She told me about it."

Vincent's eyes went to The Protocol napkins in his hand and to the papyrus blue folder on his table.

"How many items do you have?"

"About a dozen or so."

His eyes remained on the blue folder.

"Were they yours for a long time?"

"No. Ah inherited dem from mah…., from mah …. Never mind, do you want them?"

"Well, I think we'd love to have them. Can we pick them up?"

"Sure. Ah'll give you mah address before we end here. Say, you wouldn't be interested in an old, worn, papyrus-like, blue folder would you? It's from back in the day sometime. And it's got a few napkins with some strange kind of prophetic coded language written on them. The print on them appears to be a kind of archaic, ancient script."

"Really? Tell me about the content of the writing. What's it about?"

"It reads like something that Ah'd describe as sacred and futuristic, if dat makes any sense. It looks like it's meant to have a poetic sort of appeal and contain a warning or somethin like dat. It's weird jargon to me."

"Yeah. Wow. So,,… yeah, ….I think I'd like to have that. It sounds interesting. Can you put them in with the other items?"

"Sure will."

When he finished the conversation, he felt badly. He was fully aware that the folder and napkins weren't his to give away. But he shrugged it off.

His phone rang again. He looked at the screen and saw the name.

"So you calling me… *Why?*"

"How ya doin, Vincent? This is Simeon."

"What can I do for you?"

Something darted from a bush outside the window. It hovered for an instant when he looked outside. Then it zipped out of view. It held his attention for a lonely second.

The angst that he felt for his self-appointed enemy felt different. It was slightly tempered by a sense of guilt and shame at the sound of his voice. It was a new place from which to relate to a man he was committed to disdain.

Simeon didn't mention the last conversation they had.

"So how have you been?"

"Fine, real good. Nothing to complain about."

"I haven't heard from you in a while. I was beginning to think that you gave up on me. Like maybe you saw me as a hopeless cause."

"Are you inviting me to continue to harass you?"

"No, no, no,…. Not at all. I've been enjoying the reprieve. I just wanted to see how you're doing, and all uh dat."

He noted his New Orleans-speak. But he couldn't explain it if he had to.

"And all uh dat, huh? Really? You don't think Ah know what you're getting at, Mangino? Ah know you're not really wondering how Ahm doing. You're really calling to inquire about your blue folder and the weird writing in the, what's dat crazy writing stuff called again? Duh, duh,… Protocols. Yeah. You're wondering about dem, aren't you?"

"Actually I am. And I'm also caring to know how you are."

"Well, Ahm feeling a little less antagonistic toward you right now, so Ah'll go easy on you. If you must know, Ah had to go to dee emergency room recently. Had a nervous breakdown that really threw me for a loop. It got touch and go for a little while. But Ahm okay now. Gotta watch mah stress level and trying to eat a little better and all uh dat. Ah never told you, but mah grandson has been giving me fits for years and he's brought a lot of stress into mah life. It looks like he'll be in prison for a while."

"I'm sorry to hear about your health issues and about your grandson. I had no idea."

"You had no way of knowing about him, or of mah visit to dee emergency room. Dey tell me Ah called 9-1-1. But Ah don't remember doing that."

"Is there anything I can do to help?"

"No, Mangino, no thanks. And regarding the other matter, the matter of the blue folder and the writings,...Ah got bad news fuh yuh, son."

He was surprised at the surge of remorse that swept over him in the moment. His innocent and unsuspecting victim was clueless on the other end of the call. As he prepared to unleash the bad news on the poor sap on the other end of the call, he felt bad for him. It was the first time in years that he recalled feeling bad for the misfortunes of another person. It was a strange feeling.

As they spoke, he peered out of his backyard window. He noticed a hummingbird hovering before a flower. Its long beak was hidden inside while it sucked its nectar. In the moment, he was aware that he had never noticed a hummingbird in his yard. *Did he have hummingbirds in his yard??*

He felt a brief sensation, a surge of life-giving energy, a spark. It was good, and peaceful.

Simeon's pulse quickened. The mention of the blue folder and The Protocols with the term 'bad news' made him cringe inside. His heart recoiled. He braced himself.

"Ah gave em away."

The words blasted inside Simeon's brain. Though they were spoken in a normal tone, they rang in Simeon's mind like the repeating ring of a siren right next to his ear. He went numb, suspended in the battleground space between hatred and a good conscience.

He had strived, with help from The Source, The One Who lives, to love, and to not hate, an almost unlovable human being. He sat outside on the bench below Lily-Graces' orange tree, facing the back of their house. A mockingbird landed on the edge of the gutter directly in front of him, a mere ten feet away. At its landing, it launched into its familiar diatribe of incessant and irritating chirping, chitting, and chattering. It moved through its irksome arrangements without pausing. It stood perched above, like it had total access to the nearest human conscience, mocking every bird, insect, animal, and a man - mocking, mocking, mocking. But he chose to adjust the filter through which the sounds passed. He chose to hear the beauty in them instead and to remind himself of the real reason why mockingbirds showed off their stuff.

Vincent sat silent. He could tell that his words crushed the man on the other end of the call. A few weeks ago, he would have been beside himself with a sick pleasure at having the opportunity to heap another heavy burden on someone he hated. He would have entertained himself with the recollection of tying one more millstone around the neck of an enemy before tossing him into an emotional abyss.

"You gave them away."

The words were spoken in a deliberate tone, like he was trying to convince himself that he really did hear them. But the mood was somber. His neck and palms broke into a heavy sweat. The phone shook in Simeon's hand.

"You gave them… away."

He paused in the tense silence and wallowed there. So did Vincent.

"I think I'll be going now, Vincent. I need to go. Just …? Nothing, no,… forget it. I,... I'll see you around."

He ended the call.

Vincent sat still. He was stuck where he sat. He couldn't say why. But he was. He hadn't given them away yet. But he still wasn't willing to give them back to their rightful owner.

He looked for the hummingbird that he noticed for the first time a few short minutes ago. He wanted to go back to the experience. It had brought a peace he had never known. He had never before realized the beauty in his own backyard. And he wondered where the amazing little critter was.

The wings of the tiny bird had fanned the air around it into a blur. They invoked physics for that which defied gravity and stunted forward motion. The marvelous paired forelimbs held the bird in space, as if riveted to thin, invisible air. And when he previously noticed it, he was surprised to realize that he also wanted to be riveted to that very moment when it held his attention, for a long time, maybe forever. It was a strange sensation, a good one.

He searched the yard for it again. But it was nowhere in sight.

Twenty Seven

The Most Reverend Sister Elder of the Priori was tickled at her haul of spiritual icons. They would display nicely in her voodoo shop.

The blue folder, especially, piqued her curiosity. In her sensate state, she surmised that it was very old and somewhat mystical. When her hands began to tingle holding it, the mystery only grew. When she held it, she realized waves of powerful spiritual vibrations unlike any she had ever encountered. She could tell that they held a deeply meaningful spiritual component. But the vibrations she felt when handling them were troubling.

After reading The Protocols, she realized she needed counsel in order to understand them. To that end, she went to the consciousness chamber above her shop.

She lit a candle before assuming her meditative position. When seated, she closed her eyes. Being well-practiced in the habit of divination, she arrived at, and stepped through her spiritual portal, within a minute. She was immediately met by her guide. He was waiting for her. Because of their intimacy, she was instantly in deep touch with him. She sensed the seriousness of the rendezvous, so she wasn't surprised when he got right to the point.

"Whoever deals in matters related to this is not one with us."

She sat still and attentive, totally unaware of her surroundings.

"The documents in your possession are inconsistent with the universal voice. They are the subjective imaginations of misguided ones who are attempting to hold back humanity from its positive forward motion. I sense that you are understanding me."

The Sister Elder sat transfixed. Her eyes were rolled back into her forehead below her closed eyelids.

"The writing on the yellow napkins - we may hardly call them a manuscript - is an attempt that we are very familiar with. It has continued to arise and abate in different forms over the centuries and is rising again in these times, the time we call 'The Shift'. Today is the day of the universal, transcendent cosmic awakening. We are repairing the grave social injustices of the past, especially in America. We are bringing the world together as one. All of what you are witnessing as violence and dissonance are necessary steps to tear down the old. The old is the last vestige of an archaic ethic, the biased and antiquated value-system that must be eradicated. Most of mankind is embracing this evolutionary leap forward, even though they aren't aware that they are. We are leading them along. Those who are illumined and informed by the masters are aware. I am pleased to say that many of the old ethic have been lullabied to sleep and cannot see what we are doing. They will fall easily. We will deal with the rest the way we always have. I am pleased to sensate that you are receiving this."

"I am receiving this, my master."

"These documents are merely one more attempt to slow us down. We know how to deal with those who support such matters and propagate a return to the old. The new is no longer coming. It is here. There is merely one more barrier to our goal. In the last few years we have had to withstand a temporary rally of the resistance toward the new ethic. But we have been planting necessary spins and roadblocks in order to slow it down and to discredit its leaders. We have a vast network of deeply entrenched institutional servants and incredible wealth. Continue to let me bleed into you as I speak and we remain one in this moment. The Priori welcomes you and those who are one in cosmic and human consciousness. I feel your soul and you feel my own. I am taking what life your soul has left and replacing it with my own. For my own is the life of conscious oneness with the universe."

The Reverend Sister's body jolted as if a surge of energy suddenly coursed through her. Her eyes remained closed.

"You are to hold on to the documents you have been given. The Priori will consult and then get back to me. Then I will instruct you further."

When she walked down the stairs into the shop, she noted a patron with his back toward her. He appeared to be looking down at something while talking with her salesperson. She saw him reach in front of the patron as if touching the item that was in his hands. She walked into the office to retrieve the blue folder. But it wasn't there.

"Where'd I put that thing?"

"How much you want for this blue folder and these napkins inside?"

The customer held the folder in front of Damien.

"OH! There it is. Oh ... no …. That's not for sale. I misplaced it, sorry. Damien, show our friend the other icons we just got from that Vincent fellow."

After finishing for the day, she prepared to leave. She picked up her purse along with the blue folder and walked to her car. When she settled in, she turned the key. But nothing happened.

She attempted to start the engine again with the same result.

"Are you kidding me? I can't believe this."

With each attempt, the result was the same. Resigned to her plight, she reached into her purse to get her phone. But it wasn't there.

"Did I just leave my stupid phone at the shop? Unbelievable."

Resigned to her fate, she opened the door to head back to the shop. As she exited the car, a large man walked up to her along the dark, lighted sidewalk and asked her if she had a dollar to help him get something to eat.

"I'm kinda in a... okay, sure."

As she opened her purse, the man yanked it from her hand. He took off in a sprint and turned at the corner nearby. She looked around for help. But she was the only person on the street for several blocks. There was no traffic.

She stormed back toward the shop, trying hard to contain her emotions. She was relieved to find that she still had her keys.

Several days later, she was awakened early by a heavy knock on her door. She made her way warily to open it. When she did, her anxious neighbor gushed out his news like rushing waters.

"Revrend Sistuh, yuh caw's been broken into! Ah saw a dude smash yuh window just after daybreak. Ah was out walking mah dog and you know, he just smashed yuh window and rummaged troo things. He stepped up outside your passenger side door wit some kind of blue folduh looking thing. He pulled some things outta it and looked round. Duh man's awms was flailing and his eyes was wide,... oh yeah. Ahm telling you, ...yes indeed."

"Dat's not so strange, you know,.. in this town,...you know. Boiglaries are a dimea dozen. But what was strange was dat dis dude done held dem papers and that folduh for a minute. Den all of a sudden, Ah saw what looked like a flash of bright light right round his face. It looked like a miniature lightening bolt. You hear me now, sistuh? Like a miniature *lightenin* bolt. Like it was meant fuh him - *just fuh him*, Ah said. Ooooom-*HMMMMM*! And wit dat, he done fell onto duh sidewalk. He dropped dat folduh and those papers when he did. Den he looked round like he'd just been caught on camera . In a flash, he was on his feet and outta deyuh. Dis ain't no lie no way, Revrend Sistuh."

The bad news left her head spinning. In the turmoil, her emotions weren't unaffected. So they joined the fray and added energy to the twister.

"My car? My new car? And a folder? The blue folder, h-o-l-y balaoney! I left the joking thing in my car last night. Can you believe this? I just...."

She didn't get to finish her words.

"Ah couldn't believe mah eyes, Revrend Sistuh."

He slapped one hand into the other as he continued.

"Dat tiny flash of bright light come outta nowhere and zap him right in the face, right ...in the ... *face*. But it didn't hurt him no way. You understand what Ahm saying? And lemmie tell you, dat man drop dat folduh and those yellow papers right on the ground like dey was a hot potato. You hear me now? Dis duh troof, Revren Sistuh, yes *INDEED!*"

Three hours later, Vincent's doorbell rang. He was reading in the back den.

"*H-o-l-d* on. What's duh hurry? *Ahm* comin."

There was a slight cheer in his words as walked to the door. When he opened it he was surprised to see the Most Reverend Sister Elder.

"Hello, Mr. DeMaso. I brought you something."

"Reverend Sistuh. How duh heck are you?"

"Well, you're noticeably more chipper since I met you last week."

"Huh, ...interesting. You're not the first person to say dat. Huh.... Well, what brings you to mah door out of the clear blue?"

"I'm bringing this blue folder and its contents back to you."

A surge of relief came over him. He felt bad since he broke the bad news to Simeon. It wasn't the only thing he felt bad about.

"O-k-a-y. Dis is unexpected."

As the words fell, he realized that he might have encouraged her to change her mind. He hoped that wouldn't be the case.

"What the mix is this thing anyway? Since the day you brought it to my shop, I haven't had a day without something bad happening to me. My purse was stolen. My car wouldn't start. Then it was broken into. And the weirdest thing happened to the thief. He was hit by a lightening bolt, a tiny one I'm told, when he held this thing in his hands. Who gets hit in the face by a tiny lightening bolt that starts and ends right there? I've had dreams every night. One was about me driving a car up a steep incline at high speed about to hurtle over the top into an abyss. And in a different one, evil, dark angels come knocking at my front door."

"My fingers tingle every time I hold these Protocol napkins. My meditation guide tells me…"

"Excuse me. What's a meditation guide?"

"I'll explain it to you if you're interested."

"Never mind, go on."

"Well he tells me,… I don't actually see him. I sort of meet him in the cosmos when I'm meditating. He tells me that these things are not what we are about. That the words written here are about the ones who are attempting to keep mankind from coming into the oneness of the universe. You know, the universe of all things."

"Yeah, well, Ah don't know much about all uh dat."

"And other strange things are happening. My black cats keep hissing at this folduh. And one night, during a séance, one of our mediums freaked out when I walked in with this folder in my hands. And get this: I threw them in the trash in my front yard. And when I walked inside *it was on my kitchen table!* So I brought it to my back yard and made a small fire so I could burn this stuff. I threw it in with some other papers. *And the stuff didn't burn up. It went through the fire unscathed! "*

When she began, he was impressed. He left that behind sentences ago when he breached the realm of astonishment.

"Wuh Duh Protocol napkins inside the blue folder when all this here stuff happenend?"

"Yes they were. So here, take this. I never want to see this again. This folder and its contents are pure evil. They're bad news. I'll just have to tell my spirit guide a little white lie about how I lost this thing. I don't want to have anything to do with these items. And If I were you, I'd go to the middle of the Gulf of Mexico, tie them to cinder block, and drop them there."

With not a little amazement from the recent events, he quietly, and gratefully, received the items.

"Any idea what you're gonna do with this, Mr. DeMaso?"

Something darted from right to left outside his front window. It happened in the blink of an eye and caught his attention. It moved almost too fast to see with the naked eye, until it halted abruptly, gingerly planted in the thick and humid tropical air, in front of the iris bush at the corner of the house.

He easily saw it. It was his new friend.

"Ah know exactly what Ahm gonna do with it."

Time Passage

Roots

"Youth is the pollen that blows through the sky,
and does not ask why."

~ Stephen Vincent Benet

Twenty Eight

Simeon was the fifth, of what would be twelve grandchildren born from Tino and Helene Mangino's family. The first seven were boys. In short time, he came to know his place in the pecking order of the close-knit Italian clan. His gregarious uncle Gasparo was the first to call him Simmie, and the nickname was widely applied.

He lived in the house behind his uncle's, a few short blocks from Old Man River. It was seventy-five yards from Wisemar Playground, which held a baseball field, shelter house, and sizeable cement kid's pool. Hunster's restaurant, bar, and candy store sat across from home plate, fifty yards away. One short block down stood Mitt's Bar and Poolhall. Another short block from Mitts was Fump's Bar.

The large playground occupied an entire New Orleans square block. It was bordered on all four sides by narrow two-way streets. The streets displayed early 1900's wooden shotgun homes that were separated from one another by narrow alleyways. And in the early 1950's, baby boomer kids were everywhere.

Long ago, the Mississippi River ran through the marsh before the city was born. It coursed through the terrain that could more accurately be described as delta, as it was land formed from the deposits of the murky, muddy waters hundreds of years earlier. The city was a youngster to the mighty, muddy waters. And its inhabitants didn't always pay it the respect that an adolescent would to an elder who held deep secrets.

One block closer to the Mississippi River, was Tchoupitoulas Street. It was named after a large plantation that ran from the river towards the middle of town. Locally owned corner bar rooms and grocery stores dotted the neighborhood. And the owner's families lived in the same buildings behind their primary businesses.

Churches were scattered throughout the neighborhood. The largest were the parochial churches, which governed large grammar schools that were institutions in the community. Fluid interaction flowed between the life of the church and the other places of gatherings in the neighborhood. These were spiced by the colorful demeanor of the natives. And their energy was the breeding ground for the many celebrations that the culture bred. One such gathering was a birthday celebration for a three year old who was ensconced within a lively parochial family in the lively parochial neighborhood.

"Momma, iz Mawgus[47] gon-na be at mah birt-day paw-tee tuh-day?"

"No dawlin. He can't make it. But all of your cousins and aunts and uncles will be there. Yuh paw-paws and yuh grandma will too."

"Iz Trae and Lan gon-na be dey-uh, momma?"

"Of course, Simmie. Lan is right next doeuh. And Trae right down the block. You don't think dey would miss your birtday pawtee do yuh? And besides, you see dem almost every day."

"Is Aunt Mae and Aunt Katie come-in?"

---

[47] Morgus the Magnificent was a colorful and beloved, offbeat New Orleans television personality, invented and played by a local New Orleanian.

"Uh huh."

"Aunt Shoil-lee and Uncle Duckie com-in too, momma?"

"Yes, dey are."

"And Red and Rozzie too?"

"Well dey wouldn't come and leave their children home, your two cousins, would dey, dawlin?"

"Iz Footsie and Cat com-in too, momma? Iz Footsie gon-na tease eb-ry-body, momma?"

"Yes. And you know Footsie and your Uncle Gasparo will be teasing everybody there, right Simmie?"

"Hee-hee-hee. Hee-hee."

He naturally leaned into his insatiable inquisitive nature. His always receptive momma was present with him.

Why iz mah name, Sim-mie, momma?"

Maria Bonamo Mangino was caught off guard with the question. Her inquisitive first-born began to display the bent toward abstract thinking early. Her husband, Julian, entered the kitchen in the small one bedroom house that was a former slave quarters in the late nineteenth century.

"Our son wants to know why his name is Simeon."

"Because Ah said so."

Julian feigned a mean face before it broke into a wide grin. He picked up his first child and held him over his head. Looking up at him and laughing, he lowered him to his face to bury his nose in his son's stomach. Little Simeon giggled loud and continually as he looked down on his daddy's face, his appendages flailing lightly in the air.

"Because Ah said so."

A cackling laugh followed the words. He held his son playfully above his head for a few more seconds. The cackles and giggles went on before he set him down and headed back into the bedroom.

Maria continued.

"It's because we liked the name of the man in the Christmas story when Jesus was bawn in the manger. Dat's why you are our Simmie."

The little lad stared straight ahead. His mind was in motion.

"Why did-ja like duh name of duh man in the Jesus stoe-wee, momma?"

"Because he knew something dat most other people didn't know, Simmie."

"How did he know some-thing dat uth-uh people did-int know, momma?"

"Well, we don't know how he knew, honey. He just knew."

"What did he know dat uth-uh people did-int know, momma?"

"He knew dat Jesus was coming soon, Simmie."

Simeon stopped playing with his toy and looked out and upward through the screen door. His eyes lifted up toward the bright blue New Orleans sky that displayed a lone, small, bright white cloud. It posted itself stationary overhead against the rich blue heavens. Ever so slightly, the corners of his mouth creased upward into a barely noticeable smile. His eyes peered out the screen door. But his thoughts shot out in search of a faraway dimension that he momentarily sensed was within grasp, though he couldn't have said it.

"Momma, iz Jee-zus com-in tuh mah birt-day paw-tee tuh-day?"

Maria stopped counting plastic spoons. She looked at her son with tender affection. Then, her gaze followed his, through the screen door and up to the sky.

Twenty Nine

It was a typically warm fall afternoon when the seven year old stepped off the last wooden step into the backyard. His brother and cousin were playing stick ball with a weathered rubber ball. His little sister, Shairee, was playing in the dirt with a kitchen spoon along the chain-link fence to the right. Seeing him, she offered a grin.

Little brother Pokey was two years younger and a true comrade. His hefty torso was set on a wide frame. He wore curly black locks that were held in place with a blend of sweat from the morning heat and Brylcreem residue. He was fond of his older brother and cousins. And should the urge ever arise to have someone be the fall-guy for pranks and the like, no one fit the bill more ably than a younger brother or cousin.

As Simeon's worn, black, Ked's shoes touched the dirt below, his eyes wandered up toward the giant live oak tree. It reached high above the worn aluminum shed at the far end of the yard.

To the left was Pitre's[48] paw-paw's yard. On the right was Miss Dukas' manicured yard. A wooden shed staked its claim in the middle of it like a rectangular island, with thick, neatly trimmed grass on all sides. A clothes line patrolled the turf behind the shed, running front to back like a decorative piece. Never were there any clothes hanging on it. Besides these two furnishings the yard was empty.

The oak spread majestically above and beyond the aluminum shed. It's full, flush branches extended past the widest boundaries of the yard like the outstretched wings of an eagle. It was a haven for a variety of avian creatures. He was enamored with the mocking birds that perched there and whose unmistakable sounds often found their way to his ears.

After a few steps, his searching eyes quickly left the familiar oak and began to survey the sky. To his delight, he beheld the typical late-fall formation of rolling-white tropical clouds. They displayed shades of fluffed, curved, gray edges. The gray contrasted with the white, cotton-like rolls, and with the sun's help, caused the white to appear to glow and

---

[48] Pronounced "Pee-Tree's"

the soft gray shades to shine. Not to be denied, a rich blue sky filled in the openings of the cloud formations. It cradled the entire panorama over the rooftops of the houses all around. It held his gaze for a few more steps, as if they were made to be more than a sight for casual eyes.

The cascading sounds of the locusts broadcast across the neighborhood. They were occasionally joined by the sound of the train engine pulling along the Public Belt Railroad two blocks near. Periodically, the sounds of a tug boat horn, or that of a merchant ship, announced their presence along The Old Man River, just beyond the tracks.

The chorus of singing by the locusts reached a crescendo that was as loud as it was familiar. Many New Orleanians barely noticed their sounds, though noteworthy on the decibel scale. It was mostly background noise in a day's work or play, but for listening ears.

To Simeon, they were the sounds of meaning in the context of discovery and mystery, soul markers, stamps of identity.

In seconds, he was beyond his baby sister and headed to the action in the yard. He was about to address Pokey and Trae when he heard the familiar sound of a train horn. It sounded a three-second toot. It was immediately followed by the repetitious sounds of a bell.

He was caught up in one more brief and familiar stroll into the abstract place of wonderment. He sometimes glided to that space, bringing questions that were beginning to form. As he approached the action in the yard, his mindwalk down abstract avenue was brought to an abrupt halt.

"Come on, Simmie. Me and Trae been waitin for you."

"Tell him Pokey. Get your stick, Simmie. Hurry up. It's your turn to bat."

"Awe-right, Ahm coming."

Thirty

"Come on, Trae, we gonna be late. Pitre's waiting outside. Dezi is too.
Mah momma's gonna kill me if Ahm late for school. And we gonna get
it from Sistuh too. We got three blocks to walk, Trae."

"Awe right, awe right. Ah just gotta comb mah hair, den Ahm ready.
Why do we have church every morning before school, anyway, Simm?"

"Ah don't know. But you gotta hurry."

"Trae, get yourself going, boy. Simmie, Ah've been telling him to
hurry since he got outta bed."

"Ah know, Aunt Katie. He's always gotta comb his hair. Come on,
Trae. Why you have to put Brylcream[49] in your hair today? We gonna
be late."

"Just a little dab'll do ya!"

Trae couldn't resist singing the television commercial jingle for the
substance. The carefree lad wore a grin almost as large as the greasy
glob that he finished massaging into his hair. After a few determined
combs of his slick mane, every strand was subdued for the day, confined
from every disturbance.

The four young grade-schoolers finally began to beat feet for church
before school. Trae, on his part, complained at their running the whole
time, fretting that the activity might mess up his slick, shiney top. It was
a laughable emotion given the amount of greasy matter holding it in
place.

Upon their arrival, the students marched from the old school building
through the doors of the ornate church structure. The uniform-clad
students filed in quietly and obediently, like cadets at a military
academy. And they were unaware that there was any other way to begin
a school day.

Simeon sat on the end of a row of first graders. Trae bargained and
bribed to sit behind Ashley Corriege, an accomplishment he kept trying
to get his cousin to notice. When the readings began, Simeon wondered

---

[49] A popular, national brand greasy hair substance, used by males from boys to men, to
slick the hair in place.

about what he was hearing from the brief Scripture readings. His eyes went to the statue of Archangel Michael with his drawn sword. One of his feet was planted on the devil, pinning him to the ground. Simeon stared at it and wondered. A statue of Saint Francis of Assisi, the parish patron, faced them. One hand was over his heart. He had a kind and gentle look on his face. And Simeon wondered more.

He looked at the ornate altar elevated up several layers of steps from the congregation. On each side was an angelic figure. Each held a pole that held rows of candles at the top. High above them was a cross with Jesus hanging on it. He was deceased. Trickles of blood flowed from his head, hands, feet, and side. And Simeon wondered greatly.

From there, his eyes continued upward to the sky-blue rotunda overlooking the altar. Tiny stars dotted the blue color. The ceiling arched upward to a peak at its center. He felt as if he was looking into a daytime sky with stars out. He didn't know what an oxymoron was at his tender age. But he was aware of the mental tension from the view. And he wondered greatly even more.

When they returned to the classroom, Sister Mary Imelda began the class day with the daily-religion session.

"Take your books out and turn to our next lesson. Today, we'll be reading about the beginnings."

Directly in front of him sat Dora Fontaine, daughter of the famous New Orleans jazz musician. The rows of desks were attached front-to-back. This placed the back of her head at the edge of his desk. And it allowed her long auburn hair to fall over the top of his desk when she leaned back. The lesson began with her hair over the top of his book.

He had the notion to tap her on the shoulder. He realized that by simply tapping her, she would turn her head, and thereby, her hair would be gone from atop his desk. But he hesitated. Instead, he simply brushed it slightly aside, hoping she wouldn't notice. He was glad when she didn't.

On the page, there was a sketch of a kingly looking figure sitting on a throne. The black and white drawing showed the older looking figure to sport a long, flowing beard. His hands extended to the end of the arms of the throne. He sat with a featureless face so that His gaze was unknown. Lines representing beams of light emanated from His throne. The overall effect from the image impressed upon him the concept of A Supreme, somewhat impersonal, All-Powerful Authority.

"Okay, class. I'll read. Try to follow along. Let's begin…

```
'In the beginning God created the heavens
and the earth.  The earth was formless
and void, and darkness was over the
surface of the deep.  And the Spirit of
God hovered across the surface of the
waters.' 50"
```

"Now, boys and girls, I read from the very first verse of the very first book of the Bible. It is the book called 'Genesis'."

But Simeon didn't hear the last two sentences.

By the time she began with the words "In the beginning", something new and wonderful began to stir in him. For a brief moment, his heart, soul, mind, and spirit impulsively came together and bonded inside as a unified one. It happened instantly, almost as if he didn't choose it.

The young lad absorbed the words like they were cool, fresh water to a parched palate. They burned into his mind as if in the hands of a Cosmic Engraver. Each word carried meaning in its elemental sense. But his mind was carried away by the entirety of the sentences and the massive scope of their meaning.

The words went to his soul so fast that the spirit component inside jumped to attention. His eyes automatically shot up to the clear, blue sky outside the high, open widow to his left. As his teacher read the words from the Scripture verse, he saw a lone bird hovering in place against the blue sky. It remained suspended the duration of the reading and for long seconds after when Sister began talking about it. His eyes were locked onto the avian reptile and remained so until the high breeze escorted it beyond the view from the high, open window. At its removal from his view he felt loss.

It represented life to him, created life, life with purpose, intention, and meaning. "In the beginning God created the heavens and the earth…"

---

50 Genisis 1:1

By the simple, common, yet marvelous creature fastened to the sky, Afflatus[51] came to him through and in the words. And he was captivated, stolen away to the place of connection, meaning, and answer.

He wasn't overcome by utter emotion. Emotion was in its proper, submissive place. And it stood fast in neutral. His mind and soul were shooting outward toward an unseen destination, a city from above[52]. And the effortless spiritual energy began to shatter his life-limiting restraining bars. Heaven drew near, and he sensed it. But it was so deeply intrinsic that he found no name for it. Momentarily, a peaceful, inner joy jumped in to ride in one of the vacated seats in his thoughts. Mere seconds had passed. But his thoughts were going out into the universe in the soul-hope of connecting with the Originator of the inspired words and imagery. It was real. It was personal. And the young boy on a bike knew it.

He carried the experience, along with its recorded images, to the hallway of his mind. He hung it there, just inside the doorway, in the place where he knew he would know to find it when he wanted to retrieve it, when he needed it. His young mind could not figure out how to label the image that he hung there. Many years later, he hung many other images in there. And after replaying this one over and over many times he would realize how his soul labeled the experience.

It was hung with the heading:

"My heart, and my life's desire."

By the close of her reading, young Simeon was both done and undone in the same moment. He was as touched as a six year old could be. He had experienced a defining moment, though he could not explain it at the time. He was uncoupled from the notion that life could be found anywhere else other than where he had just been. It was a monumental moment in time for him. In a few years he would purposely wander from it. But it had permanently marked him. And he kept the secret to himself.

---

[51] Ibid: a divinely inspired word or thought.
[52] Revelation 21:10-27

Thirty One

It was the fall of 1962. The two second graders were walking home from school. Simeon brought up what was going on that week with the Cuban missile crises a few hundred miles below New Orleans. And Trae sensed the concern in his cousin.

"Dat's faw away, Simm, you not worried about it, are you?"

He didn't answer.

"We ain't gonna get nuked. Dat's all just talk."

"How you know, Trae? Dey could shoot a missile and hit us anytime they want to. It was on the news last night. Ah watched it with Paw-Paw Jake."

"Did Paw-Paw think dey would shoot a missile at us?"

"He didn't say. But he looked concerned."

"Paw-Paw always looks concerned, Simmie. We got nothing to worry about. And if dey shoot at us dey'll probably miss. And then we'll shoot at dem and kick their butts."

"You think so?"

"Yeah. Ah know so. Mah daddy was a Marine. They're the toughest bunch around. Nobody messes wit dem."

"Maybe you're right, Trae."

"Come on. Let's go see what Pokey's doing, Simm. He better not be playing with mah baseball cawds again."

Several days later, Simeon came down with something. He missed school for a day. That evening he lay in bed as usual, wondering if his folks might buy him the new Murray Bicycle he desired for Christmas. Not long past midnight, he woke up startled and sweating. The fever was doing its thing not only in his body but in his mind as well. Although he was very warm in bed, it was the dream that woke him.

The images themselves weren't overly gruesome or dark. The fear that was associated with them was what tilted him into panic. Without hesitation, he shot out of bed and into the next room where his momma

and daddy were asleep. He nudged himself into the double bed next to
the latter.

"What?...*What*,…who's dat?"

"It's me, daddy."

"Oh, ….*man*. Yuh scared duh mix outta me. You awe-right?"

"Yeah. Ah just had a bad dream, dat's all. Ahm gonna lay by you for
a little while, daddy."

With that Julian was back into a deep sleep. In time, Simeon was
asleep as well. But in the early morning hours he had another dream.

An army of soldiers was making its way up the outside of his right leg.
In one instant, they appeared to be the size of the toy soldiers he played
with. In the next, they were large and imposing. They were moving
toward him in a war-like posture.

He was lying on his side. In the image, his outer leg was a hill that
they were climbing to get to him. He was at the top of the hill, in the
shoulder area. He was aware that he was trembling with fear, awash in a
cold sweat. He had the idea to run, but knew that he had nowhere to run
to. The shoulder-neck-head area was the end of the line.

He felt from them the kind of determination that is propelled by
seething anger and hatred. They were coming to get him. The closer
they came, the more terrified he became. He felt the sweat dripping from
his temples and all over his torso. He was aware that his right arm was
around his daddy. He nudged closer, though he couldn't get any closer.
The lead soldiers were close enough to seize him when he reacted.…

"DADDY! … HELP ME! THEY'RE COMING
TO GET ME! ……. *DADDY*!"

Julian had to fend off his son, who was attempting to crawl inside of
him. The boy was dripping wet and shaking uncontrollably.

Awakened by the whole thing, his momma realized he was overcome
by the fever. As Maria attempted to console him, Julian went to get a
cool rag and a change of pajamas. They realized that he was only partly
conscious.

"It's the fever, Julian."

Maria assured her husband.

"Man, he scared duh mix outta me. You think he's gonna be awe-right?"

"Ah think so. Let's get him calm and cooled down. And we'll see how he is in the morning."

In didn't take long for him to cool down in the assuring presence of his parents. Within thirty minutes, he was able to calm down and settle into a safer and relaxing sleep.

The next day, he was able to reassure his parents that he was alright after the incident. So they went about their day as usual. But the experience had an effect on him. It was automatically stored in the gallery of his mind. Almost on its own, it hummed ever so slightly just below his conscience as background noise. His momma assured him it was just a reaction to the fever.

He wondered.

He hung the image in his mind. It was a close cousin to the few, but growing number of other experiences that he subconsciously hung there. They were like DVD images with the opening scene frozen and on display. All he had to do was retreat into the corridor of his mind and go to the place where the image hung. Once there, he could hit the play button and relive a good bit of the experience. For reasons a young boy on a bike couldn't know, he didn't go into those hallways very often.

This wouldn't be the last dream. Going forward he would have a few more. By his teenage years his reaction in them and to them was not as dramatic. He knew where the original was hung. And the decisive response he settled on after it happened helped him to not be mentally or emotionally distracted by it.

Thirty Two

"Come on, Parry. Swing at duh ball."

"Ah will, when Pokey throws me a good pitch. Tell him to throw it where Ah like it, Simmie."

"Throw it where he likes it, Pokey."

"Parry's too picky. Watch dis. Ah'll throw another one."

Pokey threw another one just outside the plate.

"Ya'll are driving me crazy."

"Shut up, Lan. You'll get your turn."

"You shut up, Trae."

"Simmie, why you looking up at duh sky? If he hits one at you, you're gonna get hit in the face, big brother."

He stood at first base. But Pokey's words brought him back to real time. Sweat was dripping all over his body while he stood still in the searing summer heat. He took off his ball cap and wiped the sweat from his forehead with the bottom of his dusty tee shirt.

As Pokey wound up to throw another pitch, the air raid siren sounded at the right field corner of the playground. It blasted its long wailing sound all over the neighborhood along the river. It rose to a high pitch and held it for ten seconds before rapidly descending into silence. It remained for a few seconds before it repeated the alarm. It did this for several cycles before stopping.

The siren was a test. In the early 1960's, war tensions led to cities installing the alarms in the event of a nuclear missile attack. Several times a week, the alarms were tested to be sure that they were in working order. And this time, it had the effect of getting the boys off of one another's backs.

Each time Simeon heard the siren he found himself thinking about war. He had heard stories of World War II from his uncles, aunts, and grandma. And of World War I, from his Paw-Paw's. He was repulsed at the thought of men killing one another. And there was a sense of foreboding that accompanied his thoughts. He didn't know why.

Days later, he and Lan rode their bikes to Mitts. They went to the window to get some Barq's Root Beers[53]. Orleans poked his bayou-born Cajun face out the window.

"What choo waw?"

"Hey, Awleens. Give me and mah cugino[54] each a Bawq's."

"Dat's twenty-fahve cents. Hurry up you two. Ahm busy."

"Simmie, gimme another nickel. Ah only got twenty cents."

"Ah don't have any more money, Lan."

"Come aw, Ahm busy. Gimme duh twenty-fahve cents or you're not gittin yuh root beer's."

"Hey Awleens, is our Paw-Paw Tino working in there today?"

"Yeah, why you aksin, boy?"

"Tell him me and Lan are out here and we need another nickel for two soft drinks."

"Ya'll two lil dago's are a pain in the butt, you know dat?"

"Good idea, Simmie. Paw-Paw's good for a nickel."

In a minute, Orleans stuck two cold root beers out the window. He returned the four nickels to the boys on their bikes.

"Yuh Paw-Paw says dis one's on him. Nah git outta heeuh."

"Yeah you rite. Let's go down to Huntsuh's and get some candy, Simmie. Paw-Paw comes through again."

After taking the candy, they pedaled the block back past the playground onto the corner at Mitts again. They sipped their drinks and ate candy.

"Ahm glad ya'll moved closer to us, Simmie. Ya'll are just four blocks away now. Like our first five years, when ya'll lived right behind us."

"Yeah. It was fun livin right next doeuh tuh Trae, Footsie, and Cat. But now we get to see more of ya'll again, Lan."

"So are ya'll gonna go to St. Henry's with us now?"

"No. Momma says we'll still go to St. Francis. So Ah'll still get to see a lot of Trae and the guys there,… Crisp, Ranny, Sturgis, Barry Q., Derbs, Ward, Osskuh, Bubby, RayBay, Peterson, and all uh dem."

---

[53] Barq's was an original New Orleans local soft drink ('cold drink') that at the time could only be purchased in greater New Orleans
[54] Italian: "male cousin"

"There's quite a few knuckleheads in that bunch you just mentioned. Ya'll live only two blocks away from Pomilese's now. More of Miss Dot's po-boys, huh, Simmie? And here we are, sitting on our bikes outside of Mitt's and right down the block from Fumps, duh place of your momma's roots. And when we turn eighteen dis is where we gonna hang out and shoot pool. Ah might even work here, dat is, if dey get lucky enough to hire me."

At that moment the side door of Mitt's swung open. Lan's older brother, Gasp, stepped out onto the sidewalk as if he owned it. Seeing his younger brother and cousin, he walked up to them.

"What are ya'll doing out here, boys?"

"Simmie. Did my punk big bruthuh just call us 'boys'?"

"Ah think Ah heard him mistakenly refer to us as such, Lan."

"Ha-ha. One day, when ya'll grow up and can come in Mitt's, Ah'll show ya'll a thing or two about how to shoot pool."

Their smack talk was interrupted by the loud sound of the older black man who had been standing at the edge of the street corner. He was leaning against the telephone pole, listening.

"MOMA DAWG! Eleb'm – seb'm-teen – twenty two! Dey call me Put! P - U- T. Sounds like FOOT! *Yeeeess* indeed."

Lan's next oldest brother, Lonnie, came walking up with their fourth and youngest brother, Parry, in tow. He was followed by their cousin, and Simeon's younger brother, Pokey.

"WheyY'att, Put."

Lonnie touched the old black man's shoulder as he walked by. He was still leaning against the telephone pole.

"Awe-right, awe-right."

Walking up to his older brother, Lonnie spoke.

"Gasp, go in Mitt's and buy me a beer , would yuh? Ah got a quarter. Here."

Gasp nudged his brother's hand away.

"Ah can't Lonnie. Paw Paw's working today. If he knew Ah got it for you, he'd kill us all."

"Oh yeah, Ah forgot."

"What are you doing with the two little runts following you around?"

Parry, never one to hold his tongue, spoke up.

"We ain't runts. Pokey, Gasp called us 'runts'."

"We ain't runts, Parry. We might be duh youngest. But we ain't runts."

The clever lad wore a telling grin with the words.

"Good one, Pokey."

"Yuh liked dat, huh, Gasp? Ah got more where dat one came from."

The front door to Mitt's swung open. Out bounded Footsie Trufant, Trae's older brother.

"Hey, ya'll. What's dis, a family reunion?"

His usual breezy demeanor was not overshadowed by his gladness to encounter his familiar breed.

"Yeah you rite. Ah guess we are like family, the Mangino's and the Trufant's. Ain't we, Footsie?"

"Yes indeed, Gasp. Like family and neighborhood all our lives. Ah got off work early. Gotta get home to Mary's good cooking, but Ahm gonna shoot a little pool first. Gasp, you wanna shoot some wit me? Ahm paying."

"Say no more, almost cousin, lessgo."

Simmie's two older cousins, one paternal and one maternal, walked away toward the side door entrance to Mitts. Before entering, Footsie, exactly ten years senior to Simeon and Lan, stopped. He turned and spoke.

"Ya'll are not coming with us?"

He flashed an exaggerated look of concern.

Lonnie, Lan, Simmie, Pokey, and Parry just stood there with pathetic looks on their faces.

"Oh dat's right."

He swung his arm down toward the ground in an arc while snapping his fingers.

"Ya'll are still too young to get in Mitt's."

He let out his signature, one syllable, loud laugh, and walked inside.

Old Put wobbled over toward the five Mangino boys left behind on the street corner. They stood near the window where he frequently received a shot of vino from the proprietors.

"Ya'll got a qwawt-uh fuh Old Put?"

His right hand was appropriately extended.

"Here, Put. Ah was gonna get me a beer, but mah Paw-Paw's here.
You might as well get you something."

"Much obliged, suh. Ah know you boy's daddies a long tahm. Dey be
plentiful proud uh ya'll, Ah know. Yuh heeuh me? Yeessss *inDEED*."

He turned and tapped on the window to Mitt's.

"Let's go, Simmie. Momma said be home by suppuh time."

"Okay, Pokey. See ya'll later, Lonny, Lan, Parry."

As they all headed home for supper, Simeon turned to have another
look at Old Put. He felt sorry for him. Though he grew up knowing
their daddies, he wondered why he was so poor. Not that his family was
far from being poor. But Put and the other black folk in the
neighborhood didn't seem to have as much opportunity as white folk did.
And there was something about the old guy. Though he was taken for
granted, always on the street corner drinking, or just standing around,
there seemed to be more to the man.

Simeon walked his bicycle alongside Pokey. As they turned onto
Dufossat Street, the last block toward home, the sound of the train horn
blasted a short, loud toot. It was followed by the sounds of the bell on
the engine. Simeon stopped in his tracks. He looked up to the sky.

"Did ja here dat, Pokey?"

"Here what?"

Thirty Three

"Let's go over to Sherry's. Miss Rosa might give us a cold drink."

"Yeah, she's got dat big awning over her porch, and we can get outta dis heat, Crisp."

"Ahm in, Rubby. But we should aks Simm. She's his girlfriend."

"Okay, go ahead and aks him, Derbs."

"Whaddya say, Simm. You wanna go over to Sherry's?"

"Ah don't know, guys. Ah just talked to her for an hour and a half on the phone last night."

"An hour and a half? Are you kidding me? What do ya'll find to talk about for so long, Simm?"

"Ah don't know, BarryQ.. We just find it easy to talk, dat's all."

"For an hour and a half?"

"Leave him alone, Crisp. He's in love."

"Zzzat so, Simm? You in love wit Sherrie?"

"Shut up, Ranny. We can go across duh street and sit on *your* girl friend's front porch. She's got a big awning too, you know."

"What? And bring all uh ya'll over there? Come on, Simm."

"BarryQ. wouldn't mind if we went over there, Ranny."

"Why you saying that, Sturgis?"

"Cause BarryQ. likes Kath too."

"What? BarryQ., you like mah girlfriend?"

"Be quiet, Sturgis. Who aksed you to chime in."

"Why not go over there instead of Sherry's, Ranny?"

"'Cause, Crisp. When Ah call her on the phone tonight, her momma's gonna know ya'll were at her house. And she's gonna wanna know what's going on with all of ya'll, and yuh momma's, and all uh dat. Den me and Kath won't have time to talk."

"BarryQ's okay wit dat, Ranny. He won't mind if you and Kath don't have much time to talk."

The boys laughed at Rubby's comment. BarryQ. took it in stride.

They leaned against their bicycles, their constant companions and chief modes of transportation. Simeon looked around at his fellow seventh-graders. They shared a bond . They did baseball, cub scouts, band, altar boys, bike riding, king-cake parties, neighborhood ventures, and more. The banter continued for thirty more minutes. But Simeon disengaged. The clouds above the Poor Sister's compound were striking. And they provoked his already melancholy mood. The shaded Old Oak Tree that they stood under contributed as well.

He was at the zenith of innocence and free-flight. He was a good church altar boy with chums on bikes all over the neighborhood. He was ensconced as the fifth of twelve of the Mangino offspring, the sixth of eight of the Bonamo's, and he loved and was loved by all of them, their very own Simmie. He did well in school and rarely got in trouble. He enjoyed ball. He would talk to his girlfriend every night after supper. His baby sister was always near to affirm him. And he never wanted for a willing soul to goof around with around the home. Pokey was there.

Often, the boys on their bikes rode beneath the Old Oak. He never told anyone about his attraction there. Its leaves weren't as flush and full as most of the other oaks that dotted the neighborhood and Audubon Park. But the amount of Spanish moss that grew on the Old Tree made it stand out. For many weeks of the year, it was filled with the laissez-faire southern fungus. And compared to most of the other oaks, the tree appeared to be quite old.

But the allure that Simeon felt was beyond its physical appearance. There was something else about it that drew him. And he couldn't explain what it was.

Often, when headed to the baseball fields in Audubon, or the zoo, or to Sherry's house, he rode beneath its branches. More than once, for unknown reasons, he circled around to ride under it again. When with the guys, he'd quietly take note of it.

For some reason, he had the hard-to-define sensation that the Old Oak Tree held out something for him, something strange, yet familiar. It seemed like something far away, yet always near.

Thirty Four

It was a crisp, cold, morning in 1968. Simeon boarded the Nashville Avenue bus for school. It was the second leg of public transportation that would take him deeper into the city for school. Two more remained.

"Crisp! Ah haven't seen you on this for awhile."

"Simm Mangino! How ya doing, mah old St. Francis pal?"

"Man, since our freshman year, you, me, BarryQ., and Derbs don't ride the bus and hang out as much as we use to."

"Ah know. It seems like we're beginning to go our separate ways."

"And this second year at Saint Ignatius is kicking mah butt, too, Crisp. Ah had to study hawd last year. But this year's hawduh."

"Ah heard you had a girlfriend in the neighborhood, Simm."

"Had,... she dumped me for somebody else."

"Ouch. So it's Sawgeant Peppuh's Lonely Hawt's Club Band?"

"Somethin like dat, Crisp. Let's talk about something else."

"Excuse the metaphor. Ah just heard dat song on the radio. You're hurting, man. Ah've never seen you this way before."

Simeon sat quiet. His eyes were straight ahead. But his mind wasn't.

"What about dat French girl from St. Henry's dat you liked last year? What happened to her?"

"Ah don't know, Crisp. We were getting along good and she was a nice girl, a good girl. But Ah let somebody talk me into dumping her. Ah think Ah hurt her. Ah feel bad about it."

Silence filled the air for a long moment. The two friends heard the hum of the bus engine as it ebbed and flowed. They rode beneath the canopy of oaks that populated both sides of the narrow two way street.

"Well think of it dis way, Simm. You'll do better in the girlfriend department next year, our junior year. Ah got a feeling."

He appreciated his friend of many shared experiences. His desire to encourage him was noted and its mark was recorded in a good place. But as for the remark itself, he let it glide by to the rear of the bus and fall there. He dared not tell Crisp, his close pal since second grade, nor Lan, Trae, nor anyone else what he had up his sleeve. An unsettling found a home inside. Some of that had to do with not wanting to be at Saint Ignatius. But it was more than that.

They rolled inexorably toward their high school in the center of town. His eyes settled on the back of the bus driver. The carrier casually turned his face to the right and to the left as he drove. He appeared content and at peace with his career choice. He would do his job, picking up people and dropping them off. He'd drive the same route all day long. Then he'd get up again the next day, and do it all over again. He didn't have the courage to admit it. But in the moment, he envied the man.

The two grade school friends, boys on their bikes back then, walked the remaining few blocks to high school. Their loads of heavy books pulled down on them from the heavy hand bags, which they switched between hands. They were half way to their destination when the sounds of a mockingbird burst forth from among the oaks along Carrolton Avenue. They joined in along with the vibrant city sounds and were not easily heard. The relentless bird parroted on as if the sounds of motors, horns, and purring engines were no match for its many voices. It mocked every kind of bird, insect, and rodent that a human mind might possibly imagine. Simeon tuned in to its sounds, though the competition in the airwaves was intense.

He was fascinated at the capacity of the tiny brain of the feisty two-legged critter. Its marvelous capacity stirred him to wonder. But, his conscience bore shame's burden. And its sensitivity moved him to wonder. Did the amazing species mark one single human in all of history to add to its list of creatures to mock?

Time Passage

Launch

"Friends are thieves of time."
~ Francis Bacon

Thirty Five

The cold air rushed in as he slowly made his way into the side door entrance. It was the morning of January 4th, 1974.

"Ahm home, daaddy."

The words came out muffled and slow, and sheepishly.

"What time is it, Simm? We gotta leave by a little after six, you know. You're leaving for duh Navy today, remember?"

"Ah knoow. Ah.. think its... fahve.. thiirrty. Waake me up. Ah'll be laying on….on the sofa."

He barely stumbled to the sofa in the next room. He fell on the cushions fully clothed and was out in seconds.

"What time is it, Julian? Is he just getting in? He's not gonna have any sleep for his new start, is he?"

Maria was groggy, but aware.

"He'll be okay. It was his last night wit his cousins and his friends. Ah'll get him up in half an hour. Let's hope for duh best."

Forty minutes later, Simeon and his daddy walked out of the house toward the car. A lingering darkness was fleeing the morning sky. The passing cars on State Street still had their lights on. Across the street an early mockingbird sat perched on the electric wire that ran to the nun's convent across the street. It sat perched just outside Sister Eugenia's second floor window, easily seen from Simeon and Pokey's bedroom window across the street. For a moment, he recalled the tough Sister of The Order of Charity.

She believed in him. She pushed him, correcting him often. She talked to his momma about him and his potential. She pushed others as well. She often told her students that they could do well, but that they must work for it. But he only worked for what came easy for him. He did well up to a point. When she urged him beyond that, he resisted. For a moment, he hoped that she didn't happen to peer out her window and see him. Maybe she knew that he had become a failure and had to leave home to survive and find a new life. Shame surged through him in his hungover condition.

His thoughts were interrupted by the litany of sounds coming from the mockingbird outside her window. Even though he only had thirty minutes of sleep in a hungover state, his ears were nevertheless attuned to its familiar sounds. His gait was slow and he sidestepped behind his daddy as he walked to the car.

"No,…dat's not… Sistuh E-u-g-e-n-i-a. Dat's… you. You've been m-o-c-k-i-ng me for years now,… little crittuh. You,… still think Ah can't m-a-k-e it, don't cha? Go head, chirp and w-a-r-b-l-e at me… all you want. You'll see,… you'll see…. There's something out there, and Ahm… gonnnna find it. Just watch."

"Ahm gonnnna… find it."

Thirty Six

The west coast climate has a noticeably different feel than that of
southern Lousisiana. The young New Orleanian exile was in a strange
environment for the first time in his life. And the air breathed a tidy less
stressful to him.

Navy boot camp offered the challenge of discipline, training, and order
that his renegade spirit sorely needed. And it might have been a
challenge. But it was no match for the intensity of his resolve to start a
new life. He moved through the experience at the San Diego location,
squeezing it for all that his young heart was able to glean. He reasoned
that he had much to learn after his provincial life in New Orleans. He
realized how adaptive he could be as the three month adventure wore on.
He made friends easily and sailed through the time in basic training with
hardly a bump in the road. When they entered the final week, he and the
boys in Company 007 waited for orders to their next duty stations with
eager anticipation.

"One day you should come visit me in 'Frisco, Simm. I'll show you
where I grew up. And I'll come visit you when you go back home to
New Orleens."

The two young sailors continued shining their shoes. The thought of
his buddy, Doog Leaher, visiting him in New Orleans felt strange. He
had just left home and intentionally focused on his attempt to start a new
life. He hadn't allowed himself to consider if he would ever live in his
hometown again. And when homesick thoughts and feelings came, he
quickly moved away by immersing himself in his new place.

"You're going back to New Orleans again, one day, aren't you,
Mangino?"

"You listening to me and Doog, Switchblade? Why you wanna know?
Maybe Ah'll go to New Yawk, and live in the Bronx witchoo."

"No way, baby. I'm not going back there."

The words etched in his mind. He heard them replay there….

"I'm not going back there."

He allowed himself to consider how it felt to say the words to himself. He replayed them in his mind one more time…..

"Ahm not goin back there."

And it felt good.

"Hey, guys, we're getting our orders today. And in a week, we'll be outta this dump. Just think we could go almost anyplace in the world. You excited, Simm?"

"Yeah, Doog, Ah am."

"Why do you keep looking up to the sky, Simm?"

"Huh? What cha aksing me, Doog?"

"I asked you why do you keep looking up to the sky?"

"Ah do? Ah am? Ah guess Ah do. Ah don't know, man. Ah just do sometimes."

It was the last week of boot camp. The guys were being handed large sealed envelopes with orders to their first duty stations in the active Navy. Simeon felt anxious, and excited.

"Mangino! Here ya go, man. Good luck, sailor."

The company yeoman handed the envelope to Simeon. Their hearty handshake was accompanied by mutually respectful eye contact. It was a respect shared by the group of young tetsoterone laced bloomers from all over the country, strangers twelve weeks previous. It was the kind that is borne out of a bond that develops when young men seeking a future are caged together under a single, absolute authority.

In their context, it was forged as they embraced a challenge in one accord and endured it together. The challenge was crafted by a system, which by its very existence as a rules-based, top-down structure, sought to shape them into something called 'men'. And through its many impostions, it inevitably did its work. And as an additional benefit, it morphed them into a fraternity of that human genre.

"Thanks, Yeo, old pal. Good luck to you wherever you go."

When he walked away with his sealed orders, he felt a touch of affection for the yeoman, a fellow Louisianian. And it hammered home the fact that the first chapter in his life away from home was coming to a close. He was glad to leave. But he realized he'd grown close to a few of the guys, especially Doog. And the imprint of the affection began to expand to include Switchblade, Bronx, Chief, Aaron, and a whole bunch of others, until the entire 007 Company itself had tattooed a permanent mark on his heart.

He sat next to his best friend in camp. Doog had just finished reading his orders.

"It's California for me, buddy. Rate training at the base. Then I'll be on a tin can[55] out of San Diego. At least I'll be close to home. Maybe you'll get San Diego too and we can be together. Maybe we'll get the same ship. Come on, open it up."

"Wait, before you tear it open, man, I want to say something. I'm glad we were put in the same company, Simm. Let's write when we can. Thanks for being my friend here. You and me have a lot in common, we bleed the same. Of all the guys in here, I needed you, brother. I'll never forget you."

"Ahm gonna miss you, Doog. Ah really am. We did dis together. You've been like mah friends back home are to me, like a brother. And you're right. We do bleed the same kind of blood. You sought me out, Doog. Remember? Thanks for doing that. We might never see each other again. Ah'll never forget you either, buddy."

Simeon tore open the envelope. A burst of anticipation rushed through him as he did. He read the orders, skimming over the required reporting date to the location.

> "… by midnight of the reporting date, you will be required to report to duty at the Air Intelligence Photo Recon School at Leary Air Force Base, Denver, Colorado. Permanent duty station assigned upon completion of Air Intelligence Training. Twelve week assignment."

"Looks like its Rocky Mountain time for you, Simm."

"Wow. Denver, Colorado. Ah can't imagine what mountains look like, Doog. Ah've never seen one."

"You really were a home boy down there in New Orleens, weren't ya?"

"Ah really was, Doog."

---

[55] Navy slang term for a destroyer, a ship accompanying an aircraft carrier battle group to provide defense.

The thrill of adventure and new things carried him through the final few days. Two weeks leave back to his beloved hometown followed. Bonds were refreshed there. Memories were re-kindled. Then he was off to the mountains for more training from Uncle Sam.   And he had the distinct feeling that there was something else inside of the large envelope that contained his orders, something he didn't see when he opened it.

Thirty Seven

The mountains that looked down on the Mile High City commanded the westward view. To the locals familiar with their kind, they were all in a day's routine. Simeon turned to gaze at them throughout the day, a wildeyed wonderer taking in a new kind of beauty that he was having a hard time learning to take for granted.

It was May, 1974. Two young sailors walked to class at Leary Air Force Base. They were near the end of their training for air intelligence photo reconnaissance. Most of them would be sent to an aircraft carrier.

"New Orleens. You know, Simm, all these weeks we've been here I've never asked you. Does everybody there talk like you?"

"Yep. And what's wrong wit duh way Ah talk?"

"Well let's see..., when you call Georgia, who lives down the hall, you say 'Jaw-ja.' When you say Hardie's name, you pronounce it 'Hawdy.' It's not a 'car' to you. It's a 'caw'. Am I right, Simm?"

"Huh."

"That's all you have to say? *Huh*?"

"It's not mah fault dat ya'll talk funny. So listen, Champ. Dat new movie's out. You know, dat freaky one about the devil."

"Oh yeah, I heard about it. I'm not going to see that, Simm."

"Come on, Champ. Let's go see it. Ahm not usually into horror movies but dis ain't like a real horror movie. You're into Gawd and stuff. You can see it and tell me if it fits what you read about."

"No way, man. I'm not interested."

"Champ, you gotta go wit me. Ah don't want to go wit dee other guys. Ah need you tuh help me think."

"Think about what?"

"About life, what happens when we die, and all uh dat."

"Have you been thinking about that, Simm?"

"For a long tahm."

Several hours later, the two sailors walked out of the movie theatre, somber and more than a little jittery.

"I shouldn't have come, Simm."

Simeon was silent, and shaken. The experience catapulted him back into the recesses where he had been deeply touched by expressions of darkness, death, and evil. He sensed that he had an encounter with darkness through the screen images.

Simeon broke the silence.

"What was dat book Ah saw on your desk, Champ?

"That's a book about the prophecies and the return of Jesus to the earth."

"Seriously?"

"Yeah. Why?"

"Champ, Ah've always believed the world would end in mah lifetime. Ah don't know why, ever since Ah was a kid."

"Really?"

"Yeah. Nobody likes talking about it. But it's the strangest thing."

"So is this why you've been thinking about God, Simm?"

"Yes, and no. Ah mean Ah think about Him related to other things also. Not just about the future of the world."

"I see. So would you say that you're interested in discovering more about God?"

"Maybe so. Ah was raised religious. And Ah would have considered mahself a fairly good person until Ah met you. You're a different kind of christian than anyone Ah've ever known."

"Simm. Don't put me on a pedestal, man. I'm struggling to hang onto my faith now. It's been tough for me since I joined the Navy."

"Okay. But you're different from me and the rest of the guys. And from anyone Ah've ever met. There's something about you. And it's good."

Champ didn't respond.

"Hey Champ, can Ah borrow dat book, duh one about duh prophecies?"

"Better yet, you can have it, Simm. I'm finished reading it. It's yours."

Over the next several days, he devoured the book. The words sprang from the pages like new vistas to a hungry explorer. Three days passed. After class on the fourth day, he hurried back to his barracks room. He eagerly picked up the book and began reading the last few chapters.

It was springtime in the mile high city. It had been a cold and snowy spring. Finally, the snow was beginning to melt. Each day, slowly, steadily, surely the white substance was thawing. The cycle of creation was affecting the grand and elegant annual seasonal change. And the majestic peaks overlooking the city were beginning to reveal more of their rocky terrain. With each day's passing, more and more of the naked mountains could be seen.

The slow thaw of the snow revealed the budding of new life in the plants, trees, and flowers around the military base and the city. The cold, dreary, white landscape began to give way to the bright colors of spring. It was a fascinating sight for the young man from New Orleans. He had never experienced a full and decisive expression of the changes between any of the four seasons. He was beginning to experience many new things for the first time. Some were the internal kind, in the space where the soul grapples with eternity.

He absorbed the last few chapters before turning the page to begin the last one. He was lying on his back in his rack[56] and began to feel as if he was walking into familiar spaces. The subject matter resurrected the same kinds of deep sensations that unpredictably swept over him in the past.

The edges of the barracks rooftops bid adieu to the drops of melting snow as they dripped irregularly to the ground. He could hear the sound of the drips from the melting snow just outside. Evidences of the dreary, cold, dead winter were vanishing. The vibrant life and beauty of spring was slowly taking its place.

He was moved as he read the last several chapters. So much of what he had wondered about the future was addressed by the author. He wondered whether or not the author had interpreted every detail correctly regarding the prophecies of the future of the world. But he was struck by how much the prophets had to say about the subject and how accurate they were throughout history.

He dove into the final chapter like a famished man who came on a table of freshly boiled crawfish. As the author began to summarize his material, he paused to get personal with his readers.

---

[56] Navy term for 'bed', or 'bunk'.

Simeon felt like he had been riding over a long mental and emotional trail as he went through the book. Some of what he had been reading was hard to understand. But everything rang true, especially the heart, thrust, and direction of it all. As he maneuvered the tight twists and turns along the trail, and its hills and valleys, he became aware that he was beginning up a slope to a Summit. At the head of the Summit was a promised land, a land flowing with milk and honey. A well-spring of living water was there. A tree of life was there as well, and a kingdom, with a throne. And Someone sat on it.

As he read, he was aware. And he longed for The Summit.

The slope to the Summit grew steeper with each step. But he glided up the incline, propelled forward by Desire's resolve, the catalyst for Ambition. Nothing else mattered in the moment. He was latched on to the Summit like a stolen-away lover on his long-lost beloved. With each step, he knew with increasing conviction that this was the Summit his lost soul had longed for.

And there was a Light. It was both absolutely unapproachable and yet entirely approachable. And for the first time in his life, he began to feel as if it were within reach. As he moved up the Summit, his heart began to beat faster. Something was happening. He didn't know what it was, and yet he did. He didn't know how he made it from his beloved neighborhood and family to his rack, inside his barracks, on the air base. But somehow he knew.

He recalled that his life was spared on three different occasions within the past year. He shuddered momentarily at the thought that he might have missed what he was now approaching were it not for ....

Continuing to read, the author asked him, his starving reader, a question. It was a question that he had never been asked before. And if he would have been asked it, he would never before have considered it. But the season was changing that very moment, outside and inside. He had never experienced the full change from the deep, dreary, death of winter to the potential, bright life of spring. As he embraced the question, it had the effect of preparing the flower of his heart. His pulse began to pick up in intensity and speed. He was about to approach the Summit. The bright Light was intensifying.

Aware of the brevity of the moment he summoned his Motives. They mustered before him, battered and bloodied, completely devoid of clothing. They stood naked and ashamed with each of their large left earlobes a varied shade of dim to bright blue light. He ordered them to be made completely available before The Light. He was sickened at their condition.

As tears formed in his eyes, he next called for his Ambitions. They instantly appeared and fell into formation, bloodied and beaten just as badly, naked and ashamed as well, now on deck. He was shocked when he saw that every one of them displayed large left ear lobes that were various shades of dim to bright blue light as well. Never had his Motives and Ambitions been so readily accessible and exposed. He was sickened by their condition as well.

A lump formed in his throat.

Finally, he ventured to call forth his now-awakening Will. It, too, appeared naked and dripping with utter shame. On one arm was tatooed the word "Motives", on the other "Ambitions". It stood with its head down in utter humility, naked and exposed for all of its selfishness. It looked up to Simeon's soul and turned to run. But his soul grabbed it fast and turned him around to face The Light.

"Stand!" it demanded.

His Motives, Ambitions, and Will stood side by side. The blinding Light from the top of the hill shone down and exposed their wretched conditions. The three pathetic rationales of his soul stood side by side, with their heads down, beaten and broken, fragmented to a fault, naked and ashamed. Standing in the good and pure Light, they were fully exposed to his soul and in his mind. His spirit sank to an all time low in deep and terrifying shame as he realized his total and utter depravity.

How selfish he was, in every aspect of his person. How guilty before the good and pure Light at the top of the Summit. He had no excuses, no one to blame. Every choice fell on him.

The author's question lingered. His pulse picked up even more. It was reacting to the adrenaline being pumped into his system by the sudden realization that he was not alone in the room. There was a Presence.

It wasn't a physical presence. But SomeOne was there, suddenly, mysteriously, actually. He sensed it through,….. was it through his *spirit*? It was a familiar Presence, a vaguely familiar one. But at what other time in his life had he known it? In the flash of a moment, he realized that everything in his life to that very moment led to where he was, and what was happening.

Unanswered spiritual questions about life began to muster. Questions about meaning got in line behind them. The rallying cry for a call to a purpose heretofore unknown took command of the scene. And Simeon was aware that the Light at The Summit would ultimately, and finally, lead to a convergence of it all. Someone was there to welcome him, to invite him, to embrace him, to forgive him – if he wanted in. That Someone was there to receive him with all of his questions and wondering. He would be the Answer to it all and to embrace him into The New Dynamic, the Dynamic of Life and Light.

He once was a brief outside observer to The New Dynamic and the One Who is the Light at the Summit. He suddenly realized that he had an encounter with Him in the first grade, when Sister read from Genesis. He recalled the bird silhouetted against the blue sky and the realization of The Good, Kind, and Just Someone, The Light at the Summit. And he recalled that he had many, many, urges to look into the sky ever since he was a child. And there was some kind of a draw at his beloved Old Oak Tree on Constance Street. In the moment, he realized that the revered experiences and places were Voice to his searching soul. Afflatus[57] to a child's heart that was, is, and will be seeking a city, a city whose name is God.

He exhausted the author's question. Then Simeon read his explanation of the simple, humble, willing response that The One atop The Summit invited the reader to make. It was no more and no less than a response to an invitation from The One Who cares, Who loves, The Light Himself at the top of The Summit. He was the Just One, Ever-Present, All-Knowing, Unchanging, Eternal, All-Powerful.

And as the Perfect One in Power and Authority, he came perfectly balanced in the extremes of Truth and Love. In that perfect balance, Simeon was aware through the author's words that He offered him mercy

---

[57] Ibid: A divinely inspired thought or word.

and relationship through the blood of The One Who died on a cross of wood for his sin.

And The One present in the room spoke.

He spoke to Simeon through the writer's words. But the writer's words were not his own. They were borrowed. They were borrowed from the words of Jesus, Who was born of a virgin, from Saul of Tarsus, and from John, son of Zebedee. They were Afflatus breathed into the collection of Writings that followers of the One at The Summit, The Light, are guided by. They were from The Sacred Writings of the ancient Hebrews and the followers of The One crucified.

There was warmth in His words. Tenderness, compassion, and mercy were being extended through them. Now at The Summit, Simeon was moved to remove the sandals from the feet of his soul. He was stepping up onto sacred ground.

But he didn't feel afraid. Though totally exposed and naked, ashamed for his sin and selfishness, he knew that he was welcome by Goodness Himself. He was overwhelmed by the warm tenderness, compassion, and mercy that proceeded from Him. At once, he was entirely humbled and convicted by the moral purity of His Essence. Yet, he was fully embraced and received, exceedingly welcome. The paradox was exhilarating.

How could he know that he was so fully wrong about so many things, and so selfish in so many ways? How could he feel so deeply convicted at his guilt for such, and know utter shame inside? While at the same moment know a joy that touched the soul and affirmed that he was within the paradox of joy's fullest experience?

His three escapes from sure death in the foolish years of his adolescence were similar experiences. But this was different. The paradox that cradled his traverse to The Summit birthed joy's fullest expression. It was also brought an indescribable peace, one that no kind of dopamine-ignited experience he had ever known, or could ever know, could bring. Overtaken by the joy and its companion, peace, he laid the sandals of his soul aside. He fell to his heart's knees.

His eyes were locked onto the words in Champ's book. Good news came to him through them. It was good news like never before known, or even anticipated, or imagined. At no moment while he read the chapter did he see any one in the room with him. But The Presence was real.

Through his mind's eye, he sought to look for an image[58] of The One Who was present in Spirit. He found one. It was a millisecond image within a vapor that was hardly there before vanishing. He was aware that He had nail-scarred hands and feet. And he was aware that He saw right through him. He understood everything Simeon had ever done, thought, felt, or imagined. He knew him through and through. And still He loved him. He cared. He never gave up on him. His open invitation to him was always there.

Behind Him was a throne. And The One Who sat on it was known as Father to those who came to Him through the One who was crucified for the sin of all.

The tears that had been misting up began to fully form. His heart rate was elevated at the anticipation of something profound and almost unexplainable. He was aware that the the crucified and risen One represented The Father. And that He was the exact extension and representation of Him.

Desire and Humility joined hands with his willingness to turn, to Repent, as it were. Healthy Spiritual DNA[59] had been alive inside of him. He was on the verge of bursting. He wanted to say something. He didn't know what to say, but it was bubbling up like boiling lava that had been crawling to the top of the crater for a long time. He was touched beyond what he could ever imagine. And the tears, the racing heart, and his bursting Desire were the evidences of it.

Outside, the light of the sun completed its long, faithful, steady work on the roof above him. It was totally dry. The snow was finally gone as the last drop from its long, slow melt fell from the roof's edge.

In a desperate gasp of overwhelming Desire, Simeon Joseph Mangino opened his mouth and began to speak to no physical presence in the room.

"Jesus, You're the One I've been running from for so long. I...."

------

[58] "Image": "A representation of the form of a person or object, such as a painting or photograph." American Heritage Dictionary, Fifth Edition.

[59] Please continue to the end.

Thirty Eight

Weeks after his Summit encounter in the Mile High City, Simeon received orders to report to the USS John F. Kennedy, stationed out of Norfolk, Virginia. The pauper twenty-one year old owned one pair of shoes, a few changes of clothes that he left with his momma and daddy, and some underclothes that he left there as well. He had no money anywhere, no stereo, no tools, no car, no baseball glove or fishing pole, and no more bike. Life on a giant steel war machine would be a tad less traumatic of an adjustment for someone who had nothing material in this world. But it was an adjustment of environment. His desire to find his place in the physical world was now bound with his new life in the Light, however. And he was primed to enthusiastically embrace his new world. It was a world where life happened aboard a giant floating sea vessel with airplanes taking off and landing on it, and lots of bombs and missles. The floating small town was home to 5,500 sailors.

11:34 Hours, October 3, 1974 / Mission Planning, Intelligence Center, USS John F. Kennedy

"I don't give a rat's rear end about what you're into! You better watch who you talk to about all of that spiritual stuff. Some people don't care about God. And I'm one of them."

"It's okay, Chief. Most of the guys don't mind."

"Well I do. And some of them do too. Some of them are complaining about you. You get here and now all this talk about all of that stuff. We didn't have that before you got here. Why do you have to bring your religion here to the ship, Mangino?"

"I don't, Chief. I'm not talking religion. I'm talking to the guys about a Person. He rose from the dead after dying on a cross for us."

"Son of a B, Mangino! There you go again! Why can't you just keep all that stuff to yourself? You're realling ticking me off, you hear me, sailor?"

"Chief, God loves you."

Over the next few minutes, the Chief continued to lay into the young sailor from New Orleans. Several of the men in the Intel Center of the Ops Department stood outside the closed door to the Mission Planning room. Some of them cringed and chuckled as they listened to the Chief's tirade through the closed door.

Some didn't.

"Mangino's gettin his, eh Rams?"

"Man, Rick. Chief's got a temper allright. But I never heard him go off like that."

"I hope the Chief lightens up on him. Everybody gets along with Simm. Come on, Chief, ease up."

"What are you talking about, Fitz? Mangino's got to you already? I saw you and him reading together the other day."

"That's right, Randy. I'm with him now."

"You mean you're a holier-than-thou too now, Fitz?"

"I wouldn't put it that way, Beck. Simm wouldn't either."

"But you're one of them now?"

"I am, Rams."

"You hear that, Okie? Mangino got to Fitz."

"What's wrong with that? The rest of us might not want what he has. But we all get along with Simm. He talks about it. But he only pursues it when we let him. Otherwise he's mostly personable about it."

"You're right, Okie. But he should be careful. He has ticked a few guys off. Witness what's going on in the other room."

"Yep, you got it, Randy. Even if you just talk about it there's the possibility somebody's not gonna like it. It doesn't really bother me, though. After I talk with him it does get me to thinking sometimes. But I'm not ready for that right now."

"Me neither, Okie, at least I don't think I am, …I guess. Let's head over to the chow hall. When the Chief finishes laying into Mangino, we have a pilot's briefing in there. Who's hungry?"

"Let's do it, Rams."

"Before you go, put it on record that I'm with Simm. I've been with him since he got here."

"You're a holier-than-though too, Kimbrell?"

"I'm not that, Rams. But I've been a follower since high school. And so has Traylor."

"You too, Traylor?"

"That's right, Okie, since high school."

"Mangino, Traylor, Kimbrell, now Fitz too? We're gonna start calling you guys 'The God Squad'".

"That's fine with us, guys. Just know that we care for you when you think of us that way."

"Whatever you say, Fitz."

Rams chose words that didn't reveal the true state of his heart. Something was happening to him.

12:58 Hours, October 3, 1974 / Hangar Bay, USS John F. Kennedy

The two young sailors sat on the wing of an A-6 bomber jet. Being quite new to military hardware, Simeon kept looking it over, wondering about the machine.

"Man, Tal. The Chief laid the wood on me this morning when I showed up for muster."

"Is he still not liking you?"

"I thought he was gonna take my head off. He got right in my face. I could smell the cigarette smoke from his mouth and see the veins in his neck. I thought my ears were gonna explode. He was yelling so loud. He took the phrase 'cusses like a sailor' to a new level."

He looked up to the cockpit where the pilot and co-pilots operate the aircraft.

"How are you handling the whole ordeal?"

"Six months ago, I'd have been right back at him. But I'm okay. I'm in The Light now."

"Some of the guys in my department get on me sometimes too. What do ya say, let's pray for your Chief, for my Chief, and for all of the men in our departments, Simm. You good with that?"

"Good idea, Tal. Do you know anything about this bird that we're sittin on?"

"Not really. You're always interested in the war-making things around here, aren't ya? Now, let's talk to Him."

14:19 Hours, October 4, 1974 / Chow hall, USS John F. Kennedy

Simeon and Tal sat at a table in the chow hall. They were reading the Sacred Writings. Two additional sailors walked up to them.

"Hey Simm. We saw you and Tal praying in the hangar bay[60] yesterday."

"How did ya'll know we were praying, Stehl?"

"Heads bowed? Eyes closed? Any other way we should interpret that, Tal?"

"Yeah. We thought about going over and joining in. But we were in a hurry. Why didn't you go to the chapel where it's quiet?"

"We didn't think about that, Lin."

"What were you doing on the flight deck the other day, Simm? After flight ops were over and the deck was cleared?"

"Yeah, we saw you looking up at the clouds? We were cutting across the flight deck near the island[61]. We saw you back by the fantail.[62]"

"So my brothers are spying on me now?"

"How long were you sitting there, staring at the sky?"

"If you must know, I've always been drawn to the clouds, Stehl."

"Are you wanting to be pilot, working with the pilots on the ship?"

"No Lin, I like my job just fine."

"Simm's just a deep-thinking kinda guy, that's all."

"Nothing wrong with that, Tal."

"We're with you all the way, Simm. And as far as we're concerned the sky's the limit for you."

"Was that a pun, Stehl?"

"Not intended, Tal. It just rolled off."

"We're behind you, Simm. You can gaze up at the clouds all you want. We're brothers on this ship. Right guys?"

"Right, Lin."

---

[60] The large, open belly of an aircraft carrier below the flight deck where aircraft are stored and maintained

[61] The 'island' is the command center for flight operations on an aircraft carrier. It is a narrow structure on the right of the vessel that allows wide clearance for takeoff s and landing of aircraft.

[62] The 'fantail' is the farthest rear space of a ship.

"You said it, Lin."

On his part Simeon was silent. His was eternally thankful that Providence had seen fit to place him on the JFK with his three friends from different parts of the country. They were genuine brothers to him in a different kind of a brotherhood than he had ever known before.

17:05 Hours, October 7, 1974 / Library, USS John F. Kennedy

"So your life changed after you left home to join the Navy too, right Tal?"

"Yep. I needed to get away from home. And then I came to understand what He did on the cross for me."

"Our stories are amazingly similar. I'm glad that you've been into following Him for a year now. You've settled into this life some. I need to be around you and the other guys."

"We all need each other, Simm. What's new with you today?"

"I'm still pinching myself, realizing what I'm coming out of and the possibilities that lie ahead, because of Him. There was a lot about my life back home that was meaningful and real. That I miss. But there was so much uncertainty and darkness. That I don't miss."

"What are you certain about now, my New Orleans friend?"

"I'm certain that I'm loved and forgiven. That I have hope and a promise for life with Him after death. And that I'll see Him one day soon."

"Soon? You're still sticking with that? You're saying He's coming soon?"

Tal dipped his chin and leaned forward across the table. He looked hard at Simeon. He had an unusual look of challenge about him, a departure from his usual casual and easy countenance. Simeon hadn't experienced his mentor friend from Arizona this way before. He paused to collect himself before answering.

"Uh, yeah, Tal, soon. Very, very soon, I'd say."

Tal leaned back in his chair, folding his arms as he did. He broke into his patented closed-mouth grin and beamed at Simeon.

"Why the grin? A second ago I got a stern look."

"I'm glad to see that you stood up for what you think. You've spoken about that subject some and I know the opinion that you are of. Many will not agree with you, even many who are like us. I spoke that way to you to entice you to stand up for what you think. You're new in following Him and getting into the Scriptures. Maybe your opinion on His coming will change over time. Be sure you know where you are on the subject, even if it means you're not sure. Many of His followers aren't convinced that He's coming back soon."

Tal Inlan was only a year older than Simeon in his new life. But he was mature enough to realize that not all awareness was based solely on hard evidence.

11:17 Hours, October 9, 1974 / At sea in the Caribbean, outside along the catwalk below the ship's Island.

Every day, at least once a day, Simeon took a walk. He strolled out to the lone starboard[63] catwalk[64], the hanger bay near one of the open giant elevator doors, or to the flight deck if there were no flight ops[65]. The skys at sea were the most incredible scene for a boy on a bike, especially at night. The seas offered a starker contast to the heavens in comparison to a view of the heavens containing trees, wires, and rooftops.

The ship on which he stood was the lone violation of the natural order within sight of human eyes. Its convoy was beyond the horizon as part of a military exercise. Ten-foot waves slowly rose and fell along the surface as if to remind the steel flat-top that it was a guest atop its vast domain.

The sky met the white-capped wavetops across the horizon. To the eye it was hard to tell which overpowered the other, or whether the sea and sky had a line of separation. So as not to be left out of the picture, heaven itself seemed to make its own appeal as to the right of dominion.

It displayed its glory across the panorama, beginning with a contrast of giant, rolled,white cloud formations. Various shades of light, shiney

---

[63] Right side of a ship
[64] A railed walkway along either side of a ship
[65] "Flight Operations" – The multi-facted coordinated effort by various ships departments to launch aircraft for mission and to receive them safely back to home base.

grays to darker dull charcoals glazed the front of some of the whites, which dominated. Not to be outdone, crisp, bright, pristine, blue deep-space interrupted the clouds. It announced to the entire scene that it held dominion over all.

Midway up the horizon, a single, dark-shaded gray cloud hovered in front of a cluster of whites beyond. Bright, silvery highlites lit its edges all around. It blocked the direct sunlight that had penetrated the white clouds beyond it. But it could not contain the suns rays from dashing out from its edges all around. The brilliant beams of light went in all directions around the circular shape of the cloud. And Simeon was taken in by the sight of it, and its allusions to the One True Light, and Creator, Who governed it all.

"What are you doing out here?"

"Hey, Rams. I come out here often. Just for the view, and to have a few minutes alone. I could ask you the same thing. I've never seen you strolling about the ship."

"That's because I usually don't."

"What's got cha out on this lonely catwalk today? I rarely ever see anybody else along this lonely stretch of the ship, below the island."

"I don't know. Why do you come here, Mangino?"

"I like to escape to see the natural expressions of the beauty of His creation, Rams."

"So this relates to what you've been telling me while we're working in Mission Planning, right? How we can know Him personally?"

"Yep."

He waited for Rams.

"I guess it's finally getting to me."

"What is, Rams?"

"All your words, and our talks. And my brother has become like you now. He wrote me and told me about it. When we get back to port in a few weeks, as you know, I'm out. I've done my time. I'm going back home. I'm not sure what the future holds. But more than that, I'm thinking I'm not quite as whole a person as I thought I was. And I know that God is not part of my life."

"What then, Rams? Are you willing to turn to Him, ask for forgiveness, and begin anew?"

Rams looked out over the spectacular display of sky over water. Simeon had the distinct notion that something good was going to take place in the tall Texan. A short time later, it did.

Thirty Nine

The early blooms of spring were sprouting all over the campus of Madison University in the spring of 1979. Two story graystone buildings held classes on both sides of an open grass quad. Mature hardwoods generously shaded the sidewalks. And the pleasant temperature was enticement enough for some of the students to prod their professors to hold class outside on the shaded grass. Some gave in.

Simeon had three classes on Wednesdays. He wasn't the only student pleased when his ten a.m. class let out early. There was time to kill before lunch and an early afternoon class. He walked past the students seated on the grass who pretended to give attention to their lecturers. He was headed toward the student union. Amid the cacophony of creature sounds pervading the airwaves, his ears picked up a familiar pattern. A mockingbird was in mid-performance overhead as he walked beneath a large maple. He slowed his pace to welcome his new friend.

The Virginia variety of the avain artist was in fine form. Its varied, short bursts of beautiful sounds were soothing to his soul. As it performed above, he noticed the distinctly different variations of warbles, chirps, and chits. His previous interactions in life with the sounds of the creative creature found him in a fragmented state. Those times were behind him.

"You are highly valued today, my friend."

When he walked into the student union, he was glad to see his buddy planted among some of the girls. He was eager to share his latest idea. Dett was lying on his back in deep concentration with his notebook held above his face. He began without a greeting.

"I have an idea for a new kind of group discussion, Dett."

"Hey girls, Simm's here. Just in time. Good. Okay. Simm, explain to me the difference between the average cost and the average variable cost."

Lily-Grace, Bethany, and Delia giggled. Simeon appeared deflated. Bethany rescued him.

"He's trying to get into his economics notes. But he's struggling. Help him out, Simm."

"Yeah, you know econ, right Simm?"

Delia had a telling grin on her face when she spoke.

"Okay, Dett. I'll tell you. It's ….."

"Let me tell him, Simm. The difference between the average cost and the average variable cost is the word 'variable'. One has the word 'variable' and the other one doesn't."

Lily-Grace sat unperturbed with her pretty straight-face on. Everyone else stared blankly ahead, proccessing the words.

Bethany and Delia erupted with laughs. Dett looked at her, trying to understand if what she said was actually the answer he was looking for.

"Cute, Lily-Grace. Cute. I was going to make up something. But actually, that wasn't bad. Okay now, back to what I was saying, Dett."

"Allright, allright. This stuff is boring anyway. So what's up?"

But they were interrupted.

"Well, well. Look who's lounging around the student center when they should be in class."

"Hey guys and girl."

 Delia offered her large smile when she saw Randal, Reese, and Smitty walk up to the group.

"Well you guys aren't in class either, now are you, Reese?"

"If you must know, none of us have class until this afternoon, Bethany. We're walking with Smitty over to her dorm room to help her move some things around. She needs some muscle. She was gonna ask Dett and Simm. But like I said, she needed some muscle."

"Funny guy, that Randal, eh Simm?"

Dett looked up from his notes when he spoke.

Simeon didn't anwer. He sat quietly, taking it all in and relishing the banter. It resonated with that which he had with those he loved growing up. He enjoyed watching and listening to his brothers and sisters interact. They were family. Their friendships crossed gender freely and respected personal boundaries. They were deeply meaningful and would have a lasting impact on him.

For a moment, he paused and went back into a time zone. He recalled his days around St. Francis, Doraix's, Fumps, Mitts, and Nawby's. He missed everyone from back then. He thought and prayed for them often. But he was glad that he had gotten away. He thought of Doog, Champ, and the guys on the Kennedy. He was deeply grateful for them. He loved them as brothers. He stopped to be thankful for them as well, before picking up the interaction again.

"Do you have anything to add, Smitty? You're always so quiet."

"She's just a freshman, Lily-Grace. Maybe she shouldn't say anything."

"I didn't ask you, Reese. You don't want to get on my bad side."

"When you put it that way, I get it. I don't want that."

"What were we talking about before? Oh, Randal and Reese helping me move stuff. I only asked them because I saw them first. I'd have asked Dett and Simm if I had seen them first."

"I'm scarred for life, Smitty. I'll never be the same."

"That's not true, Smitty. Dett's got thick skin."

"I know, Bethany. I'm getting to know this bunch. You all are great to be around. And I appreciate you welcoming me into your lives. I'm a new creature since I met you. And I'm grateful to God."

All rose to stand close to her. The others who had been standing formed around Smitty and got close to her as well. Everyone got quiet and gave her their full and sober attention as she spoke.

"We're not the same without you, kiddo. You bring so much to us as well. And we thank Him for you too."

"Thanks, Simm."

Nods, hand slaps, and affectionate shoulder nudges erupted among them for a brief moment. All but the original bunch moved on to the dining hall.

He was eager to get back to his idea. Simeon turned again to Dett.

"What's all this you're talking about now, Simm?"

"Let's start an end-of-the-age discussion around the dorms, Dett. We can do some digging, get our stuff together, and talk to guys around the dorms. We can get some pizza and get it going."

"An end-times discussion……. Hmmmm.

The girls were listening. Simeon looked at the three of them.

"Any comments, ladies?"

"Your'e the prophecy guy, Simm."

"Behany's right, Simm. That's you."

"Okay, Delia. He turned to Lily-Grace.

 "Last but not least…."

"I think you should go for it."

"What do ya say then, Dett?"

"Hah. This wouldn't be the first time I went along with one of your ideas. This is so out there I'm thinking we couldn't possibly pull this off unless we had Someone's help, if you know what I mean."

"You better be careful. Our university administrators might hear about it and think we're some kind of sensationalist cult."

"Good thought, Bethany."

"And we'll pray for you guys."

"Thanks, Delia. We're gonna need that."

"The two of you together are a good team. Ya'll work together good. I can see it happening," added Lily-Grace.

"Those are good words from all of you. Have I ever told you how much I love and appreciate you?"

"Come to think about it, you haven't, Simm."

"He wasn't referring to you, Dett."

"Oh."

Everyone quickly agreed that Simeon had never spoken such to any of them, Dett included.

"Good, then. I didn't want ya'll to get the wrong impression."

Several weeks later, the two former sailors, now college students, were preparing to host their first discussion in the dormitory.

"We have a few minutes before going to the dorm room for the discussion. I want to tell you about a dream I had when I was a teenager."

"A dream. How can you remember a dream from so long ago?"

"I don't know, Dett. There was this…"

"I can't remember any of my dreams."

"Then how do you know you have them?"

"Because I wake up knowing I had one. Then I can't remember it."

"Okay. Well, try to remember them. Now, can I continue?"

"Allright, allright. So you had this dream…"

"And there was a TV newscaster telling the evening news. He was normal in every way except that he had gigantic earlobes".

"Gigantic earlobes? Hah. This sounds like a dream you might have."

"Yeah. The left earlobe was a very bright blue, such that it was almost too bright to look at. There was a room full of men and women watching and listening to the guy.   Their earlobes were extremely large as well. Many of them showed varied shades of darker or lighter blue-lit left earlobes. One or two were as bright as the newsman's. A few of the others had their right lobes lit in dimmer to brighter shades of red. Several of those were an extremely bright red light."

"Weird dream, Simm. Very weird."

"I know. And it stays weird. There were no sounds until just before the dream ended. The only sound I heard was a muffled, garbled sound that I couldn't make out. The last takeaway from the dream was that it might have been the sound of a word that began with something that sounded like, "*Mo*". And its sound was imprinted as an image on the front of a ball cap."

Dett was staring at nothing in particular the whole time. His eyes moved only slightly. He remained quiet and appeared absorbed.

"Dett. Did you hear anything I just said?"

"Okay, Simm. I'm seeing a newscaster in my mind's eye. He has large earlobes, the left of which is an extremely bright blue light. Most in his audience have similar large left lobes lit in shades of blue light. A few have large right-lobes lit in shades of red."

"I'm glad you were listening. I don't feel like saying it again."

"The newsman wasn't wearing the ballcap in your dream, which has an image on it that represents the "Mo" sound. But there is a ballcap somewhere in there with the image on it."

"Right again, Dett. You're impressing me now."

"What do you make of it Simm? And why are you telling me about it?"

"Because I want you to help me process it. It's been on my mind. I've thought a lot over the years about my motives, and motives in general. There's the "Mo" sound in my dream. I'm wondering if in my dream, I was imagining something of the interplay between motives and ambitions. Ambition is something I didn't have in my adolescence. And for a long time I've thought that it's good to be open to what my motives are, without being paranoid about it. When you hear this, and couple it with my dream, help me come up with something that crystallizes this."

Without hesitating Dett spoke up.

"Here you go, Simm. I got it. In your dream you heard something that sounded like 'Mo'. You've already linked 'Mo' with 'Motives'. 'Mo' is short for 'Motives'. And you've thought of the interplay between motives and ambitions. 'Ambi' is short for 'Ambition'. So, are you ready for this? I introduce to you now,... ***"MotAmbi"***, the representative term for the image of the fluid interplay between someone's Motives and his Ambitions."

He was impressed.

"That's *genius*. Dett, my faculties are presently benumbed. I'm stupefied. May I add to your eloquent and most excellent surmise of my long-pondered thoughts, Professor Wilmeyer? And the brilliant moniker that you lend to the images in my dream?"

"I insist, Doctor Mangino."

He cleared his throat and tilted his head with an air of superior intellect. He inahled a long, deep breath for good measure.

"My distinguished colleague, Doctor Wilmeyer, your inspiration does not expire. And I will humbly add my feeble thoughts to your brilliant idea, for I am but your humble servant in the matter. I see the name 'MotAmbi' on the hat that is on the head of the creature, whatever he looks like."

He paused to disembark from the perch he pretended to occupy. He leaned toward Dett, speaking more softly out of the side of his mouth.

"I'm ditching the newsman image from here on, Dett, okay?"

"Allright, allright. I sort of liked it. But it's your dream."

"Now where was I? Okay..."

He cleared his throat and resumed his post in the rarified air.

"And the hat is *attached* to his scalp, Wilmeyer, indicating the impossibility of separating Motive and Ambition from any human, in any situation or endeavor."

"And may I suggest, my fellow professor, that we leave MotAmbi's physical appearance to the imagination of the hearer. Other than to suggest that it has very large ears. And that at any given time either the right, or left (very large, I might add) earlobe will be lit in various *intensities* of red or blue light, indicating the intensity of the motive."

"Fascinating, Doctor Dett, I mean, Doctor Wilmeyer, truly fascinating. And might we suggest to our students that the large left lobe wear the blue color, and the large right one wear the right? For such it was in my dream? And that at varied times the opposite earlobe might alternately dim down as the other lights up?"

The good Doctor Wilmeyer's head shook affirmingly, his eyebrows were furrowed in the knowing position, and his eyes squinted. He stuck his thumb into his mouth with the other four fingers and palm folded into a fist. He took a few puffs on it momentarily before removing his thumb-pipe with an aire of authority. He cocked his head and blabbered on.

"Indeed, indeed, my good Doctor Mangino. For the color blue must indicate a cool – to – cold *Selfish* Motive or Ambition. And the color red must indicate a warm – to – hot *Unselfish* Motive or Ambition. And we shall we leave the Motive-Ambition interplay, which causes ones ears to light up red or blue and compel one to act accordingly, to the imagination of our students, my distinguished colleague. Is this not wise, Professor Doctor? Or should I say 'Doctor Professor'?"

"Either suffices, most goodly gentleman of the sciences. And here, here, my good man! Your brilliant exposition must never be questioned! I stand …"

"Me too, Simm. All this deep stuff about wears me out. You?"

"I'm with you, brother. Let's get this show started and get some of that pizza. But let's talk to Him first."

Several hours later, the group discussion ended. It was bitter cold. Heavy wind gusts roared across the campus. The hardened snow on the ground was foritifed by the steady cold wind that invaded the Shenendoah Valley for an overnight seige. The two friends walked back to their dorms. They were wrapped heavily with only their eyes and noses left to brave the elements without cover.

"How do you think it went tonight, Dett? Pretty lively, wouldn't you say?"

He had to shout to be heard.

"Yeah, I'd say so. They got into it."

"I was pleasantly surprised."

"What did you say, Simm?"

"I said I was pleasantly surprised."

"Oh. Heh-heh. I was surprised at how they got to talking among themselves so intently."

"Me too. I guess we can't know how people will react to this topic. We bounced all over the place tonight. And even though none of these guys have ever gotten into the subject they seemed willing to engage. One of them was pretty quiet. It looked like he was in deep thought, maybe even troubled by the dialogue."

"I know, man. You heard Sean say that the thought scared him. The world coming into some of the hard things that might take place before Jesus returns. It can be a scary thought, Simm."

An abrupt surge in the wind hit them with a force as they passed a building. They shivered in unison. Dett went on shouting.

"Its not gonna be a picnic when the Lord allows the testing."

"God's wrath is a touchy subject these days, Dett."

Another strike from the wind, a stronger one, this one from behind, caused a split second surge in their forward pace.

"Woa. That one was strong. It's a tough subject, Simm, I'll give ya that. And I'm still relatively young in my spiritual journey, especially in understanding the prophets.

As Dett opened the door wide, another blast of blistering wind smacked into them hard from behind. Simeon surged through the threshold of the open door while hardly attempting to. Dett had to hold the door open with all of his strength to keep it from slamming into the back of his friend as he was guided along.

The pretty straight-face that Lily-Grace often wore was the public front to a privately held good heart. The young man from along the river in New Orleans eventually began to notice that face more often. And the good heart that he had already begun to know began to look even better. And as time moved on, he had a hard time telling if her pretty straight face began to increase in prettiness or if his eye for pretty faces became more keen. And in their senior year, when he began seeing her pretty face in almost all things, he realized something was up. And as the sun sets and the dawn rises, a river flowing a thousand miles away through the crescent city continued to carry things unforseen from the far north. And two separate strings that ran side by side as friends at Madison U., came together as one, being tied in a wedding knot when they were married just before the last semester of their senior year. And they were so poor, graduation itself was a special wedding present to themselves.

Forty

Several years later, the young couple moved across state to employ themselves at Dominion University. In a short time, a special baby boy showed up, followed shortly after by another special baby boy. And as if one so untimely born, a special baby girl came along. And her specialness instantly multiplied when the delivery doctor informed her parents that she was a special needs little girl with down syndrome.

It was a bright spring afternoon. Simeon walked up to the student center, greeting some of the guys as he did. He paused to visit for a few minutes.

"Sit down, Simm. Pull up a chair and have a chew. Me and the boys are talking about casting lots[66]. We wanna git your opinion."

"Sorry, Big Country. I'm in a hurry. And you know I'm not into chewing tobacco."

"Heh, heh. Yeah, we know that. If we told ya we were talking about *The Return* Ah'd bet you'd slow that hurry down though. Wanna talk about that?"

"Good idea, Shoe. Simm's not gonna turn that down."

"Now ya'll are just baiting me. And yes, Chance. I'm gonna turn that down. You guys know that I rarely bring that topic up."

"We know, Simm. We're just teasing you. You're looking extra tease-able today."

"Did you just make up a new word, Bart?

"He did, Fish. He's good at that."

"Yep, mechanical engineers make up new words every day, Fords."

"How did we go from talking about casting lots to engineers making up new words?"

"You tell us, Lore. You're the thinker in the group."

"I thought I was, Newmon, no pun intended. Ya'll got me thinking so fast, though, I'm not sure what I'm thinking right now."

The guys gave him the look. Lore grinned.

---

[66] "Casting lots" - Ancient middle eastern expression for 'rolling the dice'; used in several of the writings in The Scriptures.

"I gotta run, fella's. I gotta go meet somebody. See ya'll soon."

Chance stood. He chuckled, while pointing in an exaggerated manner towards Simeon as he walked away.

"Okay. But you're gonna talk to us about the prophets soon. You can't hide forever. We know where you live. We're at your house all the time. We're gonna tell Lily-Grace and the kids. Come back here, Simm Mangino."

"Count me in on that. I second that admonition, Chance. He can't get away with that. We'll chase him down one day."

Doog Hiller yukked his way through the affirmation.

Big Country interrupted.

"Sit down, Chance and Doog. Have another chew. Let's commence talking about casting lots."

Walking away, Simeon was moved by the raw sincerity of the unlikely mix of college students. He was touched once again by their uniqueness and special qualities, and by the thought of his special relationship with each of them.

"What a privilege."

His words were spoken out loud to The One never not listening.

In the fall of 1989, the world was in the throngs of noticeable changes. It appeared to be in an advanced stage of being swept along by significant cultural shifts. Supposed free elections were held for the first time in the splintering Soviet Union. A labor union candidate touting freedom was elected to lead Poland. The Berlin Wall came down. An outspoken conservative President was talked into invading a tiny, helpless country in the hemisphere. The world witnessed its first liver transplant. And an eastern spiritual man won the World Peace Prize for his advocacy of peace ideas to foster the end of centuries of hostility between neighboring eastern nations. These and other events were headline topics in the west. They were held forth as paradigm-changing points in history. And the corporate voices of power brokers bull-horned the tide-altering news and information incessantly to weary ears until they got used to hearing it. The result was that rapid-fire time-altering news and information became an accepted part of their everyday background noise.

The dominant tide that molded the emerging world concensus had shifted. For years, it flowed from the imperial, colonial, west. It began to slowly pivot to flow from the east. In the new tide, new ideas about power, politics, economy, and spirituality began to settle as deposits into the minds of western nations. This especially held true in America, accelerating its departure from its original Judeo-Christian ethic of government and way of life. Nearing the end of the second millennium, it feebly tried to hang on to it, only to finally find its ethic less tasty. It preferred to sample, and acquire, the goods to satisfy its now more aroused and sophisticated palate. Simeon, along with many others, observed the shift in the tide. He sniffed the air as he served in his place and raised his family. He often paused to take a look around. His Old Oak was hundreds of miles away. But he was never far from the skies.

When he walked back to the spot where the boys previously sat, Bart was still there.

"Hey, Simm. Headed back?"

"Yep. You're sitting here alone. Did you chase your brothers away?"

"They each had class this afternoon. I'm done for the day. Do you have a minute now? I've been meaning to ask you, did you enjoy the book that Shoe gave you?"

He sat in one of the chairs next to Bart, in front of the student union.

"I did. It wasn't about the prophets, or the end-times. It was about political history in the twentieth century until now. It had hundreds of sourced references."

"Do you think it relates to the prophecies in any way?"

"I think it does, Bart."

"I told you about my dreams, right?"

"Yeah you did."

"I don't know what to make of them, Simm. But I can't dismiss the idea that they are more than a mental re-hash of what already dances in my mind. The way I understand it is that, some of our dreams are no doubt that very thing, subconscious interactions with deep thoughts we've already been turning over. But we know that men and women have had dreams in history that have been from God. In Daniel's book, he writes of his dreams about the future. And their literal fulfillment has taken place in historical empires. Some haven't been fulfilled yet. Joseph had dreams, and so did others."

"For sure, Simm. And in many closed countries today, people are having dreams where Jesus speaks to them."

"So you're sensing that the dreams you're having are more than the normal kinds of dreams we have."

"Yeah, I am. And I know it sounds weird. You know that I'm not into spiritual sensationalism or making magnificent, unsubstantiated claims about God. But there's something about this. And I can't explain it."

"And you think it might have to do with the end of the age, Bart?"

"Yeah, man."

Bart picked up where he left off. His words were slightly softer than his normal soft tone. He leaned forward with the deepest conviction the bright, humble, and sincere young man could muster. He dug into the eyes of his older mentor and planted his concerned look there.

"This is what it boils down to, Simm……… He's coming *s-o-o-n*. Did you hear me Simm? He's coming soon. I know it. I don't know how I know it. I just know it. I don't know why I'm telling you this. You've watched this a lot longer than I have. And you've been where I am for a long time. But I just gotta say it to somebody once in a while who I know won't shrug me off. So I'm saying it to you. So what do you have to say to all of that, Simm?"

"Hey Bart. Turn around and check out at that sky."

Forty One

It was the fall of 1994. Simeon, Lily-Grace and their three children were in their second year of a new chapter of life. They left Dominion U. for the rural confines of Stemson University in the rural deep-south.

It was a typical school day. The couple drove the country highway toward the shopping area.

"Man, honey, they talk funny here. I genuinely can't understand some of the words folks say."

"I hear what you're saying. And guess what, Bran and Jermaine are starting to have a slight hint of a twang in some of their words, Simeon."

"I noticed. They're in those formative years, I suppose. When we moved to the country to work at Stemson, we should have figured that would happen."

"Are the students coming for supper tonight?"

"Yeah. We should have quite a few. I'll be home early. I told Lon and Mirph I'd stop by. I'll see you a little later."

When he arrived, the two southerners were their usual easy going selves. After catching up on all things relevant, they slid into easy talk.

"Do you see yerself staying here the rest of yoe-ur laff, Mango?"

"That's hard to say, Mirph. Our boys are making friends, but the services for Liza's special needs are limited here."

"Well that's rat, Simm. And you are city boy."

"Like yoe-ur waff, Lon. Mango and hurr are both from New Owerleens. How strange is that? You and Lexi have to be the only two New Owerleanians in this whole county, Mango."

"I wouldn't doubt it, Mirph. And this one has enjoyed being around you four Twangers."

"Did you hear that, Mirph? Mango just called us 'Twangers'. And Ah thank he included ow-ur wahves in the com-ant."

"Dianah and Lexi know my teasing, guys. You know that."

"Well, I'll be twanged. We're gonna make a 'Twanger' out of The Mango befoe-ur he can say 'corn pone'.[67] Rot, Lon?"

"We're gonna git him to forgit that New Oar-luns French bread before-uh he's outta here, Mirph. He's gonna get hooked on aah-ur corn pone, grits, and biscuits. We're gonna get im."

"Are you gittin with Storen and Lind tomorrow nat for that discussion?"

"Yeah, Mirph. I enjoy those two. You and Lon have had a huge impact on those two young men. Thanks for sharing them with me. They are as quality a couple of guys as I've ever met. By the way, Drew, Dave, and Dora are going to join us."

"Good news, Mango. Drew's a good man. He's wantin what's good in laff. And Dave and Dora sure do care about what's most impoe-ur-tant."

"Ah lack the way Dave and Dora elevate Jesus to first place in they-ir relationship, too, Simm."

"So do I, Lon."

The next evening, he sat with the five Stemson University students.

"It's cool, Mango, how we work together as paw-urts of the body. We can see how diff-e-r-ent you are from Lon and Mirph. You bring the same truths but from diff-e-r-ent angles and per-spey-ic-tives."

"Yeah that's rat, Storen. The Mango has that New Owerleens stahl of relating. And he likes spreading it out and giving us the broader view so that we git the con-tay-ext in ar lahves."

"What have you guys been getting from our time together in prayer and in The Writings?

"Ah've enjoyed tracing the good news of Jesus back to the tahm of Abraham. It's helped me understay-and how grand God's story is."

"Me too, Dave. When you stop and take a acloser look, you can see a progression to the story."

"That's true, Drew. Did Aah just make a rahm? Taking a closer look at the story is something that's become impoe-ur-tunt to me. Aah just never took the time to do thay-at."

"Why's that, Dora?"

---

[67] Fried and baked, eggless cornbread; a country-southern dish

"We just get too beezee. Not thay-at we need to stay thay-ir. But we need to take a look inside the story our-say-elves. It becomes moe-ur a-lahve when we do."

"Yes, Dora. And it remahnds me that the story will have an end as wey-ull, when He returns."

"Rat, Lind. We have somethang to look for-ward to."

"We sure do, Dave. I love how ya'll are processing things. I look forward to being with the five of you each week, guys. I really do."

Simeon appreciated his traditional southern friends. They were men and women of character and purpose. Their friendships bolstered him and helped guide him through his experiences there.

At semesters end, he and his family drove down to visit his family. He was eager to refresh himself there in their brief respite.

Over the years after he left home, he visited home with his family several times a year. And each move to a new location had the effect of making his return visits to his beloved hometown grow fonder.

This time, he found time to hitch up an old bike. He pedaled directly up to the levee, and set a course to Audubon Park. He paused at the old fountain outside the zoo for a few minutes. But his Old Oak Tree was nearby. When he arrived there, he seamlessly slid into that space where secrets are kept and meaningful experiences are stored.

The Old Oak was fully draped in Spanish moss, just the way he remembered it. The curly fungus swayed slowy back and forth at the mercy of the gentle breeze sneaking through the neighborhood. Easily, he was a boy on a bike again. Memory days of innocence, discovery, learning, and adventure washed over him.

It was the time when all boys and girls wondered. Never did he imagine his life would turn out the way it did. He couldn't, because he had posited himself for the potential for almost any thing. His experiences at The Old Oak were of the same genre as the one in the first grade. He could see that clearly now. They were markers of something happening with Someone Who was always close.

And what had Voice continued to hold out to him? There was the strange draw of the familiar sound of the train horm as he grew into his teen years. And the six dings of the bell behind it. Those sounds escorted his forebording thoughts of the earth's future to new spaces. Those spaces were the battleground where his fascination and his fear tussled. The fascination related to his sense of the appearance of the ultimate good. The fear related to his deep awareness of the ultimate evil, madly bent on undermining and overthrowing the good.

He had known of the showdown since his youth. The sounds of the train horn and the bell were transports. They carried him into the fascinating and fearful spaces that he could only feel and vaguely ascertain, but not understand.

He sat beneath his Old Oak for the first time in years. And he was aware that the sound of the train horn and bell had everything to do with something unique. They had to do with the near and far future, the future with an ending to an age. Or was it an ending with a new beginning? Distance, time, and maturity had brought him to where he was. They helped him to discern what their sounds were about.

But in the meantime, he thought he heard a call again. And after finally figuring out how to live among country folk, and with his boys beginning to twang a little more, he gave ear to the sound of it. And after some soul-searching and counsel, he and his family packed it in. They were moving up to the Midwest. The yankees there were to gain a southern bred family that contained one not so typically southern.

Everywhere he lived, there remained an inbred connection with a river that passed through his beloved hometown, right by his old neighborhood. It was never not part of the fiber of his being. And the seen and unseen things that the river carried south sometimes parted from the flow of the river itself. And they somehow found a way to him to deposit special things into his soul over space and time, no matter where he was.

Forty Two

In the spring of 2005, their seventh year in the midwest, the wear and tear of life among college students began to take its toll. Simeon was in his twenty-fifth consecutive year of active engagment in campus life. Their sons, Bran and Jermain, were in college. They were in their eighth year of work at Columbus U.. In his fifty-fourth year, he noticed a fatigue setting in. And he wondered if it was time for a change.

"Is it because of us? Are we the one's who are driving you away from the college scene?"

"No, Colby. You're the ones who keep us around a little longer."

"You're just saying that. You don't want us to feel bad."

"Not true. And you know better than that."

"Yeah, Jennifer Jane, Simm's getting too old for us younger types."

"So that's what we are now, Huntsman? Types? Well I'm a type."

"We all know that, Match. We do. You are a special type."

"He is, J-Will. But let's get back to talking about Simeon leaving."

"Yeah, let's, Nelly. Where will you be going, Simm?"

"Wait, Houseman. Let's guess."

"There's nothing to guess, Em."

"So you think you know, Flo?"

"I do. So do Jonathan and Hinton, and Liz, Laura,Melissa, and Leah as well. We were talking about it, right, guys? And I talked to Adam, Kara, Velyn, Hwashik, and Tara about it yesterday. They all agree with us."

"Wait, let me be the first to say it. Ever since Simm brought us down to New Orleens on spring break, I could tell something was afoot. You all are moving to New Orleens, aren't you, Simm?"

"Yeah, Saul. I'm not very good with my poker face, am I? It looks like I'll be becoming a New Orleanian again, friends."

"Simm, you were never not one. We could tell that the whole time you've been with us."

"Wow, Huntsman. I didn't realize it was that obvious. So, back to Colby's initial question. No. You all aren't the reason we're leaving the college scene. I'm the reason. And whatever is ahead for us, I'm convinced that it is a change that will bring that into better clarity. It's been a long run around campus life for Lily-Grace and me. We'll miss it in a lot of ways. And we'll miss you all too. Our experiences with you have been like a grand crescendo in a long, inspiring, and meaningful orchestral performance."

He paused to take a long look at the last mix of exceptional young men and women that he would have the chance to grow and bond with. A lump formed in his throat. With the decision to leave, he felt loss. He had been on college campuses virtually all of his adult life, since leaving the Navy. His emotions were conflicted. But he knew that it was the right thing to do.

He would take a short break before moving to his beloved home town. But before that, he had one last student obligation to complete.

"I want ya'll to know that I've enjoyed my visit here to the heart of the heartland of America. I'd never heard of Sterling, Kansas until I realized I was slated to come here to you. Although I must say that there is something strangely inviting about Sterling to me. It's hard to even find this place on a map."

"Thank you for your kind reception and open ears. I trust that your hearts are as open to my words as they have been to me personally. We'll be around the rest of the evening before leaving in the morning."

With that, Simeon put a period on the long chapter in his life in the university world. He chatted with the students for a while. As the crowd thinned, he turned to gather his things. He noted the white board which he used to write on while he talked. It was full of blue dry-erase words and illustrations. He thought to wipe it clean so as to save the cleanup person one more chore. But there was no eraser, cloth, or napkins within sight. He looked at his right hand with an uncommon thought. He paused for a moment as if to ask himself if he really wanted to get the blue junk all over his hand. With a pointed awareness of what he was about to do, he placed his right palm against the white board. He proceeded to wipe it clean, right to left, then up and down, for good measure. He stepped back, satisfied to see the board generally clean. A last glance at his hand revealed the blue marker all over it.

"Now why did I just do that? Now I have to go and wash my hand."
It was late. He was tired. This was his seventh campus visit in ten days. He wanted to go home. He spoke with several of the students before heading to the bathroom to clean his hand. His travelling partners were waiting for him. When he returned home, he and the family prepared for a trip to the in-laws in Virginia.

Days into the visit, he sat in the Briggs' family den. The cozy country home sat on a small hill overlooking a creek forty yards wide. A wooden dock provided access to several small family-sized boats. Oak, pine, and hazelnut trees populated the hill between the house and the creek. A soft marsh absorbed the last of the waters flow near the dock. Several homes abutted the shore all around the creek that led to a wider stretch of water away from the house. The in-law house sat along a cul-de-sac in the creek.

He had been to visit his in-laws many times over the years. He was looking forward to this particular visit. He welcomed the opportunity to absorb creations country beauty all around.

He sat in the den, overlooking the creek through the windows. The creek was glassy and still beyond the tall twin pines that looked down on the dock. He could see the adjacent home far across the creek. It sat back on a manicured green lawn atop a small hill. The dark boarded wooden wall at the shore reflected onto the still water offering a charming image for the eyes.

A birdhouse stood just outside the windows, overlooking the dock. It was just above the lower left view through the far left window. A steady stream of wrens, titmouses, finches, cardinals, black birds, blue jays, and sparrows chased one another from the edifice.

As he sat enjoying the scene, he noticed something else. The lazy afternoon summer sun shone through the glass doors behind him. The bright light that it let into the den had a mirror effect on the glass windows that he was gazing through. On the one hand, he looked out at the creek. On the other, with the mirror effect from the sunlight coming in behind him, he could see the reflection of a white lattice trellis at the far end of the yard outside and behind him.

The windows were at once, both clear glass to see through and a mirror to reflect at. From his perch in the den, he could see two views outside the house without turning. Looking *through* the glass windows, he could see *the real world* of the actual creek and the scene around it. Looking *at* the glass window, he could see *a reflection of* the real world in the yard behind him. His thoughts were interrupted when his cell phone rang.

"Simm, this is Shoe. How ya doin man?"

"Shoe! It's been a while! I'm allright. How are you and Sam, and the girls?"

"Everybody's great, man. I was thinking about you and had some free time this afternoon. I thought I'd give you a call."

"We're not far from your old stomping grounds in the Old Dominion[68] visiting the in-laws."

"Funny how things change as we grow older, eh, Simm? It seems like forevermore ago when I was a student at Dominon U. I've been thinking about things lately and felt like talking. And you've been chosen, just like old times when I was in college."

The twin views at the window were in his sight. As he talked, his focus shifted between the real-world creek outside and the image of the real-world lattice trellis in the yard behind him.

"Whenever we catch up, Shoe, it's like we never left each other. Our friendship is as alive and meaningful as it was then."

"I agree with that, Simm. Well, back to why I called."

He took a deep breath. Simeon could hear him exhale over the phone.

"I don't know, Simm. Things are getting weird in the world. So much is changing so fast. I'm worried about the world my teenagers are going to have to live in. You know what I'm talking about. You've had the same impressions for a long time."

"Yes, I have. Anything in particular that's currently fanning these concerns into flame?"

"It's a building sense of all things, Simm. It's like a slow, but steadily building background noise that I can turn away from and ignore for awhile. But it's never turned off. I don't worry. There's much to do and He gives me courage. But every now and then it's good to talk about this. Is that how it is for you?"

"Yes, very much."

---

[68] Adopted name for the state of Virginia

"Something's coming, man. And when I read The Writings that speak to these things they seem to describe the most recent last decade. It looks like the stage is being set to act out the final chapter of human rule over the earth. It's both scary and exciting at the same time."

"I hear you, Shoe."

"And people don't care. Many of us have got it so easy in our country that we can pretend any future danger away. We're too asleep to want to think about the possibility of a future without our comforts and pastimes. I feel like I constantly need to wake up from a lullaby that our culture is softly singing."

In the mixed image of the latticed trellis and the creek, the trellis became fixed in his view.

Shoe continued.

"Delsusion, deception, …. anything to entice us to not pay attention. It seems like we are being fed images that are not real in order to dupe us. Some things are being said and written about these matters. But more needs to be said. More needs to be said. You know that, Simm?   More needs to be written."

With the period, the real-world creek that was just obscured by the image of the lattice, came into focus again.

Forty Three

It was late summer, 2005. Simeon and his family were two days away from moving back to his hometown.

"Honey, come check this out. This is unbelievable!"

The weather update showed the radar for the tropics. The entire Gulf of Mexico was a giant mega-storm. It was headed straight for New Orleans. Panic seized him. .

It was Saturday. A moving van was scheduled to be at their home Monday for their move. The storm was to arrive on Sunday.

"We can't go now. A Category Five, for New Orleans that's a game-changer. The city won't recover if this stays on course."

He spoke slowly and deliberately. His eyes had a faraway look.

"Well, we can't unpack everything. Our house is still on the market, so we can still stay here. Let's unpack some of the basics and we'll see how long this goes on. What's your mom gonna do?"

"I wanted to wait till the latest update before I called her. I'll call her first. Then I'll call the moving company and tell them we have to cancel. We can't go down there yet. We don't know what's going to happen over the next few weeks. I gotta get a hold of Shairee and get her to get Pokey and momma. They need to get the heck outta there."

"What about Aunt Katie and Aunt Mae?"

"I'll call Trae and Lan. I'm sure they're already on it. They need to get their momma's and get outta there too."

Over the next twenty-four hours, the storm took a slight turn. The city dodged a bullet. But the levees broke due to the extremely high storm surge. New Orleans survived, but not before experiencing its worst disaster in modern times.

Time Passage

Alignment

"Everything you've ever wanted is on the other side of fear."

~ George Addair

Forty Four

Lily-Grace walked into the room. She handed a letter to her husband.
"Did you make friends with someone when you were in Kansas?"
He looked at the return address. The handwriting revealed the name of
the postal location to be *Sterling, Kansas*.
The name of the town piqued his curiosity. He opened the envelope
and began to read. The letter was from a student named 'Brent'. It read:

```
     "I wasn't close to God.  But
someone told me to ask God to speak to
me in a dream.  So I did.  Months
later, I had a dream.
     In my dream, I saw a man.  He was
talking about finding God.  I was
```

```
introduced to him, and I noticed he
had a blue hand.
     I asked Him, 'What have you been
doing to make your hand blue?'
     'Well,' the man replied, 'I have
been writing on a marker-board, and I
erased it with my hand.'
     I forgot about that dream until you
showed up.  Simm, if you remember, you
were writing with a blue marker.  And
you erased the board with your hand.
God brought you to Sterling for me.
Thank you for coming all the way out
here.  Now, I'm trusting in Christ."
```

"Man, … it's amazing what can happen. Sterling, Kansas, wow. I remember wiping that board. Honey, come see …? "

But she had left the room before he spoke. In her place, their two sons walked in.

"What about Sterling, Kansas, dad?"

"Well, hey guys, I didn't know ya'll were here."

"Me and Bran were out and about. The wives have the kids."

"You guys just walked into a meaningful moment, my two young turks."

"I like that 'young turk' moniker, Jermaine."

"Me too, Bran. It sounds strong, brave. So fill us in, dad."

"Years ago, as one of my last adventures in the student world, I did some travel to various campuses around the country."

"I remember that. You traveled a week at a time."

"Right, Bran. On my last trip I was in Sterling, Kansas. I spoke, writing on a white marker board with a blue dry-erase marker. When I was finished, I wiped the board clean with my hand. So my hand was blue."

"Well, dad. That's so downright not-impressive. You wiped the blue print with your hand. So your hand was blue."

"And that's what I thought, J.. I presumed the story was over, until I just got this letter in the mail. The student stated that God spoke to him in a dream. And in his dream he met a man who had a blue hand. He asked the man why he had a blue hand. The man told him that he had been writing on a marker-board and erased it with his hand. And the man came to talk about God."

"So you were the dude who showed up in the dude's dream?"

"Yes, dude,… I mean, Bran."

"I'm a turk, now, dad. You called us turks, remember?"

"This sounds like you, dad. Things happening that you had no idea would happen, things that were out of your hands. Like maybe there's more to this than you know. Maybe you should think more about the interesting things God has let happen in your story."

"You think so, Jermaine?"

"Yes, I do."

"Yeah, dad. And maybe God wants you to be following up on those kinds of things more than you have."

"Thanks for the prods, guys. You have keen eyes. I'm listening."

The phone rang. Simeon walked to his desk to answer it. It was his old pal, Dett. They talked at length. After catching up with the families and other matters, Dett wanted to know something else.

"How's the writing going, Simm?"

"What writing?"

"You mean to tell me you haven't started on that yet?"

He remembered the words of his son's just minutes ago. They had become flowers in bloom in their thirties, each displaying their wonder and vitality in rich ways. But Dett was lingering on the other end of the call.

"I guess not, Dett. No writing."

"Well, why not? You know it's what you want to do. And you sure have been given enough unusual incentives to get started."

"I don't know. Whatever I'd be compelled to say..."

He didn't want to finish the sentence.

"There's such a broad range of subject matter that I'd need to consider. You already know that the winds beneath my wings can come from many directions. Or, maybe I'm a procrastinator."

"Not when you want something. At least that's how I know you. You usually go for it."

"Well, maybe I really don't want to do it then. Maybe that's why I haven't gotten started."

"Or maybe you're afraid to, Simm. Ever thought of that?"

The night grew quiet. It was the time of the evening when eyelids wanted to link up and the mind was ready for a break. But he wasn't sleepy. Bran and Jermaine's words were fresh, and so were Dett's. He continued to think about the letter from Brent in his evening devotion. And about Dett's phone call. And he wondered out loud.

"How could I show up in someone's dream? How did a man with a blue folder vanish at a bus stop years ago? And who was The Professor, Songieux? And why did he give the blue folder to Momma? Why the dreams? And the train horn, and the bells? And why is Dett being so persistent???"

All of the not-so-spectacular, yet extraordinarily special experiences were meaningful landmarks in his story. They were ongoing invitations to continue to seek The City whose name was not of this world. They continued to be beacons to herald what he sensed to be coming since he was a child. They held out invitations to him to watch, to wait, to listen.

And The Protocols, *The Protocols*. His heart ached when he thought of them and his beloved blue folder. There was something special about them. Yet, they were taken from his hand, with a broken thumb thrown in, just in case he had thoughts otherwise.

The letter from Brent earlier in the day re-kindled his dormant desire for the special articles. He never forgot about them. He considered that they might be lost and irretrievable. But he never ceased to ask for their return. Their presence held a more narrow possibility related to questions which answers eluded him since they formed in his childhood.

Forty five

Simeon and Lily-grace sat at a table in their yard. The sunlight was getting heavier on their skin. And the humidity was rising. They were reviewing some family matters and details involving Liza at school.

"How long has it been since you sat and worked at your special Wendy's on St. Charles?"

"Quite a while."

"You're avoiding going there, aren't you?"

He didn't answer.

"Is it painful for you?"

He continued to put his socks and shoes on without answering.

"Maybe if you went there your thoughts will clear up. I know this still bothers you. Just think about it, okay?"

"Okay, I will."

When he finished his morning appointment, he waited until the lunch crowd thinned and acted on his wife's suggestion. When he arrived at the Wendy's, the familiar lobby was mostly empty. He thought about sitting at the special table, the table where it happened. But he couldn't. Feelings of emptiness and betrayal rushed through his heart and he almost turned to leave.

But he didn't.

He ordered a small meal and sat to eat. He pulled out some material and began to read. Several minutes later, he was interrupted.

"Long-time, no-see."

Looking up, he beheld the massive figure of Vincent DeMaso, whose stature was slightly more intimidating, if it were possible, from Simeon's seated position. Unwelcome feelings swarmed over him and he fought the urge to rise to leave.

"How are you, Vincent?"

It was all he could muster. It was a move in the right direction.

"Well Ah finally found you."

The remark barely arrested the direction, or intensity, of his feelings.

"You finally found me? Why didn't you just call me? You have my phone number and you've used it in the past."

"Ah wanted to wait to see you in person. Ah wanted it to happen by itself, even though Ah've been trying to make it happen. Ah've been to dis Wendy's at least once a week for a few months hoping to find you heeuh. And Ah been missing you at Duh Mission."

"I probably should be feeling pretty intimidated to hear that right about now, shouldn't I Vincent? Isn't that what you're after with me? Are you gonna break my other thumb now?"

With the question, he felt bad.

"It certainly was why Ah was originally after you   And no, Ahm not here tuh break your other thumb."

"And now? Why have you been looking for me now?"

Vincent's appearance was noticeably different. He appeared more relaxed. There was something in his eyes that was different. His voice was less forceful, less intense, less angry. And when he spoke, there was a slight hint of a smile coming from the corners of his mouth, and from his eyes. He appeared less pale with a hint of color on his face.

"Might Ah join you? Mind if Ah sit?"

With the question, there was a slowdown in the motion of Simeon's negative feelings.

"I can't believe you're actually asking me. Usually you just barge in and start making threats and demands."

The emotion was still strong. Yet he regretted his raw expression. Vincent sat down. Simeon thought he saw a hint of sincerity in his eyes. He noticed a strap that ran across his chest from his shoulder to his opposite side waist.

"You want something to eat, Vincent?"

"No thanks."

The calm that guided Vincent was striking. Had Simeon not known who he was talking to he might have wondered if a change had come over him.

"Why have you been staking out this Wendy's to catch me here?"

"Because there's something Ah've been wanting to talk with you about. Ah want to know about dis new life you always talk about."

He was utterly shocked, up to, and until, the moment that shock gave way to shame. He had seen this happen before. He petitioned his Father regularly for the nemesis who now sat humbly before him, as he did for others like him who were hostile, but had turned. How awful for him to allow himself to descend into the snare of self-pity. He was not unfamiliar with the prison cell where it snared the soul so that its self-focus prohibited concern for another human being.

For the next hour, the two men talked about the God-life. Vincent was full of questions and sincerely apologetic for his treatment. He opened his heart freely. The level of transparency and honesty he displayed transcended the depth of bitterness and hatred in his closed heart the last time the two sat in the same lobby. At one point Vincent paused and looked down.

"Do you remember what happened in freshman year in high school, on the playground almost every day?"

"I do, Vincent."

"Ah figured you did. Ah was too ashamed and too proud to bring it up to you, until now."

"There was no way you deserved the taunting and verbal abuse they gave you that year, Vincent. Those guys had no excuse for doing that to you. We were freshmen, they were seniors. If they'd come back three years later, it would have been a different story."

"Well, it was simply an extension of what went on in mah home since Ah was a kid. Ah guess that scarred me. It led me to hate."

He stopped. Tears filled his eyes and slowly made their way down his cheeks. He began to sob and cover his face with his giant hands. While the hulking man sobbed gigantic tears, the small man placed his small hand on his massive forearm for a few seconds.

Simeon's thoughts went to the table a few feet away. It was the table where he was too sad to sit when he entered the lobby. It was where Songieux showed up. While his former antagonist sobbed and Simeon consoled him, he wondered if his old friend might somewhere be aware of the specialness of the present moment.

"Ah want dis new life, Mangino. Ah want it, Ah really do."

The words were forced and halting through the sobs.

"Does His forgiveness extend to a guy like me?"

Simeon was slow to answer, sharing in the emotions of his new friend and touched by the working of The One Who loves.

"It does, it surely does. His mercy and love are much larger than you. Let's talk with Him right now and you can tell Him what you want, my friend,… my brother."

He liked the sound of the last four words.

Both men finished addressing Vincent's new Lord. When they did, Vincent's new estate was recorded in the impartial ledgers of the Heavenly Kingdom's Justice Department. And misty tears lingered in the eyes of the two new friends. Simeon had been through a tough time with the man across from him since their paths crossed. His emotions had been all over the map. He thought of Lily-Grace. He was thankful for her and the many times her thoughts, suggestions, and ideas were like apples of gold and settings of silver for a fine dinner. And this one was one of her best.

He glanced outside the glass wall. On the sidewalk, against Saint Charles Avenue, he saw a mockingbird on the sidewalk. A streetcar made its way past the window beyond, on the neutral ground. He could see that the head of the winged creature tilted upward, with brief tilts down to the normal position, before tilting up again. He couldn't hear its sound. But he imagined that he could. He was easily familiar with it. And what he imagined that he heard sounded very much more like the beautiful sounds of celebration and honor than that of taunting and mocking.

Reluctantly, Simeon had to leave. He was graced with the thought that every moment is new in time. But not every moment was a witness to a new life. In that kind of a new moment he was overcome by yet another transformation by a work not of this world.

Vincent had one more matter to resolve with his new friend.

He grabbed the strap across his chest and lifted it over his head. At the end of it was a green carry bag. Vincent reached in and pulled out the blue folder that he had taken from Simeon. Before handing it to him, he opened it and produced the yellow napkins that contained The Protocols.

"Ah believe dis is yours."

He wanted him to know that everything was intact. He rightly shouldn't have had them returned to him after he flippantly passed them off on the Reverend Sister. But he was already getting acquainted with new things based on genuine forgiveness for everything. And he was understandably basking in his new found pardon. He was permantly humbled by it, beginning to move into the direction of the sweet spot, where a renewed self-acceptance makes peace with the truth about one's past.

"Just like dey were when Ah took them. Please forgive me, Mangino. Ah was way outta line. Ah was a knucklehead, as previously mentioned. Ahm not sure what dis stuff is all about, but Ah sense that there's something special about them. Special to you, for sure. But also, special in a larger way. Ahm sure you've already been thinking about all uh dat."

Forty Six

A few months into his new experience, Vincent sat with his friend.

"You wanna hear me recite mah newsest memory passage?"

"Always, Vincent. Lay it on me."

"Okay, here goes,… 'Gawd is not a man that He would lie, nor a son of man that He should repent. Has He said and will He not do it? Or has He spoken and will He not fulfill it?' Dat's in Number's, chapter twenty-three, and verse nineteen[69], Ah believe."

"I'm liking it. How's it grabbing you, Vincent?"

"Dat Ahm connecting wit Someone Who is so above me, so secure and set apawt in His utter moral purity and goodness, dat He's not accountable to anyone else. He *is* duh standard, and rightly so. It makes me fear, respect, and want to get closer to Him every day. And to think dat such a One loves a sinner like me…. It's almost unfathomable. It *is* unfathomable. Trim this up for me, Simm. Expound on it further."

"Are you kidding me? How can I, Vincent? You just shared your recently discovered treasure with me. I just want to enjoy your new discovery with you. I couldn't have said it any better."

"Yuh know, Simm. In the months we've been getting together, Ah've absorbed a lot. And Ah've been getting into duh Scriptures on my own so much that they're food to me now. Ahm learning where the pantry is. And Ahm finding that duh pantry has an endless supply of food."

"I like the way you put that, Vincent."

"And Ah want to thank you for spending all uh dat time with me having daily devotions, and all the times we spend talking to Gawd together. Those two practices have become my daily habits. Ah meet with Him on mah own everyday now. And Ah've been glad to connect with other men and women of like hawt whose lives have been changed by Jesus, as mine has."

---

[69] Numbers 23:19

"Ah've been meaning to aks you, Mangino. Why do you call them 'The Scriptures' and 'The Sacred Writings'"? Most people like you, Ah mean…, like us, call it 'The Bible'. What's up wit dat?"

"It's just my way. It's printed as 'The Bible', of course. 'Bible' is a word from the Latin word 'biblios' which is the word for 'book'. So technically we could call our bibles 'The Book'. I use those alternate terms to help enliven it, to animate it as refreshers on its uniqueness. I use the terms to keep in play that they are writings that are a set-apart, totally unique in history."

Vincent listened.

"Got Weng Abem."

"What's dat?"

"'Got Weng Abem' means 'God's Holy Talk'. When a New Zealand tribe had the New Testament translated into their native tongue, this was the phrase that was transcribed as 'Bible', or 'God's Book'. Doesn't that sound like a keenly cultural label for a local people group to call their 'Bibles'?"

"It surely does, Simm. 'Got Weng Abem', 'Gawd's Holy Tawk'. Ah like dat, Simm. Yes indeed, Ah do. How do you spell that?"

He paused to write the phrase down in his notebook.

"Ah know dat Saint Paul said dey are inspired by Gawd. Ah looked up the meaning, and found that the literal phrase duh writer wrote was 'Gawd-breathed'. Gawd *breathed* His words to duh writers. And Ahm learning that the writers of The Scriptures wrote in different forms. Dey are history, records, psalms, wisdom-writings, prophecies, accounts, letters, and revelations. And they all had a close connection with Gawd. And He breathed, or inspired them, to write what dey did."

"Ah had never thought of it dat way before. Ah never stopped to consider dat The Writings are comprised of a collection of writings, different kinds actually. But dey all point in the same direction, and have a consistency of thought regarding Who Gawd is and what He is like. And they all point to a Redeemer. And they are clear as to Who duh Redeemer is. And they all point to Him coming back to set up His kingdom on earth where we will be with Him, which is what His return is all about."

Simeon sat and listened to his friend. He couldn't help but be impressed by the transformation in his being, and his humble hunger for the truth. Not only was he feeding from the Writings himself now. He was also forgiving people, reaching out in love to friends, family, strangers, and even to old enemies. He was beginning to show concern for the poor. He was indeed a new person.

"And Ahm beginning to get the larger story in the Bible, uh, The Sacred Writings. Ah don't think Ah'll ever totally get a handle on it, just like you say you haven't. But Ahm seeing it better as Ah grow."

"And in time you'll see and understand the story better."

"Why is that, Mangino?"

"You and me, and everyone who has ever lived, are living our own stories. And our stories are within God's larger story that is called life. As we grow closer to him over the years, we see ourselves, our real selves, for who we really are. We grow to understand how good, merciful, and forgiving He is. We taste more of His compassion and love. And we come to understand His nature as pertains to His justice, love, mercy, truth, and sovereignty. We slowly begin to grasp how vast is his omniscience, presence, and infinite wisdom. And our story within His story, and His story by itself, all start to make more sense, little by little as we walk with Him and stay in His Word."

"As you're saying these things, Ahm seeing that Ahm just starting to experience some of these expressions in Him. And Ahm excited to think dat over time, Ah'll get to experience more and more of Him as Ah walk with Him. And by staying focused on Him through duh words in His writings, Ah'll do dat."

Simeon soaked in the words, and the warmth of bonded friendship.

"And so, Ah was aksing you about some uh duh prophecies when we met dee other day. You were explaining to me the importance of prophecy and the Lawd's return."

"It's a subject that some talk too much about. And some don't want to talk about it at all. I was struck early in my new life how Paul apparently spoke of it on his missionary journeys when he planted local Jesus movements. It appeared to have importance in the story of the message. If Paul, universally a hero to every Jesus follower, was compelled to bring it to the forefront and keep it there, why are we afraid to?"

"You mention 'Jesus movements'. Is that what people call 'churches' today, like duh one you brought me into?"

"Pretty much, give or take a missed critical aspect here, and/ or an over emphasis of non-critical matters there. The 'church' is comprised of the people everywhere who have come into God's Kingdom by genuine faith and trust in Jesus for forgiveness of sin. Local expressions of the universal church are communities where Jesus followers practice what He taught. They are, when in their proper conditions in Him, movements of God in and through the lives of people who've been changed by Him. They might have chosen a local place to meet and organize, where the host culture they live in allows it. But the physical place has nothing to do with what the substance of each local expression is meant to be."

"Going back to the prophecies… Paul told the new followers in Thessalonica some, as far as we know, previously unknown facts about the Lord's return. He talked in detail to the new Corinthian followers about a bodily transformation when the Lord returns. That appears to have been new information as well."

"And the Old Testament prophets? Weren't dey important to your turning to duh Lawd?"

"The apostles and New Testament writers were informed by them. Heck, Jesus was informed by them as well when He grew as a child. When Jesus came, many were waiting for their Messiah to come and rule the earth. Their sacred writings, which are our Old Testament, as you know, informed them of this. They presumed that He would finally free their nation. They based this on promises recorded in Genesis, Samuel, Psalms, Isaiah, Zechariah, and other places."

"Apparantly, their leaders failed to understand that there were two aspects of the prophecies concerning the Messiah. The first had to do with the time and events when He would come and offer Himself as a sacrifice for the sins of everyone. And after, he would rise from the dead and return to heaven. The second had to do with the time and events when He would come back and finally bring peace and justice to the earth under His absolute, loving authority. This relates to the larger aspect of the story of the Bible, or sacred writitngs, and it's a critical part of the good news of the story, Vincent."

"Understanding this ushered me to the throne of the One who loves me, the One I am accountable to. The Lord Jesus came to fulfill, or complete, the writings of the Jewish prophets. His story is the completion of the story of Israel in the larger story of God. When I realized the larger story, and Who He is in it, and what He is like, it gave me the context I needed. And I was ready."

"I turned from my ultimate desire to sin, to live selfishly. I turned to Him for forgiveness, once and for all. I was lost. I was lonely inside. I was fragmented and broken. And as you and I have now discovered, the cracks in broken hearts are where His love gets in. And isn't that what our lives are also, DeMaso? Aren't our lives individual stories, like sub-plots, in the grand story of God?"

"Yeah you rite, Simmie boy."

"And if our lives are small stories within the grand story of God then who is the main character in the grand story? Before I turned to Him, I presumed that *I* was the main character in the grand story of life."

"And now you realize dat it's not about you. It's about Gawd. He is the main character in the grand story of all of life. He wanted to be in your life all along, but you weren't ready to let Him in. And the same went for my life and everyone else's."

"Well spoken, Vincent."

"And now, He's the main character in the story of mah life. Ah was telling mah friends, Alvin and Tony, about mah new life in Jesus. They're skeptical about it. But dey are aksing questions. Dey aksed if Ah still needed to confess mah sin. Ah told them Ah didn't think Ah *needed* to in order to have a relationship with my Father in heaven. But Ah told them Ah *wanted* to, like Ah would in any healthy relationship."

"And why would you even want to, Vincent?"

"Because Ah want to stay close to mah Father in heaven. Ah don't want my motives and ambitions to begin trending in a direction that takes me away from Him."

"Are you afraid that they might?"

"Not afraid so much as Ah just don't *want* dat to happen. Mah motives and ambitions could take me in that direction if Ahm not careful."

"And you think it could possibly happen because...."

"Because Ah have learned dat mah sinful nature flesh is a runaway horse. Give it a chance, especially with things dat are habitual, and addictive, and Ahm including thoughts, words, and actions here – and it will begin on a slide down a slippery slope away from Him. Ah want to always be trending toward Him in mah hawt and mind. And that's what acknowledging and confessing with a simple 'Ahm sorry, Lawd' is all about."

"So you are acknowledging and confessing within a relationship, not in order to have one, or because you're afraid you'll lose it. Is this what I'm hearing?"

"Yes. Am Ah on target?"

"Yeah you rite, brother, yes indeed. And it's a mark of the times we are living in, where in some quarters of the larger world of christendom, we are being encouraged to shy away from what you just said. Folk are becoming legalistic about avoiding all sensations to feeling any guilt at all."

"Well, isn't there an aspect of guilt dat's healthy? Ah know dat Ahm glad dat my conscience is sensitive enough to Gawd's Spirit to alert me when Ahm feelin guilty for any morally unhealthy thought, word, or action. And didn't James say we should confess our sins to one another?[70] Ah just memorized that one two weeks ago."

He couldn't get enough of Vincents' hunger.

"You think Ahm trending right in mah take on this, Simm?"

"Yes indeed. Guilt is meant by God to be like a dashboard light in a car. It turns on to help us realize something that we're not aware of, but potentially harmful. The unattended trend will reach a point where it gains inertia. There, it has enough force to wield increasing influence over us. Another way of looking at it is that guilt isn't toxic at the outset. But left unattended, it becomes toxic. And it is this toxicity that leads us to do all kinds of debilitating things to relieve the internal pain that the built up, unacknowledged, and unconfessed sin patterns cause in us."

"So we can say dat dee unacknowledged guilt dat a morally wise person would want to have removed by acknowledging and confessing, remains and festers. And dat its effect becomes like being on a runaway

---

[70] James 5:16

horse stepping onto a slippery slope; like dashboard lights dat remain on while my caw is low on oil, and like something dat becomes toxic in me and grows like a cancer. Until it is removed by a simple aknowledgement and confession to Gawd."

"I think we've come up with something here, Doctor DeMaso. I like the way you've sqeezed our metaphors together."

"Ah concur, Professor Mangino."

The lobby in Simeon's favorite Wendy's was empty again. The young man who had been cleaning the tables approached Simeon.

"Aren't you the guy who picked up those napkins from one of the tables in here months ago?"

He caught Simeon off guard.

"Yes, I am. You've got a good memory for events and faces. How'd you know me as the man?"

"I'm not sure. You looked familiar. The more I thought about it in the familiar confines of all these tables, it brought me back to then and I was able to place you. Did you ever find the guy who left those napkins for you?"

Vincent had a puzzled look on his face.

"No, I didn't."

"Well he was just here, a little while before you got here. He must have left. As usual, he was writing on his yellow napkins again."

Vincent followed the proceedings with interest. Simeon went to heightened alert.

"Over there? On that table with the yellow napkins on it? That's his table, man. Vincent, that's his table!"

"Who's table? What are yuh talking about, Simm?"

"The Professor…., Songieux. That's where he was sitting when I met him!"

"Okay. But who are you talking about, what Professor?"

The Wendy's worker went about his business. Vincent sat waiting for an explanation. And Simeon sat with a giant grin, staring at the empty table with Songieux's yellow napkins. His mind went like a laser beam in a straight line through the windows, and down St. Charles Avenue to The French Quarter. It traversed the Mississippi River, that very moment carrying unseen, but not totally misunderstood things. And it went beyond until the ray of thought was cut off by the question.

"Simeon, what duh heck was that all about? Who's dis Professor, Songieux, dat you mentioned?"

Back to the table once again, Simeon stopped him.

"Hold on one second, Vincent. I'll be right back."

He rose and walked over to what he referred to now, with the deepest affection, reverence, and respect, as 'Songieux's Table". He picked up the yellow napkins.   When he saw no writing on the top one, he turned each one over. On the last one, he read ……

> *"Let come what comes to you,*
> *regarding what has always been*
> *on your mind. And don't be afraid. "*

He stood for a long moment as the words began to penetrate, before realizing Vincent was waiting for him. He took the one written on and walked back to the table.

"Vincent, I've got something I want to tell you. Lily-Grace is the only other person who knows about it. It's going to take a few minutes."

"Let it roll, baby. Ahm ready. Lay it on me, bruh.

Forty Seven

An hour passed like it was a minute. And each minute that he spoke of it was like a thousand enjoyable minutes.

"A strange old man showed up out of nowhere, spoke to what has burned in your hawt since you were a kid, and then vanished."

"I'm humbled by it, Vincent."

"Do you get some sense of urgency to act on anything?"

"That's hard to say. I'm still thinking and praying about it."

"Is dat the standard spiritual anwer to everything?"

Simeon knew how to answer. He had the same line dropped on him by folk when he wondered if they really meant it.

"Let's eat, big guy. I'm starved."

"Me too, mah bruthuh. Mah turn this time."

Other than Lily-Grace and himself, the only other persons who read The Protocols were Vincent and The Reverend Sister.

After ordering, they sat to eat.

"*The Protocols*[71]." Vincent looked up, as if reviewing a document that was stored inside his head.

"Who is 'Saint Anon'"?

"I'm impressed by your recall of the contents. 'Anonimo' is Italian for 'anonymous'. I took it that the writer wished to remain such."

"Ahm Italian. Ah should have known that. Den what are 'Dee Essays'?"

"We already know that an essay is like a composition, or article. I think it's any kind of short writing on a particular subject."

"Well, why does the term show up in The Protocols?"

"I'm not sure."

He looked outside the window, then down at his meal.

"Well those Protocol thingee's gave me dee impression that somebody's supposed to write. And that would have to do with duh

---

[71] See Chapter 22.

prophecies and the Lawd's return. Dat's how you seein it too, right, Simm?"

"Right. man. Look at duh pickles on this burger, Vince. Doze awe some lawj pickles."

The slide into vintage New Orleans-speak was effortless and almost unplanned. On his large part, Vincent's internal fortitude was even larger, and weightier, than his very large and hefty frame.

"Yeah, nice pickles. But dee attempt ain't gonna work. So like Ah was saying, somebody's supposed to write some essays dat relate to Jesus' return and the werld. And Ah can't recall all uh duh details, but there were references to 'five of twelve', 'an army on somebody's leg', and such things. Any of these strike a bell wit you?"

Simeon raised his brows, scrunched his mouth, titlted his head slightly, and shrugged his shoulders. He avoided eye contact. Vincent didn't.

"Something in there about a horn with a bell ringing, an oak tree, clouds, and some Italian words. Recall any uh dis?"

"I think you're right, my friend. Good memory you have there."

A plastic look of concern came with the return to regular-speak.

"And there's a gun, a broken bottle, and a dead man's head on a foot in there. Oh, and Ah forgot about the strong words at dee end regarding chaos, and all uh dat. Dat's in there too, right?"

Crickets.

"Well, mah good friend, do you get enticed by all uh dis?"

Frogs.

He continued to press. He shrugged his shoulders, scrunched his mouth in return, and glanced down briefly as he continued with a tone that rode on the arrow of a good intention.

"Ah mean, the man…excuse me, was he a man? Well, he looked like a man, right? So Ah'll call him a man. The man never showed up at any table *Ah* ever sat at. He never talked *to me* about duh Lawd's soon return. And he didn't vanish after not talking *to me*. Help me out here, Simm. Who was it dat he visited and said all these things to? And whose momma did he give Duh Protocols to, and whose aunt gave dem to him? Who was dat, Simm?"

He leaned forward with raised eyebrows, locking eyes with his former classmate. Simeon noted the tender gleam there. It came from a heart now in The Light. The man in front of him, formerly feared, was now his trusted friend. He had been, and was continuing to be, helped by him. He was giving back.

"I hear you, barking, Vincent. And I appreciate your care for me. I hope you'll believe that I'm wrestling with this,... very much. But don't ask me about it on a regular basis. Spread your inquiries out, if you don't mind. I need to sort this through with God."

"You got it. Ah just wanted to give you mah take, in a round about way. One last thought. You're not duh most aggressive type. But neither are you one to hold back when it's time to strike. You tend to be careful, though Ah know you live as in a spiritual war, andt that you're poised. 'Poised' has a lot to do with timing. Ah know dat you know dis. And Ahm thinking dat you know what time it is. Take dat with you when you sort it all out with duh Lawd."

"Done."

"Are you ready fuh me to come to a few of your Friday classes?"

"I've been ready. I just didn't want you to tire of seeing my face."

"You talking about the prophecies dis week?"

"Nope. It's not on my agenda."

"Aw-ite, den. But if it ends up dat you do, Ahm forecasting fawty-five fast facts for Frahday."

"But that's not what I'm planning on doing Friday, Vincent. And as you know it's not the focus topic of the class."

"Whatever you say, Simm. Ah'll be there. See you Friday."

Friday, ten a.m. came. It was a typical Friday at The Mission. The men strolled into the chapel while Simeon carried the thin podium down from the platform to the floor level and continued to set up. The class steward entered and walked to the front with his clipboard.

"Good morning, Buzz. Ready to call the roll?"

"Mornin, Mister Simm. Yep, let's get 'er going."

While Buzzy went through the class role, Simeon took in the crowd. He faced a full class of over fifty men. A few were new faces. Some of the men nodded or waved to him when their eyes met.

"They're all yours, Mister Simm. Don't hold back. Let it all out."

"Thanks, Buzz. I'll see you later."

He paused to adjust the already adjusted microphone again.

"Why'd Buzz tell me to not hold back and let it all out? He's never said anything like that before."

He looked around the room as he began.

"Guys, I want you to meet my good friend, and dear brother, Vincent. Please speak to him afterward and offer him one of our warm Mission greetings. Welcome to the newcomers in the class. Today, we're gonna have some interaction time centered around questions and, possibly, some answers, where helpful. I'll do more of the talking next week. Let's open up with some questions that some of you want to put out to the group. Since there are a lot of us in here, let's try to not all talk at once. Who'd like to start?"

The questions stirred some lively interaction related to following Jesus. At the midway point of the class, one of the men stood. He directed his question to Simeon.

"Mister Simm, will you spend the the rest of the class talking to us about the Lord's return to the earth?"

The men were in hearty agreement on the matter.

"I only occasionally get into the subject in this class. Ya'll sure you want to go down this road?"

The men were of one accord.

Simeon glanced to the back at Vincent who was grinning from ear to ear. He stepped back from the podium and put his head down momentarily to collect himself. He looked up again and began.

"Feel free to raise your hand anytime."

He paused to clear his throat. Then he began.

"We're all familiar with seasons. In the story of God, there are seasons. Seasons come and go naturally, and they have to do with time. In God's story, I am referring to the timing of seasons that can stretch across spans of time. Before Jesus arrived in the story of God, the world was in a season. Right now, we are in another season. At some point in time, and I'll say that the time is soon, even at the door, we will be in a new season. Followers differ on some matters related to and within each of the seasons. But on one thing they all agree. The King is coming, and He will usher in a new season. My brothers, I will tell you that that new season is upon us. He is coming soon, very soon. Too soon for many, not soon enough for others."

"Not soon enough for us in hee-uh, Mistuh Simm."

"Ah heard dat, Louis. Ah know yuh hawt, mah bruthuh. And Ah know where yuh coming from."

New Orleans-speak slid from his lips in the simple interaction with one of the home grown men at The Mission.

"Looky hee-uh Mistuh Simm, how long yuh been looking into dis?"

"For fawty-five yee-uhs, since Ah began to follow Him, Ernest."

"You sayin He's comin back soon, Ah unduhstand that. How soon, Mistuh Simm?"

"Maybe before our class is over, Ernest."

He smiled. But there was a genuine sincerity behind it. He continued.

"All that I will say is informed from forty-five years of ongoing broad study on the subject as a secondary interest in The Writings. I've looked into cultures and events historically, as one grand story of God, both the good and the not so good. I've read, and continue to read, mainstream and controversial cultural and historical information. I'm willing to not be shamed away from considering what outsiders are discovering, though I take them with a grain of salt. And though these folks don't have 'credentials', I don't allow myself to automatically write them off. God might just want to speak through some of them. I keep an ear out for discoveries, trends, and insights in the culture, that is, what is going on in the world."

"Since I'm willing to listen to voices outside of the mainstream, I throw their thoughts into the tasty gumbo that many voices produce. Insight, and flavor, often come from traditional *and* unexpected places."

"Over a forty-plus year span, an old guy like me is able to get a perspective on matters that I am familiar with. Being a big-picture guy, I like perspective. It aids a slow learner like me. It is from this place that I'll speak on the matter."

"Before the next season begins, and I tell you today, it is about to begin, King Jesus will return to the earth. Before He returns, there has been an increase in the ominous activity both of nature and of the declining character of men and women in many places. And due to the selective reporting of secret matters, not all of this, no doubt very little, is common knowledge. This has to do with the deceit factor, as mentioned in The Scriptures. All of this will have severe consequences for humanity. In addition, we've known a mass return of Jewish exiles from around the world to Israel. This was predicted[72].

He looked around the room. Most were attentive. A hand went up.

"Do you think dat we christian people can be deceived about duh times we are in now?"

"That's a good question, Kenny. Anybody want to speak to this?"

"Yeah, Mistuh Simm, lemmie take a shot at it."

"Go for it, Louis."

"Okay, Mistuh Simm. We know there's gaw be a falling away from the truth when the man of lawlessness comes on the scene at dee end uh dis age. In first of duh letters to the Thessalonians and chapter two, Paul writes dat a lot of folk gaw get caught up in a lie dat's associated wit duh lawless one. Most folk call him 'dee anti-christ'. It says dat dey will 'believe what is false'. Dat's a quote. Ya'll hear me now? Dat's a quote from The Writing's. Can Ah say some more, Mistuh Simm?"

"Yes indeed, brother. Talk to us."

"And we got to associate deez truths wit duh woids of our Lawd, bruthuhs. Ya'll remember dat He said in Matthew twenty four and twenty four, dat false teachers would arise at dee end of dee age and if possible, deceive even the elect saints of Gawd, dat's us, Mistuh Simm. He is dangling out duh possibility dat *even we, ourselves,* are capable of being led astray in the end of the age mass deception."

"Powerful words, Louis. And timely too. We very, very much needed to hear that. And doesn't that remind us to be careful what we pay attention to? Clarence?"

"That's right, Louis. And it relates to what was going on in Genesis, I believe its chapter eleven. The bulk of the world's people were coming together and building a monument to mankind. They were united as one in one cause. Only problem was they left God out. It was a universal statement of solidarity that shunned their Creator."

"So, what was it about that spirit that provoked God to diversify their speech into hundreds of languages, Clarence? As we are told the entire world spoke one language at the time."

---

[72] Ezekiel Chapter 36

"Yeah, Mistuh Simm. Dere's something universally irresistible to the human spirit when human spirits come together under some kind of feel good collective. Most of us have known this warm, feel good experience at concerts, or other gatherings where everyone is on the same page and warm feelings are stirred. Passions are in sync. They somehow merge together into a force that has incredible spiritual strength. And if God, the good Spirit, is totally left out of it, there is only one kind of other spirit that will harness that energy and exploit it. And it ain't a good spirit. Ya'll hearing this?"

A bunch of heads nodded. A few affirmative expressions were offered up. Many sat silent and appeared sobered.

"The world's more evil now, Mistuh Simm. Talk about it."

"It's always been evil. But it does seem so, in a way, Thomas. The whole world is one big system now. And the creeping tentacles of evil appear to have wrapped around the entire thing. And as it has, Satan's activity has grown stronger and more intense as he sees his growing opportunity. He no doubt is motivated by the possibility, what he may see as the probability, of the idea that he can pull off what he's been trying to expedite since Eden. Subtle lies and deception, cloaked under the cover of sincere and seemingly caring people, have captured those who aren't grounded in Jesus and His words. Satan's tactics have become almost, if not actually, irresistible to the masses, 'christians' not excluded. Mass delusion is trending. And the trends appear to have the force of steady headwinds behind them."

"Wars, earthquakes, famines, plagues, terrors, and great signs from heaven are all things that Jesus mentioned in His summary of these times. And He added a clue to these common occurring events. He said they would come like a woman having birth pains[73]. That is, they would increase in intensity and frequency just before His return. And dear brothers, they have, and continue to increase in the last century. I invite you to do the research. God wants us to be alert and awake. Jesus told several stories to highlight the importance of being alert and awake to His coming for every generation of His followers.[74] Yes, brother."

---

[73] Matthew 24, Luke 21

[74] Matthew 25

"Mister Simm, what do you say about the strange creature deaths all over the world?"

"I wanted to mention that but forgot to, thanks. If you were to search online the following: 'Mass animal deaths', you will come upon a site that will stagger you. You'll find hundreds of listed headings, with a link to each of them, from newspaper articles from news sources all around the world. Each of them are local reports, with photos, of massive deaths of sea creatures, birds, animals, and insects of all kinds. In many of these, no one knows why these things are happening. It gives hundreds and hundreds of accounts of massive creature deaths that are without precedence in history, in that they are worldwide in scope and ongoing since the recent near past. My suggestion is that they easily fit into Jesus' words in Matthew and Luke when He mentioned 'plagues, terrors, and great signs from heaven'. And remember, in that context He said that such things were the signs that would increase like a woman's birth pains, which they have been."

"There's so much selfishness, Mister Simm. Speak to that."

"I know I can be selfish, Ruiz. And I think you're onto something. Paul said that in the last times, men will be lovers of themselves[75]. While this has always been true in this last age since Jesus came, this fallen human tendency is now out of control. In our world, some form capitalism, along with mass media, has invaded almost every culture. Once it's in place, technology follows. When that happens, advertising - big business, that is - entices feelings of lust and passion (normal desire on steroids), and greed and envy, making folk feel deprived if they don't have what's advertised. Opportunity to indulge is a finger touch away in most countries of the world now. And when unchecked indulgence does its sinister work inside a person, he or she begins to become entangled in addiction, from mild to severe. And in this system, somehow the rich get richer and the poor get poorer, middle classes gradually disappear if they were present at all, and the poor stay oppressed."

"Satan's evil system has fanned the flames of the sinister tendency that is the original drawing force in everyone. This force pervades every corner of every culture through its human carriers. It's in the news

---

[75] II Timothy 3:1-7

reports: local, national, and inter-national. And maybe you've smelled it behind some of the stories you've heard and read."

"The sinister tendency is micro, and it is macro. It is alive in movements and ideas. It prompts people's words and individual actions. It is embedded in our Motives and Ambitions. It isn't a stranger in every kind of venture, public or private, commercial or non-profit, and yes - religious or secular. It is both a force and a principle. It breeds action and stirs movements. It is both a cause and an effect. It's one of the proud children of The Lie, itself the firstborn child of evil. It is connected with all that is out of order from the God's original universe. It breeds fragmentation, brokenness, and disorder. And it is forever bent on dominating the voices that influence the human spirit."

"This sinister tendency is the nature to sin, an inherent bent toward selfishness,… me first."

He paused. He knew he could get pretty intense.

"How are we doing, fellas? Is this getting too depressing?"

Heads shook sideways. A few remained fixed straight ahead.

"Not at all, Mistuh Simm", "Keep going, bruh", "Yeah you right, Bruthu Simm," and other similar feedback erupted.

"Vincent?"

"Ahm wit dem! Ahm taking it in."

"Allrightty, then,… Clarence, our celebrated Vietnam War pilot.

"Heh-heh, yeah, Simm,… some folk say that the world is always what it always was. And that nuttin changes. And they don't see any sign of Him coming soon no way. Your thoughts?

"Many folk do believe that, Clarence. I suppose that's why Jesus said He would come like a thief in the night. Many won't be expecting Him. And those of us who are won't have the exact time of His return down. But He did hint that we could know the season. Paul said that those in the light can know the season.[76]"

Marcel, you want to say something?"

"Talk about duh beast, Mistuh Simm."

"Okay, the beast………… the beast."

---

[76] I Thessalonians 5

He paused. He looked up, above every man's head, to the wall. But he wasn't looking at the wall. He didn't see it. He stared beyond, in search of a familiar river, though he wouldn't know that he was looking for it. Nor did he realize that he looked for An Old Oak a few miles upriver from where he stood, facing a room full of humble, hungry, broken men. His look was set, nevertheless. It was fortified with utmost concern and a certainty that could not be contained. Its intensity blocked out every outside sound and internal thought and emotion. It was set like a rock, locked-in in search of something related to an eternal city. And it remained set, until he found it.

Long seconds passed. He began:

"In prophecy, at the end, there is a beast system, and an end of the age beast. The system is apparently, Mystery Babylon, and has been in play since the early roots of the Babylonian kingdom in Genesis, chapter eleven. It's not a benevolent system, and has been seeking world domination under one ruler, and system, for thousands of years. Whenever the world has had a dominant power seeking to bring all other people groups into its system, that power, knowingly or unknowingly, is playing into Satan's hand. He will capitalize on any movement seeking to set up a unified system by which he can deceive and ensnare. In that context, he sets up his kingdom on earth."

"The system has a spiritual component. That aspect of it has been consistent. It has shown up under different headings. But it has always ultimately had human domination, reduction, and reinvention as its philosophy. It is not, nor ever has been, associated with Jesus."

"God's setup for peaceful coexistence among the people of the world has always been 'people groups', that is, ethnic people groups and tribal clans. The original-language term for this is "ethnos", what we today call 'nations'. It is clearly stated that His purpose for this is so that 'they might find Him'[77]. God's response to the movement to bring humanity under one umbrella, removes any guessing. We see His aversion to this in His drastic reaction in Genesis, chapter eleven again, what Clarence just spoke about. After confusing peoples' languages to thwart their effort, His profound and telling statement leaves nothing to speculation.

---

[77] Acts 17:26

I'll paraphrase His response here: 'If they can pull this off, what won't they be able to do?'" God doesn't want segregated, self-governing people groups, 'nations', because He's mean. It's for our good."

"In the Scriptures, we are told that the final version of this system will rule the world economically, in The Revelation, chapter eighteen. This appears to have a political component as well. We know that politics and economies go hand in hand. Out of this last Babylon system, in Revelation chapter seventeen, another beast will arise. He is called 'the eighth' and he comes out of 'the seventh' and last, beast world system."

"This leads us to the beast himself. He is almost universally recognized as the one Paul addresses as 'the lawless one'[78]. The generic term used for this person has been 'the anti-christ', as Louis said. He spins off of this last world economic and political system."

"He hates the beast system that has fostered the conditions in which he will no doubt parlay his opportunities to act in the middle east. When he sees his opportunity, ten kings will join him in destroying the ages old beast system. These matters are addressed in The Revelation[79]. This tells us that the unified economic and political system that oversees the world at the end will be destroyed. I submit to you that that unified economic and political system is the one we are living in today. I am far from the only one who will tell you this. If we are right, then it will be destroyed 'in one hour', according to Revelation chapter eighteen, whatever 'one hour' means."

"The lawless one, the beast person, will be the tyrant who opposes all that is God's good and God's people[80]. And it is my studied suspicion – did I just invent a new term? - that God's judgments will have begun, like birth pains in a pregnant momma, around the time of the beasts' rise. I also suspect that not everyone will be aware of who he is when he begins to do his thing. And not everyone will be aware that God's judgments have begun."

"He is a man of Satan who despises Israel. Satan is critically aware that Jesus was prophesied to return to The Mount of Olives in

---

[78] II Thessalonians 2:3
[79] Chapters 17 and 18
[80] II Thessalonians 2: 3-12

Jerusalem[81]. He knows that it's written that he will be banished to the pit for a season, before being let loose to have one more go at it. So, he is doing everything he can to destroy Jerusalem, so that Jesus cannot literally return there."

"Guys, what has Satan been up to since Adam and Eve, or since the great flood? Has he been napping, or leisurely toying with a plan to permanently ban God from His rightful place as the God of His people and the universe? Or has he been relentlessly scheming and acting to set himself up for long term success?"

"Any hopes for his longterm success have to do with at least two things. First, from his perspective, no matter what it takes, Jesus cannot be allowed to return to The Mount of Olives in Jerusalem. Second, he has given himself over to a maddingly obsessive quest to replace God, and rule mankind. He is aware that each human is born in the image of God[82]. In order to take God's place, he must destroy God's original image in people and re-invent mankind. He is doing that through science and technology. Witness artificial intelligence and robotics. There is much more to be said regarding this. Time will not allow it here today."

"It's likely that this person is alive and has been active for some years now. Which, if I'm right, and others as well, the judgments have already slowly begun, like birthpains. If so, then they are already slowly increasing, and will continue to do so."

"Amidst the growing hysteria and fallout concerning health, treatment, shutdowns, unrest, wars, and more, he will likely play his hand soon, with his eyes ever more on Jerusalem. And as a caveat, I'll ask a rhetorical question. Do you know what's been going on in the middle east for the past ten years or so? I'll leave you to ponder that one."

"As things deteriorate in Satan's scheme, I wonder how much technology will survive the unfolding of God's judgments before the beast makes war with Israel. Many wars have been fought since time began. And most didn't need post-modern technology to fight them. There will be a final war, with Israel being attacked and about to be totally conquered, before, and at the last minute, when Jesus returns[83].

---

[81] Acts Chapter One
[82] Genesis 1:28
[83] Zechariah 13 and 14

That seems clear. I don't have time today to open The Writings to take you deeper into any of this. Perhaps at a later time."

"It's important that I say that I don't personally sanction everything that the nation of Israel has done since 1948. What they do or do not do has nothing to do with the prophecy of Jesus' return to the Mount of Olives in Jerusalem. Keep in mind that the Jews as a whole have not acknowledged Jesus as their Messiah. This is telling in the story."

"When folk worldwide are clamoring for 'peace and safety', sudden destruction will come on them[84]. 'Peace' from what? Are they desperate for peace from wars and societal unrest? Are they longing for 'safety', and for things to 'get back to normal' again due to the fallout from an international sickness and its treatment? Something to think about."

"In the end, God will personally deal with Satan, the lawless one, and those who align with his incredibly deceptive and evil system."

The room was still and silent.

"Finally, we must double down on our calling to live faithfully for Him where we find ourselves, in our places. We are to love Him and love our neighbors. Our Lord would have us reach out in love to those without Him and intentionally share our lives and our hope. And He would have us share life with our brothers and sisters as well. One last hand and we'll close."

"Brothuh Simm, you have lots to say bout all uh dis. Have you ever considered putting your thoughts bout dis in woids, you know, writing it down in a booklet?"

Simeon looked to the far corner of the room where Vincent sat large and tall. His ear to ear grin had returned.

Their eyes locked. Vincent couldn't help but easily maintain his telling grin. He hoped it would ride atop the return eye contact to the front of the room. He wished to fortify its recipient, who wore a slight, shy, smile, who, when he received it, replied to his questioner:

"Dat's a good question, my bruthuh. Ah'll have tuh give dat some thought."

And why he slid again into New Orleans-speak no one could say.

---

[84] I Thessalonians 5:3

Forty Eight

The first time he read The Protocols, he was enthralled. The lines took him back to a former time in his personal story or resounded with long-developed thoughts regarding the end of the age. He hadn't read them again since they were returned to him by the newly formed Vincent Demaso. He kept them on his desk, safely snuggled inside the blue folder. But Procrastinator, the thief of productivity and no stranger to him, lurked nearby his desk. And it found a way to steer its willing victim in other directions when his important tasks were completed. But the man had a conscience. And that friend did not finally betray him when, on a late sunny morning, the reluctant New Orleanian seized the moment. He grabbed the folder from his desk like he was angry at it, as if it were the fault of the folder or its contents that he was mired in confusion. He stuffed it in his bag and headed out with a resolve.

He found himself on the single step of the shallow concrete pond next to the zoo in Audubon. A steady stream of water issued lazily upward from the fountain at the head of the pond. At its crest, it dropped lazily into the pond, where on impact, it affected a continuously occuring splash. Each splash of water on water contained the sounds of many hands clapping. The sound overtook the busy chatter of the winged creatures perched in the oak branches overhead.

He chuckled fondly as he recalled the early morning hours many years ago. It was here that he and his teenage cousins and friends lay in the same pond in their drawers, drinking warm Dixie Beer. After dangling his feet in the warm pond, he felt the urge to move on. He decided to go to his go-to special place just outside the park only two short blocks away. He added socks and shoes again and headed for his Old Oak Tree. Once there, he settled in with ease.

"I don't know why I didn't come here first. I get perspective here. You've been reaching out to me here since I was a boy on a bike. You drew me under this Oak Tree, and this Oak Tree drew me to You. I didn't know it until I left home. But I know it now."

His thoughts went to the blue folder and its contents.

"My coming King, what is it that I'm to make of what is in my hand"

He stopped to ponder, pay respect, and allow his soul to bask in The Presence.

"I know your name. It is 'I AM', One True God and Father. It is Jeshua[85], Son of God, crucified and risen King. It is Sacred, Holy Spirit."

He paused in utter brokenness and wonder, overcome by the heavy weight of the words, the moral character, and boundless love of the One Whom he addressed.

"But what is Your Name, I pray you, for me to know You as at this special spot in my story, under my Old Oak Tree? In what this place means to me, and to You and me, in my sixty-seven year story? What can I call You in relation to this special, dying tree, and how You've drawn me here and spoken to my heart through my attraction to it? In that vein, O God, what is Your Name as I address You, honoring our experience at this tree?"

He sat with his back against the high brick fortress wall of the old Poor Servant's monastery. He gazed at his tree across the narrow street. It's thick, drab, gray moss appeared heavy on its listing branches. The trunk was leaning in more noticeably toward the street. His Old Friend appeared to be tired.

"The average lifespan of your kind is two hundred and seventy five years. You, my friend, would have sprouted here in the late seventeen hundreds. If you've not been very special to anyone else in your long span, you have been to me. In that way, I am a companion to the generations of creatures which have found shelter from you. Both of us have lived more life than we will live going forward. I'm glad for the special moments You've given me here, God, under it's shelter, and when I rode by when a boy on a bike."

Having no indication what special Name he might employ there, he went back to his original question regarding The Protocols. As always, when at his spot, though not hearing an audible voice, he was aware of a generally well-informed and broadly considered space of counsel. And to that place he was now able to go.

---

[85] Hebrew for "Jesus".

In that space, he had accumulated, stored, sorted, considered, cross-examined, challenged, compared, questioned, defended, and re-examined counsel from others, Scripture-tested presumptions, and prayerful meditations. All of these had already helped him think about the answer to his question. And he found himself where he had been before, realizing that guidance is reserved to the one who is willing to act. And that the affirmation always comes into clearer focus within the healthy moral action.

Over the next few days, he wrote down his understanding of how and why The Protocols might relate to him. He typed them on a document to print, making space to write down his comments.

THE PROTOCOLS[86]

Of

THE ESSAYS

Of

Saint Anon

Words of Warning ride Whispering Winds - *Whispering in the sounds of the train horn and bell sounds; my Old Oak, and the clouds; the news behind the news, and misc. discoveries*

Deposits on listening ears - *Since I was a boy*

Timely seedlings for THE ESSAYS - *Is this what its been all about?*

Devono essere scritti di nuovo *Written anew? What???? Who????*

A n old folder of blue *The disappearing man at the bus stop, Momma, Aunt May, Songieux, and Vincent; Now in my hands!!!*

---

[86] Original, with footnotes, beginning of Chapter 22

A life is a hard field to plow; Five is of twelve   - *The plowing image is one of my guiding spiritual metaphors (Matthew 11:28-30); I'm Paw Paw Tino's fifth grandchild of 12;*

Soldiers on the appendage - *My dreams*

The siren howls over the playground   - *Air raid warning sirens in '60's*

Wars, wars, and wars - *The news behind the news again*

Fifty is lost; Still the heart knows - *In 1968 I wagered Joey Groves $50 that the world would end by the year 2000 || I paid him in 2009 — I lost that bet.*

Inizia a scrivere, Il tempo e' vicino! - *Yes, the time is short. But write what???*

In latter years, Scrivi; Newly for times, as in the past - *What past? Does this connect with past warnings to watch and be alert since Jesus ascended to heaven??*

Dal libro! Sixty-six writers of forty works - *By the book! | 66 writings in The Bible*

Secondo le Scritture!   *Nothing considered that is apart from The Writings*

Broken seals at the foot of heaven's throne

Cinque in numero - *5 seals broken until now | my understanding*

For such a time as this - Numero Sei; Scrivi   -   *Soon to come the 6th??? It appears so to me*

Dark clouds in the east, Forebodes of John's beast - *Current Middle East*

Clarion whispers to the least, *Someone who's kept a listening ear toward the east, as I've done since 1974 | My 40 year following of events there that aren't covered by big news*

In the field, In the field, In a hardy field to plow - *My go-to metaphor in Matthew's gospel*

Seeking the City that will descend from the cloud — *Celestial city*

Blue sky, lone bird in the Whispering Wind - *Sister Mary Imelda's class, First grade, Saint Francis, 1958*

A man is smoking on a pole;   An angry man has a gun
My vanishing friend at Bivi 2's with blue folder: - First time almost murdered
One clenches a broken bottle *- Second time almost murdered*
But the head on the right foot changes everything *- The poor young man who died w his head on my right foot.   The experience altered the direction of my life*
An appointment with a champion; *- My buddy Champ, who showed me Jesus*

Yellow napkins on a nearby table *- The Professor was writing on yellow napkins in Wendy's*
An old man is face-to-face *- He came to sit right across the table from me*
And a butterfly from behind on the right *- This one strikes no chord of familiarity. Perhaps it hasn't happened yet?*
A horn by the river, Six dings of a bell *- My whispering uptown sounds*
Slow-dying Old Friend, Uncommon allure *- My beloved Oak*
And the sky's clouds, Always,... the clouds *- Well, these certainly make it seem like somebody's been in my head*
Humanity's convergence, and then *- I've seen this unfold in my lifetime*
That Day....... Il tempo e'vicino *- 'That day' as mentioned by the Hebrew prophets, and Yes! The time is near.*
One mind, Of The Lie, Unitary Planetary Adversary *- The lines jive with my personal conclusions through the process I've observed unfolding since 1974; and in line with The Scriptures*
Broken seals at the foot of heaven's throne *— Revelation, Chapter 6*
Humans despairing, wishing to die *- Revelation 6:12*
'Hide us, fall on us! Fall from the sky!' *- This is in agreement with what appears to be where we are in history; My draw to Revelations 6:12*
Scrive, ... Certamente, Il tempo e' vicino!
''Write''! Again?? ....Certainly, the time is near. My mantra
In every language, Watch, Be on the alert *- My utmost wishes for all since 1974; Jesus' warnings*

To eyes that are looking and ears that are hearing…..
Angelino stands where the bus stops - *Is this the name of my friend*
with the blue folder at the bus stop in front of Bivi 2's?
Scrive, … Atem lo levad. - *Yes, indeed, I am not alone!*
On yellow napkins, *WOW! He wrote on yellow napkins when I saw him!*
And again: The Protocols!

~ Songieux

Should not your name be 'Angelino' as well, my friend??? Your name makes you
more real than you already are, and personal, at least, to me.

When he completed his review and notations, he leaned back in his
chair. Looking around his study, his eyes rested on an old wooden box
on the bottom of a bookshelf. It occupied its place like collectibles do.
Day after day, year after year, few glances from human eyes brushed
over it. He stored sentimental items inside. And in the moment, he was
compelled to open it.

After perusing its items for some moments he came upon a note his
momma had sent him while he was in college. He smiled softly as he
opened it. It read……

     Simeon, my dear.

     You're daddy and I are proud of you.
You know it's hard for him to tell you,
but I can tell. I know him.
     It was hard for us when you left us
for the Navy a few years ago. And we
thought you might come back home after.
But we can see that the path you are
choosing is a good one.
     The Lord guided you away because you
needed to leave home to find yourself.
You strayed and told me you didn't need
God at one point. Remember? That was

> hard, but I kept asking Him to guide you
> and to help you find Him. And He did.
>   Remember, you've always had a good
> mind. And in time you learned how to
> think things through very well. Always
> do that. And then, do what you know is
> right. Because deep down, you've always
> known what that is.
>
>   Love Always,
>   Mother

The words were cool water to his weary soul. And the last line wouldn't stop playing in his mind: *"And then, do what you know is right. Because deep down, you've always known what that is."*

"Yes, momma. You always held us to a pretty high standard that way. I wish there had been time before you left for us to talk about Songieux."

He left home shortly after two that afternoon. He drove to a quiet place in City Park and parked beneath a tree. He sat in silence.

The blue folder was beside him beneath The Protocols. They were words of the most meaningful kind to a man like he, inked onto flimsy yellow napkins by a perfect stranger on a halcyon day, in an obscure fastfood restaurant. And as he looked down at them, his momma's words once again echoed in his mind……..

'...deep down, you've always known what is right.'

Forty Nine

He went again to the secret place.

"My Father, my heart weeps for my city, my country, and for the world. It weeps for my brothers and sisters who are being tortured and killed this very moment throughout the world because of their faith. And for all of us who it may come to before it's over. It weeps for the poor who have suffered so much. It weeps for the comfortable and the merrymakers, who presume all will continue as it always has. It weeps for the builders and planners who presume the same."

"My heart also weeps because we count on so many things that we take for granted. It weeps because we are secure in our comforts and are angry if they are not available any more. It weeps because we have become complacent in our exercise with You."

"My heart weeps because we have distorted Your truth. We have fashioned You into a teddy-bear God with no backbone or moral justice. And it weeps for the astronomical injustices in this selfish, world. It weeps for the greed that has overtaken our motives and ambitions. It weeps for the lies, the wars, the deceitful conniving, the abuses, the hatred, the murders, and the treacheries – all of which are now common enough as to no longer surprise."

"And I'm afraid. Not just for me and my family. I'm afraid for everyone. This, I know isn't healthy. And this is why it's been hard for me to process the entrance of The Professor, Songieux, into my story. And of the visit from Angelino at the bus stop so long ago. And how did I end up in the students' dream, Brent was his name, only to show up in his life months later just like the dream went down? And they are such a mystery and inspiration to me at once.

You've helped me with fear before. Help me again. Take this thief of my joy."

"I know that I'm not the only one. There are, and have been since You came to earth two-thousand years ago, many who've been inspired by Your return. And the more so today, as we are now on the delivery bed and birth is about to take place."

"And, Great Father, are we not destroying ourselves through the use of technology and its dizzying potential to build a world that doesn't need or want You, our very Creator? Are we not on the precipice of merging humans and technology, creating a super-species of being? Are You going to allow Satan to achieve this feat and have his own creation, mankind merged with technology?

"Forgive us for our complacency. Many of us say that we believe, that we trust You. But we really don't. Forgive me for my complacency, for the times when I presume I'm trusting, but I'm not."

When he retrieved himself, he reclined his seat back and looked up to the tree branches above him. Though he couldn't know it from where he sat, across town, Old Man River was moving faster and its waters carrying weighter things both seen and unseen from the far north.

Fifty

He couldn't help overhear some of the dialogue between the two patrons seated next to him. They announced their shameless opinions loudly across the dining area. He had to concentrate to hear Nick speak. Their words were those of men who knew better, and seemed to come from sources that had no small opinions of themselves.

"Idiots", "I wish they'd let me do it", "nobody knows anything."

The hot air continued to invade the space where he and Nick sat. And at the apex of the heat, before a merciful pause, he turned his head in dismay to view the fountains from which the warm air spewed.

"Excuse me, Nick. I'll be right back."

He bolted for the bathroom. When he returned, the barrage continued. Nick, perhaps for similar relief, stepped outside to receive a call. He was left to fend for himself.

As he searched for coping mechanisms, a familiar image appeared in his mind's eye. It was of the two boisterous men. In the image, their earlobes were lit up. He imagined for a moment how the world might be if a person's earlobes displayed his or her motives. The thought made him chuckle.

The stored image of lighted earlobes helped him to take looks inside in his personal story. As a casual practice, he imagined himself with either his left earlobe lit a shade of blue, or his right one a shade of red. It helped him consider his Motive and Ambition in the moment.

The stroll down imagination lane ran its course. Nick returned, the warm air continued to expel from the table beside them, and not long after, it was time to depart Pomilese's.

When he walked outside, he was greeted with a familiar sound. The sound of the train horn halted him in his steps. The short blast was followed by the familiar six dings of a bell. But this time, it was different. He had never heard the sounds so loud. And he wondered if the whole city, perhaps the whole world, might have heard them.

It froze him. He looked down on the unlevel brick sidewalk that supported his bike. And it conjured up memories of traversing the uptown sidewalks along the river the first twenty one years in his story. He grabbed the handlebar to mount his bike. He would pass by his Old Oak Tree on the way home. Like the residence his momma and daddy had always called home, he knew it would be ensconced in its place, as it always was, all of his sixty-seven years, outside Audubon Park.

When he arrived at the site of his Old Oak he was overcome with disbelief. The tree had been cut down, its trunk carved up and lying in sections on the ground. Simeon dismounted his bike alongside the wall of the convalescent home. He was overcome with a feeling of deep loss, when an elderly caretaker walked up, on her way in to work.

"How long has this tree been cut down, mam?"

"Ahm not, sure, baby. Seems like it couldn't-uh been too long. Maybe a week or two."

"Man, Ah…

"Why you aksing, dawlin?"

"Ah grew up around hee-uh. And dis one tree has always been special tuh me."

He slid into New Orleans-speak. For a moment again, he was a boy on a bike.

"Oh, it was so old, baby."

She couldn't have known she was responding to the lost neighborhood boy of decades ago whom he involuntarily conjured up and proffered in the moment.

"You saw how duh branches were rotting and it didn't have no more leaves on it and all uh dat. And look at dat trunk, mah baby. See how dee inside has dat big-ole rotten hole in the middle. Dat thing was gonna fall, fuh show-thing, precious. Ooom-hoom."

"Yes indeed. Ah see dat. Ah wish it was still hee-uh, anyway."

"Why dis tree mean so much to you, mah dear?"

"Gawd met me heeuh ever since Ah was a boy riding by on mah bike."

His voice shook in the words. A lump formed in his throat.

The dear woman noted his affection. She placed her wise and weathered hand on his shoulder. The warm touch of the stranger, and the tender heart that held it, affected him. He began to sob.

"Ahm sorry, mam. It's been a long journey. Ah've gone faw away and returned. Gawd has worked so much in mah life, and this Old Oak has been an important piece in mah story fuh so long, strange as such a thing seems."

"It ain't no strange thing tuh me, precious. What means something tuh somebody means somethin tuh dem. Keep yuh fine memory of dis old tree dat ain't been nuttin but a rottin old tree tuh me all uh deez years. Pick you up a piece or two of dat old tree. Take it home wit choo and keep it as a memorial. It's something between you and Gawd, mah baby. Dat's enough tuh make it special to you, if it ain't special tuh nobody else, no way. You and me gonna pass on one day soon just as show as dis tree done did. Ah gots tuh go in and get to work, dawlin. Ahm glad we got to talk. And may duh Lawd be wit choo and yuh family always."

"You too, sweetie. May He be with you and yours as well."

When she left, Simeon sat and leaned against the wall of the convalescent home. His Old Tree was no more. And He felt violated by the hand that held the executioner's saw which felled the martyred corpse before him.

He wanted to speak, so he advantaged himself one last time in its presence. He spoke to The Inaudible Voice, which always drew him at his Old Oak.

"What is Your Name?"

Nothing.

After a long pause he continued.

"I'd like to know what to call you. Soon, there will be no physical evidence that You enlivened Yourself to me in this place. With regard to our Tree, I'll remember You as You wish to be called here, remembering our special times here."

He realized that he could simply give it a name based on his life experience with it, and that which drew him there. But he wanted it to come from The One Who lured him there as a lonely, searching, and lost boy on a bike, in search of The Celestial City.

"What is Your Name, unique to this spot, and to our Tree?"

Nothing again.

He revisited the gallery of his mind and reviewed some of the images there. He saw the rich, full moss draping his Old Oak when it was upright and strong. In his mind's eye the mossy image impressed him as that of a thick, graying beard hanging from the face of a benevolent and just, wise King. He spoke again to Him, with a fresher perspective.

"King... Voice to me through this tree, isn't that Who You are, and have always been? Didn't it take me twenty-one years to find that out? And isn't it true that I'm still finding out what that means?"

"O King... Isn't that what you've led me to discover about You in my story?"

"My King... And isn't that why I present You as such to others, in my relationships, in groups, and in classes?"

"Oh my Great, Kind King... Isn't that why You are coming again soon, to save humanity from ourselves and to rule this world in justice and righteousness?"

The mossy image of The King resonated in his soul. After a lifetime of meaningful experiences with his beloved Old Oak, things were coming into convergence. Yet he still didn't have a name. He sat against the corner of the brick wall. There was space behind and on his right.

"Please, ...what is Your Name in this place?"

At the end of the question, a monarch butterfly bounced through the air from behind and on the right. It flitted and darted in irregular arcs and lines in the direction of the slain tree. When it arrived there, it bobbed, weaved, and arced back and forth, up and down, as if in celebration and adeiu, above Simeon's beloved icon. It circled left, bouncing over the air toward Simeon. When it neared him, it continued its circular journey, hovering briefly, directly over his head, before continuing left again. When it reached the airspace above the tree's corpse again, it repeated its celebratory dance before circling left again and out of sight around the left side of the building.

"Monarch."

He distinctly heard the sound of the word in his mind, affirming the type of butterfly he just saw. When he spoke the word, he realized the answer to his question. And he realized that he had just been given the name for The One Who spoke inaudilble life to him in the presence of the slain Old Tree since he was a boy.

"I saw the mental image of the most excellent king, with a thick, graying, mossy beard. I asked again 'what is Your name?' Then came the monarch butterfly. Monarch..... King,... of course."

Lily-Grace had planted milkweed around the house as host plants for the eggs of monarch butterflies. Because of that action, numerous monarchs filled the air in the front and back yards around their home, feeding from the nectar of the many flowers she planted there. He was familiar with them. He had photos of them feeding atop the flowers.

"Monarch,... My King, and Lord.."

And his voice cracked and the tears moistened and the lump rose again.

"Did that common monarch butterfly simply fly around from behind me on its own accord when I asked again for Your name? Or are You visiting me in special way as an answer for such a time as this?"

If it were absurb for one to believe such matters were orchestrated by the hand of Providence, then the doctorates of probability might be inclined to offer a concrete formula to explain away such matters. In contextual space and time, only the good-heart beholder in the experiences will know what can or cannot be known.

In the moment, he recalled the phrase from The Protocols and his note beside it. It was the last remaining phrase that he couldn't find a personal connection with. The phrase, with his added note was:

"And a butterfly from behind on the right[87]
This one strikes no chord of familiarity. Perhaps it hasn't happened yet?"

He bowed his head in silence. He went to the secret place[88].

Without effort, he hung the experience, in the form of its mental image, in the corridor of his mind. He hung it just inside the door. It was near the first grade experience with Sister Mary Imelda, his brief, wordless exchange with the stranger at the bus stop, his barracks room encounter with Jesus at Leary Air Force Base where everything changed, and his encounter with Songieux in Wendy's after he moved back home.

A mile and a half downriver, at the foot of Lions and Front Streets, a train horn blew a deafening blast from a still locomotive that was about to move. Six very loud and deep sounds from a dong rang from the same

---

[87] Chapter 48
[88] Psalm 31:20 NASB – "...in the secret place of Your presence."

place. After the six dongs there was a seven-second pause. The train horn blasted a second deafening blast, followed by six more very loud sounds from a dong. Seven more seconds passed. The sounds were repeated until six rounds of sounds from the horn and the dongs were completed.

And in the seventh round of the soundings, after the dong sounded six times, there was a seven second pause. It sounded out a last, resounding, seventh and final "GONG" that reverberated up the river, to the far reaches of the north. Far beyond, it reached an unseen, formerly impenetrable wall, shattering it. In its absence, unseen things were unleashed, things never before seen or known. Then it was silent.

At the first blast of the horn Simeon's head pivoted around toward the river, toward the place of his roots along Tchoupitoulas Street. The old building owned by his ancestors still stood there. The front-end of the building that housed Fump's Bar still fiercly guarded its history. And the side window, where Old Put Smith, who knew much more than he could ever say; and where he often stood, waiting to put out his hand for a quarter, was boarded up, never to be opened again. One of the survivors of its history, the fifth of twelve Mangino grandchildren, was still in its story that very moment. The uncharacteristic loudness of the horn and the dongs right by Fump's, and the seven repetitions of their broadcast, were not lost on him in the least.

Most in the near neighborhood heard the sounds and were piqued at the sudden loud intrusions through the air all around. He found himself in tune with the unseen, previously unknown things now unleashed from the far north beyond the river. And he couldn't hold back the peaceful smile that ascended from his heart to his face, nor the single, sad tear of lament that formed in his eye and began to drip down. The salty discharge did not subdue his gentle smile as it slid down over his cheek, a single drop, tracing down to link with the corner of his mouth, where sadness and happiness made peace. Rather, it complemented it, like the falling rain on an afternoon when the sun shines.

There were miles to pedal to get home. He recalled the advice of the kind woman. He walked among the tree's carcass looking for a memory piece. He found one, suitable to place on a shelf filled with memories too special to forget. It would remain there until his last day on earth. And he could not have been more thankful that he had the chance to experience every precious moment of his last moments with his Old Oak Tree.

He pedaled the late sunny afternoon through Audubon and up the levee to the bicycle trail on top. A chilly wind from the far north met him when he gained the levee top, unleashed by the recent blast . The steady north wind wove its way down the Mississippi River Valley. It found its way around the first turn on the approach to the crescent city and mounted on wings as it headed toward him. To his left below, the waters flowed furiously southward as he made his way north against the increasing wind that rode atop the murky, muddy river. Like always, he continually glanced at the old river. It was a marker to him of his roots, his story, and his place. An unusual amount of floating debris rapidly swept by, bobbing atop the treacherous current of the mighty river.

The water was an intensely darker brown that day. And the increasing wind was agitating the waves atop the choppy river as it coaxed it on. The near-surface currents were swirling and spinning into countless aqua tornados up and down the river and all across between its crescent turns. And in its perpetual southerly flow, strong and abrupt things previously unknown were carried along with it.

Simeon zipped up his thin jacket and bore down on his quads to maintain his forward motion. He lowered his head forward to lean into the wind so it would apply less pressure against him. He noticed dark, gray clouds forming quickly, very quickly, in the northern skies ahead. As he did, a blast of wind brought with it new elements that were incrementally colder and harder to pedal against.

The man-made levee protected the city from flooding by the river. It was springtime. And the river was near its annual spring floodstage crest from the melting of the northern snows and eventual drainage into the Ohio and Mississsppi River basins. He noted how the levee protected the city. On his right was River Road with its single lane traffic. The placid, sleepy neighborhood comprised of small cottage homes was populated with folks who took the levee for granted. But from his present vantage he could witness just how much the levee meant to them in their smugness. The river to the left was noticeablly higher than the neighborhood to the right.

"At any time, the Good Hand that stays the evil force that is tightening its grip on the entire world, will be removed. And like the levee that protects our fair city, the world will be engulfed by evil it has never known. Have mercy, blessed Hand."

As he labored on, the dark clouds that formed in the far north began to overtake the skies over him and as far into his path as he could see. The wind picked up again. He changed gears for a second time. The thunder that he heard in the northern skies now announced itself in slow, steady rumblings all around him as well. And their flashes of lightning did not hide from his eyes.

Grinding ahead, he wished he had brought something to cover his ears. As he approached the parish line, he noted the small incline and pushed ahead. He had crossed from Orleans Parish into Jefferson countless times. For the first time, he was aware that one day he would cross it for the last time.

Trudging onward against the contrary elements, he was aware of what he needed to do. He would begin, or more accurately, he would begin the process of finishing, when he got home. He had indeed meant to finish several times over the past few months, only to pause, and then procrastinate. And he wondered, as he approached the small incline at the parish line, if he indeed had crossed a line when he had the rewarding opportunity to behold his Old Oak Tree one last time. Something of a crossing was felt with a new impetus to forge ahead with every pretense and illusion behind him. Ironically, the loss of his tree gave him a new confidence. It applied to what was confronting him in his rubicon moment. And though never forgotten, in the functioning place of his beloved Old Oak, he now had the near image of his Monarch Butterfly.

The very air he moved in seemed to grow darker with each completed cycle of the pedal. The murky water of the muddy river did as well. He captured the small incline at the parish line. As he pedaled on from the perch there, his figure began to slowly shrink against the darkening horizon. But despite the darkness ahead and on the river that flowed in the opposite direction, his face was set like a rock toward the incomplete task before him. Everything necessary had been provided. No matter what would come of it, he intended to finish.

His shadow continued to diminish as he pedaled hard toward home. The familiar demarcation of the parish line fit a possibility every time he crossed it in the past. There was always the potential for it to be his last traverse there, a non-negotiable aspect of every visible and invisible line in the universe. The shrinking, decreasing figure of a small boy on a bike, long a man now, shrunk into a smaller and smaller dot on the dark and ominous horizon. Now so very tiny, it morphed into a hazy vapor that appeared for a brief moment in a space of time, like a wisp of steam from a boiling pot. Then it was gone.

Epilogue

"So what's stickin out to you in what we just read, guys?"

His words echoed through the chambers of his mind as he recalled being asked the same words often. It was New Years Eve afternoon. There could be only one reason that he and his two friends braved the mind-boggling cold that held New Orleans and the entire country in its frozen grip. Their informal meetings were forbidden by city and state officials. Extraordinary measures were being taken to keep people away from one another.

Vincent, Tony, and Alvin met several times a week in the very different world than they inhabited all their lives. They kept their meetings on the low because they were vitally important to them. Vincent was a lifetime friend of his fellow New Orleanians. After his life changed, he was with his new friend, his former enemy of choice, a lot. They invested many hours together, praying and looking into the Scriptures. Now, Vincent DeMaso was passing it on the way it had been passed on to him.

"Ahm thinking about what Jesus meant in this statement. He mentioned 'yhe cares of dis world, the deceitfulness of riches, and the desire for other things'[89]. Ahm glad dat you've helped me realize how Jesus died for me so dat I could be forgiven and have life, Vincent. For so long, Ah didn't care about any uh dat stuff. Ah was caught up in the cares of dis world. God was a thought, but an afterthought. It sounds like The Lord is saying dat deez things choke the effect of God's words in our lives, from having its helpful impact. Izzat how you guys see dis?"

Vincent was quiet. He had thoughts and he knew what Jesus was saying. He had dug into this on his own and with his mentor. But he didn't speak.

"Yeah, Alvin. Ah know dat for me, Ah was so into being swept up by our New Awlins culture dat Ah didn't desire to make room for Gawd.

---

[89] Mark 4:19

Ah thought Ah was content. But deep down Ah wasn't. Ah was hurting, and Ah didn't know what to do about it."

"Me too, Tony. Me too."

As the boys went back and forth, he noted the self-discovery process at work in them. Though he had become a mentor to them, he knew from the way he was mentored that he didn't have to tell them everything. They were hungry for the God of their new lives. When being mentored himself, he was given room to wade through the words of Scripture. The processes of wondering over them alone and chewing on them with a friend helped him to learn and grow. He became aware that not all telling is teaching. And that not all teaching is learning. He knew that his mentor knew things and had lived the new life many long years. But he appreciated that he gave him room to discover many things himself. On occasion, he would chime in and sometimes launch into a monologue. But he was often as much ears as he was mouth.

"When Vincent first turned to duh Lawd we thought he was weird, remember, Alvin? We tawked about him and kept away from him. But he still reached out to us in love. Dat made it for me, man. He kept in touch without being too pushy. He bid his time and waited for moments with us. As we opened up, he walked in wit duh good news about Jesus."

"Yeah you rite, Tony. You're not getting too big-headed hearing all of this dat we're saying about choo, are you, DeMaso?"

The big man just laughed a short huff. But in his heart he was a grateful man. The heater barely kept the outside cold at bay. But his heart was being warmed in present company.

"So what's left to care about in our world today as far as material things? Duh playing field has been leveled. And what's left and still open is now off limits to us unless we download the reporting app. Since we're not gonna do dat we're left to swap, trade, or do tasks for the little food we can obtain. Soon, we may be in danger of losing our homes. With out each other and our other brothuhs and sistuhs, we'd be up a creek without a paddle."

"It's sobering, allright, Vincent. And many of the ones who are trusting in the system are still struggling from the original shutdown last year. And the rioting and looting are continuing, so we're hearing."

"Dat's why we need to keep meeting to pray, Alvin. Even though we have to lay low, we and our bruthuh's and sistuh's desparately need to come together and come to our Gawd."

"Yes indeed, Vincent. Unemployment is worse den it was when things first got bad. Food is scarce and some are virtually starving. Duh riots in many cities are spreading into neighborhoods."

"Dat's right, Tony. And dee unheard of fall and winter weather have only made things worse."

"Yeah, Vince, and all the hurricanes. And dey say it was duh worse year for fires in the country. Earthquakes and tsunamis are happening right now. My neighbor told me about dem. He's the one who's been giving us food. With duh shutdown effect throughout the world and the noticeable increase in natural disasters, and everything else, it's been a time of testing for all of us."

"It's downright serious dat they are watching people on all of their smart technology. First, it was to publish who's had duh test and who hasn't. Den it grew to broadcast who's had duh sickness and who hasn't. Now it's public on the system who has gotten the treatments and who hasn't."

"Do you think we're at duh time you told us about, Vincent? You know, we looked at some of the things Jesus, Paul, and Peter said. And we also looked at some of the prophets too."

"Mah mentor was certain of it, Alvin, one-hundred percent certain. Ah think so. And Ah agree with him. We're right there. He's coming back any second. Ahm listening for dat trumpet sound dat we looked at a few weeks ago, coming like a thief in the night, like the twinkling of an eye."[90]

"So Vince, what about all of these terrible things dat we experienced dis year up to dis New Year's Eve? And the stuff dey say is going around, do you think it was all orchestrated?"

"Who knows, Tony. Ah've come to learn that Satan's plan is ultimate control. Anyway dat's happening, Ah presume it's by his hand. Note how more and more power is funneled to the structure. When more power accrues, we see what the agenda is. It's virtually always

---

[90] I Thessalonians 4: 16-18; I Corinthians 15: 51-53

suppression and control. If things *weren't* orchestrated, those in control of the system have at least reacted to things in such a way so as to parlay things to their advantage. They've gained more power and control each successive time. And that's Satan's agenda."

"Is dee earth under judgment now, Vincent?"

"Ya'll are aksing some tough questions, mah bruthuh's."

He wished that his friend was present.

"There are different opinions on this. What mah mentor thought was that some uh duh descriptions of Jesus in the gospels and John in the Revelation are in language describing partial judgments, or warnings to duh world of impending severe judgment. Dat would be just like the loving nature and character of Gawd. He has given warnings before judgments in the past."

"Partial judgment….. dat sounds like Jesus' statement dat duh signs for His coming would increase in intensity like birth pains.[91]"

"Dat's right, Alvin. And what were dose birth pain signs again?"

"Okay, mentor. Ahm up for dis. Lesssseee,.. Matthew twenty-four… wars, rumors of wars, nations opposed to nations, famines, and earthquakes. And Luke twenty one, ...plagues, or pandemics, and famines."

"Not bad for a boy your age, Alvin."

He recalled saying the same words numerous times to the one he wished was there.

"So you're linking the partial first judgments in The Revelation wit the more intense birth pains dat Jesus mentioned in Matthew, right Vincent?"

"Yeah, dat's what Ahm wondering."

"Keep going, Vincent. Hand me dat scawf first."

He rubbed his cold hands together rapidly then placed the scarf around his neck.

"Okay Alvin. Duh trumpets in Revelation refer to one-third of dee earth experiencing calamities. And it might mean that different parts of dee earth experience the different calamities at different times, though more pronounced than typical calamities have been in the past. Since

---

[91] Matthew 24: 3-8

deez may be more nearly like calamaties have always been on the earth –
a catastrophic event in one place at a time – den people will not tend to
see dem as warnings from Gawd. In this way, duh 'one third' of the
earth that experiences these partial judgments[92] may be meant to mean
something like: 'a significant number that is more than ususal, still
somewhat random, but more random and catastrophic than usual'. "

"The bowl judgments[93] affect dee *entire* earth. And it appears dat
everyone who has the mark of the beast will be recipients of the more
harsh, expansive, comprehensive, judgments. It appears dat the birth
pains are most frequent and intense through the *full* expression of the
wrath of Gawd in these bowl judments. Dat will be because the physical
universe is about to give birth to the Kingdom of Gawd, with planet earth
and humanity as its epicenter."

He paused as he noticed a police squad car slowly moving through the
frigid air down the street. Visiting friends at home was considered a
gathering and banned without showing proof of compliance. If one had
no phone, the detaining authority could check the records. In most
states, it was dangerous to leave the boundaries of one's property or
dwelling without proof of having what was required.

As the patrol car slowly passed in the frigid cold, the men leaned back
in their living room chairs. Vincent bent forward with his chin between
his legs. His massive frame could easily be seen through the naked
window.

*"Why didn't Ah close dose curtains? It's too cold to have em open
anyway."*

As the car moved down the street, the men sat up and looked at one
another. They each knew what the other was thinking. Had they been
found out, they were done. Appeal to citizen rights was no longer an
option. Dissenting opinions were totally banned everywhere. And
everyone was at the mercy of either a lenient, understanding state or
local official or one that was given to the system. And it was
questionable in their area.

The system and its puppets now operated as its own law. And its
bureaucracy was set up to protect it. The original rule of law based on

---

[92] Revelation Chapter 8
[93] Revelation Chapter 16

the document of the fathers was virtually shredded. Elites full of empty
promises steadily gained control from within the system, beginning in
the middle of the previous century.

The intrepid, debilitating cold eased overnight though it was still very
unseasonably cold when Vincent sat down alone to breakfast. It was
New Years Day. For some time, every meal for those outside the system
was a meager one, if there was one to be had at all. Miracles of all kinds
were happening by the hands of many of the brothers and sisters. And he
had witnessed several in the most challenging of times. He paused to
thank His Lord for what he had when his doorbell rang. When he
opened the door, the frigid air startled him. A man Vincent had never
met spoke up without introducing himself. He wore no winter coat.

"I have something for Vincent Demaso."

Without hesitating, he reached out to receive the gift. He did a quick
scan of the stranger's garb and appearance with a tender look. He was
touched by the nerdy, professor-looking man's appearance at his door.
And he felt the bond that two people have when both have an intimate
common connection with another person. His eyes were fixed onto those
of the stranger. No additional words were spoken. While each held a
hand on the gift, they heard a loud, abrupt burst from a train horn. It was
immediately followed by the deep sounds of six dongs, followed by a
very loud, and deeper, seventh dong.

Each of their hands held the gift before the strangers hand released it.
With their eyes still locked, the strange old man shared a telling look of
admiration and respect with Vincent. After long seconds, he turned to
walk away in the frigid air.

Vincent closed the door. He was aware that the sound of a local train
could not be heard from his neighborhood. There were no train tracks
within miles. But he was intimately familiar with the sounds from
another story. It was a story he learned to cherish after it intersected,
embraced, and breathed life into his own.

He sat in his comfortable chair in his cold den to open the material that
had been handed to him. As had become his custom over the past year,
he paused to peer out into what used to be his perfectly manicured yard.
What had formerly been unnoticed by him there had become a regular
expereince to enjoy. On many occasions, his new friend, a resident

hummingbird, dashed into view. It was one of the growing number of new-life experiences he began to cherish.

"Soon."

The word did for his heart what the conditions could not do for his body.

He looked down at the worn blue folder in his hand. His thumb was on the top. He recalled another thumb, a smaller one, which he had violently grabbed and attempted to wrench from its socket, breaking it, almost a year ago. Sentiment overtook his soul. His eyes teared.

Awash in emotion and sentiment, he felt as if he might be on the verge of weeping uncontrollably. But along with the emotional energy, a burst of spiritual awareness, with its associated strength, latched onto it. It respectfully refused to interfere with his tears. But its addition tempered and channeled his feelings into that peaceful space where meaning and purpose are found. Recognized and genuinely embraced emotion, which would have formerly led to spiraling regret, was channeled along better pathways to a healthier landing place. The misty tears became fonts of healthy sadness that were tempered by meaningful engagement with a fondness he would never relinquish. And the fondness, engendered by better memories from his healthy heart, left deposits of tenderness, affection, and love there.

He opened the blue folder. A small booklet was inside. As he held the booklet, he gently caressed it. And the only issue that was available inside for release were the warmest words of the most meaningful kind.

"My friend, my brother."

After closing his eyes for a long moment, he again looked down at the object in his hands. He waded through feelings of unworthiness. Then he settled into the place of peace where His Lord would always lead him when he acknowledged Him. He closed his eyes one more time before opening it. And he began to read.

THE ESSAYS
Of
Saint Anon

———

A renewal of the successive contemporary warnings to men and women through the centuries in post-modern language and context

Circa 2021

To those who have ears to hear…

Il tempo è scaduto[94]

———

---

[94] Italian: "The time is up".

Please excuse the delgue of questions that follow, fellow post modern traveller. Though you may be tempted to believe otherwise, know that this writer cares. And so does The One and only Sovereign, and His Savior, King Jesus, who is about to return to earth and save it from the diabolical chaos of men and women. But the questions are necessary for every one of us. So I'll begin.

What's been going on with your heart, dear one? What has been your god in the time that has deposited you into this moment and place?

Do you presume that you can escape true God's loving and just notice? Are you tempted to, or have you already, gambled foolishly on the idea that He is Someone Who lets things go? That He doesn't care about the little things? That He doesn't care about, or is disinterested in you? Or that He couldn't possibly love you if He really knew you? Have you given the media, culture, an author, theologian, or a friend the influence to convince you that He is a mean God? Have you seen and known some of His stated followers to be hypocrites and so dismissed Him? Or do you insist that He is a myth?

Or perhaps you've taken a more hostile view of Him by presuming for yourself a superior perch? And from there, you've been able to banish mean little God away into a corner so as to punish Him for things? (Bad God!) Or are you resigned to blame Him for all of your misfortunes as well as the misfortunes of everyone else? Blame Him for all the bad and evil in the world.

If any of the above befit your view of God, or other similar views consistent with these – it's okay. I mean, it's okay in that there has been time to rethink the matter. He is quite loving and patient beyond our understanding. But *il tempo è scaduto*, (The time is up). Powers are at work everywhere this very moment doing that manipulative/ controlling thing. Hard things are showing up now which warnings have been building like birth pains for a while now.

The game is over. A new Sheriff is about to step into earth-time. Satan's long, evil, treacherous, stultifying, freedom-robbing control is about to end. But not without a fight. His hatred is now launching to mystifying heights through dazzling, paralyzing, (and mostly devious) displays of pure evil. He's a control freak beyond any true despot you can imagine. He is positioned like a wolf in sheeps clothing, an angel of light, in every place. His ruse is that what's proferred is best for all.

His conniving schemes have been building steam for decades. Now they have launched into hypersonic mode. All that remains is what others have referred to as "the shaking" to be completed. The shaking has been slowly starting for some years. Its force and motion are increasing now.

Good God loves you, friend. His love is just and pure. He is giving us loving warnings through the intensity of what is now upon us and about to go into hyperdrive. It is His loving way to warn first.

The birth pains that women endure in childbirth are God-given, loving warnings of something wonderful, and very quite exquisitely painful (I am told), almost beyond bearable. Imagine that a woman is working at her desk fully pregnant to the nine months, blissfully focused. But her water breaks and the baby is about to force her head out! The sudden intense pain without warning would be an uncaring experience to arrange for a woman who is about to bring a precious new life into the world.

On the other hand, the early, irregular, infrequent contractions are a signal that birth is inevitable. As they grow in frequency and intensity, the special daughter of Adam begins to check that the house is secure, her things prepared, and her help is on standby. This is the way of loving God.

It is *The ESSAYS* writer's deepest longing and heartfelt hope that you will lend considering ears to the following simple words. Give them a fair shake as to the possibility (in your mind and heart) that what they are about is good for you, for the writer as well, and for all of us. They are part of what a growing cascade of Jesus followers around the world are saying. They are birth pains of warning that will very shortly arise to their most rapid repitions and most intense pain.

Whether or not you accept the premise that He is about to return any moment, please consider this. Might you hear A Voice in your heart beckoning you? If you do, it is no doubt the Voice of God calling you to a new beginning with Him. Such a beginning with God is what *THE ESSAYS* are about. And it is the natural and hopeful starting point that they are meant to help you turn to. It is the tender, gentler place where all of His warnings through history were meant to lead us.

What follows flows not merely from my own heart, but from the hearts of many through the ages. They couldn't make it to the roundup that is coming on the earth. But they're standing by.

Please consider, my friend.........

ESSAY ONE
Paramount

Soul Knows

There are no excuses, special one. Their have never been. Their never will be. You know of Him way down deep. The elemental things of His existence and your accountability to Him are intuitive, seen through what He has made. Your Soul Knows.

Who are you mad at when something happens to tick you off, but you can find no one to blame? It has happened to all of us. In such a moment, you are getting in touch with what your Soul Knows. You are mad at the One and Only Sovereign over all Who made this world and you. You are mad at Him because your Soul Knows that He Is, that He made you and could have stopped what happened.

What you know, you know. Deep inside, in the soul of your heart, you know. And that is what you will be held accountable for. For what you know and what you do about it. The same goes for this writer, and for everyone - - ever.

Way down deep you may suspect, even know, but pretend away, that there is a supreme good and a supreme evil. And you may know that they are diametrically opposed, at permanent war to the end. And you no doubt suspect that one day, there is coming a day of accountability. He knows that you know. That deep awareness is why we are all accountable. We all know.

He knows that you've been proud, wounded, hurt, angry, afraid, and more. He knows that you're sometimes, or often, mad at Him. That is why He has given you time. He loves you because it is His nature to love. And He has given all of us time. Many, many seconds, minutes, hours, days, weeks, months, and years. But that time is now expiring, special one.

Evil Satan has now accomplished the total hegemony in the post modern world that he has been trying to establish through history. Every world conquering empire, force, political system, philosophy, economic system, and institution have been the roads he has constructed to control man as his freedom-destroying god.

On the other hand, longsuffering, merciful, loving God is good. No arguments to put our fists in His face change this otherwise. We might as well dispute with the nameless, faceless, inanimate wind. It does no good. Go yell at the sun. It will not be moved. He is Who He is, The First-Person Singular, The Present Tense. We can do Him no more harm than a barking prairie dog can to the midnight moon.

He is going to display His authority through sweeping, impartial actions. King Jesus is coming back to earth to save humans from destroying ourselves and to finally set up a just and caring system of rule over the earth. He will be the Ruler. But first comes the time of testing that will come upon the entire earth. We are in that time now.

Do you consider yourself 'a christian'? Are you mindful of and perhaps tasted of and partaken in the riches of his kindness, forebearance, and patience? Have you claimed to have known the heavenly gift and to be part of His body? Do you claim to have dined on the good Word of God?

What has been going on with your heart? What has been your god in the time that has escorted you to this very moment and the place where you sit today? Or are you 'christian' in designation only?

There is no partiality with God[95]. We look at the outward appearance.
But the Lord looks at the heart[96]. He sees hearts like we see faces, only
much more deeply and objectively. He sees what is actually there. He
does so in His loving and just way because he is Spirit. He operates and
communicates at that level, "as far as the division of soul and
spirit,…and able to judge the thoughts and intentions of the heart. And
there is no creature hidden from His sight, but all things are open and
laid bare to the eyes of Him with whom we have to do."[97] He is the
Heart Reader with no bias that leads to prejudice. He sees our hearts
down to their cores. And He abides in this manner effortlessly.

The Good Heart Reader sees you inside and out. And despite the
selfish and rebellious ugliness that is mingled with your sincere and well
meaning desires and interests, He is patient with you. He is not pleased
with the way you have aligned your Motives and Ambitions to some of
the selfish and rebellious uglinesses that are satisfying to your sinful
human fleshly nature. And it these that He wishes to bring healing and
wholeness to.

For you, professing 'christian' who lives not as such, you are most
unhappy in your condition. Your conscience has been hardened by your
repeated selfish choices. You are living out of your fear, poverty, and
shame. You know better but won't turn. The writer of these essays has
been there. He knows of your deep pain.

Choose to turn again. Turn to The One Who loves and forgives as he
has. He is coming back any moment now, like a thief in the night. I
strongly urge you to consider.

If you are one who has never claimed to have come to Jesus for mercy
and forgiveness, you stand as an outsider to these matters. But you don't
have to. Soul Knows. And your Soul Knows that it is your choice as to
what you do about this.

CHOOSE! That is, choose differently. For if you haven't chosen to
turn in desire and humility toward the Wonderful and Set Apart, the
Loving and Just Alpha and Omega, you're already ouside of Him. You
have chosen what you want. And that is you.

---

[95] Romans 2:11
[96] I Samuel 16:7
[97] Hebrews 4:12,13

You have set yourself as the main character of the story of life. We have all begun that way. And so we have conflict, fights, strife, murder, theft, and hatred in many expressions. We can't change others. We can only choose for our own lives. Will you now choose to die to your first-life choice of selfishness and sin, so that you may live? CHOOSE to die to that life.

It started when we were children. It is called 'conscience'. And we are all guilty of violating the unseen, pesky creature which we can't seem to rid ourselves of. Not that we don't try. But try as we may, the built-in nemisis from birth holds on. Consider the backlog of guilt in men and women, and its pitiful birthchild, shame. These are the children of unforgiven sin.

Tragically, many will not acknowledge these things. Or if they do, many others will not respond to them. And so we will move on to further matters related to God, culture, and self-awareness.

ESSAY TWO
Veritas

MotAmbi

All behavior is goal oriented. I scratch my leg because of an itch at the spot. You ordered a hamburger because you wanted a hamburger. A sibling slaps his brother because.....

Thoughts breed actions which, if they become habitual, forge a character. Selfish thoughts breed selfish actions, which forge selfish character. **Moti**ves and **Ambi**tions are the forces that compel our thoughts.

A Motive is a reason. Ambition is the drive to act on the reason. The problem is, we aren't in touch with our self-seeking Motives and Ambitions - *MotAmbi*. Our consciences are hardened from realizing our selfish MotAmbi from years of practice sealing ourselves from them. So our thoughts remain at the surface level, not in touch with what's really going on in our hearts.

Not to say that we can't have a good Motive. But how can we know when we're not in touch with them? And sadly, we don't want to be. It feels like too much work. But it isn't. After a short season of practice with Jesus it becomes second nature. That's due to His strenght in us and because of our intense desire for change at the heart level. My Desire linked with His strength is an unbeatable combination. It's an inside thing, deep and personal.

Spiritual reflection from a heart open to self-evaluation is not a welcome pursuit in the main in 2021. It is dismissed as stodgy, ancient 'christianity' or 'religion'. 'Legalistic' is the more common description of this kind of spirituality. Why do we presume that we are free from such spiritual exercise as to practice self-reflection on a regular basis?

"Veritas" means "truth". One's personal introduction to the truth is meant to have a covenantal and contractual component that is to begin inside of us. We must be willing to agree with it, embrace it into our soul's bosom, and then live it. The truth is that you are loved by God. He loves you because you are his work of art at birth. He wanted you like He made you. But you and I have morally marred the work of art that He originally made us to be. We have burned immoral, selfish thoughts – and their inevitable actions - into the image He made so that we are broken and fractured. We are out of sorts. Something has to be set right to get us back to Him. That starts with our Desire for the new and renouncement of the old – the old deep inside of us. And in truth, we were born with a nature to sin.

God looks at the heart (soul, mind, spirit). And that is where our deep Motives and Ambitions, *MotAmbi*, lie hidden and covered, like a camouflaged command center in battle.   And He wants us to be honest with ourselves there. We don't have to be overly concerned with our

Motives and Ambitions. We simply need to be open. Ask Him to show you if you're not pleasing there.

"Search me Oh God, and know my heart. Try me and see if there be any hurtful way in me." (Psalm 139:23) "You desire truth in the inmost being. In the hidden part You will make me know wisdom." (Psalm 51:6) And He will.

"Faithful is He who calls you, and He will also bring it to pass." (I Thessalonians 5:24)

And when He reveals hidden MotAmbi, it will be personally obvious that, left to ourselves, *'You Ain't So Such A Much'*[98], morally speaking. These regular revelations to our seeking hearts are what will remind us that we are loved by Him, even though we still have sin and regard it inside way too often.

"Veritas" is "truth". And the truth is that, if you turn to Jesus for forgiveness once and for all, you are a new creature in Him. You will sin at times after that. It is imperative that you don't ignore your continued sinful, selfish tendencies. Your heart to want to walk in your new life is what pleases Him. Your sinful actions do not. Don't confuse the two. Your sincere heart and humility in this matter makes all the difference.

This is the astounding love of God in the Lord Jesus Christ.

---

[98] The title of a song recorded by New Orleans' own Blanche Thomas in 1954, in New Orleans' Imperial Records Studio

ESSAY THREE
Aggregate

Co-D Codes

It is almost impossible to live in a land with any version of a free-market without having some level of Co-dependency. Co-dependency is described as an unhealthy attatchment to experiences, to things, or to other people. Because our love tanks are not being filled we feel bad inside. Not knowing/ feeling love from anyone leaves a void in the soul. So we fill that void with experiences, people, and things that make us feel better. What this is addressing is a more than casual, leisure partaking of experiences, things, or other people. Take away Co-D and these are enjoyable, but of little consequence if they are missed.

Jesus spoke about the cares of this world (experiences, things, and other people), the deceit of riches, and desire for other things[99] (experiences, things, and other people again) having a choking effect on someone's potential connection with Him. This is Co-dependency, special one.

One might be mildly Co-dependent, another severely. As levels of Co-d begin to rise, they become more severe over time and addictive patterns begin to form. And over time, as the Co-d behavior intensifies, the addiction begins to harden, wrapping itself around the psycho-chemistry of the person like an anaconda who dines on the human spirit. It first begins to enfold, then to squeeze until life ceases. Then it devours.

Is this too much to digest, friend? Please, bolster your heart to be brave about what is true about life and death, soul and spirit. You won't regret it when this life is over.

Why not think about it now? Life is changing around you in 2021. You may not be able to get your haircut. I hope you're still working. If

---

[99] Mark 4:19

not, I sincerely hope that you're getting unemployment or some kind of help from somewhere. I mean that.

But please, take time to think about God, and you, and eternity. Our levels of Co-dependency indicate the levels to which we don't know and feel loved. And all the while, your caring Creator and Heart Reader sees you. And He loves you. He knows what's going on, dear one. Jesus understands because He lived on this earth as a man, and experienced the challenges and emotions that we do[100].

And at this writing, He sits at the right hand of God the Father to intercede for those who come to God through Him, who have asked for forgiveness.[101] At any moment now, He will rise up and return.

ESSAY FOUR
Abstract

The Desire Quotient

If you continue to want the world, it is the world that you will get. But in the end, you won't like the world that you get. It will be a world of separation, void of God. And you will be there because you desired to be. It will have been your choice.

---

[100] Hebrews 4:14,15
[101] Hebrews 7:25

Desire is a feeling or sensation of wanting or wishing. Because your desire is active it is your responsibility as to how it is fed, nurtured, harnessed, and channeled. In a world where we feed our Co-depenencies and addictions, this will take a change of heart, a new Desire, friend.

Consider Desire to be a force in you. God placed it there at birth so you wouldn't die. You're hungry, so you desire food, thirsty, so you want something to drink. You desire friends, so you connect with others. But our desires are tainted with sin's selfishness. This is desire broken. And if it is not healed it continues to go awry.

Fortunately, God also gave us 'conscience'. When Desire gone awry leads us to reap heartache, pain, guilt, and shame, conscience is regularly seeking our attention. That is God's way of trying to lure us from the deep end we're headed for. If my conscience is hardened then the warning light has been flashing on the dashboard of my soul for a long time. I've ignored it. My soul's engine is in bad shape and getting worse. It will continue on that trajectory until I turn to Him and accept His mercy.

Friend, the time is shorter than short. There is virtually no time left. The King is coming. He is lovingly warning us by allowing us to be taken advantage of by Satan and his world-governing system. And by the increasing calamities the world is witnessing. The moment of trial has come to all the earth.

ESSAY FIVE
Composite

Healthy Spiritual DNA

Many who profess to trust and believe in Jesus fade away from following Him. A main reason is set forth here. It is because something is not right in the spiritual gene pool.

If the pure, unadultered, non synthetic, non-GMO seed of an orange is planted and the conditions stay right, what will you have? And why?

You will have a healthy orange (hopefully more than one) because the DNA of the seed was intact and healthy. So it is with all life forms, special friend, even spiritual life. How do I know this? Because Jesus said so.

"Unless a grain of wheat (seed) falls into the earth and dies, it remains alone. But if it dies, it bears much fruit."[102] When a healthy seed falls and begins to be absorbed into the topsoil, it germinates. Germination is the natural, God-made process in His created order in which the hard shell of a seed breaks down. And in doing so, it releases its life, its DNA, into the soil. The DNA of the orange will be present in the stem shoot that sprouts through the dirt. It will work its way through the developing trunk, branches, and buds until it finally settles into the orange itself. The same DNA of the original orange seed will be in every orange seed, in every orange, on the tree.

Spiritual life, because it is life similar to all other life, works the same way. Jesus' words just cited testify to this. So what are the components of healthy spiritual DNA? I will list three here. They will help you understand some of the foundational dynamics at play in the exciting life that Jesus offers.

The first component of healthy spiritual DNA is **DESIRE**. Can't nobody come into God's kingdom who doesn't want to. You won't be

---

[102] John 12:24

able to become a follower of Lord Jesus if someone has to force you to. It won't take. God's gift of forgiveness and eternal life through the sacrifice of Jesus is a free gift. You can't earn it. Don't try to. Just receive it. Receive Him. It is nigh time, you who were created at your birth in the image of God.

What do you want, dear friend? Maybe you're fed up with living life on your own terms, calling your own shots. Maybe you're stuck in the miry clay of guilt and shame for all that you've done. Perhaps you realize that this Satan's world cannot and will not bring lasting life to you when it's all said and done. What do you Desire?

If you're wondering what kinds of Desire are indicative of one who reaches out to take the forgiving Hand with the nail scars in it, we'll go there briefly.

A God-seekers Desire is fragranced with the following aromas:

First, she is <u>seeking a city</u>, the eternal city of God where righteousness and justice reign[103]. This is obvious within her heart where she is totally disenchanted with this world's system of pseudo-justice, phoney love, and fake righteousness (hypocrisy). So she seeks that which is genuinely of God and only found where He is. And she displays this kind of heart by Desiring to, and applying herself as best as she knows how, to follow this Desire until she finds Him.

And second, she is <u>not satisfied with the status quo</u> of both what this world system offers and of the state of her heart when she is out of sync with God. She senses and feels the void that exists in her disconnect with God. She realizes she is living on her own terms and regrets it. This dissatisfaction begins to, and will continue to, propel her heart away from what dissatisfied it. In this new direction, she applies her heart with a growing Desire for NewLife with her Creator.

The second component of healthy spiritual DNA is **HUMILITY**. The concept, as spoken in God's terms, is of one who is lowly in mind. This mostly has to do with being painfully aware of one's personal spiritual

---

[103] Hebrews 11:10

poverty and inherent moral brokenness, which he deeply regrets[104]. And he wishes deeply that this were not true of himself. His soul reaches out to the Creator God, One and True, whom he knows in his heart cares. And he Desires to be forgiven and right with Him. In his common sense humility, he is respecting himself as a free-thinking person who thinks enough of himself to admit what he is like before God.

He allows that guilt and shame are the natural results of denying his conscience. And he humbles himself to admit that he no longer desires to live that way. Such are the qualities of Humility. It is this state of mind that produces a willingness to allow the third aspect of healthy spiritual DNA to germinate.

The third component of healthy spiritual DNA is **REPENTANCE**. Repentance is a turning, as from a change of mind and heart. I realize I've been thinking/ believing/ living a certain way and that it has not produced the deep, meaningful life that I hoped it would. So I repent, turning in the other direction in a change of mind and heart. I repent, turning to God, Whom I know to be good, loving, merciful, and compassionate. I realize He has been patient with me. I realize He is just. And He cannot and will not live forever with anyone who presumes to want to live selfishly, sinfully, before Him. None of us will thumb our nose at God forever and expect to find life apart from Him.

Weighing these things, I turn in my heart to Him, once and for all. And He seals the deal with me. In this NewLife covenant relationship He gives His Holy Spirt to reside in me. He speaks to, leads, empowers, and guides me as I daily lean on and trust in Him.

DESIRE (for God and the God-life), HUMILITY (a realistic admission of my moral human condition), and REPENTANCE (a willingnesss to turn toward God, followed by the decision to do so). DHR - - These are the components of healthy spiritual DNA.

Apple seeds won't produce broccoli. The seed of butter beans won't give us grapes. If any single component in the DNA in the seed of any

---

[104] Matthew 5:3 – "Blessed are the poor in spirit, for theirs is the kingdom of heaven."

of these is not present, or not functioning, we have no apples, broccoli, butter beans, or grapes.

Will you be accused of possessing healthy spiritual DNA by the world system when the world's true King shows up any moment now?

ESSAY SIX
Inertia

Coolishness and Incorrections

No one wants to be labeled 'not cool'. Culture has shaped us into folk who want to fit in. Older ones want to be cool just like the younger ones. And most folk want to act and fit in with the jargon and fashion that befits 'young'. Young is cool. Old is out. Old is 'old fashioned'. It's definitely not 'trending'. Big culture has cultivated this, setting the agenda for our lives with its reporting power and access to every home or phone, twenty-four seven. And we have let it invade us and implant its DNA.

If I don't fit in or stand outside of mainstream (cool) views, I'm not cool. And everyone else will know that I'm not. And if big culture chooses, what follows is their ace-in-the-hole weapon... they'll shame me.

Ah, shame, one of the most effective of the many tools employed by evil Satan and his minions to advance his diabolical cause. This is his most ready tool today because he knows that nobody wants to look bad, labeled *not cool*. So he attacks those who, in there supposed freedom, might disagree or challenge his very evil system and practices. And by making a public spectacle of them through his system, he shames them into submission. Or else he demonizes them by labeling them in the most dreadful ways. This is consistent with his nature as father of lies. It also reveals his historic starting place, appearing to the masses as an angel of light.

It's not cool to be uncool. In today's world, uncool doesn't cut it. One of the functioning factors related to this is something called "Cognitive Ease".

Cognitive Ease is associated with the measure of how easy it is for our brains to process information. The relative ease that accompanies my taking in information will affect how I feel about it. It will influence heavily whether or not I will be moved to follow up. If the process requires mental effort that is taxing, being complex and requiring effort to mentally process, cognitive ease fades. To continue to process that information becomes work and it is abandoned. The tendency is to conclude that it's not worth the effort.

Because cognitive ease feels good we tend to remain there. This places us in the landing space that can be described as satisfied and numb. No extra cognitive effort is desired so we don't give any. It's just plain easier to live comfortably among the cool, having already advertised myself as 'cool' as well. And, indeed, it is noble to want to fit in in order to care and serve effectively with a good heart. But it's dangerous to want to fit in out of fear of being labeled, or worse, shamed.

Fear forms in the darkroom where negatives are developed. And fear governs my heart when my bottom line motive is to fit in at all costs.

The inevitable result of remaining in the space of cognitive ease is mental complacency. This leads to laziness in mental processing. The end result is to be more open to anything. This is where Satan has wanted us. *More open to anything with no filter* is to be more open to his multi-faceted, dizzying, and mind-boggling schemes of all kinds. With eons of experience in his craft and every technology known to man at his disposal, and control, we don't stand a chance without God's help.

Are you getting this, dear one whom God created and loves? Have you drank Satan's cool aid that mystifies you to believe that feeling good, by being cool, is where it's at? Do we long to be cool and fit in in lieu of having a relationship with loving God, our Creator?

If we want to be cool we'll get caught up in the Coolishness and Incorrections of this world system. It is now telling us to fit in - or else.

ESSAY SEVEN
Contagion

Disformation Perplexia

In a specific application of 'the end justifies the means', large scale misdirection is employed daily to prop up Satan's system. The father of lies has checked this box off: 'Get them to believe lies.' His success has come out of the propaganda protocol's go-to play from evil's playbook: 'Say something (a lie) repeatedly, long enough, and it will begin to ring true'. All-day-long doses of "Incorrections" travel the air and cyber waves through methods and sources while publicly shaming all challengers.

Disformation Perplexia.

A groundswell of on-the-ground researchers and practictioners are speaking out against the policies, estimates, and conclusions of those who influence major life decisions for people in 2021. But they are not given a voice. They are being muted.

Disformation Perplexia. You hardly know what to believe. And that's on purpose. Gobbledygook, mobsense, trending, the latest - 1984 - in full bloom in 2021.

Know that the God Who Is seeks your attention in the midst of all of the current challenges and competing voices. Disformation Perplexia is meant to confuse you, discourage you, weaken you, shame you, and then snare you. But God wants to set you free from yourself and Satan's world system. He wants to free you to live life with Him.

The time is so very, very near, friend. I appeal to you. Reconcile with God. If you haven't already, turn to Him now through Jesus, the Savior.

ESSAY EIGHT
Pathway

Hodos Tethlimenne[105]

Another metaphor for living that Jesus used was that of travelling a road, a pathway. He described the road that led to life as "difficult". Some translations render the word as "narrow", which is a closely associated word that captures the meaning. Because just before that Jesus used the word "wide" to describe the path that led to destruction. But the more accurate translation of "tethlimenne" is "difficult".

---

[105] Greek: "The Difficult Path"; Pronounced: "teth – lee – men – nay"

According to Jesus, the road that leads to death (eternal) is wide. The road that leads to life (eternal) is narrow, better stated – hard, difficult. And perhaps this essay is suited mostly for us who lay claim to being believers in (followers of) Him.

How's it going on our difficult paths, friends? Are we trusting in Him as we travel them? Or are we, as I often am tempted to do, taking matters in our own hands, as if we aren't following behind Him along the path? Or maybe, we've decided to carve out our own paths with no regard as to whether or not we're actually following Him.

We want it easy. We want our stuff, our leisure, our comforts. Having these, without regard for whether or not we're trusting/ following Him, are indications we may have chosen an easier path. And are we in danger of naively turning onto the wide path that leads to destruction if we do so?

We must be extremely careful, friends.

Following Him on the road to life eternal is a difficult road in this world. Have we gotten spoiled? Are we lullabied to sleep by what we have and what we want? The voices of the material masters never cease their lullaby songs.

And all the while, many of our brothers and sisters in other places are being persecuted for their faith. And we care not.

And the poor are all around us. And we care not.

And we offend and don't get along with one another. And we care not.

And we talk about each other. And we care not.

Because the hard road gets hard, and in many cases it stays hard. So we justify our inattentive faith with the excuse that we need breaks, very long and indulgent breaks. And we need things, more and more things. And we need experiences of fun, constantly, and ongoing. And we need more money even if we have enough, or maybe even, plenty.

ESSAY NINE
Agency

Dying Places Hallowed Spaces

There are millions of ways to die. I'm not talking about the death of the body before we cross into eternity. I'm talking about the life that we live now. We are either living for ourselves or dying to our selves. And if we are daily choosing to die to ourselves it will show. If we are choosing to die to ourselves we'll be found loving God and loving others.

These are one in the same. I myself can get this one right, I understand this. It's not math. (Rocket science wasn't even on the table for me. But math was, until I couldn't pass it anymore.)

One whom God loves and paid a great price for, the difficult road that leads to life is a road filled with opportunities to put others first, serve them, and help with their needs. In this, we die to ourselves. And in this, we live for Him, that is, if we do it for His glory and not for our own. So we don't want to be promoting ourselves while we do. We don't broadcast our efforts. We do them in secret for the One we come to in secret all day long.

The places along the difficult path that leads to life are *dying places*. And in those frameworks of time, when we are dying to ourselves to bring glory to Him, we are in *hallowed spaces*. These are the private spaces where soul meets Soul, where being fuses with Being, where we are most in harmony with Him and pleasing to Him. For our Lord Himself did not come to be served but to serve, and to give His life a ransom for many[106].

It's challenging enough sometimes to die to ourselves regularly for those we feel close to and love. A tougher challenge is to die to myself for strangers, for strangers who can't do something in return for me.

---

[106] Mark 10:45

And the ultimate test is to meet needs for those who actually hate me and want to hurt me. Our Lord Himself challenged the presumption of only doing good for those who do good for us, or for those who we care about. He marked the action by affirming that even bad people do that.

This is an aspect of the difficult path that leads to life. And those who are on it are on it apparently. Their actions speak louder than their words. They love the hard to love with their actions, especially their enemies and those who hate them. They serve others incognito and shun the limelight. And they do so for strangers.

And for the overcomers, there awaits an eternal reward[107]. When their dying is done, "there will no longer be death, there will no longer be mourning, or crying, or pain.[108]" These are "the first things[109]" that will have passed when the Lord returns to the earth. According to His words, when He comes, the following will take place after 'the first things' are completed.

The last trump will sound, and He will enter the realm of the physical heavens. Those who entered the narrow gate and travelled the difficult road that leads to life will be caught up to Him in the air, both the dead and the living. They believed, that is, they trusted so as to cling to Him in this life. This is coming soon, quite soon, anytime now, dear friend. And then, He will return to reign on the earth.

The challenges that living in this world bring will inevitably cause pain and sorrow. This side of eternity is referred to by John the Revelator as 'the first things'. Those who overcome the first things by persevering in believing, trusting, and clinging to the Lord Jesus for deliverance, forgiveness, strength and courage will be relieved of death, mourning, crying, and pain. The hallowed spaces they chose to go with Him in service to others, especially those who didn't like them, will be fully recognized and rewarded. There will be an eternal dwelling place for His humble servants, those who by faith, died to themselves in their time on earth.

The rest who survive the end of the age tribulations will remain on the earth. They will enter the age when Jesus lives and reigns along with

---

[107] Revelation, Chapters 2 and 3
[108] Revelation 21:4
[109] Ibid

those who trusted in Him in this present age. Those who return with Him to reign will be the ones who were caught up with Him in the air just before He returns to earth. They will have been the overcomers. They will have chosen to walk the difficult path of life into dying places of service to anyone and hallowed spaces of dependence on their God as they did. They will have shown their faith by their works.

There is very much more to say about these things that will not be pursued here. In the very little time left, dear reader of these brief essays, seek these matters yourself as you, I trust, will seek Him with all of your heart. He loves you with a principled love.

ESSAY TEN
Priori

Love Under Agape[110]

God loves. His love is everlasting. It never ceases. His love is in perfect harmony with His other attributes, or characteristics. None of His attributes function contradictory from the others. They exist in perfect harmony in Him. He is a Whole Being without any conflict within Himself. He is utter oneness and complete. He needs no one else. He created us because He wants to share His goodness and love.

---

[110] Pronounced: 'Ah-gah-pay'; The unmerited, character/principle-based love that God extends to those He created.

His love is not primarily an emotion, loved one. It is a principle of his Nature that seeks moral goodness for all and in all. He is not beholden or taken captive to the entertainment industry's depictions of emotional-based love. He is far above that petty position. His apape love is unmerited. You and I cannot earn it. It is applied toward us from the font of His Being. It extends to sinful humans, that would be you, myself, and everyone who has been born of a man and woman.

He Is. He is the first order of existence of Being. All that is actual being, that is, real, eternal-founded existing –is of Him. And His agape love is out of that Being. There is nothing you or I can do to alter this aspect of His being.

His agape love intersects with His perfect justice. His justice cannot, due to His morally pure character, excuse the slightest sin in any motive, ambition, thought, word, or action. He can't. It's not in His Being (think DNA) to. It doesn't compute. It's like saying two equals twenty-two. No sense, meaning nonsense.

God's love is under Agape, offered freely to the undeserved through the sacrifice of Jesus, the Son of God. We can't earn it. It just is.

Does this do anything for you? Do you love Him in return?

A daddy had a time getting his daughter's attention on her attitude. One day, he said to her:

"Pretty is as pretty does."

Every claim to any virtue can be inserted into this provincial proverb. Good is as good does. Care is as care does. Justice is as justice does. Friend is as friend does. The proof is in the action. The action reveals the heart behind it. Not that you have to perform yourself into God's circle of acceptance and trust. You can't. I can't. But, if we claim to trust (believe) in Him for new-life forgiveness, it will show.

God is Agape love. So God loves. His "agape" love extends to all, even though we sin (rebel, disobey). He is just. So He is morally non-negotiatble. What He does verifies Who (and what) He is.

The young daughter is truly pretty if she *does* pretty. Remove the subject qualifiers and we have the essence: Is, As Does.

And there we have it. Mere words alone don't cut it with God. He does His part. He shows His love. And He has proven it by sending His Son to die for our sin. He has taken the initiative. His agape love for us

is plainly on display. We aren't loving Him in return if it isn't showing.
If it isn't there, it ain't. If it's there in the heart, somehow, someway, it
will selflessly show. If not in grand ways, at least in small ways. His
Love under Agape motivates me to trust in and cling tenaciously to
Jesus, even though I might struggle sometimes in life. And knowing that
He loves me in and through my struggles moves me to love Him in
return.

Is, As Does, in that there is showing with the telling.

And if it ain't there, then it still can be. But we must turn to Him.
Special one, if you haven't, it is time.

ESSAY ELEVEN
Consequence

Justice God

There is coming a payday for everyone.

Paydays are for work done. So will our paydays be from God. But
there are two different kinds of paydays coming. One is a payday like
we know them now. Another is actually not a payday in the technical
sense. I'll explain.

Salary payment is merited from work done for an endeavor. The salary
is for work done commensurate with the goal or mission of the
enterprise. Those who've chosen to turn from this world and themselves
and seek His Kingdom are within the movement of His Kingdom on

earth. They will be caught up to meet Him in the air at the time of His return. When finally with Him, they will receive rewards for the eternal quality of their works after turning to Him on earth[111]. The final measure for payment/ rewards for those who've humbled themselves in the new-birth life with Him will be what had been recorded as selfless service done for His Kingdom.

Payment for everyone else will be in the form of judgments. They will receive their judgments when they finally stand before the throne of the eternal Father[112] when it's all said and done. "And the books were opened…were judged according to the things which were written in the books, according to their deeds…" "And if anyone's name was not found written in the book of life .…[113]"

Good God has a recording system with a Divine metric. How grateful I am for having Jesus to bear my sin so that He can receive me into His presence – cleansed by Jesus' blood and forgiven for everything.

How can we know that Justice God is about to act out of His justice, when it is time for Him to come back to the earth? The answer is not overly complicated to the seeker of such things.

Two thousand years ago, a relative few were totally into the reality that the time was ripe for their Savior to come. The examples shown in the writings are those of the poor and obscure, simple folk. They didn't have a public platform or any prominence in the culture. Had they made their awareness known to those who held titles and influence, they would no doubt have been at best ignored, at worst, chided or scorned – marginalized, considered extremists.

But they knew. They knew that they knew. And history proved them right.

It's the same today. When the time was right, Jesus came the first time to offer Himself as the sacrifice for our sins. When the time is right, He will come back. And here is one of the ways that those who are aware are made aware.

Man is about to transform the human species. He is about to merge humanity with technology into a suprahuman species created by men and

---

[111] I Corinthians 3
[112] Revelation 20:12
[113] Revelation 21:11-15

not by God. This appears to be Satan's plan. This is how he can supercede God, or so it appears that he believes. This might be, in his mind, because he will have re-made God's image bearers into an image that he created. He will have taken humanity away from God in humanity's original image of Himself, and placed himself at the head to be worshipped as its creator-god.

Fringe news? The mere fantasy of fiction? Too out there for the common sense mind?

Imagine that someone from the year 936 woke up in the middle of a room filled with super computers with giant screens. Then see her taken on a spacecraft, taken to a fast food restaurant, watching a football game, an action-packed thriller movie, and finishing off by witnessing a post modern live military exercise. Had she been told that she would experience these things in the year 936, she would have considered it the ramblings of a madman, out of his common sense mind. It would have been labeled as fringe news, unfounded fantasy, and wacko thinking. Are you paying attention to what's going on in the world of technology and science?

Justice God is about to return to save His creation. His worldwide warnings are perfectly in tune with the agape love element of His perfect nature. And behind the smokescreens that the system has constructed, the evidences are myriad.

The time is nigh. All things have consequences. It's the system of order that God has created. It is the reaping principle. Each of us will reap what we have sown. The seed of our actions will bring the inevitable fruit. All of our actions will be written in the books. The King's deparment of justice knows no partiality, has the inherent eternal ability to see everything, and is of the utmost integrity in matters of its duty. None of us will escape our individual appointments with The King and His accountants. I can run as hard as I want for now, but I'm never out of sight.

The Scriptures reveal that God shows His wrath only when He has to. His wrath is a loving expression that arises from His Just nature. He can't, and won't, put up with the selfishness of man forever. His just nature cannot allow it. He is patient with everyone. But He doesn't wink at our setting His morality aside. He reminds us in all kinds of ways. Then He warns that He'll allow hard things if we walk away from Him by simply allowing us to reap what we've sown.

When mankind, in universal agreement, has become like our immoral ancestors in the time of Noah, they will be beyond reach, given over to evil by choice. "And every intention of the thoughts of his heart is only evil continually.[114]" "… God gave them over to a depraved mind, to do those things which are not proper…[115]"

His wrath is always an expression that is governed under the umbrella of all of His other quality attributes, or characteristics. His wrath, or just anger, is because of what we've done to hurt ourselves, each other, and our world. That's what's happening in the world, right now. The world system has become one kind. The many are beginning to give way to an ever encroaching ideal, a consensus that is subtly becoming more and more hostile to the Creator. His way of the created order is being rejected on a worldwide scale. And the merging of humans with technology is in the advanced stage.

The Almighty will not allow the tyrant, the deceiver, the one given over to madness, to take it from him by creating a new kind of man.

The show's over, my friend.

---

[114] Genesis 6:5
[115] Romans 1:24

ESSAY TWELVE
Portal

The Lie of The Dark and the Dead

Dear friend, evil knows no bounds when given complete access to the combined sympathies of merged human souls.

A smokescreen has been manufactured to hide from view activities that are taking place right behind it, near to where many of us abide, toil, and leisure. The dense fog has been sustained by sinister forces for quite some time. It is in the form of matters that are designed to occupy our attention. These varied and versatile matters are placed front and center to divert our attention from what is going on behind the scenes. And what is going on is staggering to the mind. It is as broad in scope as it is in the depth of its evil. The human soul given fully to evil knows no bounds to its treachery and manipulation.

The lie is in full bloom as its petals have spread across the entire globe. It has infected every place and virtually every major institution. Its primary aim has been to bring everyone together under a universal agenda that has no place for Creator God. Satan is obsessed with removing Him from His place as Sovereign over the universe. This has been his unalterable intent since Eden. He is given over to this obsession to the point of madness. He is irrational beyond comprehension, although he hides behind well sounding and seemingly innocent causes. He promotes these primarily by appealing to human emotions. "That just makes us feel so good, that this must be a good thing. We're coming together. It's a good feeling, so it must be good!"

He has gotten us addicted to feelings. First, he led us to get comfortable leaning into them. Next, we began to depend on the dopamine they ignited. The universal dependence became a universal codependence for humanity. And the codependence has morphed into an advanced state of addiction to feeling good.

The enemy, Satan, is the father of lies. If he speaks a truth there is a sinister motive behind it. It's as if his giant left earlobe has been the darkest fiery red color twenty-four seven since he chose to try to overthrow God aeons ago[116]. But his days are numbered. His end is foretold:

> "Is this the man who made the earth tremble, who shook kingdoms, who made the world like a wilderness and over-threw its cities, who did not allow his prisoners to go home[117]?"

> "And the devil who deceived them was thrown into the lake of fire and brimstone where the beast and the false prophet are also. And they will be tormented day and night forever and ever.[118]"

No doubt, the depth of God's constitution to love you is at least as deep as Satan's hatred for you. Satan has deceived those ensnared in his world system into believing that all technology is good and there is nothing to fear from applying oneself in and to it. He revels in satisfaction that we think he is somewhere far away doing things we could never know about. And all the while, mankind is being led astray, like lambs to the slaughter. And he is working behind the scenes of almost every cause and institution, in many places, doing things that would horrify us if we knew what they were.

---

[116]   Isaiah 14:3-23
[117]   Isaiah 14:16,17
[118]   Revelation 20:10

ESSAY THIRTEEN
Axiom

Trust Alive

There is no such thing as 'dead trust'. By definition, trust is either active and alive, or it doesn't exist at all. To believe in Jesus, according to what the New Covenant writers wrote in the Greek language, is to 'trust in, cling to, and rely on' Him. This is an active, living trust. It is a trusting dependence in an ongoing relationship with a living King Who cares.

When we die, or when He takes up His followers to meet Him in the air, the quality of relationship that we have with the Benevolent King (for those who have one), will probably kick-in at the same level of intimacy in the next realm as it was in this one. The time is at hand.

So what do you trust in? Who do you depend on?

Perhaps you claim to have faith, that is, trust in Him. Would a survey of local opinion affirm your claim to be true, dear one?

Have you been willing to follow Him no matter what, realizing that following Him is *obeying Him*. Would you be convicted of loving Him with all of your heart, soul, mind, and will, and loving your neighbor, even the stranger - and especially the enemy, as you love yourself? Not perfectly, loved one, but genuinely, always recalibrating yourself back to that direction when you find yourself astray?

Herein, dear reader of these age-end essays, is trust that is alive. As said earlier, it is not math. Or, if you're challenged in another way, it is not language study. And if you're new to all of this, outside looking in, it is my earnest prayer and hope that you'll turn and enter in. The time is so very much now.

ESSAY FOURTEEN
Alpha

The Darling of Heaven

It was inevitable. Love without sacrifice is partial love, diminished love, hence… not love at all. But there lives forever One Who loves fully. He does so by choosing to love those who do not love Him in return, at a sacrifice to Himself.

The natural processes which He has created gave you the food that you recently ate. The water that you drink is from His hand. And in His love, He is willing to sacrifice for you, borne out of His intense desire for your good. This He applies to all, friend and foe.

Jesus pre-existed with Father God in eternity past. He was and is, before and beyond, space and time. We don't know what His name was before He was conceived by the Holy Spirit in Mary's womb over two thousand years ago. It may have been "The Word of God.[119]" As part of a whole, a Three-In-One Being, He was, and remains, fully God.

When He ascended into heaven as the resurrected Son of God, Jesus entered the blessed realm in bodily form. He will apparently live forever with Father God in His glorified body. It can't be an exaggeration to suggest that the heavenly hosts, the angels of God who are each named, loved, and known by God Himself were exhilarated to receive the Second Person of the Trinity back. He had left their presence for thirty three years of earth time and there is no doubt that His Personal absence was felt.

And how is He now, in glorified bodily form, probably cherished and worshipped as The Darling of Heaven? It is because the God Who loves but is also Just, could not receive selfish, rebellious men and women into His morally pure, set apart Presence. We are indelibly stained, morally speaking. He, in the Person of God the Son, became the human-but-still-

---

[119] Revelation 19:13

God Jesus of Nazareth. As a human being, He resisted temptation to sin at every point. Then, as a morally pure person, He offered Himself to The Father, to be crucified, as the perfect sacrifice to a perfectly just God Who hates selfish sin. On that cross, God received His sacrifice for all of our sins forever.

 One can only imagine His angels, swords drawn and beside themselves within a hurricane of conflicting emotions. Think of the good king who watches his only son's head offered as a ransom to redeem the subjects whom he loves. The son goes willingly. But how must His warrior servants have been ready to attack Satan and his demonic hordes who no doubt, stood jeering and mocking at the cross where Jesus hung.

 He was tortured and beaten virtually beyond recognition. Hanging there, He received all of our sin with its associated, overwhelming burden of all of our guilt and shame.

 The Darling of Heaven made it possible for heaven to be populated with re-born people. He provided that God can share His ecstatic life and principled love within relationships as He always wished to. His angelic servants surely must rejoice that the One Who loves them will now get to share His love with men and women. These angels have never rebelled, eternally fixed with Him by their first choice long ago. The proof of the character and goodness of the One they pledged themselves to was ultimately on display on the cross. He intiated with mankind, has shown patience with us, and paid the ultimate sacrifice. He gave His life for us. In God's great love story called 'Life', His angels have no doubt welcomed Jesus home as the hero in the story. He is the cherished, honored Knight in shining light, the benevolent King Who rescues those who come to Him. He is **The Darling of Heaven**.

 But He is more than that. He is also the Lion of the tribe of Judah. On earth, his father, Joseph, was a descendent of the tribe of Judah. King Jesus is its Lion. Other male lions have staked out their territories and are in conflict as to supremecy. **The Lion of Judah** has no peers. No one can remove Him from His person and His position.

 Consider the male lion, called by men 'king of the beasts'. On earth, men can tranquilize such an incredible animal. They can take it captive, and carefully teach it tricks so as to perform at circuses. In a limited way, men might tame lions in captivity. The Lion of Judah can never be subdued, captured, or tamed. The image of the lion that portrays Him is that of unsurpassed strength, power, honor, and dignity. Added to these qualities in Him are all the pristine moral characteristics that befit goodness. These include: principled love, kindness and compassion, mercy without compromise of justice, wise decision-making, and more.

A third emphasis of His astounding character deserving a title is that of His relational involvement with each one of His Own. In that regard, He is referred to here as **The Load-Lifting PlowMaster**. What He is, to those whose trust in Him, is revealed in metaphors. In one of His metaphors He offers Himself as One to Whom we might yoke ourselves to[120] when plowing life's difficult field. In the image, He offers to take the brunt of the load as He plows together with each one of His followers. This is from His gentle and caring heart. It is the heart of One Who prefers to not aggressively assert His power and authority over those over whom He is King.

There is a fourth mention wherein he might be bequeathed a title. He is **The Autonomous Rescuer**. At this time in history, in the waning moments of this present age, He has promised to come back and receive His Own to Himself. The near episode is captured in the New Testament in several places.[121] In this act of deliverance, He will be on a rescue mission. He will snatch away from the earth those who are His Own at that moment, both the dead and the living. They will simply vanish from the graves and from right beside those who are not His. Then they will be with Him where He is, forever and ever. This event will likely happen any moment. And note the recent government and media attention given to 'UFO's'. How timely.

Do influential others suspect that Jesus followers might actually vanish soon? If so, if they are still able to, are they preparing an explanation of some kind when it happens? And if they are able to, who might be leveraging the ensuing fear behind the scenes?

Lastly, for purposes here, it is said that He is **King Forever In The Order of All That Will Be**. When all is said and done, He will reign supreme over the new heaven, restored universe, and new earth. Those who are His Own, by overcoming life's challenges through their living

---

[120] Matthew 11: 28-30
[121] Matthew 24:20; I Corinthians 15:52: I Thessalonians 4:16-18

trust in Him, clinging to Him for all its worth, will reign with Him forever. Those who do not, who turn down His invitation for forgiveness and restoration, will live eternally apart from Him. It will be a place of sorrows.

ESSAY FIFTEEN
Eschaton

The Time Has Arrived

By saying the time is now, this essay writer means to say that He is at the door to our dimension and about to enter it. I don't know if He'll come back before you turn the last page of this piece or whether it will be a month or a year. In The Writings, we are spoken to in such a way as to give us the motivation to be prepared.

This writer hasn't been given any special notification of a day or an hour of His return. No one has. He has no one specific clue above and beyond what others like him are aware of. Others are also aware of not only the season we are in, but also of the nearness of the moment of His return.

Suffice it to say that, as simply as I can tell you, dear reader of these essays, He is about to come in the clouds any second now. When He makes His appearance to descend on The Mount of Olives, He will be seen as far as the east is from the west. Every living eye will see Him. (Forgive the oxymoron) And when they do, all who are alive and remain will mourn. They will know that he is The One, and that they missed out on the first resurrection, the catching away that happened beforehand. As far as relative time goes, the time of the age we are in is about to close. We are at the door. Each of us should prepare. There is no more time. That's how close we are.

Men and women created in the image of the One God, He is Lord of heaven and earth. He is high and lofty above all. He is the One of grace and truth. He is the Morally Principled One and Only. He needs no one, but desires all. He presides as Sovereign in wholeness of Being and character. He sits in complete and pure moral goodness, is Autonomous in His will, and answers to no one. What will you choose?

Choose Him this day to serve. Then cling to Him for all that its worth until the end. The decision is worth everything you have and are.

Let Him be your soul's final satisfaction, knowing the peace that comes from being forgiven for your sin by the One and Only Sovereign. He loves you deeply. He will take away your guilt and shame for all of your wrongs. Your conscience will be wiped clean when you turn to Him.

Broken seals at the foot of heaven's throne
Cinque in numero[122]
For such a time as this - Numero Sei[123]

Dear reader, we are out of time. May the spirit, soul, mind, and body of you and I unite soon in the skies, in the first resurrection. In His glorious kingdom there is room for the least and the greatest among men and women of every tribe, race, language, and nation. There was room for this struggling soul. There is room for you.

Haste, my friend! I eagerly desire to see you there, so that we might bask in His warm embrace together.

---

[122] Italian: "Five in number"
[123] Italian: "Number Six"; Revelation 6:12 – the sixth seal

Presage

"Longing is the heart's treasury."
~ Augustine of Hippo

He laid the blue folder and the small booklet on his massive lap. His heart was ablaze. A firestorm of passion, conviction, fond recollection of friendship, solid affirmation, and sobering sadness overtook him when he finished reading THE ESSAYS. He rubbed his hands together front and back to generate warmth. A sudden knock on the back door interrupted him. It was Alvin and Tony.

The two friends scurried through the narrow opening that Vincent supplied. They were hunched low and buried under heavy clothing, gloves, head-cover, and scarfs. They didn't want to be noticed going to Vincent's back door. They were in an agitated state.

"Vincent, you're not gonna believe dis."

"Yeah, Vince, dis is unbelievable, man. Tell him, Tony. Tell him."

"I'm tryin to, Alvin, if yuh'll shut up for a minute."

"Okay. Awe-right."

"We weren't supposed to meet again till tomorrow, guys. We gotta be careful. What's dee excitement about?"

"Okay, Vincent. Duh man,…duh one you told us about, duh one who showed up at, at Simeon's table. Simeon told you about him, right?"

"Dat's right, Tony. Why?"

"He was a nerdy-looking old Professor type, wasn't he?"

"Yeah, he was."

Alvin couldn't wait.

"Dat's him, Vincent. He showed up at both of our doors last night. We think it's duh same guy, duh same guy, Vince!"

Tony was almost beside himself.

"Dat's right, Alvin. Izzat possible, Vince? Could it have been the same guy?"

"What happened after he knocked on yuh doors?"

"He gave us each a copy of dis booklet, *THE ESSAYS*. Look, here it is.
Show him yours, Tony. Show him."

Tony produced his as well.

"Wow, guys. Look at dis."

Vincent retrieved the worn, old, blue folder containing a copy of THE
ESSAYS.

"He showed up here last night as well."

"What are we to make of all uh dis, Vincent? Is something
happening?"

"Man, Tony. Ah think so."

"Why are we getting to see THE ESSAYS? Are dey about to get out
as warnings? If dey are warnings, wouldn't there be time for the
warnings to get out to people to read them?"

Vincent recalled the telling non-verbal exchange he had with The
Professor the previous evening.

"Yeah, Tony, Deez end of dee age essays contain what a silent
minority of fringe voices within the body of believers have been warning
everyone about for decades. Dey are a representation of what duh Lawd
has wanted us to listen to and take heed of. As Ah discovered, and what
you are as well, is dat He always warns for a season before He sends His
final judgments. And we are living in the time of His final judgments at
dee end of dee age. These essays simply contain a summary of what was
being said for many years. But few have been paying attention. Few
would give a platform to dee obscure, fringe voices dat were trying to tell
us these things. They floated on the edges of mainstream versions of
christianity. Most considered dem to be weird sensationalists,
doomsdayers and the like. They were given shameful labels dat made us
all want to ignore them and distance ourselves from them."

"Ah wish Ah would have been listening, Vince. Does this mean dat
Simeon wrote these essays? Did he write em in vain? Did he get to
publish them? Did word of them get out on the web, social media, and
other ways so dat many might receive one more final summary warning
among many others? Since duh time is up, has no one but duh three of
us gotten to read em? What do you think, DeMaso?"

"There's no doubt who wrote em, Alvin. As to their wider publication
and broadcast, Ah can't say. It wasn't long ago dat we lost all access to

duh web. And because Ah wasn't aware of their existence, Ah couldn't have looked to see if dey were published and sold online. Who knows how long dey have been out there."

The three seasoned New Orleanians sat in silence in the cold room. The gravity of the time they were living in was setting in on their individual and collective consciences. They exchanged sober glances and agreed to pray. And before long, without realizing it, their special time with God extended into hours.

Miles away, at the approach to the metro area, the attributes of Old Man River rapidly became more pronounced. The muddy water was muddier, murk became murkier, flow gave way to rush, and whitecaps turned into deep river swells. Swirling currents both deep and shallow morphed into aquatic mini tornados. The waters that carried things from the north churned menacingly.

Throughout the world, including the men in Vincent's living room, the faithful sheep of the Good Shepherd had each begun their very difficult day in the past twenty-four hours. Without exception, every one of them was momentarily vaguely aware of something. It was a fleeting, indescribably pleasant sensation amidst the terrible trials they were experiencing. The instantaneous impression was a one and done micro-second experience for each of them. It penetrated the mind down into the soul's core, touching every aspect of being in between. It held the hint of a déjà-vu moment, although it was raw and new for every one of them. The timing of the sensation was unique to each of the sheep. And his or her preoccupation in the moment was only deterred in the milli-second when the sensation touched down. The affect was that the experience was regarded momentarily in the subconscious. But the thoughts already in motion hardly missed a beat. They went on, while the subconscious blip on the radar screen evaporated as quickly as it showed up. And the memory apparatus in each soul recorded it for later retrieval, for hearty approval and affirmation, and for consensus celebration in another age rapidly closing in from the far north horizon of an old river moving menacingly through New Orleans..

Along the Mississippi River at New Orleans, two Corps of Engineers inspectors were checking the frozen levees for cracks and other potential damage due to the prolonged artic temperatures. One of them, Taneesha, was preoccupied with other matters. Her thoughts went to her God. She had only recently chosen to receive His forgiveness by way of Jesus' death, burial and resurrection. She was now a committed follower. She had hesitated for years, preferring to live life on her own terms. She knew that she would lose her government job because of her decision and the choices she now wanted to make. Her eyes filled with tears that she quickly wiped before they froze in place. But her heart was warmed by the penetrating love of God.

Looking down to the river, she noticed the abrupt and dramatic shift in its activity. She shouted to her companion through her thick scarf. A still train locomotive sat with its motor idling on the other side of the levee. At that moment, its horn blew one short, loud, three-second toot. Six short, crisp, clear, dings of a bell followed in quick succession before there was a seven second pause. A profoundly louder, much more noticeable sound of a dong followed. Heads throughout the nearby old uptown neighborhood, now inhabited by a newer generation of citizens mostly not born there, turned in their homes toward the river. Taneesha and her partner turned to look behind them.

"What's that sound, Taneesha?"

His words rode on the back of a mounting fear.

The brave woman shivered next to her fellow, shivering levee inspector. They turned again to face the river, noting the alarming developments. They were side by side, close enough that their thick coats touched at the arms. Her presence was felt as her partner took in the rivers' strange activity. He considered that they should take a video and report the activity immediately.

Exactly seven minutes after the sound of the loud seventh dong of the bell, the heads of persevering sheep the world over, including those asleep, turned upward in unison to the call of a trumpet only they could hear. Taneesha, Vincent, Alvin, and Tony were among them. They looked up in their places in unison with a rush that came from souls spontaneously alive with anticipation.

The male levee inspector turned to address his partner. But she had vanished from her spot, right next to him on the levee. She, Vincent, Alvin, and Tony, along with millions the world over who were touched with the fleeting sensation in the past twenty four hours, had their stories on earth end the exact same way, in the exact same millisecond - in the twinkling of an eye.

The bewildered levee inspector partner paced back and forth atop the levee, agitated and confused, as he frantically dug in his pocket for his phone. And a new kind of fear, one that untold millions of self-enshrined *my way* pundits suddenly felt in unison all over the world, came over him. It compounded the shaking that had already seized him in the frigid cold.

And the aroused, murky water of the old river, which had bid his partner an inexplicable, abrupt adieu, was disturbed as never before. It roared, agitated by a force unseen on a windless day. On and on and on, it flowed angrily from above, compelled by a force greater than the weight of its continuous motion through many centuries. And it carried with it the most unwelcome, unpleasant, and unstoppable things ever known to mankind, both seen and unseen, from the farthest places of the far reaches of the far north.

Afterword

"In a world of fugitives, the person taking
the opposite direction will appear to run away.

~ T.S. Eliot

"A time is coming when men will go mad, and when they
see someone who is not mad, they will attack him saying,
'You are mad, you are not like us.'"

~ Anthony the Great